SEEING DOUBLE

Lucinda Edmonds, a full-time author, trained as an actress. *Seeing Double* is her eighth novel, following her latest successes *Losing You* and *Playing with Fire*. She now lives in Rutland, with her husband and three young children.

LUCINDA EDMONDS

seeing double

PAN BOOKS

First published 2000 by Pan Books
an imprint of Macmillan Publishers Ltd
25 Eccleston Place, London SW1W 9NF
Basingstoke and Oxford
Associated companies throughout the world
www.macmillan.co.uk

ISBN 0 330 39080 5

1 3 5 7 9 8 6 4 2

A CIP catalogue record for this book is available from
the British Library.

Typeset by SetSystems Ltd, Saffron Walden, Essex
Printed and bound in Great Britain by
Mackays of Chatham plc, Chatham, Kent

for my godmother,
Joan Besant
(1927–1999)

prologue

20th November, 1995

'James, darling, what are you doing here?'

He looked around him, not sure where he was.

She caught him, just before he fell. 'You've been sleepwalking, haven't you? Come on, let's take you back to bed.' The gentle voice of his granddaughter told him he was still on earth. He nodded desolately, knowing he'd been standing here for a reason, there was something urgent he must do that he'd been leaving right until the last moment . . . He let her half-carry him to his bed, loathing his wasted, fragile limbs that rendered him as helpless as a baby.

'There now. How's the pain? Would you like a little more morphine?'

'No.' It was the morphine that was turning his brain to jelly. Tomorrow, he'd have none and then he'd remember what it was that must be done before he died.

Her hand stroked his forehead. 'You're burning up, darling.' A cool flannel was placed on his temples. James began to dream of faces, events, dislocated memories that had no coherence, no relevance to what it was imperative he remember . . .

Then he saw her, as clear as the day he'd first met her.

'Remember? The letter, my darling,' she whispered.
Of course!

He opened his eyes and saw the concerned face of
his granddaughter staring down at him. He could feel
something rubbing against the inside of his elbow.

'The doctor's going to give you something to calm
you down, darling James,' she whispered.

'*No! No!*' Yet somehow, the words would not form
on his lips. The needle slipped into his arm. He knew
then that he'd left it too late.

'I'm so sorry, so very sorry,' he whispered.

Zoe watched as his lids closed for the last time. She
pressed her cheek against his and found it wet with
tears.

*

He stared in disbelief at the headline:

LIVING LEGEND IS DEAD
Sir James Harrison, perhaps the greatest actor of his
generation, died yesterday at his London home. He
was 95.

A smile spread across his face. Was it possible after
all these years that the matter would now be closed? By
God, he hoped so. Flicking through the rest of the
article, briefly documenting James Harrison's life and
career, his attention was caught by the headline directly
beneath it:

RAVENS MISSING FROM TOWER
It was announced last night that the Tower of
London ravens, in residence for almost 900 years, have

vanished. The raven keeper was alerted to their disappearance when he arrived to feed them at their lodgings last night . . .

His blood ran cold. Surely, this was just an unhappy coincidence? He swallowed hard. For he knew the legend all too well . . .

chapter one

Joanna Haslam ran full pelt through Covent Garden Market, her breathing heavy, her chest rattling with the effort. As she emerged into the square in front of the church, she saw a limousine draw up outside. Photographers surrounded the car as the chauffeur stepped out of the driver's seat to open the back door.

'Damn, damn!'

With the last iota of strength she had left, Joanna sprinted across the square, cast her gaze over the huddle of paparazzi and saw that Steve, her photographer, was in prime position. Waving at him, he gave her a thumbs-up sign and she made her way inside the church.

Flashing her press card at the usher and still digging for breath, she slipped into the back pew of the packed church and sat down gratefully, her shoulders rising and falling exaggeratedly as she fumbled in her rucksack for her notepad and pen. Although the church was frosty-cold, Joanna could feel the beads of sweat on her forehead, the roll-neck of the lambswool sweater she'd thrown on in her panic sticking uncomfortably to her clammy neck. She took out a tissue and blew her nose loudly. Sweeping a hand through her tangled mass of long dark hair, she leaned back against the pew and closed her eyes for a couple of seconds, taking deep gulps of air to slow her still uneven breathing.

5th January, 1996.

So far, the new year was not holding out much promise of happiness. Joanna swallowed hard, willing herself not to cry. Yesterday afternoon, she'd not been so much chucked, but rather hurled off the top of the Empire State Building. At speed. Without warning.

Why?

Joanna bit her lip, opening one eye to check that the people who the congregation were waiting for had not yet made their entry through the door of the church behind her.

Matthew: the love of her life, now the *ex*-love of her life, according to him.

A few minutes on a Sunday afternoon, when most people were settling down to read the papers after a large, satisfying roast lunch. A few minutes during which Joanna's whole existence, her very vision of herself had been blown into tiny fragments.

Matthew had turned up on the doorstep of her flat in Crouch End unexpectedly. After the heavy revelry of Christmas and New Year, the two of them had agreed to adjourn to their own flats and have a quiet weekend calming down before work began the following week. Typically, Joanna was nursing the nastiest cold she'd had in years. She'd opened the door to Matthew, clutching her Winnie the Pooh hot-water bottle, fetchingly clad in her favourite ancient thermal pyjamas and a pair of stripy bedsocks.

She'd known there was something wrong when he'd hovered near her sitting-room door, refusing to take his coat off. Usually it was slung over a chair within seconds and she was wrapped in his arms, taking pleasure in the warm words of greeting he'd mutter in her ear.

Not yesterday, oh no, not yesterday.

Yesterday, Matthew had informed her nervously that he couldn't see their relationship going anywhere and that maybe it was time to call it a day. She'd listened as he'd explained how he felt. That they'd been together since their second year at Durham, almost five years now. That although he'd contemplated the thought of marriage to her, it had never quite sat right with him. He'd said he'd thought it was probably a time thing, that at some point, as they both matured, he'd have an urge to make her his bride, to tie the separate bits of their lives together. But that feeling hadn't happened. And quite honestly, he'd shrugged, if it hadn't by now, then he doubted it ever would.

Joanna had stared at him; shocked, silent. She measured his words with the guilt on his face. Then she'd pulled out a damp tissue from her pyjama pocket and blown her nose hard.

'Who is she?'

The blush had spread right across Matthew's handsome brow and seeped into his already ruddy cheeks. He'd sat down then and started to cry. He hadn't meant it to happen, he'd said, but it had and he couldn't go on pretending any longer.

Joanna remembered the New Year's Eve they'd

shared four nights ago and thought he'd done a bloody good job.

She was called Samantha, apparently. Worked at the same advertising agency as he did. An account director, no less. It had begun the night Joanna had been doorstepping the Conservative MP on the sleaze story and hadn't made it in time to the agency's Christmas party. The word 'cliché' whirled round Joanna's head. But then, where did clichés come from, if not because they were the common denominators of human behaviour?

Matthew insisted he'd tried to stop thinking about Sam, all through the Christmas they'd so recently spent together in Yorkshire at Joanna's parents. But they'd met again for a 'drink' last night, and he'd known then that he could not continue a relationship with Joanna.

Joanna was out. Samantha was in. It was as simple as that.

He'd admitted it might well be infatuation, but the point was, he'd said, if he felt this way about another woman now, it was obvious that there was a major problem with his committing to a lifetime with Joanna.

Joanna had agreed this was an honest and sensible statement. Then she'd burst into floods of coldy, Lemsip-induced tears, told him he was an evil, low-down, double-crossing, two-timing bastard and ordered him to leave immediately. What had really mortified her was that he'd taken no further persuading. He'd stood up, muttering stuff about various possessions that might still be in the other one's flat, getting together for a chat once the dust had settled and virtually charged for the front door.

Joanna had spent the rest of the afternoon alternately crying down the telephone to her mother, her best friend Simon's answering machine, a whole army of mutual friends that Matthew and she had made over the years, and into the increasingly soggy fur of her Winnie the Pooh hot-water bottle.

Later, due to large amounts of Night Nurse and brandy, she'd eventually passed out, grateful only that she had the next couple of days off from work in lieu of hours she'd worked on the newsdesk before Christmas.

Then the telephone had rung this morning. Joanna had raised herself from her drug-induced slumber and raced for the phone, realizing it might just be a devastated, recalcitrant Matthew realizing the enormity of what he'd just done.

'It's me,' the voice had barked.

Joanna had sworn silently at the ceiling. ''Lo Tom,' she'd snuffled. 'What do you want? I'm off.'

'Sorry, love, but you're not. Alice, Richie and Bill have all called in sick. You'll have to take your days in lieu another time.'

Joanna had given a loud, exaggerated cough down the telephone. 'They can join the club. Sorry, Tom, but I'm dying too.'

'Well, look at it this way; work today, then when you're fit you'll be able to enjoy the time off owing to you.'

'No, I'm sorry, I really can't. I've got a temperature, Tom. I can hardly stand.'

'Well that's okay. It's a sitting-down job, at the Actors' Church in Covent Garden. There's a memorial service for Sir James Harrison at eleven.'

Joanna had groaned. 'You can't do this to me, Tom, *please*. The last thing I need is to sit in a draughty church. I've already caught my death. You'll end up at a memorial service for me.'

'Sorry, Jo, love, no choice. I'll pay for a cab though. You can go straight home afterwards and send the piece on your modem. Try and talk to Zoe Harrison, will you? I've sent Steve to do shots. Should make a nice piccie if she's all dressed up. Right, love, speak later.'

Joanna had hung her aching head in despair, then looked at the clock. It was ten past ten. 'Shit!'

She had dialled the number of the local mini-cab company, booked a taxi for twenty past and staggered into the bedroom to dress.

Most of the time she loved her job, *lived* for it, as Matthew had often commented. After a stint on a regional paper, she'd been taken on as a junior reporter a year ago by the *Morning Mail*, one of the top-selling national daily newspapers in the country. However, her hard-won but lowly position at the bottom of the pile meant she was never in a position to refuse. There were a thousand wannabes right behind her. Her two month stint in the newsroom had been the hardest so far. The hours were unremitting and Tom, the newsroom editor, a true dedicated professional, expected nothing less from those who worked for him than he was prepared to give himself.

'Give me the bloody women's pages any day,' Joanna had snuffled as she pulled on a not terribly clean black jumper, a thick pair of woolly tights and a black miniskirt in deference to the sombre occasion.

The cab had arrived ten minutes late, then had got stuck in the most monumental traffic jam in Charing Cross Road. Joanna had looked at her watch, jumped out of the cab and hared through the streets to reach her destination on time, her chest labouring under the pressure of such exertion.

*

The organ stopped playing and the congregation ceased their quiet chatter. Joanna opened her eyes and turned round as Sir James Harrison's family members began to file into the church.

Leading the party was Charles Harrison, Sir James's only child, now well into his sixties. He lived a reclusive life in Los Angeles, and was an acclaimed director of intelligent, picturesque, big-budget films.

By Charles Harrison's side was Zoe Harrison, his daughter. As Tom had hoped, Zoe looked stunning in a black suit with a short skirt that showed off her long legs, and a wide-brimmed hat that set off her classic English rose beauty to perfection. Matthew had always been mad about her, going to see every film she made. He always said Zoe reminded him of Grace Kelly, his dream woman. Joanna had often wondered why, if that was the case, Matthew was going out with a dark-eyed brunette such as herself. She swallowed a lump in her throat, betting her Winnie the Pooh hot-water bottle that Samantha was a blonde.

Holding Zoe Harrison's hand was a young boy of around nine or ten, looking uncomfortable in a black suit and tie: Jamie Harrison, named after his great-grandfather and Zoe's illegitimate son. Zoe had given birth to Jamie when she was only eighteen and refused to name the father. Sir James had loyally defended his granddaughter and her decision both to have the baby and remain silent about his paternity. Since then, Zoe's acting career had steadily gathered momentum and, although not in the same stratosphere as her grandfather, she was one of the UK's most beautiful and talented actresses.

Joanna thought how alike Jamie was to his mother, the same fine features, milk and roses complexion, and big blue eyes. Zoe kept him away from the cameras as much as possible – Joanna hoped Steve had taken a shot of mother and son together. It might even make the front page tomorrow morning.

Behind them, dressed in an overtly unsuitable (in terms of both weather and occasion) cotton safari suit and wearing an insouciant expression on his mesmerically handsome face, came Marcus Harrison. Joanna watched him as he came level with her pew. Even in her poor physical and mental state, she recognized that Marcus Harrison was drop-dead, groin-tinglingly gorgeous. As dark as his sister was fair, but sharing the same huge blue eyes, Marcus oozed sex appeal. In his unsuitable suit, with his black hair almost touching his beige cotton-covered shoulders, Joanna knew he was a man that would slay 'em in the aisles, a heartbreaker that would have no problems finding new victims – exactly the kind of man Joanna herself fell for. Matthew had a similar charisma . . .

Joanna dragged her gaze away from Marcus as he followed the family to the front of the church. Next time, she was going for the kind of man who counted bird-watching and stamp-collecting amongst his hobbies. She tried to recall what exactly Marcus Harrison did with himself. It was surprising that with his looks and impeccable family connections he had not achieved a higher profile.

'Good morning, ladies and gentlemen. Sir James Harrison's family and I, the Dean of Westminster, welcome you all here and thank you for coming to pay tribute to one of the finest actors this century. Sir James has left explicit instructions in his will for any memorial service that might take place after his death. He was adamant that the occasion was not to be sombre, but in fact a celebration. Both his family and I have of course honoured his wishes. Therefore, we start with hymn number two six nine, "I Vow to Thee My Country", Sir James's favourite hymn. Please stand.'

Joanna pushed her aching legs into action, glad that the organ began the introduction just as her chest heaved and she coughed loudly. Reaching for her service sheet on the ledge in front of her, a tiny, spidery hand, the skin almost translucent, revealing the blue veins beneath it, got there before hers did.

For the first time, Joanna looked to her left and studied the owner of the hand. Bent double with age, although the woman was standing, she only came up to Joanna's ribs. Resting on the ledge to support herself, the hand in which she held the service sheet shook continuously. It was the only part of her body that was visible. She was dressed in a black coat that touched her ankles, and a hat with a black net veil shielding her face.

Devoid of her service sheet, Joanna bent down to place her lips by the woman's ear. 'May I share with you?'

The hand offered her the sheet, Joanna took it and placed it low so the old woman could see it too. At the end of the hymn, the woman struggled to sit down. Joanna silently offered her arm but the help was ignored.

'Our first reading today is Sir James's favourite sonnet, read by Sir Laurence Sullivan.'

The congregation waited as the old actor made his way to the front of the church. Crocks anonymous, thought Joanna, as the famous voice that had once held thousands spellbound in theatres across the globe read the sonnet in his still rich, honeyed tones.

The door at the back of the church behind her opened. An usher pushed a wheelchair through it and placed it at the end of the pew opposite Joanna. She scribbled a few words in shorthand in her notebook, feeling particularly uninspired. She then became aware of a rattling noise that made her own earlier chest problems seem inconsequential. The old woman next to her was having what sounded like an asthma attack. She was staring past Joanna, her gaze locked on the figure in the wheelchair.

'Are you okay?' Joanna asked rhetorically, as the woman put her hand to her chest, her focus still not leaving the wheelchair. Suddenly, the woman grasped at Joanna and indicated the door behind them. She was digging for breath.

'I'll help you out,' Joanna said as the Dean announced the next hymn and the congregation stood.

She helped the woman stand, then holding her by her waist, she virtually carried her to the end of the pew. The woman turned her face into Joanna like a child wanting protection as they came adjacent to the man in the wheelchair. A pair of steely grey eyes studied both of them. Joanna shuddered involuntarily, unlocked her gaze from his and helped the woman the few paces to the door. An usher stood on the other side.

'This woman . . . I . . . she needs . . .'

'Air!' the old woman cried between gasps.

Joanna took the woman into the grey January day, spotted a bench and sat them both down on it. The old woman sat with her head bent almost to her knees.

'Should I call an ambulance? You really don't sound very well.'

'*No!*' the woman gasped, the strength of her voice at odds with the frailty of her body. 'Call a taxi,' she panted. 'Take me home. *Now!* Please.'

'I really think you should—'

The bony fingers locked around Joanna's wrist in a vice-like grip. 'Please! A taxi, now!'

'All right, you wait there.'

Joanna sprinted round the corner and hailed a passing black cab. The driver gallantly helped the woman inside.

'She okay? The old duck's breathing sounds a bit off,' he said to Joanna.

'I know, but she insists she wants to go home.' Joanna lent into the cab. 'Where is home by the way?'

'I . . .' The effort of getting into the cab had obviously exacerbated her condition. She sat there, panting, speechless.

The cabbie shook his head. 'Sorry, love. 'Fraid I can't take her anywhere in that state, not by herself, like. Don't want a death in the back of me car. Far too messy. Could take her if you come with her, of course. Then it's your responsibility rather than mine.'

'But . . . I don't know her . . . I mean . . . I'm working . . . I should be in that church now, listening, so I can write a report on it.'

'Sorry, love,' he said to the old woman. 'You'll have to get out.'

The old woman looked at him, then, still unable to speak, she lifted her veil. Her terrified eyes sent a silent message to Joanna.

Help me, please.

'Okay, okay.' Joanna sighed with resignation and popped into the back of the cab.

The driver shut the door behind her and Joanna sat down next to the woman.

'Where to?' she asked gently.

'. . . Mary . . . Mary . . .'

'No, where to?' Joanna tried again.

'Mary . . . le . . .'

'Do you mean Marylebone, love?' the cabbie asked.

The woman nodded with visible relief.

'Right you are.'

Joanna watched the woman stare anxiously out of the window as they passed the church, then visibly relax as the cab sped away. Her breathing began to ease. She put her head back against the black leather seat and closed her eyes.

Joanna sighed. The day was getting better and better. Tom would crucify her if he thought she'd snuck off early. The story of the little old lady sitting next to her being taken ill really would not wash with him. Little old ladies were only of interest to Tom if they'd been beaten up by some skinhead after their pension money and left for dead.

'We're nearly there now. Could you try and find out where we're going?' said the cabbie.

'Nineteen, Marylebone High Street.' The clipped voice rang out crisp and clear. Joanna turned to look at the old woman in surprise. Her breathing had become normal and a little colour had returned to her cheeks.

'Feeling better?' Joanna asked gently.

'Yes, thank you. Sorry to put you to so much trouble. You should get out here. I'll be fine.'

'No. I'll see you home. I've come this far.'

The woman shook her head as firmly as she could. 'Please, for your own sake, I—'

'We're nearly there now. I'll help you inside your house and then go.'

The old woman sighed, then, as if the small amount of energy at her disposal had been utilized, sank further down into her coat and said no more until the taxi came to a halt.

'Here we are, love.' The cabbie opened the door, a look of relief that the woman was still alive written on his face.

'Take this.' The woman held out a fifty pound note.

'Don't think I've got change for that.' He shrugged as he helped the old woman down on to the pavement and supported her until Joanna stood beside her.

'Here. I've got it.' Joanna handed the driver a five pound note. The woman had already slipped from her grasp and was walking unsteadily towards a door wedged between a newsagent's and a florist's.

'Shall I do that?' Joanna watched as the woman's arthritic fingers failed to put the key in the lock.

'Thank you.'

Joanna turned the lock and opened the door. The woman almost threw herself through it.

'Come in, come in, *quickly!*'

Having delivered the woman home, Joanna's intention was to get back to the Covent Garden church as soon as she possibly could. She stepped inside. Immediately the woman banged the door shut behind her.

'Follow me. Please.' The woman was heading for a door on the left-hand side of a damp hallway. Another key was fumbled with, then finally fitted into the lock.

Joanna followed her into complete darkness.

'Lights are just behind you on the right-hand side.'

Joanna felt for the switch, pressed it and saw she was standing in a small, dank-smelling lobby. There were three doors in front of her and a flight of stairs to her right.

The old woman opened a door and switched on another light. Standing just behind her, Joanna could see that the room was full of tea chests, stacked on top of one another. In the centre of the room was an old single bed, its iron bedstead rusting at both top and bottom. Against one wall, wedged in between the tea chests, was an old sofa. The smell of urine was distinct. Joanna felt her stomach turn.

The old woman headed for the sofa and sank on to it with a sigh of relief. She indicated an upturned tea chest by the bed.

'Tablets, my tablets. Could you pass them please?'

'Of course.' Joanna made her way through the tea chests and retrieved the pills. She noticed the directions for use were written in French.

'Thank you.' The woman nodded as she opened the screw top of the bottle, emptied out two tablets into her shaking hands and put them in her mouth.

'Do you need water?'

'No. They dissolve under my tongue,' the woman nodded, then closed her eyes. Joanna stood watching her, wondering if she was now okay to leave. She shivered, the fetid smell and dismal atmosphere of the room closing in on her.

'Are you sure you don't need a doctor?'

'Quite, quite sure.' The woman's eyes were still closed.

'Well then. I'm afraid I'd better be going back to the service. I have to file my piece for my newspaper.'

The woman's eyelids popped open and she regarded Joanna quizzically. 'You're a journalist?'

'Yes. On the *Morning Mail*. Very junior at the moment.'

'What's your name, dear?'

'Joanna, Joanna Haslam. Are you sure you'll be okay?'

'Yes.'

Joanna studied the boxes. 'Are you moving?'

The woman smiled. 'I suppose you could put it like that, yes.' She stared off into space. 'I won't be here for much longer. Maybe it's right that it ends like this . . .'

Joanna's head was spinning and her stomach was churning. She sat down on a box. 'What do you mean? Please, if you are ill, let me take you to someone who can help you.'

'No, no. It's too late for all that now.' She shrugged, then looked at Joanna. 'You go now, dear, back to your life. Goodbye.' The woman closed her eyes again. Joanna watched her. A few seconds later she heard soft snores emanating from her mouth.

Feeling horribly guilty, but unable to stand the atmosphere of the room any longer, Joanna stood up and quietly let herself out.

The memorial service was over by the time she arrived back in Covent Garden. The limousine containing the Harrison family had left and there were a few minor celebrities milling around outside. Her cold and her aching head were making her feel really ill now, Joanna just managed to take a couple of quotes from those still present before dizziness began to overtake her. Giving up the entire morning as a bad job, Joanna hailed a taxi and headed home.

chapter two

The bell was ringing. Again and again, searing through Joanna's throbbing head.

'Oooh Go ... d,' she groaned, as she realized whoever was at the door was determined not to go away.

Matthew? For a split second, her spirits rose, then sank again instantly. Matthew was probably toasting his freedom with a glass of champagne, in a bed somewhere with Samantha.

'Go away, go away,' she moaned, blowing her nose on Matthew's T-shirt to clear her nasal passages and allow her to breathe.

The bell rang again.

'Bugger, bugger, bugger.'

Joanna gave in, crawled out of bed and staggered to the front door.

'Hello, sex-kitten.' It was Simon, smiling ironically at her.

'Fuck off,' she whimpered, hanging on to the front door for support.

'Come here.'

A pair of thick, muscled, comfortingly familiar arms closed round her shoulders. Tall herself, Simon, at six foot four, was one of the only men she knew who could make her feel like a fragile, vulnerable female.

'I got your message yesterday. Sorry I wasn't there to play agony aunt.'

'It's okay.' She snuffled into his shoulder.

'Let's go inside before icicles start forming on our clothes, shall we?' Simon led her in, an arm still firmly around her shoulder. He shivered in the small sitting room. 'Jesus, it's cold in here.'

'Sorry. I've been in bed all afternoon. I've got a really terrible cold.'

He pulled her away from him and studied her. 'You look like hammered shit, sweetheart.'

Joanna sank on to the uncomfortably narrow lime-green sofa. She'd only bought it because Matthew had liked the colour and had regretted the purchase ever since. Matthew had always sat in the armchair when he came round.

'I feel like it. On top of being dumped by Matthew yesterday, Tom sent me out to cover a memorial service this morning on my precious day off and I ended up in Marylebone High Street with a weird old lady who lives in a room full of tea chests.'

'Wow. There's me in Whitehall, and the most exciting thing that happened to me today was a different kind of filling from the sandwich lady.'

Joanna usually giggled at Simon's dry sense of humour, but tonight, she could not even raise a smile.

'Sweetheart.' Simon sat next to her and took her hands in his. 'I'm so very sorry, really.'

She nodded, the tears pricking in her eyes.

'Is it over for ever, or do you think it's a blip on the road to marital bliss?'

Joanna sighed deeply. 'It's over, Simon. He's found someone else.'

'Want me to go and give him a good kicking to make you feel better?'

'Truthfully, yes, but reasonably, no.' Joanna put her hands to her face and wiped them up and down her cheeks slowly. 'The worst thing is that at times like this you're meant to react in a dignified manner. You know, if people ask you how you are, you're meant to brush it off, lie and say "Oh, absolutely fine thank you. He meant nothing to me anyway and his leaving has been the best thing that's ever happened to me. I've so much more time now for myself and my friends and I've even taken up basket weaving at night school which has always been something I've wanted to do," but it's all *rubbish*! At this moment in time, I'd crawl across burning coals if it would mean Matthew would come back to me, so that life could go on as normal. I . . . I . . . love him. I need him. He's mine, he be . . . belongs to m . . . me.'

Simon sat while she cried like a baby in his arms. He stroked her hair gently and listened as the shock, surprise, hurt and confusion poured out of her. After a while he patted her hand. 'You light the fire while I boil the kettle for some tea.'

Joanna turned on the gas flames in the fireplace and followed Simon into the small kitchen. She slumped down at the table in the corner, over which she and Matthew had shared so many lazy Sunday morning

breakfasts and intimate candlelit suppers. As Simon
busied himself making the tea, Joanna gazed at the glass
jars placed neatly along the work top.

'I've always loathed sun-dried tomatoes,' she mused.
'Matthew adored them.'

'Well.' Simon took the glass jar full of the offending
tomatoes and tipped them into the bin. 'There's one
positive thing to come out of this, then.'

'In fact, now I think about it, there were lots of
things Matthew liked and I just pretended to.' Joanna
put her hands, gnome-like, under her chin.

'Such as?' asked Simon.

'Oh, going to see weird, foreign art-house movies
on Sunday at the Lumiere when I'd have preferred to
stay at home and watch children's TV. Music, that was
another thing. I mean, I like classical in small doses,
but I was never allowed to play my Abba Gold or Take
That CD.'

'I hate to admit it, but I'm afraid I'm with Matthew
on that one,' chuckled Simon, pouring boiling water
over the tea-bags. 'The point I think you're trying to
make is that Matthew was aspiring to be who he
thought he *should* be and you should be too. His taste
probably bore no resemblance to what he actually liked
or enjoyed.'

'Yes.' Joanna sighed. 'At the end of the day, I think
I was just too ordinary for him. But that's who I am,
just a boring middle-class Yorkshire girl.'

'Sweetheart, I promise you, the one thing you're
not is ordinary. Or boring. Honest, maybe; down to
earth, yes, but those are qualities that are to be admired.

Here.' He handed her a mug of tea. 'Let's adjourn to the sitting room and some heat from that gas fire.'

Having drunk the tea, warmed up and calmed down somewhat, Joanna was sitting in front of the gas fire between Simon's knees. 'The thought of going through the whole courting process all over again is awful.' Joanna sighed. 'I'm twenty-seven, too old to start afresh.'

'Jo, really.' Simon raised his eyebrows.

'It's going to take me ages to get used to being a singleton again.'

'The problem with the human race is that they dislike change of any kind. I'm sure that's why so many unhappy couples stay together when they'd be much better off apart.'

'Talking of couples, have you heard from Theresa?'

'Yes. I got a postcard from Perth last week. She's going up-country apple-picking or some such.' Simon sighed. 'It's been a long year. Anyway, she's back in March, only nine weeks and three days left to go.'

Joanna patted one of Simon's knees. 'You've been awfully good to wait for her the way you have.'

'Yeah, well, the way I see it is that if she still wants me by the time she arrives home, we'll know that it's right and for real.'

Joanna sighed. 'Well, don't bank on it. I thought Matthew and I were right and for real.'

'Well, you have your career, your home, me. You're a survivor, Jo. You'll come out the other side, you wait and see.'

'That's if I still have a job to go back to. The piece

I filed this morning was crap. What with Matthew, and the cold, and that weird old lady . . .'

'You say she was living in a room full of tea chests?'

'Yes. She said something about her not being here long enough to unpack.' Joanna bit her lip. 'The whole thing completely depressed me. I sat in that room thinking that if this was what life brought you, then what the hell is the point of struggling through anyway?'

'She's probably one of those mad eccentrics who lives in a dump and has millions stuffed away in the bank. Or in tea chests for that matter. You should have checked.'

'She was fine until she looked at this chap in the wheelchair at the end of the pew opposite us. She freaked when she saw him,' Joanna mused.

'Probably her ex-husband. Maybe *his* millions really were stashed away in those tea chests,' chuckled Simon. 'Anyway, sweetheart, I must be on my way. I have some work to do before tomorrow.'

Joanna followed Simon to the door and he clasped her in his arms. 'Thanks for everything.' She kissed him on the cheek.

'Anytime. I'm always there if you need me. I'll call you from work tomorrow. Bye, Butch.'

She nodded. 'Night, Sundance.'

Joanna closed the door behind him and ambled back into the sitting room. She'd known Simon all of her life. He'd lived on the farm across the road in Yorkshire with his family. Even though he was a couple of years older than her, living in such an isolated environment with other playmates not at hand, Joanna and Simon had spent much of their childhood together. An only child and a tomboy by nature, Joanna had thrilled to Simon's company. Simon had taught her to climb trees, play football and understand cricket. During the long summer holidays, the two of them had taken their ponies up on to the moors and played lengthy games of Cowboys and Indians. It was the only time they ever fought, as Simon always and most unfairly demanded that he live and she die. When he was thirteen, Simon had gone to boarding school in Sedburgh and they naturally saw less of each other. The old closeness still remained but both made new friends and had their own individual worlds. They'd celebrated when Simon had won a place at Trinity College, Cambridge, Joanna following him to university two years later at Durham.

Then their lives had separated almost completely. Simon had met Theresa at Cambridge; in her final year, Joanna had found Matthew. It wasn't until they'd both found themselves in London, and coincidentally living only ten minutes apart, that their friendship had blossomed once more.

Matthew had never liked Simon. Joanna had recognized male jealousy immediately. Apart from towering over him physically, Simon had won a first at Cambridge and had been offered some kind of high-flying job in the Civil Service. Simon modestly said he was just an office bod, but that was Simon all over. Whereas Matthew had received a second from Durham and had to gofer at an ad agency before being offered a junior position and slowly working his way up through the ranks.

Maybe Matthew was hoping Samantha's superior position at the agency would enhance his own career . . .

Joanna shook her head. She refused to think about him any more tonight. Setting her jaw, she put Alanis Morissette on her portable CD player and carried it into the bathroom to run a hot bath. Singing 'You Learn' at the top of her voice, the water pouring out of the taps, Joanna did not hear the footsteps or see the face peering into the uncurtained windows of her ground-floor sitting room. She emerged from the bathroom as the footsteps receded down the path.

Feeling calmer and cleaner, Joanna drew the curtains, made herself a cheese sandwich and sat in front of the fire toasting her toes. She was suddenly filled with a strange kind of optimism for the future. Some of the things she'd said to Simon in the kitchen earlier sounded flippant, but they were actually true. In retrospect, she and Matthew had shared very little in common. And now she was a free agent with no one to please but herself. No more putting her own feelings second. This was her call, her life and she was damned if she was going to let him ruin her future.

Before her more positive mood left her and depression descended once more, Joanna took a couple of paracetamol and headed for bed.

chapter three

His secretary came through the door with the post and his habitual cup of freshly ground Moroccan coffee.

'Thank you.' He nodded at her, then sipped the coffee slowly. Once he had drained the cup, he went carefully through the post. Maybe today . . .

'Damn!' He slammed his fist on the leather-bound desktop, then picked up the telephone. 'Jenkins, what did your boys find out last night?'

'We know where the girl lives. Clive followed her to her flat in Crouch End.'

'Did she take our old lady to her home?'

'We don't know. Our man saw them getting in a taxi together outside the church and put out a call. But the cab was well gone before anyone could get on their tail. We're still checking all the hospitals to see if that's where they went. She was in a pretty bad state. But so far nothing. Want us to question the girl?'

'No, not yet. Keep an eye on her, will you? Let's give her time to make a return visit.'

'Understood. We'll keep on searching. From the state the old lady was in, we may not find her before she goes anyway.'

'We will. We *must*. It's imperative.'

'We'll keep on it, sir.'

'Do that. I'll telephone you later.'

He put the telephone down and drummed his fingers on his desk, then manoeuvred his chair so he could look out of his vast window, with its superb view of the Mall. Time was of the essence. She had returned from the dead just as he had died. It was too much of a coincidence.

chapter four

'Bye-bye, darling.' She hugged him to her, breathing in his very specific smell, only accessible to herself.

'Bye, Mumma.' He snuggled into her coat for a few more seconds, then pulled away, watching her face for signs of unwelcome emotion.

Zoe Harrison cleared her throat and blinked back tears. This moment became no easier, no matter how many times she went through it. But it just was not done to cry in front of other parents and Jamie's friends. So she smiled at him bravely. 'So, I'll be down to take you out to lunch two weeks on Sunday. Bring Ben if he'd like to come.'

'Sure.' Jamie stood by the car, looking uncomfortable, and Zoe knew it was her moment to leave.

'Right. I'll be off. Ring me if you need anything.'

'I will, Mumma.'

'Okay.' Zoe nodded at him and climbed behind the wheel. She closed the door, started the engine, then wound down the window.

'I love you, sweetheart. You take care now, and remember to wear your vest and *don't* leave your wet rugby socks on for any longer than you have to.'

Jamie grinned. 'Yes, Mumma. Bye.'

'Bye.'

Zoe pulled off out of the drive, watching Jamie waving cheerfully in her rear-view mirror. She turned a bend and her son was lost from sight. Turning on to the main road, Zoe brushed the tears away harshly and ferreted for a tissue in her coat pocket. Whilst trying to navigate the narrow high street, Zoe told herself for the hundredth time that she suffered more on these occasions than Jamie did. Especially today, with James gone too.

Zoe followed signs for the motorway and blew her nose hard on the tissue, once more asking whether she was completely selfish to confine a nine-year-old boy to a boarding school, especially one who had suffered a tragic bereavement a few weeks before. Yet Jamie loved his prep school, his friends, his rugby, his *routine*, which was something that was just impossible to give him at home with her. He was thriving at the school, growing up, becoming ever more independent.

When she had found herself pregnant at eighteen, she had nearly died of shock and devastation. Just out of boarding school and with a place at a good university to head for, it seemed ridiculous to even contemplate having a baby. And yet, throughout the barrage of negative reaction from her father, her brother, her friends and those paid to counsel in such situations, coupled with pressure from a completely different source, Zoe knew, somewhere in her heart, that the baby inside her had to be born. Jamie was the product of love, a special, magical gift. A love from which, after almost ten years, she had still not fully recovered.

Zoe joined the other cars streaking towards London

on the motorway. She thought how dismissive others could be about love that happened at a young age. After all, it was only in modern society that one waited until one's mid to late twenties before feeling mature enough to take the plunge. Fifty years previously it had been completely acceptable to be married at eighteen, before that, even younger.

Not that there had ever been any chance of marriage, she thought ruefully. Zoe sighed. She did not dwell on it much anymore. It was pointless and emotive. Yet it was interesting that amongst those who had every right to be shocked by her condition, James, her darling grandfather, had remained calm; a quiet presence of reason and support when all those around her seemed to be screaming at the top of their voices.

Zoe had always been James's special girl, the first female to arrive in the family after her father and her older brother Marcus. As a child, she had no idea that the kind, elderly man with the rich deep voice, who refused to be addressed as 'Grandpa' because he said it made him feel old, was one of the most lauded actors in the country. Zoe had lived with her mother and Marcus in a comfortable house in Blackheath. Her father seemed to be rarely at home, and so it was James who became the father figure in her world, his rambling country house in Kent with its huge orchard and cosy attic bedrooms that formed her most pleasurable childhood memories.

In semi-retirement, only popping off Stateside occasionally to appear in a cameo role, her grandfather was always there. Especially after Zoe's mother had been killed suddenly and shockingly in a freak road accident only a few yards from their house in Black-heath. Zoe had been ten, only a year older than Jamie was now. Charles, her father, had returned from his work in LA and tried to comfort a son and daughter he hardly knew. It had been James who had wiped away the tears of grief and hugged her as she wept far into the night. James had tried to comfort Marcus too, but Marcus preferred to deal with it himself. Outwardly, he'd seemed almost untouched by his mother's death, laughing and joking in the same way he always had. Like every other emotion, any grief Marcus felt for the loss of his mother was locked away.

After the funeral, Charles suggested that his two children come to live with him permanently in the States. The usually easy-going, thirteen-year-old Marcus had put his foot down and point-blank refused. He wanted to stay at his boarding school in England with all his friends. Charles agreed that if he was happy to do that, it was probably the best thing. Marcus could fly out to LA for the holidays.

At the age of ten, Zoe had no such sway. She travelled to LA with her father three weeks after her mother had died. When she arrived at the comfortable hacienda-style house high up in the Hollywood Hills, Zoe discovered she had an 'Auntie Debbie'. Auntie Debbie apparently lived with her daddy and even slept in the same bed as he did. Auntie Debbie was very blonde, very voluptuous and not happy having to take on the responsibility of a young child.

Zoe had been sent to a school in Beverly Hills and had hated every moment of it. She rarely saw her father, who at the time was carving a serious niche for himself as a movie director. Instead she saw Debbie, whose idea of child-rearing was a TV dinner and wall to wall cartoons. She wrote long letters to her grandfather, begging him to come and fetch her and asking if she could possibly come and live with him, that she could look after herself and, really, would be no trouble, if he'd only let her come back home.

Six months after Zoe had arrived in LA, a taxi-cab arrived in the drive. Out of it had stepped James. Zoe still remembered the feeling of overwhelming joy as she ran down the drive and threw herself into his arms. Her protector had heeded her call and had arrived to rescue her. With Auntie Debbie banished to sulk by the pool, Zoe had poured out her woes into her grandfather's ears. Three days later, her father had arrived back from location. Zoe had been sent to bed early, but that did not stop her from hearing raised voices from the terrace below her room.

The following morning at breakfast, her father had asked Zoe whether she wanted to stay in LA with him and Debbie or move back to England and live with James. There had been no contest. Zoe had whooped for joy, hugged and kissed James, barely noticing the pain etched on her father's face.

It was agreed that Zoe should attend a weekly boarding school near her grandfather's house in Kent and spend weekends at home with him. Holidays would be split between England and the States.

Five days later, she kissed her father and Auntie Debbie goodbye and sat happily next to James, her small hand clutched in his big one on the long flight back to England. As her eyes closed with tiredness and she leaned on his firm, capable shoulder, she knew that home was wherever he was.

Her boarding school had been a happy, fun experience. James had always been glad to welcome her friends into his home, either in London or the country. It was only when Zoe watched her companions wide-eyed wonderment as they shook hands with Sir James Harrison, legend, that she began to realize just how famous a man her grandfather was. It was during this time that James had begun to pass on to her his love for Shakespeare, Shaw, Wilde, Brecht and Ibsen. The two of them would go up to London on a Saturday night to take in a play at the RSC, the National Theatre or the Old Vic. They'd overnight at James's house in Welbeck Street, then spend Sunday in front of the fire going through the text, discussing it, reading it, until Zoe's knowledge and love of classical theatre was extensive and mature beyond her years.

By the time Zoe was seventeen, she knew she wanted to become an actress. James sent off for all the prospectuses from drama schools and they pored over each, weighing up their pros and cons, until it was decided that really Zoe should go to a good university and take a degree first, in English, then apply for drama school when she was twenty-one.

'Not only will you study the classics at university, which will help you in the future, but you will also be older and ready to suck up all the information on offer by the time you get to drama school. Besides, a degree gives you something to fall back on.'

Zoe recalled looking in fear at James.

'You think I'll fail as an actress?'

'No, my dear, of course not. You're my grand-daughter for a start,' he'd chuckled. 'But you're so damned lovely looking that unless you've got a bloody degree, they'll class you as a brainless bimbo.'

They'd agreed between them that Zoe, if her A level results were as good as expected, should apply to Oxford to study English.

And then she'd fallen in love. Right in the middle of her A levels. Four months later she was pregnant, devastated and her carefully mapped out future was in tatters.

Uncertain and terrified of her grandfather's reaction, Zoe had blurted it out over supper one night. James had paled a little, but had nodded calmly and asked her what she wanted to do about it. Zoe had shrugged and burst into tears. The situation was so dreadful, so complex, that she could not even tell her beloved grandfather the whole truth. James had eventually explained calmly that her father would have to be told, that Zoe was his daughter and he had a right to know.

All through that awful week when her father had arrived with Debbie in tow, shouting at her, calling her an idiot and demanding to know who the father was, James had been there, somewhere near, giving her strength and the courage to take the decision to have her baby. And he had never once asked who the father might be. Nor questioned the trip to London that had left Zoe drained, ghostly white and tearful as he'd picked her up from the local railway station and she'd fallen sobbing into his arms.

If it hadn't been for his love, support and his complete faith in her ability to make the right decision, Zoe knew she would not have made it.

*

Zoe negotiated the roundabout at the end of the motorway and headed for central London. Further tears filled her eyes as she thought of entering the empty house in Welbeck Street; a house that only two months ago had been filled with the pleasant aroma of Old Holborn tobacco, which James had smoked up until the day he finally gave in and died, a house that was no longer home because James was gone. In the last few months, he'd been awfully sick, his ears and eyes failing, his ninety-five-year-old bones begging to be given a rest. But his charisma, his sense of humour, his *life force*, had still filled the house.

The doctor had diagnosed his cancer two years ago. Because of James's age and frailty, chemotherapy had been ruled out. The doctor thought it more helpful to hide the true extent of his illness from him, let him have the time he did have left spent in a positive frame of mind, free of tubes and drips which would only extend for a short time a life that was soon to end. Zoe had agreed wholeheartedly with the doctor. If, as James deteriorated, that kind of equipment was needed for his comfort, then it would be provided.

It was at this point Zoe made the heart-breaking decision to send Jamie away to school. Not only did she feel strongly that after all his tender care, James had a right to receive Zoe's in return now he needed it, but also for the sake of Jamie himself.

At Jamie's birth Zoe had watched his famed, faded-blue eyes fill with tears as he kissed his great-grandson. The labour had been early and so swift that there had been no time for Zoe to make the half-hour journey from the Kent house to the nearest hospital. So Jamie had been born on his great-grandfather's old four-poster bed, a local midwife in charge. Zoe had lain there, panting with exhaustion and elation, and watched as her tiny, squalling son was lifted into his great-grandfather's arms.

'Welcome to the world, little man,' he'd whispered.

Whether the bond had formed at that moment, or in the following few weeks as grandfather and granddaughter took it in turns to get up at night and comfort a colicky, tearful baby, Zoe didn't know. All she did know was that the bond had strengthened and grown down the years. James had been a father, a friend and a male ally to her son. The two were inseparable from the beginning. As she had started to pursue a career as an actress, Zoe had not needed to employ a babysitter. She had been able to leave her son without the smallest hint of anxiety. Young boy and old man had spent many hours together, James somehow galvanizing the energy to play Jamie's favourite game of hide and seek, increasingly confined to the lower floor of the large house as his legs became weaker. Zoe would arrive home and find them out in the orchard, James throwing the football for Jamie to kick. He'd take him off on nature hunts through the winding lanes of the rambling Kent countryside.

And it was because of that bond that Zoe had known she must extricate Jamie from his all-abiding love for his namesake. Ease him into a life without Great-James, as Jamie had always called him, slowly, gently and with as little pain as possible. For Zoe knew how she had never regarded James as old while she was growing up. She remembered being shocked when she read a piece about him in the newspaper at the age of fourteen and discovered that he was celebrating his eighty-third birthday. Nor did Jamie see the age etched on his face, nor the way he'd fall asleep in his armchair after lunch and not wake until the evening. Death was a foreign phenomenon to a nine-year-old boy, especially one as sensitive and bright as Jamie.

So Jamie had gone away to school and thankfully settled down happily, while Zoe had nursed and cared for an increasingly frail and sick old man. James refused to go into hospital and the doctor had agreed that, as long as Zoe could cope, James was just as well off at home. However, Zoe had persuaded him they should move to the Welbeck Street house, which had immediate access to the hospital facilities James might need in an emergency.

One cold November evening, just a week before he died, James had caught Zoe's hand. 'Where's Jamie?'

'He's at school.'

'Then can he come home this weekend? I need to see him.'

'James, I don't know whether that's such a good idea.'

'You mean you're worried about my condition upsetting him?'

'Yes.'

'Don't be. We've discussed it plenty. I've known

since Jamie was first born that I wasn't immortal, my darling. It was obvious I was unlikely to be around beyond his early years. Therefore, Jamie has been prepared most of his life for my departure.'

'I see.'

'So? You'll get him home?'

'Yes.'

Reluctantly, Zoe had collected Jamie from school on Friday evening. On the drive home, she'd told him how ill James was. Jamie had nodded. 'I know. He's going to die soon. He told me at half-term, actually; said he'd call for me when it was near.'

When Jamie ran upstairs, Zoe had paced the kitchen, worrying how Jamie would react to seeing Great-James so ill. She heard a couple of bumps and thumps and raced up the stairs to find Jamie grinning on the landing.

'Go away, Mumma. We're having a private, secret game.'

That night, as the three of them had supper in James's room, Zoe thought the old man had brightened considerably. Jamie spent much of the weekend ensconced in James's bedroom. When she finally went upstairs and told Jamie they had to leave to get back in time for school curfew, James threw his arms out to his great-grandson.

'Bye, old chap. You take care of yourself and that mother of yours.'

Jamie nodded, hugged his great-grandfather tightly, and left the room.

They hadn't talked much on the journey down to Jamie's Berkshire prep school. Just as they pulled into the school gates, Jamie had spoken. 'I'll never see Great-James again, you know.'

'Darling! Of course you will.'

'No, Mumma. He's going soon, he told me.'

Zoe had pulled the car to a stop. She turned and looked at her son, at his serious little face.

'Don't worry, Mumma. I'll be there to look after you.'

And with a wave he was off up the steps and inside.

*

Less than twenty-four hours later, Great-James, better known as Sir James Oliver Harrison, was dead.

*

Zoe unlocked the front door of the house in Welbeck Street and closed it behind her, picking up the post from the mat. The house was cold. She shivered, wishing she could retreat back to the comforting, semi-isolation of her home in Kent. But work had to be done. Just before he'd died, James had insisted that Zoe agree to take the leading part in a film by an up-and-coming young British director. Zoe, who'd only given James the script to keep him from boredom, and never expecting him to read it anyway because of his bad eyes, had shaken her head. In the past year she'd put her burgeoning career on hold to care for James, only taking a few weeks' work in a film being shot conveniently in the Kent countryside, which meant she hadn't had to stay away from home. James had grabbed her hand and held it, telling her that a part such as this was not likely to land in her lap every day, that he thought the script was exceptional and she *must, must* do it, if he had to emotionally blackmail her into saying yes.

He hadn't needed to say 'last request'. She'd seen it in his eyes. She'd nodded reluctantly, agreed to call her agent and take the part.

Zoe took off her coat and wandered into the kitchen. Wine glasses and dirty ashtrays were stacked by the sink, left over from the drinks party she'd felt obliged to hold after the memorial service yesterday. The answering machine was bleeping. Zoe pressed 'play' and listened to the two messages. One was from her agent, asking Zoe to call her about the shoot next week, the other was from Marcus. A very drunken Marcus from the sound of things. He wanted her to ring him at home, immediately, urgently. Zoe sighed, took off her coat and slung it over the back of one of the kitchen chairs.

She'd been horrified when she'd seen what Marcus had turned up wearing at the church yesterday. And he'd not even had the decency to come back to the house afterwards, just skulked off without even saying goodbye. Marcus was sulking. Heavily. And there was not a damned thing Zoe could do about it.

Sir James Harrison had decided to leave virtually all his money and the house in Kent in trust for Jamie until he was twenty-one. The Welbeck Street house had been bequeathed to Zoe, along with his theatrical memorabilia that took up most of the attic space in Kent and a lump sum of money. There was also an insurance policy to pay for Jamie's school fees and university education, but *not* enough for the two of them to actually live on. Zoe smiled. Her grandfather had been a wily old buzzard. He knew, had he given her more, that Zoe might not have had the financial need to pursue her acting career, his dearest wish for her. There was also a large lump sum of money in trust specifically to set up the Sir James Harrison Memorial Scholarship. This was to pay the fees of, in the trust's opinion, two talented youngsters who would not normally be able to attend a reputable drama school. Zoe had been asked to set the scheme up.

Marcus, on the other hand, had received very little in proportion to his grandfather's fortune, which was substantial. Admittedly the two of them had never been particularly close. Their personalities had been very different and James had disapproved of what he saw as Marcus's lack of focus and flamboyant lifestyle. Sensing this, Marcus had steered clear of his grandfather in recent years and had only bothered to visit a couple of times in the last month of James's life. James had left him ten thousand pounds, a 'paltry token gesture', as Marcus had put it after the reading of the will. Zoe understood Marcus's shock and devastation, but, as usual, Marcus had been his own worst enemy.

Charles, her father, had also received much less than an only son should have done. Zoe had never quite been able to work out the relationship between father and son, but it had never been close. Charles had been left a small sum of money, some antiques and a Picasso Zoe knew James had never really liked. Not that her father needed an inheritance. He was himself now worth millions. But still, after the reading of the will, she could feel her father's hurt, and animosity crackling like electricity from Marcus.

'Looks like all that creeping and sucking up to Sir Jim did you some good after all,' he'd sneered.

Even though Marcus had called the following day to apologize for his outburst, Zoe could not forget the look of bitterness on his face. She switched the kettle on to boil, weighing up whether to call Marcus back, knowing if she didn't he was likely to call her at some ungodly hour of the morning, half-cut. She loved her brother, however excruciatingly difficult and unreasonable he could be. His temperament was quixotic; he was capable of being the most charming, caring individual when it suited him. At other times he exasperated Zoe with his wanton arrogance and selfishness. But she knew, deep down that Marcus had a good heart. He'd not had an easy time growing up. An absentee father and a dead mother was not the launching pad a child needed to grow into secure adulthood. Even if her brother had not helped himself, Zoe felt a great deal of guilt for the fact that she and her son had been so favoured by her grandfather. She picked up the portable telephone.

'Hi, it's me.' Holding the phone between her ear and her shoulder, Zoe made herself a cup of tea. 'What's up?'

Zoe listened as Marcus filled her in on the latest crisis to hit Marc One Films, her brother's fledgling and already ailing film company.

'Look, Marcus, you can't blame Dad for saying no. He's helped you out so many times before . . . *Yes*, I'm

sure it's a great film and it'll make you a squillionaire
overnight if you could only get that extra hundred
grand but—'

Zoe held the phone away from her ear as Marcus
shouted at her. She took a sip of her tea, then opened
one of the two envelopes in front of her.

'Marcus, you know all the money is in trust for
Jamie . . . What?' Zoe put the envelope inviting her to
the preview of the Nicole Farhi January sale to one side
and tore open the other envelope. 'You can forget that.
There's no way I'm remortgaging this house, Marcus.'
Zoe gritted her teeth to stem her anger as Marcus
launched another tirade at her down the line.

'Jesus! Enough is enough, Marcus! Listen to yourself! Are you really surprised James didn't leave you a
house when he knew you'd sell it toute de suite to
make a fast buck? I . . .' She stared down at the wording
on the invitation in her hand and suddenly felt very
faint. 'Look I have to go now, Marcus. Sober up and
we'll speak tomorrow. Bye.'

Zoe clicked the phone off and let it fall out of her
hand on to the table. The other words on the thick
vellum invitation swam in front of her as the name
came into sharp clear focus.

'Oh my God.'

chapter five

Marcus Harrison unlocked the front door to his rented flat in Holland Park, picked up the pile of letters, each one no doubt threatening to pull out all his pubic hairs individually with tweezers if he did not pay the enclosed amount immediately, and closed the door behind him.

He had a raging hangover, yet again, which had still not cleared, even though it was twenty to six the following evening. Dumping the bills on the table in the kitchen to gather dust with the rest, Marcus headed for the sitting room and the half-empty whisky bottle. Pouring a hefty amount into his glass, he sat down and knocked it back. He felt the warmth flow through his veins and calm him somewhat.

Marcus groaned and topped up his glass.

Where had it all gone wrong?

There he was, the – and there was no denying it – handsome son of a hugely successful, not to mention loaded, father, and grandson of the most lauded actor in the country. Almost a dynasty.

Not only was he good-looking, but he was bright, witty, kind to children (except that insipid, fey little nephew of his whom he couldn't bear), and generally the kind of person with whom success should walk hand in hand. And yet, it didn't. And it never had.

What was it his father had called him the other night? A lazy ligger with no staying power. God, that had hurt, really bloody hurt.

Whatever his father thought of him, Marcus knew he had always done his best. It wasn't his fault that life seemed to throw constant struggle in his way. Okay, so when he'd left school and decided to try his luck as an actor in LA, it hadn't been in his life plan to get the daughter of a studio president pregnant. Surely it had been fairer to her to suggest a termination? He didn't love her, she didn't love him, they'd been too young . . . but the girl's father had understood none of this. He had treated Marcus as though he'd *raped* his daughter, which was about as far from the truth as you could get.

'I'll make sure you never work in this town again' had been the attitude.

And sure enough, Marcus hadn't.

At the time, Dad had been pretty understanding. It was one of those things, he'd said, unfortunate as the chap in question happened to be the most powerful man in Tinseltown. Dad had given him a hefty amount to buy a flat in London and had suggested he try his luck there. Marcus had agreed and bought a swish bachelor pad in Chelsea, done bugger-all work and proceeded to hold noisy, drunken parties every night until the neighbours put in a petition to the council to have him evicted.

The borrowing from the bank to fund his Porsche and his extravagant lifestyle began to mount up. Marcus took out a mortgage on the flat to pay it back. Then he fell in love with a beautiful, blonde-haired Sloane who liked to dress in designer labels to watch TV at home and expected endless foreign holidays on private yachts as her due. Two years later, she'd left him for an Italian prince, and Marcus had had to crawl to his father to bail him out of the heavy debt she'd left in her wake.

Charles had written the cheque reluctantly and told his son that this was the very last and final time he was prepared to save Marcus's hide. He told him to curb his ridiculously excessive lifestyle and find a job.

Marcus had done just that, meeting an old school-friend at his club one night who told him of a film project that he and a few other chaps in the City were backing. He'd offered Marcus the chance to throw his hat into the ring too. Marcus, rather fancying the idea of becoming a film mogul and having to do sod-all work to boot, had remortgaged his flat to provide the necessary capital needed. The eventual film had been a huge and terrifying flop and Marcus had lost every penny of his one hundred and fifty thousand pound investment. But he *had* learned something through the experience. The production side of movie-making was what he wanted to do.

For the first time in his life, Marcus had found some discipline. He'd sold his flat to pay off the mortgage he could no longer afford and put the small remaining capital into an account to fund the new business, Marc One Films. The problem was that none of the banks would touch him because of his appalling financial track-record and his dad had point-blank refused to 'throw away' any more money. He also had the most amazing script handed to him by a friend of a friend. Not only was it a wonderful, sensitive story, just right for the 'caring' nineties, but it was going to be bloody cheap to make.

Marcus knew his situation was an extremely unfortunate case of crying wolf once too often. Everyone had lost their faith in him and Marcus was at his wits' end to know how to change their attitude. Of course, he'd been mightily excited when Sir James had finally popped his clogs. Even though there'd been little real love or affection between the two of them over the years, Marcus was, after all, one of only two grandchildren. With the fortune the old bugger had amassed over the years there had to be *something* substantial for him. He'd gone to the solicitor's office with Zoe, the brat Jamie and his Dad, feeling chirpier than he should for such a sombre occasion. That feeling had soon been replaced by astonishment and devastation when he heard the solicitor read his legacy, and utter disbelief at the thought of all that money being held in trust for Jamie, the golden child of the family. Never mind that he was illegitimate, born out of wedlock, the identity of his father a heavily guarded secret.

Up until the reading of the will, the fact that Marcus seemed to be regarded as the black sheep of the family by his dad, his dead grandfather and, to a lesser extent, his sister had rarely fazed him. Independent since he was a small boy and without a firm hand to guide him through his childhood or teenage life, Marcus had learned to rely on himself, growing a thick outer hide that protected him from the unwelcome opinions of others. But since the reading of the will, it had begun to dawn on him what a rotten time he'd had. No mother and a father and grandfather who so obviously favoured his sister and her bastard offspring. For the first time in his life, Marcus had begun to feel real bitterness towards his family. And the fact that he'd been so obviously snubbed by Sir Jim in the financial stakes just when he really was prepared to graft as hard as was necessary, if only he had the capital to do it, was chewing him up inside.

Never before more than a social drinker, Marcus had turned to the bottle to help him pass out at night, then revitalize him the following morning. Feelings he'd never experienced were stirring inside him. White-hot anger, hurt, misery and frustration were only some of the emotions he drank to remove. His inner confidence, his optimism and his relaxed, open personality seemed to have disappeared in a puff of smoke. He felt like a failure.

Was he having some kind of breakdown, he wondered?

The telephone rang. Marcus picked it up. ''Lo, Zo.'

'Look, Marcus, have you remembered you're taking me to this première tonight?'

'No.'

'Oh Marcus! Don't say you can't come. I really need you.'

'I'm glad someone does.'

'Marcus, come on. This isn't like you.'

'Maybe I'm not like me at the moment.' He shrugged.

'Go and get out your DJ, have a shower and meet me in the American Bar in an hour. My treat.'

'That's big of you, Zoe. Thanks.'

'I'll see you at seven. We can talk then, okay?'

'Anything you say, sis,' he drawled. 'Beggars can't be choosers, can they?'

'Bye, Marcus.'

The line went dead. Sighing heavily, Marcus did as he had been bid and went upstairs to dig out his dinner suit.

*

Marcus thought he'd never seen Zoe look more beautiful. He watched her as she walked through the bar towards him. Every head, male or female, turned to admire her.

'Wow, Zoe. You look radiant tonight.'

'Do I?' she asked nervously as she kissed him and sat down. She put a hand to her hair. 'What do you think? I don't look too old-fashioned, do I?'

Marcus appraised the sleek golden hair which had been expertly styled into an elegant chignon.

'You look fab, sweetheart, elegant and very sexy.' He eyed her. 'Okay? Can I stop now?'

'Yes, of course,' Zoe replied, a trifle irritably.

'You're not usually paranoid about your looks. What's up?'

'Nothing, it's nothing. Give me a glass of champagne.'

Marcus did as he was bid. Zoe raised the glass to her lips and he noticed her hand shook slightly. She emptied half the glass and put it down on the table.

'God, I needed that.'

'You sound like me, darling.' Marcus chuckled.

'Well, let's hope my half-glass of champagne does not have the same effect on my appearance as it seems to have had on yours. You look like hell.'

'Bitch,' Marcus quipped, feeling much brighter after three whiskies and two glasses of champagne. He ran a hand through his dark hair. 'To be honest, I feel like it too.'

'Still searching for the elusive hundred grand?'

'Yeah. Not that I have a cat in hell's chance of acquiring it, no thanks to dear old Sir Jim. I mean, what does a nine-year-old want with nearly three million quid? Can you imagine how much that will be in twelve years' time? Jesus, I only need a measly hundred grand.'

'I understand how hurt you are about the will, Marcus, but really, it's not fair to blame anyone, especially not Jamie.'

'Look, sis, I really don't mean to. I'm just . . . at the end of my tether I suppose. Everything's going wrong. I'm thirty next month. Maybe that's it, maybe I'm suddenly staring middle-age in the face.'

'Hardly,' laughed Zoe. 'But you must be down. I haven't seen you with a new woman in weeks.'

'Nope.' Marcus took a Marlboro Light out of the packet on the table and lit it up morosely. 'I've even gone off sex.'

'Oh my God!' Zoe's eyes twinkled. 'Now that is a sobering thought.'

'You know,' Marcus pointed his cigarette at Zoe, 'that kind of reaction is just what I expect from my family. Nobody has ever taken me seriously. You all patronize me, treat me as though I'm a child who has to be sometimes indulged, other times rapped across the knuckles.'

Zoe studied his pouty, spoilt expression and thought how accurately Marcus had described himself.

'Is that all our fault? Let's face it, Marcus, you have got yourself into some scrapes over the years.'

'Granted, but now when I suddenly feel I've matured, that I have a project I'm totally committed to, you lot won't either believe or support me.'

Zoe sipped her champagne, checking her watch as she did so. Twenty-five minutes before the première began . . . twenty-five minutes before she saw him once more in the flesh . . . her heart rate gathered pace and she felt suddenly and horribly sick.

'Look Marcus, we've got to be going. Get the bill will you?'

Marcus signalled a waiter and Zoe took one of his cigarettes out of the packet.

'Didn't think you smoked,' Marcus mumbled.

'I don't. Often. Listen.' Zoe inhaled, felt even sicker and irritably stubbed the cigarette out in the ashtray. 'I've had an idea about how we might be able to sort out your problem. I'll have to speak to Dad about it first—'

'Then it's a non-runner to begin with. Dad's as down on me as he could be.'

'Not necessarily, and besides, it's something that I make the final decision on. You may not like it, but it's the best I can do under the circumstances.'

Marcus brightened considerably. 'What is it? Tell me now, Zoe, please. Let me sleep tonight.'

'No, not until I've talked to Dad. Thanks.' The waiter handed Zoe the bill and she tucked her credit card inside the leather folder. 'What about immediately? Do you need some money to see you through?'

'Yeah, I do to be honest. I had no idea probate took so damned long. I'm down to my last few pounds and I'm about to be chucked out of my flat for non-payment of rent.'

Zoe reached into her clutch bag and drew out a cheque. She handed it to Marcus. 'There. It's a loan, mind you. I took it out of my savings account and I want it paid back when your ten thousand comes through.'

Marcus studied the cheque and smiled at his sister. 'Thanks, Zoe. I appreciate it.' He folded the cheque and tucked it away in his inside jacket pocket.

'Don't spend it on bottles of whisky, please, Marcus. Right, let's go.'

The two of them took a taxi to Leicester Square.

'How big is your part in this?' Marcus enquired.

'Second lead.' Zoe shrugged. 'You'll enjoy it. It's a good film.'

The cab pulled up outside the cinema. Zoe stepped out on to the pavement and surveyed the rather thin crowd of onlookers herded behind the barriers. This was an English, low-budget, quality production without a Hollywood star or special effect in sight.

Zoe grabbed Marcus's hand instinctively as they walked on to the red carpet.

'Stay close tonight, will you?' She squeezed his hand.

Marcus looked at her oddly and shrugged. 'If you want.'

'I want.'

A couple of flashbulbs popped in the drizzle as they walked inside the foyer, which was buzzing with the usual first-night mixture of soap stars, comedians, models and those famous purely for being famous. Zoe accepted a glass of wine from the tray and looked around nervously. He'd obviously not arrived yet.

Mike, the director, pounced on her and kissed her enthusiastically. 'Darling, sorry about poor Sir James. I would have come to his memorial service but I was horribly caught up with all this.'

'Don't worry, Mike. It was for the best. He was very poorly towards the end.'

Grief obviously suits you, Zoe.' Mike looked at her admiringly. 'You're looking stunning. There really is a buzz about the film, and doing this royal charity première was a stroke of genius by the PR people. We'll get oodles of newspaper coverage tomorrow, especially with you in that dress.' He kissed her hand and smiled. 'Enjoy, darling. See you later.'

Zoe turned round, Marcus, despite her plea, had disappeared.

'Shit.'

Zoe could feel the adrenalin pumping round her veins and making her head spin. It was then she decided she had every right to behave in a cowardly and immature way. So she went and hid in the ladies' toilet.

*

Zoe crept to her seat in the cinema, timing it just as the lights went down.

'Where did you get to?' asked Marcus.

'The loo. I've got the runs.'

'Charming.' He sniffed, as the opening credits began to roll.

Zoe sat through the really very good film in a daze. The thought that he was here, in the auditorium, possibly only a few yards away from her, breathing the same air as her for the first time in ten years, sent such confusing, intense shafts of emotion through her that she doubted she'd make it to the end of the film without passing out. As she sat there in the dark, Zoe admitted to herself that after all these years of telling herself it was some kind of adolescent fixation when she was young enough to know no better, those sharp, deep feelings had still not left her. She'd used Jamie as an excuse for the lack of boyfriends in her life, citing the fact that it would unsettle him to see his mother with a string of different men. But tonight Zoe knew she'd only been fooling herself.

And how exactly did one exorcize a ghost? One met it straight on and looked it deep in the eyes.

'Fuck,' Zoe mumbled under her breath as the credits rolled at the end and a roar of applause broke out in the auditorium. She'd been planning to grab Marcus and exit at high speed before any confrontation had a chance to take place.

No . . . she shook her head. If she was ever to free herself from his invisible grasp on her, she had to destroy the fantasy of him that she had built up in her head over the years. Maybe meeting him in the flesh, studying him for signs of imperfection was the only hope of a cure. There was every chance he would have forgotten who she was by now. It had been a long time ago and he met so many people, especially women.

The lights came up. Zoe gripped the seat with her hands, holding herself in it so she would not run away. Marcus kissed her and gave her a friendly punch. 'You were great, sis. The camera makes love to you, it really does.'

'Thanks.' Zoe sat in her chair as those around her began to leave the auditorium. Her courage left her.

'Shall we go, Marcus? My stomach really isn't good.'

'Oh Zoe! I was chatting to Jane just before we went upstairs and we agreed to meet afterwards at the party.'

Jane Donohue was the star of tonight's movie. Young, very voluptuous and, Zoe thought privately, overrated as an actress.

'Marcus, you promised! Take me home now, please. I'm really not well.'

Marcus sighed heavily. 'Okay. I'll just go find Jane, tell her I have to leave and extract her telephone number.'

Zoe stood in the crowd, counting the seconds until Marcus returned and she could retreat. She felt a tap on her shoulder.

'Zoe?'

She turned round, actually hearing the blood rushing round her body. And there he was. He looked a little older, a few creases beneath his warm green eyes, laugh-lines etched into the skin on either side of his mouth. But his body seemed as sleek and trim in his dinner suit as it had been ten years before. All these things she noticed as she gazed at him, thirstily drinking in every detail.

'How are you?'

'We . . .' she cleared her throat. 'Well, thank you.'

'You look . . . radiant. You're even more beautiful than you used to be.' He spoke in hushed tones, leaning forward slightly to reach her ear. She smelt him, the aroma so familiar and so frighteningly intoxicating. She could not speak to thank him for his compliments.

'I enjoyed the film. Thought you were excellent.'

'Thank you,' she managed.

'Sir . . .' A grey-suited man appeared next to him and indicated his watch.

'All right. I'll be along in a few seconds.'

The grey suit melted into the crowd.

'It's been so long,' he said wistfully.

Zoe nodded.

'How have you been?'

'Fine. Just fine.'

'I read about your grandfather. Nearly wrote to you but I didn't know your, er, circumstances.' He looked at her in askance and she shook her head accordingly.

'I'm not attached.' She hated herself for wanting to impart such information.

'Look, I have to run I'm afraid. Could I . . . ring you, maybe?'

The grey suit was approaching once more.

He reached out a hand to touch her cheek but stopped himself before it reached her face.

'I'm the last Harrison in the book.'

'Zoe . . . I . . .' The pain was visible in his eyes. 'Goodbye.' With a resigned wave he was gone.

She stood in the now almost empty auditorium, oblivious to everything except him, walking away from her, leaving her for matters that took priority over her, that always had and always would. Every bone in her body, every sinew and nerve ending screamed in horror at what she had just done. Yet her heart rejoiced.

Zoe went to the Ladies to powder her nose and recover her composure. And as she stared at her reflection in the mirror, she could see that the light which had been turned off so suddenly and abruptly ten years ago, had started burning in her eyes once more.

Marcus was kicking his heels outside in the empty foyer. 'Blimey, you do have a problem. Going to make it home?'

Zoe smiled and linked her arm through his. 'Of course I am.'

chapter six

Joanna sat down at her overflowing desk and searched amongst the paperwork for her keyboard. Switching it on, she dumped the newspapers, magazines, old copy, unanswered letters and photos into her in-tray. Telling herself she'd stay late one night this week to clear things up, she took an apple out of her bag and began to open her post.

'*Dear Miss Haslem . . .*'

'Spelt wrongly,' murmured Joanna.

'*I wanted to write and thank you for the nice piece you did about my son who had his Airfix model plane glued to his cheek. I was wondering whether I could ask you for a copy of the photograph that appeared with the article . . .*'

Joanna put the letter in the in-tray, bit into her apple and opened the next one, an invitation to the launch of a 'revolutionary kind of sanitary towel'.

'Pass,' she murmured, throwing that into the in-tray too.

The next envelope was big and creased and brown, the spidery writing almost indecipherable. Joanna was amazed it had reached her. She tore it open and took out its contents. There were two further envelopes inside, with a piece of notepaper paperclipped to the front of them. Joanna recognized the same spidery writing.

Dear Joanna,
    You may remember the old lady you helped home a few days ago. I would like it very much if you would come to my flat very urgently as I don't have long now. I have enclosed two things for you. Keep them under lock and key until you see me and let no one else look at them. I'll have more for you when you come.
    I am warning you it is dangerous but you are a young woman of integrity, I know, and the story must be told. If I have already gone, then you must talk to the White Knight's lady. It's all I can tell you now. I pray you are in time.
    I am waiting for you here.
    I trust you, Joanna.

The signature beneath was illegible.

Joanna read then reread the letter, chewing thoughtfully on a piece of apple. Throwing the core into the bin, Joanna opened the smaller brown envelope and drew out the contents. The piece of cream vellum folded notepaper felt flimsy beneath her fingers. As she opened it, she felt it almost crackle with age. Joanna scanned the page. It was a letter, written in ink in a flowing, old-fashioned hand. There was no date at the top and no address.

My darling Sam,
    I sit here, pen in hand, and wonder how I can begin to describe how I am feeling. A few months

ago, I did not know you, did not know how my life
would be changed, altered beyond recognition. Even
though I know we have no future, in fact no past
that any other can discover, I yearn for your touch.
Being beside me, sheltering me, loving me the way
that only you can.

I live a lie and that lie will last for eternity.

I don't know how much longer it is safe to write
to you, or whether you will receive this letter. I put
my trust in God, and in the loyal hands that will
deliver my words of love to you.

Reply in the usual way.

My darling, even my words to you are guarded.
How can I stand it?

Your true, true love.

The letter was signed with an initial. It could have
been a B an E an R or an F. Joanna could not decide.
She breathed out, feeling the intensity contained within
the words. Who to? Who from? There seemed to be no
clues, other than that the love was obviously clandestine. Joanna opened the other envelope and drew out
an old programme.

> *The Hackney Empire is proud to present,*
> THE GRAND AGE OF MUSIC HALL.

The date was 4 October, 1923. Joanna opened the
programme and flicked through the cast list, looking
for names she recognized. Sir James Harrison, possibly,
as his memorial was where she'd first met the old lady,
or perhaps the old lady herself was one of the young
actresses. She studied the old, grainy group photograph

of performers, but there was no one who caught her eye.

Joanna picked up the love letter again and reread it. She could only surmise she was looking at a letter written by someone who was, at the time, well known enough for the affair to cause a scandal. Two people in the theatre, perhaps?

As the old woman had presumed, the letter had whetted her journalist's appetite. Joanna rose from her desk and photocopied both letters several times, then tucked them, the originals and the programme safely back into the innocuous brown envelope, slid it into her rucksack and headed for the lift.

'Jo! Here!'

Tom caught her just as she pushed open the door to freedom. She swung a left and sauntered towards his desk.

'Where you off to? Got a job for you, doorstepping the Redhead and her lover.'

'I'm going to check out a story.'

'Yeah? What?'

'It's a tip-off, Tom, could be good.'

He looked at her, his eyes barely cleared from last night's hangover, and smiled. 'You got contacts already?'

'No, not really, but my gut tells me I have to go.' Joanna nodded at him.

'Your gut, eh?' He patted his substantial belly. 'One day, if you're lucky, yours'll be the same size as mine.'

'Please, Tom?' she pleaded with him. 'I did cover for you that day when I was dying.'

'Okay, bugger off. Be back by two though. I'll send Alice till then.'

'Thanks.' She smiled at him.

Outside her South Bank offices, Joanna hailed a cab and directed it to Marylebone High Street.

Fifteen minutes later, Joanna arrived outside the flat where the old woman lived. Paying the driver, she jumped out and went to study the bells. She had a choice of two, both unnamed. She pressed the lower bell and waited anxiously for an internal response.

None was forthcoming.

She tried again.

Nothing.

Joanna tried the top bell. Again her call was not heeded.

Once more, for luck . . .

The front door was pulled centimetres ajar.

'Who is it?'

It was not the old woman's voice.

'Erm, I'm here to see the old lady who lives in the downstairs flat.'

'Yeah? Well she's not here any more.'

'Really? Has she moved away?'

'You could say that, yes.'

'Oh.' Joanna physically drooped on the doorstep. 'Do you know where she's gone? I got a letter from her this morning, telling me to come and see her.'

The door opened a few more inches and pair of elderly female eyes peered out.

'Where are you from? The police?'

'No. As a matter of fact, I'm her great-niece. I've been away in Australia for months.'

The bright eyes studied Joanna thoughtfully. The door was opened wide.

'Well then, you'd better come in.'

Joanna stepped inside the dark corridor. The door on the right-hand side was ajar. She followed the woman through it and into a similarly designed maisonette to that on the opposite side of the passage. Except this one was very much a home.

'Step inside.' The woman beckoned her into the over-warm, rather cluttered sitting room and indicated the worn Dralon sofa. 'Make yourself comfortable.'

'Thank you.' Joanna watched her as she struggled to sit in the easy chair by the gas fire opposite her. She was a big woman, somewhere in her sixties, Joanna would guess, with a pleasant, open face. Her grey hair had recently been permed, for it coiled in tight, unnatural curls all over her head.

'I'm Joanna Haslam, by the way.' She smiled. 'And you?'

'Muriel, Muriel Bateman.' Muriel stared at Joanna hard. 'You don't look nothing like your aunt.'

'No, well, that's because she married my blood great-uncle, if you see what I mean.'

The woman nodded.

'Er, do you know where . . . Auntie is?'

'Yes dear, I'm afraid I do.' Muriel reached forward and patted Joanna's hand. 'It was me that found her, see.'

'Found her? I . . .'

Muriel nodded. 'She's dead, Joanna, I'm really sorry.'

'Oh. Oh no!' Joanna did not have to fake her shock. 'When?'

'Last Wednesday. A week ago now.'

'Bu . . . But, I got a letter from her this morning! How could she possibly have died and still have sent this?' Joanna fumbled in her bag and studied the postmark on the old woman's letter. 'See? It was sent on Monday of this week, five days after you said she died.'

Muriel blushed. 'I'm afraid that was my fault. You see, Rose gave me the letter to post last Tuesday evening. Then, of course, with the shock of finding her the next day, and the police and all, I quite forgot about it. I didn't post it until a couple of days ago. I really am sorry. I'll make some tea, shall I? You've just had a nasty shock.'

Muriel came back with a tray containing a teapot dressed in a lurid pink and orange tea-cosy, cups, milk, sugar and a plate of chocolate digestives.

'Thanks.' Joanna sipped the hot, sweet liquid as Muriel eased herself back into her chair. 'Whe . . . where did you find her? In bed?'

'No. At the bottom of the stairs in the hall. Crumpled, like a tiny doll, she was . . .' Muriel shuddered. 'I shall never forget the terror in the poor lamb's eyes . . . sorry. The whole thing's kept me awake for the past few nights.'

'I'm sure it has. Poor Auntie. Tell me, Muriel, if you wouldn't mind, how she seemed in the past few weeks. With me being away and everything, I'm afraid I've rather lost touch.'

'Well,' Muriel reached for a biscuit and bit into it, 'as I'm sure you know, your aunt had only been here for a few weeks. That flat next door had been empty for ages and suddenly, at the end of November, I see this frail old lady arrive. And then, a few days later, all them tea chests – ' Muriel stared into space ' – and she never unpacked them. I think she knew she was a-goner ages before she died . . .'

Joanna bit her lip silently and waited for Muriel to continue.

'I didn't bother her for a few days after that, thought I'd let her settle in before I'd make myself known to her as her neighbour. But she never seemed to leave the house, so one day I knocked on the door. I was worried, see, with her being so frail and no one coming in or out of that awful, damp old place, but I got no reply. Then, it must have been the middle of December when I heard a cry from the passage. Like a kitten it was, so weak and small. And there she was, on the floor of the passageway, in her coat an' all. She'd stumbled over her doorstep and couldn't get up. Naturally I helped her, brought her in here, sat her down and made her a cup of tea, just like I've made you today.'

'Oh dear.' Joanna sighed. 'If only I'd known she was so frail.'

'Well, if it's any comfort we all say that, dear. I had a bloomin' great big row with my Stanley and he dropped down dead the next day of a heart attack. Anyway, I asked her name that day and where she'd moved from. She said she'd been abroad for many, many years and had only come back recently. I asked if she had relatives here and she shook her head, saying most of them were still abroad. She must have meant you, dear.' Muriel nodded. 'Then I told her if she wanted bits of shopping done or medicines fetching she only had to ask. I remember her thanking me very polite-like for my offer and asking if I'd get her some tins of soup. That's where she'd been going when she fell, see.' Muriel shook her head. 'I asked her whether she wanted me to call the doctor to see about her fall, but she refused. When it was time to take her back to her flat, the poor old girl could hardly stand. I had to help her every inch of the way. Well, when I saw that miserable, miserable room that she lived in, with all them tea chests and that awful pong, I tell you, I was shocked.'

'Auntie always was eccentric,' Joanna threw in lamely.

'Yeah well, excuse me for saying, but I'd reckon unhygienic too. My cat lives better than she did, poor old biddy. Of course, I suggested I call the social services, see if they could send someone in, get meals on wheels and a district nurse to bath her but she got so upset about it I thought she'd peg out then and there. So I left that but I insisted I should have a key to her front door. I said to her, what if you was to fall again inside the flat and the door was locked and I couldn't get in to help you? She finally agreed. I promised that all I'd do was to pop in once in a while and check on her. She went on an' on about the key and keeping it safe and telling no one I had a spare.' Muriel sighed and shook her head. 'Funny old buzzard all round. More tea?'

'Yes please. She did always value her independence.'

'Yeah, and look where it left her.' Muriel sniffed as she topped up Joanna's cup. 'Well now, I did pop in to check on her once a day from then on in. She was usually in bed, propped up with cushions, writing letters that I'd pop in the box for her or sometimes dozing. I got into the habit of taking her a cup of tea, or a cup-a-soup and a piece of toast. I didn't stay very long, I admit. The smell made me queasy. And then Christmas arrived. I went off to my daughter down in Southend, but I came back on Boxing Day. And sitting on the table in the passage was a card. I took it inside to open it.'

Joanna leaned forward. 'Was it from Auntie?'

'Yes. A beautiful Christmas card, you know, one of them ones you buy separately from a newsagent and not in a pack. She'd written inside in ink, in that old-fashioned style of hers. "Muriel, thank you for your friendship. I will treasure it always, Rose." Muriel wiped a tear away from her eye. 'Made me cry, that card did. Your auntie must have been a lady, well educated. And to see her brought to that . . .' Muriel shook her head. 'I went to knock on her door to say thank you for the card. I persuaded her to come in for a warm by the fire and a mince pie.'

Joanna nodded. 'I'm glad. You've been so kind to her, Muriel.'

'Least I could do. She was no bother. We had a nice chat, actually. I asked her about her family again, if she'd had kids. She turned dead pale, then shook her head and changed the subject. I didn't press her. I could see that she'd got even weaker that night. There was nothing of her, just skin and bone. I tried to suggest calling the social again, but she got all funny and said she was perfectly fine on her own and that was the way she wanted to stay. Then, just after Christmas my sister in Epping took ill and asked me if I could go and stay with her for a week to look after her. I went and got back only a couple of days before the poor old thing died.'

'And she gave you the letter to post?'

'Yes. I went in to check on her the evening I arrived back. In a shocking state she was, shaking, shivering, jumpy as a cat on a tin roof. And her eyes . . . they had this look . . . I dunno.' Muriel shuddered. 'Anyway, she handed me the letter, begged me to post it for her urgently. I said I would of course. Then she grabbed my hand and squeezed it, really tight, and handed me a small box. She asked me to open it and there inside was a beautiful gold locket. Not my style, of course, too delicate for me, but you could see the workmanship was good and the gold was solid. Of course, I said immediately I couldn't accept such an expensive gift but she insisted I keep the locket, got really upset when I tried to give it back to her. Quite affected me, it did. I went back to my own place and decided then and there that I was getting a doctor to her the next day, whatever she said. But of course, the next day, it was too late.'

'Oh Muriel, if only . . .'

Muriel shook her head. 'Don't go blaming yourself. I should have posted the letter. But if it's any comfort to you, she was a-goner before it would have arrived. I found her at ten the next morning, lying at the bottom of the stairs, like I told you. Do you want a brandy? I could do with one, I tell you.'

Whilst Muriel went into the kitchen to fix herself the drink, Joanna pondered what she had learned so far. She was desperate to write it all down, but of course that was totally impossible.

'Ciggie?' Muriel was back with her brandy and packet of Embassy.

'No thanks.'

'Always like a fag when I drink, me.' She sat down again.

'I wonder what Auntie was doing at the foot of the stairs?' mused Joanna. 'If she was that frail, there was surely no way she could have climbed them alone?'

'Absolutely what I said to the ambulance man when he arrived.' Muriel nodded. 'He told me he thought she'd broken her neck, and the big bruises on her head and her arms and legs said to him that she had fallen right the way down. I said then and there that Rose could never have got up the stairs alone. Besides' – Muriel shrugged – 'why would she want to? The upstairs was deserted.' She blushed. 'I went and had a dekko once, just out of curiosity, like.'

Joanna shook her head. 'That really is very odd.'

'Yeah.' Muriel took a drag of her cigarette. 'Well, of course, the police had to be called and they all trooped in and started asking me lots of questions, like who she was and how long she'd lived there and stuff. The whole thing really upset me, it did. When they'd taken her away, I packed a case, called my daughter and went to stay with her for a couple of days . . .' Muriel reached for her brandy. 'I was only trying to do my best.'

'I know. Do you know where they took her?'

'To the morgue, I s'pose, to wait for someone to claim her, poor old thing.'

The two women sat silently, staring into the fire. There was so much more Joanna wanted to ask, but knew she could not. Eventually she said, 'Well, I suppose I'd better go and see the flat, decide what to do with Auntie's things.'

'They've gone,' said Muriel abruptly.

'What? Where?'

'I dunno. I told you I stayed down at my daughter's for a couple of days afterwards. When I came back I let myself into her flat, to lay the ghost as much as anything else, and the whole place had been emptied. There's nothing there, nothing at all.'

'But . . . who would have taken them?'

'I thought that maybe the family had been notified and come to clear the place out. Have you got any family over here that might have done it?'

'Er . . . no, no, I haven't. They're all abroad like Rose said. There's only me here . . .' Joanna's voice tailed off. 'Why?' she pondered out loud.

'Search me,' Muriel shrugged. 'I've still got the key. Want to go and take a look for yourself? Smell's not too bad now. Whoever took the stuff gave the place a thorough going over with the disinfectant bottle too.'

Joanna followed Muriel out of her flat and into the passage. She watched as Muriel unlocked the door opposite.

'You don't mind if I leave you to it, do you? That place spooks me out. Be glad when they get another tenant. A young family would be nice, breathe some life back into the place again.'

'Of course not. I've disturbed you long enough anyway. Would you mind if I took your telephone number, just in case I need to get any other details?'

'No, not at all. I'll write it down for you. Come and collect it when you drop the key back in.'

Joanna stepped inside Rose's flat, pulling the door to behind her. She switched on the light and stood in the small hall, looking up at the steep, uneven staircase to her right. The woman she had helped out of the church two weeks back was no more capable of mounting those stairs than a newborn baby. Slowly, Joanna walked up them. Each step creaked noisily. At the top of the stairs was a small landing. Two deserted rooms lay beyond, one on each side. Joanna paced them, looking for something but finding nothing save four walls and bare boards. She left the room and stood on the landing, her toes on the very edge of the top step. No more than fifteen feet, the drop seemed much, much further . . .

Joanna walked back downstairs and entered the sitting room where Rose had lived for the last days of her life amongst her tea chests. She sniffed. There was still a faintly unpleasant aroma in the room. But that was all. The room had been stripped bare. Joanna got down on her hands and knees and crawled across the floorboards, looking for anything that previous eyes might have missed.

Nothing.

Joanna inspected the bathroom and the kitchen then went and stood at the foot of the stairs, the place where Muriel had found poor Rose.

'. . . I don't have long now . . . I am warning you it is dangerous . . . if I have already gone . . .'

Joanna shuddered. There was every possibility Rose had been murdered. The question was, why?

*

The car started its engine as Joanna came out of the front door. The traffic was solid all the way down Marylebone High Street. They watched her as she stood uncertainly for a few seconds, then turned to her left and walked off along the road.

chapter seven

Joanna spent a long, wet afternoon in the driving rain, standing huddled with other journalists and photographers outside the Chelsea house of the Redhead, as she was nicknamed by Joanna's fellow hacks.

The flame-haired supermodel, who was reportedly lovenesting with another female model of equal renown, finally made a run for it through her front door. The flashbulbs popped as the Redhead broke through the crowd and ran for her taxi.

'Right. I'm off to follow her,' said Steve, Joanna's photographer. 'I'll call you when I find out where she's going. My bet is the airport, so don't hold your breath.'

Joanna nodded. She watched the other photographers climbing on to their motorbikes and the cluster of reporters dispersing into the rainy night. She sighed with fatigue and frustration and headed for the Underground. On the tube, she stared blankly at the advertising panels above her. Doorstepping was such a thankless task. All that hanging around for hours, sometimes days, when you knew damned well the most you'd get out of the person at that point was 'no comment'. And it rather affronted her sense of basic human decency. If the Redhead wanted to have a rampaging affair with a sheep, for God's sake, surely it was no one's business but her own? But, as Joanna was constantly being told by Tom, the public had an insatiable appetite for all things scandalous, beautiful and sexy. The Redhead's picture on the front page tomorrow would sell an extra fifty thousand copies.

Coming through the tunnel at Finsbury Park, Joanna left the tube and headed for the escalator. At the top she checked her mobile. There was a short message from Steve waiting for her.

'I was right. She's on a plane to the States in an hour. Night.'

Joanna tucked away her mobile and headed for the bus queue, grateful she could go home and have a long hot bath before heading for Simon's flat, a ten-minute walk from her flat up the hill towards Highgate.

Too busy since her conversation with Muriel to think through what the woman had told her, Joanna wanted to pick Simon's brains, see what he thought. She'd scribbled everything she could remember Muriel had said down on her notepad on the journey back to the newspaper offices and just hoped there was nothing she'd forgotten.

Eventually the bus arrived and slowly made its way through the rush-hour traffic to Crouch End. Joanna alighted, then walked briskly along the street before turning into her own wide road, lined by large Victorian villas. Reaching number thirty-three, Joanna walked up the path and put the key in the lock.

Every step she took was silently watched by the men sitting in the grey Rover.

*

Simon's flat was on the top floor of a large converted villa at the top of Highgate Hill with wonderful views over the green spaces and rooftops of north London. He'd bought it two years ago, saying that what it lacked in footage on the inside was more than made up for by the feeling of space on the outside. Living in London was an enormous sacrifice for Simon. He was still a country boy at heart, yearning for the peace, tranquillity and emptiness of the moors on which he had been raised.

Joanna rang the buzzer and the security lock opened. She traipsed up the seventy-six stairs and, panting, arrived on the small landing that led to Simon's studio. The door was open, delicious cooking smells wafting through it, the sound of Fats Waller emanating from the speakers inside.

'Hi.'

'Hello, sweetheart, come in,' Simon called from the small but user-friendly kitchen in one corner of the room.

Joanna plonked a bottle of wine down on the breakfast bar that acted as buffer between the kitchen and the sitting room. Simon, face red from the contents of a saucepan he was stirring, put down his wooden spoon and came to give her a hug.

'How are we?'

'Er . . . fine. Just fine.'

He held her by the shoulders and looked at her. 'Still pining for Matthew?'

'A little, yes. But I'm much, much better than I was, really.'

'Good. Heard from him at all?'

'Not a word.' Joanna pulled up a stool from the breakfast bar as Simon went back to his stirring. 'I've put all his belongings in four rubbish sacks and left them in the hall. If he doesn't come for them in the next month, they're going to the dump.'

'Well said,' nodded Simon, reaching up into a cupboard above him and retrieving a wine glass. He poured some wine from the half-empty bottle standing by the hob and handed it to her.

'Thanks.' Joanna took a sip. 'How are you?'

'Well.' Simon topped up his own half-full wine glass. 'Tired, as usual. Sit down and I'll serve the soup.'

Joanna sat at the table by the window, which provided a pretty view over the twinkling lights of the capital.

'God, this is good,' Joanna praised, as she hoovered up the thick, tasty black bean soup. 'I think you should forget about the Civil Service and give Marco Pierre a run for his money.'

'Absolutely not.' Simon looked horrified. 'Cooking is my pleasure, my hobby, my sanity after a long day in the nuthouse. So,' he topped up Joanna's wine, 'how's work?'

'Fine.'

'Not stumbled on a major scandal recently then? Discovered a famous soap star has changed her perfume recently?'

Simon had a passionate dislike for the tabloids. Joanna shrugged good-naturedly. 'No, but there is something I want to discuss with you.'

'Really?' He wandered into the kitchen and put the soup bowls into the sink.

Joanna studied him as he bent over to extract a large casserole dish from the oven. 'Yes. A little mystery I managed to stumble on. It could be something, or nothing.'

Simon procured a ladle and filled two plates with the casserole. He added wild rice from a saucepan and brought the steaming plates over to the table. 'There you are, modom. It's bouillabaisse, commonly known as fish stew.'

'You really are going to make someone an excellent wife one day,' Joanna teased as she forked up a mouthful. 'This is delicious.'

'Thanks. Anyway, what's the story?'

'Oh God, let's eat first, shall we? It's so weird and complicated that I need my full concentration to even know where to begin.'

'Sounds intriguing.' Simon raised an eyebrow. 'Right. Let's nosh.'

*

After supper, Joanna washed up while Simon made the coffee. She sat down in a comfortable armchair and curled her legs underneath herself. Simon poured them both a brandy, sat down and lit a cigar.

'Okay. Shoot.'

'Well, remember the day you came round to the flat and I was so distraught about Matthew dumping me? And I told you I'd been to Sir James Harrison's memorial service and sat next to that strange old lady who almost keeled over and I had to help her home?'

Simon nodded. 'The one who lived in a room full of tea chests.'

'Spot on. Well this morning at work, I received an envelope from her and . . .'

Joanna went through the day she'd had as chronologically and as carefully as she could. Simon sat silently, listening to her until she had finished.

'Whichever way you look at it, her death points to one thing.'

'And that is?'

'Murder.'

'That's a very dramatic assumption, Jo.'

'No, Si, I don't think it is. I stood at the bottom of the stairs. There is just no way that Rose could have mounted them by herself. Besides, why should she want to? Muriel said the top floor was deserted.'

'Mmm. I think, Jo, that in these situations you have to think as laterally as you can. For example, have you considered that this old dear's quality of life was such that she really couldn't stand it any longer? The logical explanation is that she committed suicide.'

'But what about the letter she sent me? And the theatre programme?'

'Have you brought them with you?'

'Yes.' Joanna rifled through her rucksack and drew out the envelope. She passed Rose's letter to him and left the mysterious love letter and the programme on the table.

Simon scanned it quickly. He nodded and passed it back to her.

'The other letter?'

'There.' Joanna indicated the table. 'Be careful. The paper's delicate.'

'Of course.' Simon slid it out of its envelope and read that too.

'Well, well,' he murmured. 'Fascinating. Absolutely fascinating.' He brought the letter closer to his eyes and studied it. 'Have you noticed these?'

'What?'

Simon handed her the letter and pointed to what he'd seen. 'Look, all round the edge there are tiny, almost invisible holes.'

Joanna looked and saw he was right. 'How odd. They look like pin-pricks.'

'Yes. Pass the programme, Jo.'

She did so and he studied it for a while, then put it back down on the coffee table.

'So, Sherlock, what do you deduce?' she asked.

Simon took a sip of his brandy and sat back in his chair. He rubbed his nose, as he always did when he was thinking. 'We . . . ell, there is the chance that the old biddy was off her trolley and senile dementia had set in. That letter could have easily been something written to her from an admirer, of absolutely no importance at all. Except to her, of course. Maybe her lover was in the cast of the play or something.'

Joanna looked doubtful. 'But why send them to me? Why say it was dangerous? Rose's letter's a pretty intelligently composed dialogue for someone who's supposedly lost their marbles.'

'I agree. The whole thing is decidedly fishy. All I'm trying to do is to suggest alternatives.'

'And if there are no plausible ones?'

Simon leaned forward. 'Then, my dear Watson, it seems we have a mystery on our hands.'

'I am truly convinced that Rose was not mad. I am also dead certain she was terrified of someone or something. But where on earth do I go from here?' Joanna sighed. 'I was thinking that maybe I should show what I have to Tom at work, see what he thinks.'

'No.' Simon shook his head. 'You haven't got enough yet. I think the first thing you have to try and establish is who Rose was.'

'How on earth do I do that?'

'Well, you could start by going down to the local cop shop and spinning the same story you spun to Muriel, about being the great-niece just back from the land of koalas. They'll probably point you in the direction of the morgue, if she's not already been buried by her family, that is.'

'She told Muriel her family were all abroad.'

'Someone must have taken those tea chests away. The police may well have traced her relatives.'

Joanna shook her head. 'Even if they had, it seems odd that those rooms were swept clean within forty-eight hours. But I can hardly go down to the police station in search of an aunt whose surname I don't know.'

'Course you can. You can say she lost touch with the family years ago, that she may have remarried since and you're not sure what surname she might go under.'

'Good one. Okay, I'll do that as soon as I can.'

'Another brandy?'

Joanna checked her watch. 'No. I'd better be on my way home.'

'Want me to spin you down the hill?'

'I'll be fine, thanks. It's a dry night and the walk'll help work off some of those calories.' She placed the letter and the programme back in their envelopes and stuffed them into her rucksack. Then she stood up and headed for the door. 'Another culinary triumph, Simon. And thanks for the advice.'

'Anytime. But just watch yourself, Jo, until it's all been logically explained.'

'You sound like Mr Spock,' laughed Joanna as she kissed Simon on the cheek. 'Night.'

*

Joanna put the key into the lock of her front door. The flat was in darkness. She cursed, feeling sure she'd left the hall light on earlier and wondering if the bulb had blown. Closing the door, Joanna groped along the wall for the light switch. Turning it on, she walked into the sitting room and let out a gasp of horror.

The place had been ransacked. There was no other word for it. Her floor to ceiling bookshelf had been cleared, the hundreds of books scattered across the room. Her sofa had been knifed, the material covering both frame and cushions violently ripped to pieces. Plant pots were overturned, the soil spilling out on to the floor, her collection of old Wedgwood plates smashed on to the tiles of the fireplace.

Choking back a sob, Joanna ran through to the

bedroom to find a similar scene. The mattress of her bed had been ripped apart, her clothes torn from the cupboards and drawers. In the bathroom, her pills and potions and make-up had been opened and flung into the bath, forming a colourful, congealing mess that any modern artist might have been proud of. The floor of the kitchen was a sea of milk, orange juice and broken crockery.

'Noooo . . .' she groaned, as she staggered through to the sitting room, huge, guttural sobs emanating from her. She reached for the telephone and discovered the wire had been wrenched out of the back of it. Shaking violently, Joanna searched through the wreckage to discover where she had left her rucksack. She found it in the hall. Delving inside, she pulled out her mobile phone and with fingers that shook so hard she dialled the wrong number three times she called Simon.

*

He found her standing in the hall, shaking and sobbing uncontrollably.

'Sweetheart, oh sweetheart. I'm so sorry.' He pulled her to him, but she was too hysterical to be comforted.

'Go in there!' she shouted. 'See what the bastards have done! They've destroyed everything, *everything*! There's nothing left, nothing. Go and see.'

Simon stepped into the sitting room and took in the devastation, moving into the bedroom, bathroom and kitchen. 'Jesus,' he muttered under his breath, stepping over the detritus to return to Joanna in the hall. 'Have you called the police like I told you to?'

'Yes, yes I have.' Joanna sank down on to the heap of Matthew's clothes that had spilled out of one of the slashed black bin bags stacked in a corner of the hall.

'Did you notice whether they've taken anything? Your TV or video, for instance?'

'No, not really.'

'I'll go check.'

Simon was back three minutes later. 'Fraid so. They've taken the TV, video, your laptop computer and printer, hi-fi . . . the lot.'

Joanna shook her head in despair as they both saw the blue lights of a panda car twinkling through the glazed glass panel in the front door.

Simon stepped over her to open the door. He went out into the lobby and greeted the police on the path outside. 'Hello, officer. I'm Simon Warburton.' He dug in his pocket and produced an identity card.

'That kind of a job, is it, sir?' the officer asked.

'No, I'm a friend of the victim and she is . . . er . . . unaware of my position.'

'Righto, sir. I get your drift.'

'I just wanted a word before you go in. This was a most frenzied and violent attack. The lady was out at the time, thank God, but I would suggest that you take this very seriously and do as much as you can to find the culprit, or culprits, as the case may be.'

'Of course, sir. Lead the way then.'

*

An hour later, after Joanna had been calmed by the bottle of brandy Simon had brought from his flat, and had given as clear a statement to the police as her dazed brain would allow, Simon suggested he take her to his place for what was left of the night.

'Fine by me, Miss Haslam. Forensic should be down here any minute to go over the place with a fine-tooth comb,' the officer said. 'Best to leave the clearing up 'til morning anyway.'

'He's right, Jo. Come on, let's get you out of here.'

Simon put an arm round her shoulder and led her out of the front door, down the path and into his car. She slumped into the front seat. Simon walked round to the driver's door and opened it. Climbing inside, he turned on the engine and the headlights. Pulling out from the kerb, his left-hand headlight caught the number plate of a car parked on the other side of the road in its beam. How very odd, he thought, as he swung the car left, glancing into the darkened interior as he passed the vehicle. It was probably just coincidence, he told himself, as he drove up the hill towards his flat.

But he'd check it out tomorrow anyway.

chapter eight

The telephone rang just as Zoe had finished mopping the floor. Swearing because the device was on the other side of the kitchen, which meant she had to walk back over her hard work, she sprinted across and reached it just before the answering machine clicked in.

'I'm here,' she said breathlessly, hopefully.

'It's me.'

Her heart sank. 'Oh, hi, Marcus.'

'Don't be so chuffed to hear from me, will you?'

'Sorry.'

'I'm only returning your call, anyway.'

'Yes, thanks. Do you want to pop round this evening for a drink?'

'Sure, have you spoken to Dad?'

'Yes.'

'And?'

'Tell you later.'

'Okey-dokey. See you around seven.'

'Yes. Bye.' Zoe slammed the receiver down and let out a howl of frustration. Time was running short. Next week she was off on location to East Anglia to begin shooting *Tess*, the adaptation of *Tess of the D'Urbervilles* she had agreed to star in. But he wasn't to know that, was he? And even though she could leave her mobile number on the answering machine, the fact that she wasn't in situ, immediately available, and instead in a place where he would be so horribly noticeable would mean he wouldn't come to visit her. Instead he'd say something like 'we'll get together as soon as you're back in London', and then it would drift and the moment would have gone and Zoe just didn't think she could stand it.

'Please, *please* ring,' she begged the telephone.

Zoe looked at her reflection in the corner of a Bell's whisky mirror and sighed. She looked like hell. She'd done what she always did in times of high tension and crisis; she'd cleaned and scrubbed and polished and dusted manically, trying to wear herself out and keep herself from dwelling on the situation.

And she was totally unused to being by herself, which wasn't helping. Up until two months ago, there'd always been James to talk to. God, she missed him. And Jamie. She was only grateful that she *had* done as James had asked and accepted the part of Tess, especially as the call she so desired to take looked more and more unlikely to come as further time passed.

*

Marcus rang the doorbell at half past seven that evening.

Zoe greeted him at the door.

''Lo, Zo.'

She eyed him. 'You been drinking?'

'Only a couple, honest.'

'Mmm, a couple of bottles from the look of you.' Zoe led Marcus into the sitting room. G&T?'

'Whisky if you've got it.'

'Fine.' Zoe went to the antique drinks cabinet, a piece of furniture that was obviously worth a fortune but which she'd always thought was incredibly ugly, and retrieved the whisky. She filled a glass a quarter full and handed it to her brother.

'Come on, sis. That's a bit of a stingy measure.'

'Help yourself then.' Zoe sighed, pouring herself a gin and tonic. 'I'll just go and get some ice. Want some?'

'No thanks.' Marcus poured himself an almost full glass and waited for Zoe to come back into the sitting room.

'Making yourself at home, then?'

'Yes.'

'Nice to have a legacy like this,' he remarked.

'Marcus, I hate to remind you, but Dad did buy you an awfully nice flat in Chelsea not so long ago. It's hardly my fault if you managed your financial affairs so badly that you had to sell it.'

Marcus nodded. 'Okay. Fair point. I'll stop the bitter and twisted bit. Tell me what you and Dad discussed the other night.'

'Well' – Zoe curled up on the sofa – 'even though you really have been ungracious, not to mention downright nasty to me and Jamie over the business of the will, I can understand how you've felt.'

'That's very perceptive of you, sister dear.'

'Don't patronize me, Marcus. I'm only trying to help.'

'I would have said you're the one doing the patronizing, sweetheart.'

'Jesus! You are so bloody impossible! Now just shut
up for five minutes while I explain how I might be able
to help.'

'All right, all right.' He nodded. 'Pray continue.'

'I can sort of understand why James decided not to
give you very much out of the will. I think the deal has
always been that you were looked after by Dad, and me
and Jamie were taken care of by him. And because of
Jamie's lack of a male parent, I think James wanted to
make absolutely sure that whatever happened, he'd be
okay.'

'Fair enough,' nodded Marcus.

'But – ' Zoe took a sip of her gin ' – I still think
that it was unfair to give you so little and I hope
wherever he is, he won't mind me for saying so. The
trouble is that all the money and the Kent house are
tied up in trust for Jamie. Even if I wanted to, it would
be impossible for me to give you even a gift, shall we
say. I have this house, which is where I want to live.
The lump sum I've been left directly isn't that much.
Okay, so I'm working now, but what if my acting work
dries up in two years' time? With Jamie to care for
financially until he's eighteen at least, I just couldn't
take the risk of giving that money away.'

'No. I accept that,' Marcus said reasonably. 'But
there is always Dad to turn to. You haven't blotted
your copy book like I have.'

'True, but that really isn't the point. I want to be
independent – '

'Hear, hear . . .'

' – And I know that you do too.' Zoe sighed. 'So, there is only one area of the will in which I can legally and honestly extract some money for you.'

'And that is?'

Zoe shook her head. 'I really don't think you're going to like this, Marcus, but it really is the best I can do to try and help.'

'Come on then, shoot.'

'Well, do you remember at the reading of the will the bit about the memorial fund?'

'Yes, I think so, although by then I'd heard what Sir Jim had left me and was about to blow a gasket.'

'It's basically an amount held in trust to provide fees to drama school for one talented male and one female actor.'

'Oh. You're going to suggest I use that and go back to college, are you?'

'No, silly. What I'm suggesting is that we put you in charge of the trust and pay you a good salary to organize and administer it.'

Marcus stared at her. 'Is that it?'

'Yes. Oh Marcus, I knew you'd react like this! I'm offering you a job that will probably take up, maximum, a couple of months a year. Of course, you'll need to do the initial promotion and get the media interested in it to encourage would-be scholarship holders to come forward. Then there'll have to be a week or two of auditions in front of a panel and some administration, but really, it's money for old rope. You could do it standing on your head. It'll also make those that have doubted you in the business stand up and take notice. You'd really be helping the future of British theatre.

And there's no reason why you can't use the media coverage you'd receive to raise your own profile and your production company alongside.'

Marcus was silent. Then he said, 'How much?'

'Dad and I thought thirty thousand a year. I know it's not a massive amount but it's not bad for a few weeks' work. And you can have the first year's salary upfront if you want. There. The paperwork concerning the trust is in the envelope on the table. Take it home and have a look at it. You don't have to decide now.'

Marcus leaned forward and fingered the envelope. 'That's awfully kind of you, Zoe. I thank you for your generosity.'

Zoe genuinely did not know whether Marcus was being gracious or sarcastic.

'That's okay. I've really tried to sort something out for you. I know it's not the hundred grand you wanted but you'll have your ten, and thirty, which makes forty. Plus whatever amount you managed to salvage from the sale of your flat.'

'I've been living on that,' growled Marcus. 'There's not a penny left.'

'Whatever, you're nearly halfway there already. I'm sure it wouldn't be too hard to raise the other sixty.'

'No, no, you're probably right, as usual.' He sighed, standing up. 'Tell me, Zoe, where do you get off?'

'What do you mean?'

'You sit there smugly, a modern-day Goody-Two-Shoes, with your ordered life and money in the bank and you look *down* on me from your fucking celestial eyrie: the poor sinner who's lost his way but can be rescued with a bit of time and patience from angel Zoe.

And yet, *and yet*' – Marcus scratched his head in disbelief – 'it's *you* who's the fucking sinner, *you* who had the child at eighteen, an illegitimate fatherless child. Unless it really was the bloody immaculate conception, I'd reckon you knew more about sin then than I do now.'

Zoe's face drained of colour. She stood up, shaking with anger.

'How dare you insult me and Jamie like that! I know you're hurt and angry but I really have tried to do everything I can to help. Well, this is where I get off. I've had it up to here with your laziness and your pathetic self-pity. Now *get lost!*'

'Don't worry, I'm going.' Marcus stood up and headed for the door. 'And you can stick your wanky memorial fund where the sun don't shine!' The door slammed behind him.

Zoe burst into tears. She was crying so hard she only just heard the sound of the telephone ringing. She stopped crying and listened as the answering machine took the call.

'Er, hello, Zoe. It's me. I . . .'

Zoe almost vaulted off the sofa and sprinted into the kitchen to pick up the receiver. 'I'm here, Pip.' The family nickname she'd used in the past was out of her mouth before she could stop herself.

'How are you?'

Zoe looked at her rather pathetic, tear-stained reflection in the Bell's whisky mirror and said, 'I'm well, very well.'

'Good, good. Er, I was wondering, would it be too rude to invite myself to your place for a drink? You know how it is with me and I'd love to see you, Zoe, I really would.'

'Of course. When would you like to come?'

'Friday evening, maybe?'

'Perfect.'

'Around eight?'

'Suits me.'

'Right then. I look forward to it. Goodnight, Zoe. Sleep well.'

'Night, Pip.' Zoe put down the receiver slowly, not sure whether to carry on crying or to whoop for joy.

She chose the latter. Doing an Irish jig round the kitchen, Zoe made mental plans to spend tomorrow beautifying herself. Hairdressers and clothes shops were most definitely on the agenda.

Contemplating her complete and utter *shit* of a brother was not.

chapter nine

Marcus had fallen out of Zoe's house in Welbeck Street and proceeded to get satisfyingly and revoltingly pissed. Drunk enough to end up in some seedy Oxford Street night-club and meet a girl who, he'd been convinced at the time, was the image of Claudia Schiffer. When he woke up the following morning and glanced at the face on the pillow next to him, he'd known just how out of his mind he'd been. The girl had the kind of plump, undefined features that one would immediately associate with puberty.

He'd gone to the bathroom and promptly been very ill indeed. He'd showered, trying to clear the cobwebs from his head, and groaned when he remembered just exactly what he had said to his sister last night. He was a first-class, low-down, rotten asshole.

Insisting the girl in his bed refrain from playing truant from whichever comprehensive she would normally attend, he bundled her out of the house, drank large amounts of black coffee which made his stomach churn even more, then decided to take a walk in Holland Park.

It was a bright, crisp, frosty day. The weathermen were predicting snow. Marcus walked fast along the footpaths through the park and let the lump in his throat turn to tears. He really didn't like himself any more. Zoe had only been trying to help and he'd treated her like shit. It had been the booze talking, yet again.

So, his pride had been hurt, but what else did he have? And was what Zoe had offered him really so awful? As she'd said, it was money for old rope. Marcus had no idea how much was actually in the memorial fund, but he'd bet it was substantial. And surely, if it was managed well, there was room for expansion . . . Marcus pictured himself in the role of generous bene-factor, not only to students, but maybe to struggling theatres, young film-makers and, of course, himself as administrator. He would become known in the business as a man with sensitivity, insight and money to spend.

The only problem was, he'd have to go and grovel to Zoe big time. Then he'd get hold of the envelope he'd left at Welbeck Street last night and run through the figures.

Yes.

Marcus turned on his heel and headed for home.

*

Leaving Zoe to simmer down for a day and knowing how she absolutely hated arguments anyway, Marcus decided to call unannounced at Welbeck Street on Friday evening.

Bunch of flowers in hand, he rang the bell.

Zoe answered it almost immediately. Her face dropped when she saw him.

'What are you doing here?'

He stared at his sister's beautiful, subtly made-up face, her long blonde hair shining like a halo to her shoulders. She was wearing a royal-blue velvet dress that matched her eyes and encased her sylph-like figure, stopping just above her knees, revealing her long, slim legs.

'Blimey, Zo, you look stunning! Expecting company?'

'Yes ... no ... I mean, I have to go out in ten minutes.'

'Okay, this won't take long, I promise. Can I come in?'

She seemed agitated, nervous. 'No, this really isn't a good time.'

'Fine. I'll say what I need to here. Look, I was a total and utter bastard to you the other night. I am truly, truly sorry. I'd go down on my hands and knees if it would mean you would forgive me. I'm not excusing myself, but I was a drunk, angry, ungrateful shit. And over the past two days I've seen the error of my ways. I'd love to take over the memorial fund if you'd still let me. It's a great opportunity, and now I've calmed down I can see how good it was of you to trust me enough to offer it to me. Here.' He thrust the flowers into her hands. 'These are for you.'

He watched her eyes darting up along the street.

'So, do you forgive me?'

'Yes, yes, of course I do.'

Marcus was staggered. He'd planned on a good few days, at least, of serious grovelling while Zoe extracted her rightful pound of flesh.

'Enough to let me take over the memorial fund?'

'If you really want to.'

'I do, I do.'

'Fine.' Zoe surreptitiously glanced down at her watch. 'Look, can we discuss this another time?'

'Sure, as long as you won't change your mind.'

'No, of course I won't.'

'Do you have that brown envelope handy by any chance? I thought I could take it home and study it over the weekend, plan my media campaign, etcetera.'

'Okay.' Zoe flew inside, took the envelope out of the bureau in the study and ran back to the front door. 'There.' She handed it to Marcus.

'Thanks, Zo. I won't forget this. I'll call you tomorrow.'

'Yes. Night, Marcus.'

The door was shut hurriedly in his face. Marcus shrugged, amazed at how easy it had been, and walked off along the road whistling as the first few flakes of snow began to descend on the streets of London.

*

Joanna watched the snow fall in fat white flakes from the window of Simon's flat. She remembered how, as a child up on the moors, the farmers had dreaded its arrival, knowing it would mean long hard nights rounding up the flocks and taking them to the safety of the barns, then digging out those they'd missed, the ewes usually dead or dying. For Joanna, snow had meant fun and no school, sometimes for days, until the narrow roads had been ploughed and were once more passable.

She did not often yearn for her childhood home, but that Wednesday night she wished she was once again snuggled up in the attic bedroom of her parents' comfortable farmhouse, safe and untroubled by adult pressures.

On Thursday morning, when she had woken up, Simon had insisted on calling Tom at the newspaper before he left for work. He had explained about her break-in as Joanna had sat wrapped up in the duvet on Simon's sofa-bed, waiting for Tom to insist Joanna turned up for work at the usual time. Instead, Simon had put down the receiver and said that Tom had been very sympathetic. He had also suggested that Joanna take a further three days that were owing to her from Christmas, and use them to recover from the initial shock and set about the practical side of things, such as insurance, and the massive clearing-up operation she'd have to face before the flat was habitable once more. That meant she didn't have to return to work until next Wednesday. And Joanna had spent the rest of Thursday in bed recovering.

On Friday Simon had suggested she go home to Yorkshire for the weekend, receive some TLC from her mum and dad and take time out, but Joanna had refused. The thought of her flat in its present state would haunt her and make her unable to relax. It was like falling off a horse. You had to get straight back on or else you never would.

It looked no better in the light of day. Joanna hardened her heart and began in the kitchen, setting to work on the stinking mess covering the floor. Three hours later, the kitchen was back to normal, minus the crockery, the bathroom was gleaming and the sitting room had everything broken stacked neatly on the slashed sofa waiting for the insurance assessor. Joanna felt too exhausted to contemplate the bedroom. She walked in and packed a change of clothes into a holdall. Simon had said he was happy for her to stay with him for as long as she felt she wanted to. As she was reaching down to stuff her underwear back in a drawer, Joanna noticed something gleaming on the carpet, half-hidden by a pair of her jeans which had been wrenched from the wardrobe. She picked it up and saw it was a slim, gold Cross fountain pen. On the side of the ink barrel were the initials 'I. C. S.'.

'Some classy kind of a thief,' she muttered, putting it away carefully in her rucksack to hand on to the police.

*

'Morning, Warburton. Do sit down.' Lawrence Jenkins, Simon's boss, indicated a chair placed in front of his desk.

'Now, it seems you might be able to help us with a little problem that's come up.'

'I'll do my best, as always, sir.'

'Good chap.' Lawrence nodded. 'I hear your girl-friend had a bit of bother on Wednesday night.'

'Not my girlfriend, sir, but a very close friend.'

'Ah. So you're not . . .?'

'No.'

'Goodo. That makes the situation a little less delicate.'

Simon frowned. 'What exactly do you mean?'

'Well now, the thing is that we think your friend may well have been given something which contains information so delicate, that if it fell into the wrong hands could cause us all a lot of problems.' Lawrence's hawk-like eyes appraised Simon. 'Have you any idea what this something might be?'

'I . . . no, sir. I have no idea.'

'Well, we are sure that your friend has received a letter that was posted to her by a troublemaker. Our department have been instructed to retrieve that letter as soon as possible.'

'I see,' nodded Simon.

'It's very likely she doesn't appreciate its significance.'

'Which is what? If I may ask.'

Lawrence shook his head. 'Classified, I'm afraid, Warburton. Rest assured, if she does have it, it is absolutely imperative she returns it forthwith.'

'To whom, sir?'

'To us, Warburton.'

'You want me to ask her if she has it?'

'I would try a less blatant tactic than that. She's staying with you at the moment, isn't she?'

'Yes.' Simon looked at him in surprise.

'We checked her flat for the letter and it wasn't there.'

Simon tried to keep the shock and revulsion from his face. Tore it to pieces more like, he thought angrily.

'So, I would suggest that if she does have it, it may well be with her, possibly at your flat. Now, rather than subject her to more unpleasantness, I thought I could leave it to you to retrieve it for us. Rather fortuitous, really, you being her, er, friend. She trusts you, I presume?'

'Yes, of course. That's what most friendships are based on, sir.' Simon could not help the sarcasm that dripped out of his voice. He was being put in an impossible position.

'Good. Then I'll leave it to you to sort it out. Unfortunately, if you don't, then others must. Warn her off, Warburton, for good and for all. It really would be in her best interests for her to desist from further investigation. Righto, I think that's everything.'

'Thank you, sir.'

Simon left the office feeling angered and confused. He walked back through the maze of corridors to his own section and sat down at his desk.

'You've been to see Jenkins?' Ian, one of his colleagues, stood behind him.

'How did you know?'

'It's that glazed look in your eyes, the slightly slackened jaw.' Ian smirked. 'I think you need a good stiff gin to help you recover. The boys are having a shindig over at the Lord George.'

'Thought it was deserted in here.'

'It is Friday evening, Simon.' Ian started to put on his coat.

'I might join you later.' Simon nodded. 'I have some bits and pieces to tidy up.'

'Okay. Night.'

'Night.'

Simon rubbed his face with his hands.

'Shit,' he muttered.

Admittedly, the conversation had not been much of a surprise. He'd already been aware that there was something odd about the situation. Yesterday, at lunchtime, he'd gone to the car pool, smiled sweetly at the receptionist and handed her the letters of the number plate he'd spotted in his headlights the night before.

'Pranged it, I'm afraid, only slightly. It's going to need some minor repairs, but it's nothing urgent.'

'Okay.' The receptionist looked up the registration number on her computer. 'There we are. Grey Rover, yes?'

'Yes.'

'Right, I'll just get you a form. Fill it in and bring it back to me and we'll process it.'

'Will do. Thanks a lot.'

Simon had walked out of the office and made his way to St James's Park. He'd sat on a bench, eating his roll and thinking. The reason he'd known the number plate belonged to one of their cars was sheer coincidence. His own car was P_041 JMR. The number he'd seen on Wednesday night was P_042 JMR. The chances were that the car pool had bought in quantity at the same time and that the number plates had been given in numerical order.

Now Simon stared at his computer screen. Whatever it was Joanna had stumbled on was major, of that there was no doubt.

Wednesday night's incident and his meeting earlier had convinced him that Joanna was in danger all the time she had that letter.

*

Joanna was looking much better when Simon arrived home. Something was simmering on the stove.

'Blimey, are you sure you're okay? You? Cooking?' Simon laughed.

'Only spag-bol, I'm afraid. I'm not even going to start competing with you.'

'How are you?' he asked, removing his coat.

'Okay. I went to the flat today . . .'

'Oh, Joanna!'

'I know, but I had to. And I feel much better. Most of the mess was peripheral. Besides,' Joanna licked the wooden spoon, 'at least I can get a nice new comfy sofa out of all this.' She smiled.

'That's the spirit. Look, you pour me a drink and I'll take a shower.'

'Okay.'

Twenty minutes later they sat down to eat the spaghetti bolognese.

'Not bad, for an amateur,' smirked Simon.

'Cheers, big ears. I won't bother again.'

'Jo, where is Rose's letter?'

'In my rucksack. Why?'

'Can I see it?'

'Of course.' Joanna stood up from the table and went to fetch the envelope. 'There. Come up with something, have you?'

'Er, maybe. Look, I was wondering, would you mind if I took it into work with me? I have a friend who works down at the Yard in the forensic lab who might be able to give us some information on the type of notepaper, the ink and the approximate year in which it was written.'

'Really?' Joanna looked surprised. 'That's a pretty impressive friend for a mere civil servant.'

'I knew him at Cambridge, actually.'

'Oh, I see.' Joanna poured some more wine into her glass and sighed. 'I don't know, Simon. Rose specifically said to keep the letter close to me, not to let either that or the programme out of my sight.'

'Are you saying you don't trust me?'

'No, of course not. I'm torn, that's all. I mean, it would be great to get some details on it, but what if it fell into the wrong hands?'

'Mine, you mean?'

'Don't be silly. Look, Si, Rose was murdered, I'm absolutely positive about that.'

'Oh, come on, Jo. You have no proof. A mad old dear and you're seeing "Tinker-Tailor-Soldier-Spy".'

'I'm not at all!'

'Then why don't we leave it like this? You give me the letter and I'll take it to my mate. If he comes up with anything, we'll take it from there. If not, I think you should drop the whole thing and forget about it.'

Joanna took a sip of her wine as she pondered the situation. 'The thing is, I just don't think I *can* leave it. I mean, Rose trusted me. It would be a betrayal.'

'Jo, you'd never met the woman before that day. You've no idea who she is, where she's from or what she might have been involved with.'

'You think she might have been Europe's biggest crack-cocaine baron, do you?' she giggled. 'Maybe *that's* what was in those tea chests.'

Simon smiled. 'So, is that a deal? I'll take the letter into work on Monday and give it to my mate. I'm away on a God-awful boring seminar from Monday afternoon, but when I get back I'll pick the letter up and we'll see what they've had to say.'

Joanna sighed. 'Okay. This guy you know is trustworthy, isn't he?'

'Good God! Of course. I'll spin some story about a friend of mine wanting to trace her family heritage, that kind of thing.' Simon folded the letter, went to the kitchen and put it away in a drawer.

'Right then,' said Joanna. 'A little Viennetta for dessert?'

*

The two of them spent most of Saturday doing the remainder of the clearing up in Joanna's flat. Simon was going to be away for the next week and Joanna had agreed to stay at his flat until the insurance money came through.

On Sunday evening, Simon locked himself in the bedroom, saying he had some work to run over. He dialled the number and the line was answered on the second ring.

'I have it, sir.'

'Good.'

'I'm at Heathrow tomorrow at eight. Can someone pick it up from me there?'

'Of course.'

'I'll see them in the usual place. Goodnight, sir.'

'Yes. Job well done, Simon. I won't forget it.'

And neither will Joanna, Simon sighed, when he had to spin some excuse about the letter being so flimsy it had disintegrated during the chemical process. He felt like a Judas, betraying her trust. But he had done it to protect her. It was as simple as that.

Joanna flopped on the sofa watching *The Antiques Road Show* and relishing the fact she didn't have to get up for work tomorrow morning. There were other things she had to do, mind you . . .

'Right.' Simon emerged from the bedroom. 'All done and dusted. Oh, let me give you a telephone number, for emergency use only, just in case you get into trouble while I'm away. You seem to be attracting it at the moment.' Simon grinned and handed her a card.

Ian Simpson,' she repeated.

'A pal of mine from work. Good chap. I've given you his work and mobile numbers just in case.'

'Thanks.'

Simon sat down on the sofa next to her. Joanna put her arms round his neck and hugged him.

'Thanks, Simon, for everything.'

'You're my best mate, my honorary sister. You know you don't have to thank me.'

She nuzzled his nose with her own, enjoying the familiarity of him, then out of the blue, felt a sudden sharp stirring in her groin. Her lips moved towards his automatically. Joanna closed her eyes as they kissed lightly, then deeper as their mouths opened. It was Simon who stopped it. He pulled away and leapt off the sofa.

'Jesus, Jo! What am I doing! Theresa . . . I . . .'

Joanna hung her head. 'Sorry, I'm sorry. It's not your fault, it's mine.'

'No. I was as much to blame.' Simon paced the floor. 'We're best friends, this kind of thing shouldn't happen, ever.'

'No, I know. It'll never happen again, promise.'

'Good . . . I mean, not that I didn't enjoy it' – he blushed – 'but, I'd hate to see our friendship ruined by a quick fling.'

'So would I.'

'Right then. I . . . I'll go and do my packing.'

Joanna nodded and Simon left the room. She gazed at the television, the screen a blur through her damp eyes. It was probably because she was in shock, vulnerable, maybe still missing Matthew. She'd known Simon since childhood and even though she'd always acknowledged his good looks, the thought of taking it further had never seriously crossed her mind.

But just now, Joanna pressed her fingers to her lips, she'd not wanted the kiss to end.

chapter ten

Zoe lay in her bed daydreaming. It must have been at least half past eleven on Saturday morning. It was unheard of for her to be up later than half past eight; she left the badge of sloth in the mornings to Marcus, but today was different.

It had dawned on her when she'd woken up that she was entering a whole new phase in her life. Up until now, she had been first a child, with natural restrictions placed on one's freedom, then she had been a mother, a state that necessitated complete unselfishness, always putting Jamie's needs before her own. And lately she had been a carer, helping and comforting James through his final weeks. But this morning, finally, Zoe had realized that, apart from her never-ending role as mother, she was freer than she had been in all her twenty-eight years. Free to live as she wished, take her own decisions and then live with the consequences . . .

Although Pip had left at eleven last night, and their lips had only met in a chaste kiss goodnight, this morning she felt wrapped up by love in the calm, contented way that one associated with a night of satisfying love-making. If they had not touched physically, mentally they'd imagined it. Even the brush of his jacket against her side as he'd moved past her to open the champagne he'd brought with him had sent hot desire through Zoe's body.

They'd sat down in the sitting-room and talked, at first both shy and uncertain, but soon relaxing into the easy intimacy of two people who had once known each other well. It had always been that way with Pip, from the first moment they'd met. While others around him treated him with deferential uncertainty, Zoe had looked at him and seen his vulnerability, his humanness.

Last night, they'd both purposely steered clear of the past. Instead they talked of nothing in particular and generally revelled in each other's company.

Pip had finally and sadly glanced at his watch. 'I have to go, Zoe.'

'I know,' she'd answered lightly.

'You say you're filming in Norfolk for the next few weeks?'

'Yes.'

'I can easily be down at our place for a weekend. In fact, how about next weekend? I'll have the car pick you up on Friday evening. Do you know where you're staying?'

Zoe had walked to the bureau and pulled out details of the inn where she'd be staying for the next six weeks. She wrote the information on a postcard and handed it to him.

'Perfect.' He'd nodded with satisfaction. 'I'll give you my mobile phone number too.' He pulled a card out of his breast pocket. 'Here. If there's one modern invention that has revolutionized my life, it's my mobile friend.'

They'd stood in the hall, for the first time that night, uncomfortable.

'Bye, Pip. It was lovely to see you.'

'And you.' He'd nodded, then reached forward, squeezed her hand and kissed her lips chastely. 'See you next weekend. We'll have more time then. Goodnight, Zoe.'

*

Eventually Zoe got out of her bed, showered and dressed. She went shopping for groceries and came home, having forgotten half of the things she'd gone out to buy. Dreamily, she played a record dating back ten years which she'd not put on the turntable since.

On Sunday, having taken a long stroll through Hyde Park, enjoying the snow-covered trees and walking on the white grass to avoid the treacherous icy paths, Zoe returned home to call Jamie at school. He sounded very perky, having just won a place in the junior rugby team. Zoe gave him her number in Norfolk to pass on to Matron in case of emergency and discussed where he and his friend Ben would like to go for lunch in two weeks' time. She packed much more carefully than she usually would for location filming, thinking about what she might need for next weekend. Good underwear, she giggled, packing the La Perla set that Auntie Debbie had bought her for Christmas.

That night in bed for a few moments she allowed herself to consider the consequences of what she was beginning all over again. And the raw fact that, as before, there was no hope of any future.

But, Zoe thought sleepily as she turned over, she loved him.

And love conquered all, didn't it?

*

On Monday morning, Joanna waved Simon off to work, relieved at his departure. That morning there'd been none of their usual easy banter, and tension had hung thick around them. However, it was very likely that after a couple of weeks apart, the air would be cleared and they'd settle down once more into their old, comfortable friendship.

Joanna closed her mind to how she had felt about last night's kiss. It had been a very difficult few weeks and she was vulnerable and overwrought. Besides, there were other matters to attend to. And she'd been presented with the perfect opportunity. She had two whole days off.

As soon as Simon left, Joanna pulled the photocopy of the letter she'd taken at work, the programme and the covering note from Rose. As she did so, her hands touched cold steel and she retrieved the gold Cross fountain pen. She'd forgotten all about it, what with everything else.

I. C. S. The initials rang a bell, but Joanna could not think from where. Taking the top off, she pulled out her notebook. She sat cross-legged on the sofa bed, studying both the letters and the programme and began to jot down the events of the past few days. If Simon really thought she was going to curtail her interest in this whole business, then he really didn't know her as well as he thought. He'd seemed agitated and nervous on Friday night, most unlike his usual self. Why was he so dead set on her not following this up?

Joanna studied her letter yet again. Who was 'Sam' and 'the White Knight'? And who the hell had Rose been, for that matter?

She made herself a coffee and mulled over the few facts she had at her disposal. Was there anyone else who might know of Rose's surname? Muriel. Maybe she had seen letters addressed to Rose. And surely Rose would have had to sign some sort of tenancy agreement when she took the flat in Marylebone? Joanna flicked through her notebook, looking for Muriel's telephone number. If she could garner Rose's surname it would make her trip to the local police station that much easier.

She picked up the telephone and dialled.

*

Joanna opened the swing door that led to the front desk of Marylebone police station. Muriel had been unable to help her with Rose's surname. She said she'd never seen Rose receive a single item of post, not even for utilities. The electricity ran on a coin meter and Rose had not had a telephone. However, Muriel had passed on the telephone number of the landlord. Joanna had called the number and left a message on George Cyrapopolis's answering machine. This meant she had to busk the next few minutes at the police station and act as Simon had originally suggested.

The waiting area was deserted, and there was no one on the desk. She pressed the bell.

'Yes, miss?' A middle-aged constable strolled out of the office behind the desk.

'Good morning, constable. I'm here because I think your station might be able to help me discover what's happened to my great-aunt.'

'Right, madam. Has she disappeared?'

'Er, not exactly, no. She's dead, actually.'

'I see.'

'She was found a couple of weeks ago in her flat in Marylebone. She'd fallen down the stairs and broken her neck. The neighbour called the police and—'

'You think the call might have been taken by one of our officers?'

'Yes. I'm recently back from Australia. I'd got her address from my dad and thought I'd go and visit her. But when I arrived, it was too late.' Joanna sighed. 'If only I'd have called round sooner, then . . .'

'We all say that in retrospect,' nodded the constable kindly. 'I presume you want to know where she was taken, that kind of thing.'

'Yes. Only there's a problem. I've no idea what her surname might be. It's likely that she had remarried.'

'Well, let's try and find her under the name you knew her by. Which was?'

'Taylor.' Joanna plucked a name out of thin air.

'And the date she was found dead?'

'The thirteenth of January.'

'And the address at which she was found?'

'Nine Marylebone High Street.'

'Righto.' The constable tapped into a computer on the desk. 'Taylor, Taylor . . .' He scanned the screen, then shook his head. 'Nope, nothing doing. Nobody of that name died that day, not that our station dealt with anyway.'

'Could you try Rose?'

'Yep.' The constable scanned the screen. 'We have a Rachel, a Ruth, but no Rose.'

'Those ladies both died on that day too?'

'Yep. And there's a good ten more listed here. Terrible time of year for old people. Christmas is just past, the weather's cold ... Anyway, I'll tap in the address. If we were called to an incident that day, it'll be listed here.'

Joanna waited patiently as the constable studied his screen.

'Mmmm.' The constable scratched his chin. 'Nothing there either. You sure you got the right date?'

'Positive.'

The constable shook his head. 'It might have been another station took the call. You could try Paddington Green, or better still, the local meat facto ... I mean the public morgue. Even if it wasn't us who dealt with the incident, your aunt's body would have certainly been taken there. I'll write down the address. I think you should pay them a visit.'

'Thanks for all your help.'

'Righto. Hope you find her. Rich was she?' He grinned.

'I have absolutely no idea. Bye.'

Joanna walked out of the swing door, hailed a passing taxi and directed the driver to the morgue.

*

'Can I help you?' It was a young girl on the front desk, this time. What a God-awful depressing job, Joanna thought as she explained her story again.

'. . . So the constable thought my great-aunt's body would probably have been brought here.'

'Yes.'

The young girl took similar details to the constable. She looked up the name, the date and the address. 'No, I don't have a single Rose on that day, I'm afraid.'

'Maybe she was using another name?' Joanna searched for alternatives.

'I've put in the address you've given me and that's not showing anything up. Maybe she was brought here a day later, though it's doubtful.'

'Check anyway, would you?'

The young girl did so. 'No, still nothing.'

Joanna sighed. 'Then, if she didn't come here, where would her body have gone?'

The young girl shrugged. 'You could try some of the local funeral homes. If there was family you were unaware of, they might have had her taken away privately. But usually, if there's been a death and a body is unclaimed, they'll end up here.'

'Okay.' Joanna nodded. 'Thanks very much.'

Joanna caught a bus back to Crouch End and went to her flat to pick up her post. Shuddering, she closed the door behind her and thought how sad it was that a place which had been her pride and joy, her refuge and her security, now invoked antithetical feelings. Walking up the hill towards Simon's flat, Joanna wondered whether the best thing might be to put it up for sale and look for somewhere else. She doubted she'd ever be comfortable there again.

When she arrived at Simon's flat, she saw there was a message on the machine. It was from George Cyrapopolis, Rose and Muriel's landlord. Joanna picked up the telephone and dialled his number.

'Hello?'

Joanna could hear the crash of crockery in the background.

'Hello, Mr Cyrapopolis, it's Joanna Haslam here. I'm your deceased tenant's great-niece.'

'Ah yes, 'ello.' George Cyrapopolis had a deep, booming voice with a caricature Greek accent. 'What is eet you'd be wanting to know?'

'Whether Rose signed a tenancy agreement with you when she first moved into the flat she rented from you.'

'I – ' there was a pause ' – you're not the Eenland Revenue, are you?'

'No, I promise, Mr Cyrapopolis.'

'Hmmm. Well, you come 'ere to my restaurant and show yourself to me. Then we can talk, okay?'

'Okay, what is your address?'

'I am number forty-six, Wood Green. The Aphrodite Restaurant, opposite the shopping centre.'

'Fine.'

'You come at five, before we open, okay?'

'Yes. See you then. Thanks, Mr Cyrapopolis.' Joanna put the telephone down. She made herself a coffee and a peanut-butter sandwich and spent the next hour calling every funeral director listed in central and north London. No Rose was listed, either on that day, or two days after. 'Then where on earth did they take her?' she mused, then called Muriel once more.

'Hello, Muriel. It's Joanna. Sorry to bother you again.'

'That's all right, love. *Take the High Road* doesn't start for a few minutes. Any joy findin' your aunt?'

'No, nothing. I just wanted to double-check who it actually was that took Rose away.'

'I told you, an ambulance came for her. Said they were taking her to the local morgue.'

'Well, they didn't. I've tried that and the police station and every single funeral home in the district.'

'Ooh-er. A lost body, eh?'

'And they didn't ask you if you knew of any family?'

'No. I did tell 'em the old duck had mentioned they lived abroad though.'

'Mmm.' Joanna mulled this over.

'Tell you what, though. Have you tried the local registrar's office? You have to go and register the death there. I did it after my Stanley passed on. Someone would have had to register Rose's death.'

'That's a good idea, Muriel. I'll try it. Thanks.'

'Any time, love.'

Joanna hung up, then looked up the address of the local registrar's office in the telephone book, grabbed her coat and left the flat.

*

Two hours later, she emerged from the registrar's office, feeling totally bemused. She had tried every possible permutation that her information would allow. There had been three dead Roses registered in the two weeks after the eighteenth of January, but none at the right address and certainly not of the right age. A young baby, only four days old; just reading of her death brought a lump to Joanna's throat, a twenty-year-old and a forty-nine-year-old, none of whom could even conceivably be the Rose she was looking for.

The woman who had helped her said there was a chance that the death had still not been registered. But that would mean, surely, that the body was still lying unclaimed in the public morgue?

Joanna shook her head in agitation as she headed for the tube station and Wood Green. It was as if Rose had never existed. Her body *had* to be somewhere. But why was it that someone, obviously in a position of authority, had managed to cover their tracks so thoroughly? Or was there an avenue that was still yet unexplored?

Joanna walked along Wood Green High Street looking for the Aphrodite Restaurant. She found it and opened the front door.

'Hello?' The small, cheerfully decorated interior was deserted.

''Ello.' A balding, overweight, middle-aged Greek emerged from the beads strung across the doorway at the back of the restaurant.

'Mr Cyrapopolis?'

'Yes.'

'I'm Joanna Haslam, Rose's great-niece.'

'Okay. Sit down?' He pulled two wooden chairs out from the table.

'Thanks.' Joanna sat. 'I am sorry to bother you, but

as I explained over the telephone, I'm trying to find my great-aunt.'

'What? You 'ave lost the body, ees it?' George could not stop himself from grinning.

'Er, it's a complicated situation. All I wanted to ask you is whether my aunt Rose signed a tenancy agreement with you. I'm trying to discover her married name, you see. And I thought it might have been on the tenancy agreement.'

'No. There was no agreement.' George shook his head.

'Why? If you don't mind me asking? I would have thought it in the landlord's best interests to have one.'

'Of course, usually I do.' George removed a packet of cigarettes from the breast pocket of his shirt. He offered one to Joanna, who declined, then lit up.

'Then why not with my great-aunt?'

George shrugged. 'I place an advertisement in the *Standard* as usual. First call ees from old lady who wants to view. I meet her there that evening. She gives me one and a half thousand pound cash, on the head . . . nail.' George shrugged. 'Three months' rent up front. I know she was safe. I mean, not likely to throw wild parties or vandalize the place, eh?'

Joanna gave a small sigh of disappointment. 'I see. So you wouldn't know her surname?'

'No. She said she deedn't need no receipt.'

'Or where she moved from?'

'Aha!' George tapped his nose as he thought. 'Maybe. I was at the flat a few days after she move een. I see van coming. The lady – Rose, you say? – direct van men to put tea chests in flat. I stand at the door and help men and I notice they have foreign stickers on them. French, I think.'

Joanna suddenly remembered the pills she'd picked up from the table by Rose's bed. 'Can you by any chance remember when exactly it was Rose moved in?'

George scratched his head. 'Er, eet was November sometime.'

She nodded. 'Well, thanks very much for your help, Mr Cyrapopolis.' She stood up and so did he. They wandered towards the front door.

'Oh, just one last thing, did you clear out the flat after Rose had died? I mean, for new tenants?'

'No.' George shrugged in genuine puzzlement. 'I went down a couple of days later to see what was happeneeng and poof! Everything had gone.' He regarded Joanna. 'I thought eet was her family who had taken her theengs and cleaned up, but eet could not have been, could eet?'

'No.' She held out her hand to him. 'Thanks for your time anyway.'

'That's okay.'

'Have you rented out the flat again now?'

He nodded sheepishly. 'Someone called. No point in haveeng it empty, was there?'

'No, of course not – thanks again!' Joanna smiled weakly and left the restaurant.

chapter eleven

There was a knock on the door.

'Come,' he replied.

'Sir, this has just arrived for you.'

'Thank you.'

'Anything else, sir?'

'No, that will be all.'

He waited until the door closed behind her, then, with trembling hands, removed the contents from the envelope. He unfolded the paper and read the words through slowly. When he had finished reading he momentarily rested his head in his hands before picking up the telephone.

'Jenkins. It's me.'

'Hello, sir. You got the letter, I presume?'

'Oh yes, I got it all right.'

'Then can we assume that the case is closed? Pull the team off?'

'Oh no, Jenkins. I'm afraid we can't do that at all.'

'Oh dear, sir. Why not?'

'Because it's the wrong bloody letter, that's why!'

There was a pause at the other end of the line.

'I see. Well, we'll have to redouble our efforts. I'll put some more men on the trail.'

'You do that. Take as many as you need. It must be found.'

He slammed the receiver down in frustration, cursing the day the bastard had ever been born. As far as he was concerned, a deal was a deal, especially in a case such as this. And the man had welched on it, revealing his true, common stock. He may have given himself airs and graces, titles which had been bestowed on him in good faith, but at heart he was rubbish.

Today, finally, he'd been hoping against hope that he would finally be relieved of the burden he'd shouldered for nearly sixty years. It had been partly his own fault that things had been delayed. He'd seen that woman at the funeral and presumed ... He sighed. Such a waste of bloody precious time. He'd been barking up the wrong tree all along. The problem was that he was asking his men to work blind. Hunt for something it was imperative they knew nothing of. He cursed his age, his physical frailty, which prevented him from searching himself.

Time was running short. Every day it remained undiscovered was another day nearer catastrophe. The moment had come to share the facts. What he needed was someone to be his legs and his eyes, one person to whom he must pass on all that he knew. A man or woman who could be trusted completely, whose integrity and excellence at their job was second to none.

He picked up the telephone again.

chapter twelve

Joanna went into work on Wednesday morning feeling deflated. In the past two days she'd got nowhere fast, had gathered no further information about Rose than she'd begun with, other than the fact that the tea chests had arrived from France. Not quite enough, Joanna mused, to go to Tom and say she'd uncovered a major scandal, involving those at the very top of the pile.

'Morning, Joanna,' smiled Tom, patting her on the shoulder in a fatherly manner, 'how are you?'

'Better thanks.'

'Sorted out the mess at home yet?'

'Yes.' She nodded. 'They did an excellent job. I've got virtually nothing left.'

'Ah well. The only thing to be said is that at least you weren't there when it happened, or walked in on them for that matter.'

'Yes.' She leaned over his desk and smiled. 'Thanks for being so good about it.'

'No.' He shook his head. 'I know how frightening it can be.'

Blimey, thought Joanna. He's human after all. 'What do you have for me today?'

'Now then, I thought I'd let you back in gently. So,

you can either have "My Rottweiler is kitty-cat really", even though he took a chunk out of an OAP's leg in the park yesterday, or you can have a nice lunch with Marcus Harrison. He's starting up some memorial fund in remembrance of his granddad, old Sir James.'

'I'll take Marcus,' nodded Joanna.

'I was thinking you might.' He wrote down the details for her, handed them to her, then grinned.

'What?' Joanna asked, feeling her face colour up.

'Put it this way, Marcus Harrison is more likely to chew you up and spit you out than the Rottweiler. Take good care, now.' Tom smiled.

Joanna went to her desk and called Marcus Harrison, thinking this would be one of the more pleasant jobs she'd done since arriving on the newsdesk, not to mention coincidental. They agreed to meet for lunch in a trendy restaurant just round the corner from Marcus's flat in Holland Park. She hoped it might give her the opportunity to ask him whether his revered grandfather had known a little old lady called Rose . . .

*

Marcus ordered a good bottle of wine from the maître'd. Zoe had already said he could charge all expenses associated with the memorial fund to the trust. She had issued him with a float of £500 to organize publicity. Marcus sipped the burgundy with pleasure. Every time he had called Zoe on her mobile in Norfolk about his plans for the fund, she had been sweetness and light, never once alluding sarcastically to his appalling behaviour of the week before. Something was going on in her life, he just knew it. Whatever it was that had given her that sparkle in her eyes the last time he'd seen her, the happiness that made its presence felt in her voice, Marcus was glad of it. It had made his life so very much easier.

The amount in the trust amounted to nearly £750,000. An awful lot of money. Marcus had clapped his hands with glee when he'd read the documents enclosed in the brown envelope. He realized, of course, that the money was not his exactly, and that every move he made with the funds had to be okayed by Zoe, cheques drawn on the fund countersigned by her etcetera, but he was sure it was possible, as time went by and he earned his stripes, for further leeway. Apart from anything else, the money he had to dispense made him feel solvent and important.

He lit a cigarette and watched the door for Joanna Haslam, the journalist, to arrive.

At three minutes past one, a young woman entered the restaurant. She was wearing a pair of black jeans and a white sweater that clung to her firm breasts. She was tall and very slim. Her thick, shiny brown hair hung beyond her shoulders, the curly ends caressing her breasts. She turned round and followed the maître'd to Marcus's table. He stood up and smiled.

'Joanna Haslam?'

'Yes.' She smiled, showing a set of pearly white teeth.

'I'm Marcus Harrison. Thanks for coming.'

'Not at all.' Joanna sat down.

Marcus felt a shudder of desire as he noticed her

large, inquisitive hazel eyes, framed by dark, curly eyelashes and her lovely clear complexion, untarnished by make-up. Joanna Haslam was an absolute knockout.

'A glass of burgundy?'

'Thank you.' She nodded, her cheeks dimpling as she smiled.

'Here's to you.' He raised his glass.

'Here's to the memorial fund,' reciprocated Joanna.

'Now, before we get down to business, why don't we order? Get it out of the way so we can chat.'

'Absolutely.'

From behind the safety of her menu, Joanna studied Marcus. Her stored mental picture had not been inaccurate. In fact, if anything, it had underplayed his attractiveness. Today, instead of the creased safari suit, Marcus was wearing a casual soft wool royal-blue jacket and black poloneck sweater. She was mentally undressing him when his voice broke into her thoughts.

'. . . and the lamb. How about you?'

'Er, I'll have the soup and join you in the lamb, I think.' Joanna met his enquiring eyes.

'No baby lettuce leaves arranged on a plate and fashionably called a radicchio salad, then? I thought that was all you girls ate these days.'

'Forget it. I was raised in Yorkshire. I'm a meat and two veg girl myself.' She grinned.

'Are you now?' He looked amused and Joanna realized what she had said.

'I mean,' she blushed, 'I enjoy my food.'

'Good.' Marcus nodded. 'I like that in a woman.'

He was flirting with her already. Trying to concentrate on the job in hand, she reached into her rucksack and took out her tape recorder, notebook and pen.

'Do you mind if I record the conversation?'

'Not at all.'

'Right.' Joanna put the tape recorder near Marcus. 'We'll turn it off when we eat, otherwise you only pick up the crashing of cutlery.' She switched the recorder on. 'So, you're launching a memorial fund in memory of your grandfather, Sir James Harrison?'

'Yes.' Marcus nodded. He leaned forward and stared at her intensely. 'You know Joanna, you have the most wonderful, unusual eyes. They're tawny coloured, intelligent, like an owl's.'

'Thanks. Er, tell me more about the memorial fund.'

'Sorry,' he smiled disarmingly, 'your beauty is distracting me. Grandpa, dear Sir Jim, or Old Siam, as he was known to his friends in the theatre business, left a large amount of money in trust to fund two scholarships a year for talented young actors and actresses, who would not otherwise be able to go due to lack of funds. You know how few and far between government grants are these days. Each county council has an extremely limited number on offer to drama students. Once they've gone, you're out of luck. Even those who do receive a grant will have to work during their time at drama school to fund their living expenses. A lot of them end up either dropping out early, or in a heap of debt when they've completed the course.'

Joanna had hardly heard a word Marcus had said. To her embarrassment, she was highly aroused. Dragging her thoughts back to the business in hand, she thanked God she'd taped Marcus and could listen to it later. She cleared her throat. 'Right. So, will you be accepting applications from any young actor or actress?'

'Absolutely.' Marcus lit up a cigarette, inhaled and exhaled slowly.

'Surely you'll be inundated?'

'Oh, I'm sure we will. We'll be auditioning in May, and the more candidates, the merrier. The only stipulation is that they've been accepted at an accredited drama school and they've applied to the local council for funding and been either refused, or offered an amount that is too small to make a difference.'

'I see.'

The soup arrived and Joanna switched the tape recorder off.

'This smells good,' said Marcus, taking a mouthful. 'So Joanna Haslam, tell me a little about you.'

'But I'm the one doing the interview.' She smiled.

'Well I'm sure you're much more interesting than I am.'

'I doubt it, compared with your illustrious background. I'm just a straightforward, middle-class Yorkshire girl, who has a dream of becoming a solid, excellent journalist whose writing and opinions are respected by her peers and the public.'

'So, what are you doing with the *Morning Mail*? From the sound of things, the broadsheets would be more your style.'

'I'm earning my stripes and learning all I can. One day I'd love to move to a more up-market newspaper, but it's almost impossible to get in with no experience.'

Joanna sipped her wine. 'What I need is a great scoop to get me noticed.'

'Oh dear,' sighed Marcus. 'I don't think me and my memorial fund is going to do that.'

'No, but I like the fact that, for a change, we'll be helping to publicize something worthwhile that could really make a difference to someone.'

'I see,' Marcus's eyes twinkled, 'a hack with morals. That is unusual.'

'Don't make me sound twee, Marcus. I'm not, I assure you. I've doorstepped and hassled celebrities with the rest of the mob, but I don't like the way journalism is going. It's intrusive, cynical and sometimes extremely destructive. I'd welcome the new privacy laws if they were approved, which they won't be of course. Too many editors are in bed with those that run the country. How can the public ever hope to receive neutral information and form their own opinions when everything in the media has a political bias?'

'Not just a pretty face, are we, Miss Haslam?'

'Sorry, I'll get down from my high horse now.' She smiled. 'Actually, most of the time, I love my job.'

Marcus raised his glass. 'Well, here's to the new broom of young, ethical journalists.'

The soup dishes were removed and the lamb arrived. Joanna's normally healthy appetite had deserted her. She picked at her food, while Marcus swept his plate clean.

'Do you mind if we continue?' Joanna asked, once their plates had been removed.

'Not at all.' Marcus lit up a cigarette.

'Right.' Joanna pressed the record button on the

tape recorder once more. 'So, in his will, did Sir James specifically ask you to run the memorial fund?'

'No, not exactly. It was left to the family, my father, my sister and myself, to organize the trust. We decided at a family meeting that it should be me, as Sir James's only grandson, that looked after it.'

'And of course your sister Zoe is so busy with her acting career. I was reading the other day she's playing Tess in a film remake. Are you and your sister close?'

'Very. We always have been. Our childhood was – how can I put this – varied, so we always clung together for security and support.'

'And you were obviously very close to Sir James?'

'Oh yes,' nodded Marcus without guile, 'very'.

'Do you think being part of such an illustrious family has helped or hindered you? I mean, did it put you under pressure to achieve?'

He looked at her. 'On or off the record?'

'Off, if you'd prefer.' Joanna was eager to know as much about what made him tick for herself as she was for the interview.

'It's been a bloody burden, to be honest. I know how others might look at me and think, lucky bastard, but in reality, having famous relatives is damned hard. It's pretty impossible to outstrip or better what my grandfather did, and now my father. So I'll have to do something pretty spectacular unless I want to be thought of as second rate.' Suddenly he looked vulnerable, unsure of himself.

'I can imagine.' She nodded.

'Can you?' He looked at her. 'Then you'll be the first woman that has.'

'I'm sure that's not true, Marcus.'

'As a matter of fact, it is. I mean, I'm quite a catch, aren't I? Wealthy, famous family, reasonable looking – '

Joanna suppressed a giggle at his disingenuous estimation of himself.

' – it's entirely possible that no woman has liked me for myself. I've not exactly had the most high-flying career, you know.'

'What have you done in the past?'

'Oh, a bit of acting, directing, etcetera. Floated around on the outskirts of the family "firm". As a matter of fact, it's only recently I've found my niche.'

'Which is?'

'I'm trying to start a film production company and raise funds for my first script. I think, rather than being involved on the artistic, creative side, like the rest of my family, that maybe my gifts lie on a more practical level.' His eyes glittered. 'It's something that no one in the family has touched before and maybe an area of the business I can actually call my own.'

Joanna nodded. 'Well, I wish you luck. I'm sure it'll all work out for you. Now I'd better get some further details on the memorial fund. Can you give me the date on which the applications have to be in by, an address and what candidates need to submit?'

Marcus talked swiftly and concisely for ten minutes, telling Joanna all she needed to know for the article.

'Thanks, Marcus, that's great. Oh, one last thing, we will be needing a photograph of you and Zoe together.'

'Zoe's in Norfolk on location. She's there for ages.

I know I'm not as famous or anything, but you might just have to make do with me.' Marcus was pouting.

'That'll do just fine,' she said quickly. 'If they want Zoe, they can always use a still from her file.' She reached to turn the tape recorder off, but Marcus stopped her hand by putting his on her forearm. An almighty burst of electricity shot up her arm at his touch. Marcus put his voice low to the tiny microphone and whispered something into it.

He lifted his head and smiled at her. 'You can turn it off now. A spirit for you? Brandy maybe?'

Joanna glanced at her watch and shook her head. 'I'd love to, but I'm afraid I have to get back to the office.'

'Okay.' Marcus looked deflated. She watched as he signalled for the bill.

She stood up. 'I'll be in touch about the photographs and really, thanks for lunch.'

*

Back at the office, she sat down at her desk and rewound the tape recorder a little, then pressed 'Play'. She couldn't resist discovering what it was Marcus had whispered into the microphone.

'Joanna Haslam. You are quite gorgeous. I want to take you out to dinner. Please ring me on 0171 932 4841 to arrange this as a matter of urgency.'

She giggled. Alice, the reporter who sat at the next desk, looked at her.

'What?'

Joanna shook her head. 'Nothing.'

'You went to lunch with old hands-on Harrison, didn't you?'

'Yes. So what?'

'Leave well alone, Jo. I had a friend who endured the Marcus Harrison Experience. He's a cad and a layabout without an ounce of moral fibre in his body.'

'I know, but he is . . .'

'Handsome, charismatic, sex-on-legs, yeah, I know.' Alice chewed on a sandwich. 'My mate spent a year in therapy getting over him.'

'It's all right, Alice, really. I have no intention of getting involved with Marcus. I'll probably never see him again.'

'Oh? So he didn't ask you out to dinner then? Or give you his telephone number?'

Joanna lowered her eyes but said nothing.

'Of course he did!' Alice smirked. 'Well, just watch yourself, Jo. You've had enough heartbreak recently.'

'Yes. I know. Excuse me, Alice, I've got to get this typed up.' Irritated both by Alice's patronizing manner and by her accurate assessment of Joanna's reaction to Marcus, she stuck on her headphones, plugged them into the socket of the tape recorder and cleared her computer screen.

Five minutes later, the colour had drained from Joanna's face. She sat staring at the blank screen, her fingers constantly pressing rewind on the tape recorder and returning continuously to the same words Marcus had spoken.

She'd been so busy drooling over him that she'd missed the moment he'd said it. '*Old Siam . . .*' Sir

James Harrison's nickname. Joanna took off her head-phones and drew the by-now creased photocopy of the love letter Rose had sent her out of her rucksack. She studied the first line of the letter. Could it be . . .?

Joanna wasn't sure. She needed a magnifying glass. She left her chair and wandered round the open-plan office in search of one. Having eventually purloined what she needed from Archie, the ageing sports reporter on the other side of the office, Joanna returned to her seat. Her hands shook as she studied the word through the glass. 'My darling *Sam.*' She searched the space between the top left-hand corner of the S, and the right hand corner of the A. *Yes!* Joanna studied the dot again, aware it could be ink or a mark of some kind from the photocopier. No. There was absolutely, definitely, a small dot between the S and the A. Joanna took a pen and copied, as exactly as she could, the flowing writing of the word. And then she was sure. There was an unnecessary upward stroke after the capital S and before the A. Putting a dot directly above the stroke, the word instantly changed. Sam. *Siam.*

Joanna gulped, a tingle of excitement running up her spine. She knew now who the love letter had been written to.

chapter thirteen

Joanna had decided to strike while the iron was hot and utilize Tom's sympathy and current good humour to her advantage. Before she left the office, she went up to his desk. His shirtsleeves were rolled up, the perennial Rothman's hanging out of a corner of his mouth, sweat on his brow as he cursed the screen in front of him.

'Tom.' She leaned over the desk and smiled at him.

'Not now, love. We're behind deadline and fucking Sebastian hasn't rung in with his report from Miami and the Redhead. I can't hold the front page for much longer. The Ed's wetting himself as it is.'

'Oh. How long before you're finished? I've got something I want to talk through with you.'

'Midnight do, will it?' he said, not removing his eyes from the screen.

'I see.'

Tom glanced up. 'Is it important? Like world-threateningly, we're gonna sell another hundred thousand copies of the paper, type thing?'

'It might be a previously uncovered sex scandal, yes.'

Tom's expression changed. 'Okay. If it's sex, you got ten minutes. Seven, in the local.'

'Thanks.' Joanna nodded, then went back to her desk and spent the next hour tidying up the bits and pieces in her in-tray that she'd left for too long.

She walked round the corner to the seedy pub which was frequented by journalists only because of its proximity to the office. It certainly had nothing else to its credit. She sat on a bar stool and ordered herself a gin and tonic, knowing that calling her bit of a story a 'sex-scandal' was a slight over exaggeration, but it was the only way to get Tom's attention.

He strolled in at a quarter past seven, still in his shirtsleeves, even though the night was bitterly cold. 'Usual.' He nodded to the barman. 'Okay, Jo, shoot.'

So Joanna went right back to the beginning, to the day of the funeral. Tom drained his whisky and listened to her intently until she had finished.

'To be honest, I was going to give up on the whole episode. I was getting nowhere fast and then suddenly, today, out of sheer coincidence, I discovered who the letter was written to.'

Tom ordered another whisky. His tired, red eyes appraised Joanna. 'There might be something there. What interests me is the fact that someone has obviously gone to great lengths to make your old dear disappear, along with her tea chests. That would say to me a cover-up. Bodies don't just vanish into thin air.' He lit a cigarette. 'Joanna, just out of interest, did you have the letter on you that night your flat was turned over?'

'Yes. It was in my rucksack.'

'It hasn't struck you that it may not have been a chance burglary? From what you say there was a high degree of needless destruction. They knifed your sofa and your mattress, didn't they?'

'Yes. What are you saying?'

'That someone was looking for something they thought you might have? Possibly hidden?'

'Even the police seemed shocked at the devastation,' she murmured quietly. She looked up at Tom, a sudden fear in her eyes. 'Oh God, I think you might be right.'

'Christ, Jo, you've some way to go before you become a suspicious, cynical bastard like me. In other words, a great newshound.' He smiled and patted her hand. 'You'll learn. Where is the letter now?'

'Simon took it to work to have his forensic lab run some tests on it.'

'Is he a copper?'

'No, he's something in the Civil Service.'

'Fuck, Jo! Grow up!' Tom slammed his glass on to the bar. He shook his head. 'I'll bet a pound to a piece of pig shit you'll never see that letter again.'

'You're wrong, Tom.' Joanna's eyes flashed with anger. 'I trust Simon implicitly. He's my oldest and best friend. He was only trying to help and I know he'd never deceive me.'

Tom shook his head in a condescending manner. 'Caesar and Cleopatra were mates until an arsehole and an asp got in the way. All right, so the love letter's gone but you say you have a photocopy?'

'Yes. I took another one for you to keep.' Joanna handed it over.

'Thanks.' Tom unfolded it. 'Let's have a look-see,

then.' He read it through quickly then studied the name at the top. 'Could definitely be Siam. Yep.' He nodded. 'The initial at the bottom is illegible. But it doesn't look like an R to me.'

'Maybe Rose changed her name, or maybe the letter isn't from her. There's definitely some kind of theatrical connection, but neither Rose or Sir James are listed anywhere in that programme.'

Tom checked his watch and ordered another whisky. 'Five minutes and I'll have to scoot. Look, Jo, I honestly can't say whether you're on to something or not. When I've been in these situations, I've followed my gut. What is your gut telling you?'

'That I am.' Joanna nodded her head definitely.

'And how do you intend to progress from here?'

'I need to speak to the Harrison family, learn what I can about Sir James's life. It may be as simple as him having an affair with Rose. But why would she send me that letter? I don't know.' Joanna sighed. 'If my flat was turned over because they thought I'd got the letter, then surely this must mean it's quite a big deal to someone.'

'Yeah. Look, I can't give you company time to investigate this—'

'I was wondering how a profile on a British theatrical dynasty would appeal to you. Starting with Sir James and Charles his son, then looking at Zoe and Marcus. Then I'd have the perfect excuse to get as much information out of them as possible.'

'Bit girls' pages for the newsdesk, Jo.'

'It wouldn't be if I discovered some kind of huge scandal. A few days, *please*, Tom,' she begged. 'I'll do all the research in my own time, I swear.'

'Go on then,' Tom capitulated. 'On one condition.'
'What?'

'I want to be kept informed every step of the way.
Not because I can't keep my big red nose out of it, but
for your own protection.' Tom shrugged. 'You're young
and inexperienced. I don't want you getting yourself in
so deep you can't get out. No heroics, okay?'

'I promise. Thanks, Tom. I'm off to get going. See
you tomorrow.' Impulsively, Joanna kissed him on the
cheek and left the bar.

Tom watched her go, then looked down at the
letter in his hand. Nine times out of ten when a cub
reporter came to him with a 'great' lead, he'd shoot it
down in flames within a few seconds, send them away
with their tail between their legs. But just now, as
Joanna had reported her story to him, his famous gut
had twitched like billy-o. She had something. Christ
knew what, but something.

*

Even Marcus had been surprised at how quickly Joanna
had called him back. She'd used the excuse of wanting
to do some kind of feature on the entire Harrison
family to back up the memorial fund piece. Marcus
had, of course, complied with her request to visit him
at his flat the following evening. In honour of her visit,
Marcus had spent the day clearing the detritus of his
disorganized, bachelor existence. He'd swept what
lurked under his bed straight into a bin bag and even
changed the sheets.

It was a long time since a woman's imminent
presence had stirred such lust in him. If he hadn't

bedded her by ten o'clock, Marcus reckoned he'd lost his touch.

*

The bell rang at half past seven. He opened the door and saw Joanna had made very little effort to dress up, which disappointed him somewhat.

He reached forward and kissed her on both cheeks. 'Joanna. Lovely to see you again. Come in.'

She followed Marcus along the narrow corridor and into a small, basically furnished sitting room. She was surprised. She'd expected something much more luxurious.

'Drink?'

'Er, I'd prefer a cup of coffee, if you wouldn't mind,' Joanna replied. She felt exhausted. She'd been up most of the previous night making notes and determining the kind of questions about Sir James that she needed Marcus's answers to.

'Spoilsport,' said Marcus. 'Well, I'm going to have a drink, anyway.'

'Okay. Just a half a glass.' She nodded.

Marcus came back into the sitting room and sat very close to her on the sofa. He stroked her long hair. 'Are you tired, Jo? You look it.'

Joanna edged away from him. She had to concentrate. 'Yes, I am, a bit.'

'Well, you just relax. Hungry? I have some pasta I could knock together for you.'

'No, please don't go to any trouble.' Joanna set up her tape recorder and placed it on the coffee table in front of them.

'It's no trouble at all, really.'

'Well, could we get started and see how we go?'

'Of course, whatever you want.'

She could smell the musky scent of his aftershave as he reached forward and poured them both a glass of wine. No, No, No, Joanna.

'Right, as I told you on the telephone, I'm going to be writing a big retrospective on Sir James and his family to back up the launch of the memorial fund.'

'Wow. I'm truly grateful, Jo, I really am. The more publicity the better.'

'Absolutely. I'm going to need your help. I want to discover what your grandfather was really like, where he came from and how his meteoric rise to fame affected and changed him.'

'Blimey, Jo, surely you can go and get one of three biographies on him, can't you?'

'Oh, I have those from the library already. I admit I haven't yet begun doing much more than leafing through them, but that's not the point. I want to see him from the family's perspective, get to know the little details. For example, Siam, that pet name you say his old acting friends used. Where did that come from?'

Marcus shrugged. 'I've absolutely no idea.'

'I mean, he had no connections with the Orient or anything?'

'No, I don't think so.' Marcus emptied his glass and poured himself more. 'Come on, Jo. You've hardly touched your drink.' He rubbed her shoulders gently. 'You're awfully tense.'

'Sorry, I am, a bit.' Joanna sighed, picking up her

wine glass and taking a sip. 'It's been a funny few weeks, one way and another.'

'Tell me all about it.'

The pressure on her shoulders increased. She shrugged his hands off and turned to him, an eyebrow raised. 'No. I have to get this all buttoned under for the middle of next week and you're not exactly helping, Marcus. It's in your interests too, you know.'

'Yes, yes.' Marcus hung his head like a chastened schoolboy. 'I'm sorry, I just can't stop finding you attractive, Jo.'

She couldn't help but smile. 'Look, half an hour maximum, okay?'

'I'll concentrate, I promise.'

'Good. Now, what I really want to know is what you know of Sir James's life, right from the beginning.'

'We . . . ell . . .' Marcus thought he had never had to work so hard for the chance of a fuck. He'd really not taken a great deal of interest in his grandfather and his life, but he racked his brains to try and remember as much as he could.

'You know, it's Zoe you need to speak to really. She knew him better than I did because she lived with him.'

'Yes, I will speak to her, but it's always interesting getting different perspectives on the same person. Did you, by any chance, ever hear your grandfather talk of someone called Rose?'

Marcus shrugged and shook his head. 'No. Why?'

'Oh, her name came up in one of the biographies, that's all.'

'Well, I'm sure James had lots of lady loves in his time.'

'Yes. Did you know your grandmother?'

'No. She died before either Zoe or I were born. She died abroad. My dad was only a few years old, if I remember rightly.'

'Were they happily married?'

'Very, so the legend has it. But you can probably get a better idea of that kind of stuff from the biographies,' Marcus replied, unable to curb his impatience.

'Yes, possibly. By any chance, did your grandfather keep his papers? You know, old programmes, newspaper cuttings, that kind of thing?'

'Did he ever!' Marcus chuckled. 'There's an entire attic-full in Kent. They were all bequeathed to Zoe.'

Joanna's ears pricked up. 'Really?'

'Yeah. Zo's been saying for ages she's going to go to Kent for the weekend and sort through the attic where James stashed all that kind of stuff. Most of it's probably rubbish, but there might be a programme or two that's quite valuable now. A real hoarder, was Sir James.'

'Marcus, there's no way that maybe Zoe would allow me to look through that stuff, is there? I mean, I wouldn't take anything, or tamper with it, but it might be a great way of discovering who your grandfather was behind the acclaim.'

Marcus had a brainwave. His face lit up. 'Well now, how about I organize for you to come to Kent this weekend? I'll give Zoe a call. I'm sure she won't say no, as it's all in a good cause. Of course, we'll both insist on a minder being present, so you don't steal the family silver, or any long hidden secrets for that matter.' He grinned.

'And who would that minder be?'

'Er . . .' Marcus scratched his head. 'What with Dad in LA and Zoe in Norfolk, I suppose it'll have to be me. We could drive down on Saturday morning and spend the night there. You'll need a good couple of days at it.'

'Well, if you're sure,' said Joanna, uncertain herself. 'You'll ask Zoe then?'

'Of course.'

'Super. I really am grateful.' Joanna packed her tape recorder into her rucksack and stood up.

'You're not going, are you? What about the pasta?' Marcus looked horrified.

'It's really sweet of you to offer, but really, if I don't get some sleep tonight I'll be fit for nothing tomorrow.'

'Okay,' sighed Marcus. 'Spurn me and my spaghetti. I don't care.'

Joanna walked to the front door and handed him a card. 'There's my number at work. Would you call me tomorrow and let me know what Zoe said?' She pecked him on the cheek. 'Thanks, Marcus. I appreciate it. Bye.'

Marcus watched her as she left the flat. Surely Joanna would soon tire of searching through fusty, dusty boxes of yellowing paper down in Kent and allow him to amuse and entertain her. Whistling with antici-pation and thinking how some things really were worth waiting for, Marcus grabbed his coat and set out for a pizza round the corner.

*

As Joanna walked towards Holland Park tube station she accepted that she was deeply attracted to Marcus. His flattery boosted her flattened, bruised ego, his obvious desire for her made her feel sexy again. It was years since she'd even glanced at another man. The feelings Marcus had stirred in her were exciting yet troubling. She was determined not to be another notch on his bedpost. A quick fling might be physically satisfying, but mentally wounding. But despite herself, a tingle ran up her spine as she thought about the weekend; being with Marcus and at the same time, maybe, just maybe, discovering further clues to the mystery. And Tom, cynic that he was, thinking there might be something in it, had given her the confidence to take her story seriously.

Joanna arrived home at Simon's flat and crawled into bed almost immediately with a biography on the life and times of Sir James Harrison. She noted there was not a single photograph of him as either a child or a young man. The biographer attributed this to James Harrison's parents having their house bombed during the Blitz, which had destroyed everything they'd owned. The first photograph was of James and his wife, Kitty, after their marriage in 1930. Although Joanna did her best to take in the words on the page in front of her, her eyes drooped and she fell asleep upright, the biography still in her hand.

chapter fourteen

Zoe had spent a vast amount of her first week in Norfolk kicking her heels, with too much time to think. A lot of the outside location filming had been curtailed by the presence of a thick blanket of snow. Although pretty and atmospheric, it would be impossible to film continuity wise. Instead, they'd done what they could in the ancient cottage the company had rented out for the duration of the shoot. The actor playing Zoe's father had not been booked until the week after and was unavailable earlier as his pantomime finished in Birmingham that week. She'd contemplated going back to London, but given that Pip had arranged for her to be picked up from Norfolk anyway, it seemed a pointless journey.

On Friday morning, Zoe woke up suddenly, dripping in sweat, with a gut-wrenching fear gnawing at her. Gone were the rose-coloured glasses, the sense of wonder that fate, after all this time, had drawn them back together. Replacing those feelings was sheer disbelief that she had even stupidly allowed herself to consider seriously the possibility of a liaison. What about Jamie?

'Oh God,' she muttered, blind panic gripping her.

Zoe climbed out of bed, pulled on her jeans and wellies and went for a walk round the picturesque, snow-covered village. It was all very well declaring herself at last independent, free of the shackles that had bound her previously, but she had to be realistic. What she was doing – *about* to do – could affect the rest of Jamie's life. How could she keep the secret from Pip? Surely, once they talked, got to know each other better, he'd realize. And then where would that leave the three of them?

'Shit!' Zoe kicked some slush into the ditch. She'd lived with it for so long herself, but it was going to be one hell of a shock for others . . .

Could she subject her precious child to the furore that would surround him?

No.

Never.

What on earth had she been thinking of?

That afternoon, Zoe packed her bags into the car and headed back to London. When she arrived home, she turned off her mobile and let the answering machine take any calls that might come through, welcome or unwelcome. Then she uncharacteristically drank an entire bottle of wine and went to bed with a love story that did not in any way match up to the velocity and drama of her own life.'

*

Marcus drove his Volkswagen Golf steadily down the M2 towards Kent. He only hoped the key was where he remembered it had always been. He'd tried Zoe on numerous occasions in the past twenty-four hours, leaving messages for her to call him on both her mobile and her answering machine, but she had not got back to him. In the end he'd decided that she couldn't say he hadn't tried to reach her and gone ahead with the weekend as planned.

Joanna sat next to him quietly, her thoughts very much on what she might find in the next twenty-four hours. She'd been genuinely surprised when Marcus had called on Friday morning to say he'd got the okay from Zoe and they were all set for the weekend. She'd been convinced Sir James's granddaughter would refuse to let a reporter troll through his private life.

She glanced at Marcus, at his perfect profile. She wondered whether Sir James had looked similar when he'd been younger.

Marcus pulled off the motorway and drove the car down a series of narrow country lanes. Finally, he turned the car into a gated drive and the oast house came into view. It was a lovely, ancient Kentish house, built in redbrick. The oast house itself, a circular, domed building, was attached to the house by what was obviously a fairly recent but very tasteful extension. The recent snow had been set by a hard night frost on the roof and window ledges, and the house was glistening in the emerging morning sun.

'It's beautiful.'

'Sure is. Worth a packet on the open market,' commented Marcus, rather bitterly. 'Sir Jim bequeathed it to Zoe's son Jamie. Stay there while I get the key.' He jumped out of the car and headed for the water barrel, situated around the back of the house. He only hoped the key was still where it used to be. Digging underneath the left hand-side of the barrel, Marcus's fingers had to break through solid ice before he felt the large, old-fashioned key that would gain them access to the front door. 'Thank fuck for that,' he muttered, blowing on his numbed fingers and returning round to the front of the house.

Joanna was out of the car, peeping through the mullioned windows.

'Got it.' He smiled as he put the key in the lock and turned it.

They entered a large, dark, galleried hall. Marcus switched the light on and Joanna saw a fierce bear's head glaring down from above her. The house was possibly colder inside than it was out.

Marcus shivered. 'Come on. We'll light a fire in the sitting room.' He looked at her. 'I've never known this house to properly warm up, even in summer. Could be a case of body heat to prevent hypothermia, you know.'

Purposely ignoring his comment, Joanna followed Marcus into the vast, baronial sitting room. Its high vaulted roof was heavily beamed, the huge stone fire-place making the room resemble a set from a Tudor banqueting scene. Half trees were stacked at the side of the walk-in fireplace. Marcus knelt down in front of it, grabbed a packet of firelighters, threw them into the grate and lit them. They flared up, sending shadows dancing up the walls. He added some tinder, then threw on a couple of huge logs.

'Right, that'll soon warm the place up. Now for the heating.'

Joanna followed Marcus through to a huge kitchen, complete with grey-flagged floors and an ancient Aga.

Marcus studied the dial, then leaned inside. When his head came out there were smeary soot marks on his face. There was some newspaper next to the fire. Marcus stuffed that in and lit it, then threw in some coal from the bucket.

'It may not look impressive and I can assure you it isn't.' He grinned. 'Oh for good old gas central heating. Dad went on at Sir Jim for years to install a proper system and he point-blank refused. I think he rather enjoyed freezing his nuts off. Right, I'll nip and get the supplies.'

Joanna wandered round the kitchen, enjoying its original rustic qualities. The airer, strapped by string above the Aga, was not there for its charm, nor was the herb rack, still full of dry, cracked plants, meant to create atmosphere. The scrubbed pine table had seen years of use, the cream painted cupboards were still full of tins. It was the real McCoy, the country kitchen every suburban housewife oohed and aahed over in interior magazines, yet not one of them would want its basicness, it's lack of modern, time-saving essentials.

Marcus was back with a large cardboard box full of supplies. Joanna noticed the two bottles of champagne, the other delicacies such as smoked salmon, which she loathed, caviar, which she loathed even more, and wondered whether she'd either starve or freeze to death this weekend. From the amount of alcohol Marcus seemed to have brought at least she could do it drunk. Joanna unpacked the booty and returned to the rather pathetic warmth of the Aga.

'Right,' Marcus said. 'What about we go and get out some of the boxes from the attic? The best thing is to bring them down and work through them in front of the fire.'

Joanna followed Marcus up the creaking wooden stairs until they stood on the galleried landing. Marcus took an iron rod that was placed against a nearby wall and hooked it into the handle above him. A set of stairs appeared as he pulled on the rod. He climbed them and pulled a piece of string that immediately flooded the attic above them with light.

He offered her his hand. 'Want to come and see just what you've decided to take on?'

Joanna took his hand and climbed the stairs behind him. She stepped out on to the hardboard floor of the attic and gasped. The entire space, which must run from one end of the house to the other, was filled with tea chests and cardboard boxes.

'Told you he was a hoarder. There's enough stuff to fill an entire museum up here.'

'Have you any idea if it works in any chronological order?'

Marcus shrugged. 'No, but I'd presume the stuff nearest us, the most accessible, is also the most recent.'

'Well, I really need to start from the beginning, as far back as we can possibly find.'

'Very good, milady.' Marcus pretended to doff his cap. 'You have a wander and point out the boxes you want down first.'

Joanna picked her way through the boxes, choosing one of the corners furthest away from the steps in which to start. Twenty minutes later, she had settled for two boxes from the 1940s and an old suitcase whose cracked yellow newspaper cuttings indicated the 1930s.

She sat as close to the fire as she could without being engulfed by it and sipped the hot tea that Marcus had made them both. 'I am fr . . . freezing!' she laughed as she shivered uncontrollably.

'Shall we give all this up as a bad job and retire to the nice warm country hotel just down the road?' Marcus's eyes were twinkling.

'No!' Joanna smiled, putting her mug down and heading for the suitcase. 'Now, I'll get started.'

'Right, I think I'll pop off and have a pint or two at the local, unless you want any help.'

'That's fine, Marcus.'

'Right, don't secrete anything on your person or I might have to find it later.' He grinned and left the room. As he drove out of the gates of the oast house he noticed a grey car parked in the entrance of the drive just a few yards up the lane. Marcus glanced in as he passed and noticed the occupants. There were two men sitting inside, their backs straight, both of them staring ahead. Marcus wondered whether he should call the police. They might be casing local houses for a robbery.

*

Joanna, in spite of the now leaping flames of the fire, still felt chilled to the bone. She could not chance sitting too close because of the fragile, yellowing paper she was dealing with. She had so far discovered absolutely nothing that she had not already gleaned from the four biographies.

Sir James had begun to make a name for himself as an actor in the late twenties, starring in a string of Noël Coward plays in the West End. In 1929, he'd married

Kitty, the marriage ending in 1937 when Kitty had so tragically died in France, pneumonia turning to emphysema and killing her in a matter of days. According to friends who the biographer had interviewed, the death of Kitty was something from which he had never fully recovered. She had been the love of his life and he'd never married again.

James had been left to care for Charles, his son of only five years old. The biographer noted that the child had been put in the care of a nurse, and sent to boarding school at the age of seven. Father and son had never been close, a fact which James had later attributed to his son's resemblance to his wife. 'It pained me to even see Charles,' he'd admitted. 'I kept him at a distance. I know I was a bad father, which has caused me great pain in my later years.'

In the thirties, James had made a number of successful films for Rank in England, and it was this that had really brought him to the public's attention. He'd had a brief fling with Hollywood, then when war gripped Europe, James had gone abroad as part of ENSA, visiting British troops and boosting morale.

Once the war had ended, Sir James had worked at the Old Vic, taking some of the big classic roles. His portrayal of Hamlet, followed two years later by Henry Vs had moved him into the élite ranks of the great. It was then he'd bought the Kent house, preferring to spend time alone there rather than circulate in the glitterati of the London theatrical scene.

In 1955, James had moved to Hollywood on a permanent basis. He'd spent fifteen years there making some good and some very bad pictures. He'd returned to the UK in 1970 to play King Lear with the RSC, his swansong, as he'd announced to the media. After that, he'd devoted himself to his family, especially his granddaughter, Zoe. Perhaps, the biographer had suggested, trying to pay penance for the earlier neglect of his own son. Charles had at the time separated from his wife and had moved to America to pursue his career as a film director. James seemed to have taken on a new lease of life being the father figure to both Marcus and Zoe.

Joanna sighed, her lap and the floor covered in ageing newspaper, photographs, letters . . . none of which bore any resemblance to the one she had either in writing style or content, although Siam was most definitely confirmed as Sir James's nickname, used constantly throughout the mass of correspondence Sir James had kept.

Joanna glanced at her watch. It was ten to three already and she was only halfway through the first suitcase, studying every single photo, letter and newspaper item carefully to see if it threw up any clues. The point was, she really had no idea what exactly it was she was looking for.

Working her way through to the bottom of the suitcase, thinking how much a historian would give to be sitting where she was now and cursing the lack of time, Joanna was just about to dump the stuff back in when she noticed a photograph sticking out of an old programme. Pulling it out, she saw the familiar faces of Noël Coward and Gertie Lawrence, and standing next to them, a man who she also recognized.

Joanna rummaged through the pile for the photograph of James Harrison on his wedding day. She put the photograph next to the one she'd just found and compared them. With his black hair and trademark moustache, James Harrison was instantly recognizable as he stood next to his bride. But yet, surely the man standing next to Noel Coward, despite his blonde hair and clean-shaven face, was also James Harrison? Joanna compared the nose, the mouth, the similar smile and, yes, the eyes were what convinced her. Joanna shrugged. It meant nothing. Perhaps James had dyed his hair blonde and removed his moustache for a particular role in one of Coward's plays.

She put the photo to one side as she heard the key in the lock.

'Hello.' Marcus entered the sitting room, bent down and rubbed her shoulders. 'Find anything yet?'

'No, not really, but it's been absolutely fascinating.'

'Good. Fancy some smoked-salmon sandwiches? You must be starving and beer always gives me an appetite.' He wandered towards the door.

'No smoked salmon for me,' she called after him, 'bread and butter and a nice hot cup of tea would be wonderful.'

'I have caviar too. Want some of that?'

'No thanks.'

Joanna went back to her boxes.

*

At six o'clock that evening, Joanna stood up and stretched her aching limbs. What I need now is a nice hot bath.' She smiled.

'Yep, we can just about manage that. The Aga may

have roused itself to produce at least half a tank of warm water. Come on, I'll show you the bathroom and where you're sleeping tonight.'

Pulling her up the stairs, Marcus showed her the large but rather shabby bedroom she'd be sleeping in, then took her along the corridor to another room. In it stood an old-fashioned four-poster bed.

'James's room, where I shall be kipping.' He pulled her down on to the bed and tickled her. 'Wouldn't you prefer to spend the night in the actual bed that Sir James Harrison, your hero, slept in every night for years?'

Joanna chuckled. 'Alone, yes.' She was below him, looking into his eyes, the weight of his body on hers.

He pushed a strand of her hair away from her face. 'Joanna, you have no idea how much I want you.'

'Marcus, you hardly know me.'

'That's because you won't let me get to know you. Joanna, you are so very, very lovely.' He brought his lips down to hers but in the nick of time, Joanna rolled away from him and Marcus kissed the eiderdown that had been lying beneath her. He sighed and rolled over on to his back, legs and arms splayed. 'Okay, I surrender,' he chuckled good-naturedly. He propped himself up on his elbows and studied her. 'Tell me now, so I can stop torturing myself. Is it just that you don't fancy me or are you saving yourself until I propose?'

Joanna folded her arms and shook her head. 'You are incorrigible, Marcus Harrison. Now, I'm going to have a bath, if you'll kindly show me where the bathroom is.'

*

Joanna lay soaking herself in the old-fashioned claw-foot bath. She felt like a Victorian virgin contemplating her wedding night. She groaned as she thought of the self-control it had taken to roll away from Marcus's kiss. And anyway, why was she being so old-fashioned? Didn't nineties women grab men by the balls and swing them round the bedroom if they so wished? She was shit-scared, plainly and simply. If she gave Marcus what he so obviously wanted and she wanted too, wouldn't he tire of her, as he had all the others? Well, there was no point analysing it any more, she thought as she stepped from the bath. She'd follow her instincts and see how she felt when the inevitable moment came. Joanna went back to her bedroom, shivering. She threw on her woolliest jumper and climbed back into her jeans.

'Joanna!'

'Yes?' she shouted.

'I'm pouring the champagne. Come on, or I shall have to come upstairs and get you.'

'There.' Marcus was sat on the leather sofa in front of the fire. He'd changed into a heather-coloured sweater and a pair of black cords. He handed her a glass and patted the cushion next to him. She sat down. 'Look, Jo, I'm really sorry for behaving like a teenager. If you don't want me in that way, it's absolutely fine. I'm sure I'm mature enough to enjoy your friendship, if that's all you want to offer me. What I'm saying is that you'll be perfectly safe tonight. I promise I will not creep into your bedroom and ravage you. Now, I hope now we can relax and have a nice evening. I've booked a table at the inn in the village. They have nice plain

English fare, none of this sophisticated foreign muck that I rather gather you don't like. Anyway cheers. Here's to you being your own woman.' He raised his glass and smiled at her.

*

Half an hour later, they drove the mile or so to the local village.

The ancient inn was low-roofed, cosy and quintessentially English. Marcus ordered a couple of gin and tonics, chatted to the barman and the two of them took their seats at a table in the dining area near the fire.

'By the way, this is my treat,' said Joanna as they studied the menus, 'to say thank you for arranging all this for me.'

'My pleasure.' Marcus nodded. 'As it's your treat, I'm going to have the steak.' He grinned.

'Me too.'

The young waitress came to take their order and Joanna chose a bottle of claret from the surprisingly extensive wine list.

'So, tell me about your idyllic childhood in Yorkshire,' Marcus suggested.

Joanna did so. Marcus listened with more than a little envy as she described family Christmases, celebrations, the tight-knit community that supported each other and worked together to help their neighbours through the long, hard winters.

'The farm's been in my family for generations. My grandfather died about ten years ago and Dora, my granny, handed the place over to my dad. She still came and helped out at lambing time up until last year.'

'What will happen when your dad retires?'

'Oh, he'll keep the farmhouse and rent out a lot of the land to the neighbouring farmers. He'd never sell. Talking of which' – Joanna cut into her steak – 'some of that stuff I was looking through today I would think was fairly valuable. Those programmes and photos . . . I mean, should they really be left up in the attic to rot?'

'No. James wouldn't have it touched when he was alive, but you're right, now he's gone we should do something with it.'

'I'm sure the London Theatre Museum, for example, would be terribly interested. Or I suppose you could hold an auction, raise money for the memorial fund, maybe.'

'That's a good idea. Mind you, whether Zoe would approve, I just don't know. Those boxes were willed to her, after all. But there's no harm in putting the idea to her, anyway.'

'Excuse me for being blunt, but the way you describe her makes your sister sound like quite a tough cookie,' commented Joanna.

'Zoe? No.' Marcus shook his head. 'I'm sorry if I gave you the wrong impression. Granted she's had to grow up pretty fast, what with Jamie arriving at such a tender age in her life . . .'

'Do you know who the father is?'

'No. And even if I did, I'd never tell, certainly not you,' he said abruptly.

'Sorry. I can't help wearing my journalist's hat just occasionally,' she apologized.

'Anyway, Zoe is a sweetie, fiercely protective of those she loves and terribly insecure underneath.'

'Who isn't?' sighed Joanna.

'So, what's the score with your love life, Miss Haslam? I detect a deep distrust of the male species lurking in your psyche.'

'You'd possibly be right. I had a long relationship with someone that ended just after Christmas. I thought it was for life, but it wasn't, of course.' Joanna sipped her wine. 'I'm getting over it now, but these things take time.'

Marcus reached over and took her hand in his. 'You're a real old-fashioned girl at heart, aren't you?'

'Yes, I suppose I am. God that makes me sound dull, though.'

'Not at all. It makes you refreshing and very real. Now, I fancy one of those enormous desserts with lashings of cream and glacé cherries that you'd never see gracing the tables of any of London's so-called fashionable restaurants. How about you?'

After coffee and liqueurs, they made their way back to the oast house. Marcus made Joanna sit by the fire while he went off to the kitchen. He arrived a few minutes later clutching a furry hot-water bottle under each arm.

'There you go. If I can't keep you warm, then this will have to do instead.'

'Thanks, Marcus.' She took the hot-water bottle and cuddled it to her chest. 'I think I'm going to retire if you don't mind. I'm exhausted.'

He nodded.

'Goodnight.' She moved towards him and kissed

him on the cheek. He drew her into his arms gently and held her for a while. Then he returned the kiss, dropping it lightly on to her lips.

'Night, Joanna,' he murmured.

He watched her as she left the room, then sat down on the sofa and stared into the fire. This girl was doing something to him. Apart from the fact he wanted to bend her naked in all sorts of outrageous positions, there was something stirring in his heart. Joanna was by far the most balanced, intelligent woman he'd ever met. Her sensible, straightforward honesty appealed to him in a way that surprised him. She took none of his nonsense and did not seem to be the least impressed by himself or his family. There was just the tiniest possibility, he admitted to himself, that he was falling in love.

*

Joanna closed the bedroom door behind her. She swallowed, trying to still her heart beat. God, she'd wanted him just then – the thought of them both naked in front of that glorious fire endangering her resolve. She shook her head. No, this was a job. She could not mix business with pleasure. It was dangerous to become emotionally involved with Marcus at present. It might cloud her judgement, complicate things.

Joanna took off her jeans and climbed into the big bed still wearing everything else. She tucked the hot-water bottle under her sweater, closed her eyes and tried to sleep.

chapter fifteen

Zoe was upstairs in her bedroom sorting the laundry. She heard the doorbell ring and decided to ignore it. Whoever it was, she couldn't face them tonight. It rang again and again. She tweaked the net curtain that separated her from the busy West End street beneath her.

'Oh God,' she whispered when she saw who was standing on the doorstep directly below her. She dropped the curtain back into place quickly, but not before he'd looked up and seen her.

The doorbell rang again.

Zoe looked down at her tracksuit pants and ancient sweatshirt. Her hair was piled untidily on the top of her head and she wasn't wearing a stroke of make-up.

'Go away,' she whispered, 'please go away.'

A few minutes later, Zoe reluctantly opened the door.

'Hello, Pip.' She gazed at the floor.

'Can I come in?'

'Yes.' She shrugged.

He stepped inside and closed the door behind him.

'What happened yesterday?'

'Pip, I . . .' She shook her head and shrugged.

'Oh my darling, oh darling.' He pulled her into his arms and held her close to him.

'Don't, *please*, it's wrong, *we're* wrong . . .' She tried to pull away from him, but he held her firmly.

'I nearly went mad when I couldn't get through to you, when I realized you were running away again. Zoe, my Zoe' – he smoothed away a lock of blonde hair that had fallen over one eye – 'I've never stopped thinking about you, wanting you, wondering why . . .'

'Pip, I . . .' Tears were pouring down her cheeks now. She shook her head.

'Jamie's mine, isn't he? Isn't he? Christ, Zoe, however much you deny it, I've always known, always.'

'No . . . no!'

'It didn't matter that you spun me some ridiculous story about another man. I never believed you, never. Besides, after what we shared together, even at our tender ages, I knew you couldn't have done that to me. I knew you loved me too much to deceive me in that way . . .'

'*Stop! Stop! Stop!*' She was sobbing uncontrollably, trying to break free of his grasp, but he held her tight.

'I have to know, Zoe, is Jamie mine? Is he?!'

'*Yes! Yes! Jamie's yours!*' she screamed at him, then suddenly, all her energy gone, she physically sagged in his arms. 'He's yours,' she whimpered.

'Oh darling, my love, my angel.' Again he pulled her tightly to him as his own tears dropped on to her blonde hair.

They stood in the hallway, crying for themselves and for the son who could never know his father. Then he kissed her, first on the forehead, then on her cheeks, her nose and eventually her mouth. Salt tears mingled as their tongues entwined with a ferocity, an animal passion that mirrored their feelings.

'Zoe, Zoe, have you any idea how I've dreamed of this moment, longed for it, prayed for it, oh God . . . oh God . . .' He caressed her ears, her neck, then in one easy movement pulled off her sweatshirt so his lips could touch the soft skin of her shoulders and her small, rounded breasts.

Zoe groaned in pleasure as he removed the rest of her clothes. She nuzzled into his neck, breathing him in, her arms wrapped tightly around his shoulders as though she was frightened he might leave her. She wrenched his sweater from his torso and undid his jeans, their mouths only parted for a few necessary seconds. He put his hands on her buttocks, drawing her into him. They both stumbled back against the wall, a detritus of clothes at their feet.

'I love you, God, I love you,' he panted as he lifted her on to him and her legs wrapped tightly around his waist.

She joined him on his ascent, helping him physically, yet hardly noticing him for she knew he was there too, fused to her, their ecstasy only possible because it was shared between them. They screamed at almost exactly the same moment, their bodies tensed to the smallest muscle, before the heaviness of relaxation made it necessary for them to crumple to the floor, amidst the heap of discarded clothes. There was no talk as they lay, legs and arms entwined in an ungainly heap of humanness. Their brains still fuzzy, the chemicals trying to deal with the unprepared for, physically and emotionally shattering, explosion of love.

Pip was the first to speak. He had to clear his throat before he could talk. 'Zoe, forgive me. I . . .'

She managed to hoist herself into a position that enabled her to put a finger to his lips. 'No. Don't. Don't spoil something so wonderful, please.'

His hands roamed her back. He was still unable to stop touching her, confirming her physical presence next to him. 'I love you. I always have and I always will.'

She knew then that he had to go. She nodded, sat up and began rooting around beneath them for his clothes.

'Can I see you again? Please? Oh darling, I understand how impossible this is for you, for both of us . . .'

She offered him his boxer shorts and his socks, revelling in the intimacy of seeing him put on these mundane, rather ugly items.

He stood up when he was dressed and offered his arms to her. 'There is a way. I know it's not how it should be, but please, at least let's try for a while.'

She leaned into his chest. 'Jamie . . . I'm so scared for him. I don't want anything in his life to alter.'

'It won't, I promise. Jamie is our precious secret.' Pip smiled down at her. 'I am so very glad you told me, Zoe. My love,' he murmured, then headed for the door, opened it and was gone.

Zoe staggered to the sitting room and sank on to the sofa. She stared into space for a while, reliving every second of the past half-hour. Then the demons with their doubts and their warnings and the ramifications of breaking the promise she'd vowed to keep for eternity began threatening to invade her tranquillity. Not tonight. She wouldn't let the past or the present torture her. She would take the moment and wrap its pleasure and its peace around her for as long as she could.

Zoe went to bed a little later and slept like a baby.

chapter sixteen

Joanna was awake bright and early on Sunday morning. She shivered her way down the stairs and donned her coat which hung over the banister at the bottom. She went into the sitting room and stirring the still-burning embers of yesterday's fire added firelighters, tinder and logs to get it going again.

She sighed in frustration at the little amount of time she had to look through such a mountain of possible further information. She'd need a couple of months to work through the boxes carefully and systematically. But, as she didn't have that luxury, Joanna decided to confine herself to the early stages of Sir James's life, the part all four biographies seemed rather vague about.

At eleven o'clock, Marcus appeared, his face creased from sleep, an eiderdown wrapped round his shoulders, but somehow managing to look sexy as hell.

'Morning.'

'Morning.' Joanna smiled up at him.

'Been up long?'

'Since seven.'

'Blimey, the middle of the night. Still at it, I see.' He indicated the half-empty box next to her.

'Yep. I've just found some unused clothing coupons.' She smiled, flapping the pieces of paper at him. 'I wonder if Harvey Nicks would still accept them?'

Marcus chuckled. 'No, but they must be worth a few bob in their own right. I think Zoe and me'll have to seriously wade our way through that stuff soon. Could be worth a fortune. Tea? Coffee?'

'I'd love a coffee.' She nodded.

'Right.' Marcus shuffled out in the direction of the kitchen. Joanna, in need of a break, followed him and took a seat at the old pine table.

'I don't think your grandfather started collecting stuff until the mid-nineteen thirties, which is a real pain because the biographies are all very vague about his childhood and early adulthood. Do you know anything about it?'

'Not really.' Marcus shrugged as he lifted a hob cover and put the old-fashioned kettle on to boil. He sat down opposite her and lit a cigarette. 'Born somewhere near here and ran away to London town to tread the boards at sixteen. At least that's the folklore, anyway.'

Joanna nodded. 'I'm surprised he didn't marry again after Kitty died. Ninety-five years is a long time for just one marriage of eight years.'

'One of those cases of true love. Kitty and James worshipped each other, apparently.' Marcus stood up to take the whistling kettle off the hob. 'There you go.' Marcus put a coffee down in front of Joanna.

'Your poor dad, losing his mother so young.'

'Yeah.' Marcus nodded. 'At least I had the pleasure of my mother until I was thirteen.' He sighed. 'The women in our family seem to be accident prone, while the men thrive and live to grand old ages.'

'Don't tell Zoe.' She grinned, taking a sip of the hot coffee.

'Or any prospective wife of mine, for that matter. Anyway, are you going to take time out for a traditional Sunday roast at the local pub, or do I have to go by myself?'

'Marcus, you've only just got up! How can you even think about beer and roast beef!'

'I was only thinking of you actually, how hungry you must be,' he countered.

She raised an eyebrow. 'That's very thoughtful of you, Marcus. Okay then, I think I've got enough to write a halfway decent article now anyway. I was wondering though, whether you'd allow me to take one photo that I found with me to put in the article. It's of Sir James in the early days, with Noël Coward and Gertie Lawrence, really atmospheric. I thought the idea of having a photo of him as a young actor would mirror nicely the fact that the memorial fund is for the young actors of today. I'd send it straight back of course.'

'I don't see why not,' nodded Marcus. 'I'll obviously just okay it with Zoe before you print it.'

'Thanks.' Joanna stood up. 'I'm going back to my boxes.'

*

He was just carving the pheasant when his mobile rang.

'Yes?' he barked in irritation, holding the carving knife in the other hand.

'Jenkins here. It's most definitely our girl with him,

sir. We couldn't be positive last night, but we caught a good look at her just now.'

'Have they left?'

'We saw no luggage going into the car. My guess is they've gone out for lunch.'

'Right. Keep me informed.' He tucked the mobile back in his trouser pocket and carried on carving.

*

After a pleasant lunch, Joanna spent a further hour searching through another four boxes in an arbitrary fashion, before it was time to repack them and think about heading back to London. While Marcus heaved the boxes back into the attic, Joanna tidied the kitchen and damped down the fire.

'All set?' Marcus stood in the hall.

They went outside and Joanna flung her holdall in the boot while Marcus returned the key to its hiding place, before jumping behind the wheel next to her and starting the engine.

*

A pair of binoculars tracked the Golf as it sped away.

Static crackled over the line. 'They've gone, sir. We've a car following them.'

'Okay. Give them an hour to come back for anything they've forgotten, then go in. Not a thing out of place when you've finished. Take every precaution possible.'

'Of course, sir.'

'Call me immediately with any news.'

'Will do, sir.'

The pheasant, as it always did, had given him chronic indigestion. He stared unseeingly at the Sunday magazine in front of him. This girl journalist was becoming a serious problem. It was obvious from her sudden appearance with Harrison Minor at the house in Kent that she'd made the connection. As far as the grandson went, his report indicated the boy was a layabout with a trail of debt as long as his arm. It might be that he could be encouraged to help out, without being told too much, of course. But the girl, now she was bright. How much did she know? He doubted they would find anything amongst the boxes in the attic. They'd been checked out before. Unless, of course, something had been placed up there since . . .

He wheeled himself into his study and opened the file on Simon Warburton. Jenkins had suggested that the man might be just who he was looking for. His connection with Haslam was helpful too. He stared out of the window and into the dark, bitter night. The security sources at Buckingham Palace had also presented him with another problem. It might just be possible that this could be used to his advantage and that Warburton could kill two birds with one stone. In the meantime, he'd have someone else warn Haslam off.

*

Marcus parked the Golf in front of Simon's flat.

'Thanks, Marcus. I can't tell you how grateful I am for all you've done.'

'Well, just make sure you get me at least a double-page spread in that rag of yours. Listen, Jo.' Marcus leaned over the gearstick and gripped her hand before she could escape. 'Can I see you again? Maybe dinner on Thursday evening?'

She nodded, then leaned over and kissed him, on the lips. He folded his arms round her shoulders and prised her mouth open with his tongue.

'Okay.' She pulled away from him gently. 'I'd better be going. I'll see you on Thursday. Goodbye.'

'Bye, Jo,' Marcus answered wistfully.

She opened the boot and pulled out her luggage, then waved at Marcus as she set off up the path to the entrance to Simon's flat. Soldiering up the long flight of stairs, she decided that either Marcus really was as great an actor as his grandfather had been or, in fact, he was smitten. The fact that she should have had such an effect on him, mirroring her own feelings, pleased and comforted her.

Joanna took off her coat with a renewed gratitude for the modern convenience of timed central heating, then placed the photograph she had acquired from the oast house on the coffee table. As she went into the kitchen to put on the kettle and make a sandwich, Joanna pondered Tom's words about the possibility that Simon had procured the letter from her under false pretences and that it was doubtful she'd ever see it again. No. How could Simon have known that the letter was significant in any way? Joanna was convinced she'd prove Tom wrong.

Taking her sandwich and her mug of tea, Joanna collected her biographies from the bedroom, the music hall programme and the photocopy of the love letter Rose had given her. With everything on the table in front of her, she pressed the remote-control button and turned the television on to see the news.

More political and royal scandal . . . it was all that seemed to fill the headlines these days. Joanna pressed 'mute' and reread both Rose's note and the love letter, then flicked through the old programme. She studied the blurred photographs of the cast. And her heart began to pound as she recognized a face.

'Mr Michael O'Connell' the programme read beneath the picture of the man.

Joanna put the photo she had brought back from Kent beside it and compared James Harrison and Michael O'Connell. Even though the photo in the programme was old and grainy, there was absolutely no doubt at all. With his blonde hair and devoid of his moustache, there was no doubting it. James Harrison was a double for the actor calling himself Michael O'Connell. Unless they were twins, surely they had to be one and the same man?

But why? Why would Michael O'Connell alter his name? Yes, it was quite possible he would have acquired a stage name that he felt suited him better, but surely he'd have done that right at the beginning of his career, not a few years later? By the time he'd married Kitty in 1929, he'd dyed his hair, grown a moustache and called himself James Harrison. Besides, none of the biographies noted any change of name. The early details all related to the 'Harrison' family.

Joanna shook her head. Maybe it was just coincidence that the two men looked so alike. And yet, it would finally explain the significance of the programme, the reason why Rose had sent it to her.

Had Sir James Harrison once been someone else? Someone with a past he wished himself and others to forget? She sighed and wished Simon were there to mull over the facts with. In the light of the fact he wasn't, she'd have to do the next best thing.

chapter seventeen

Tom was not at his desk when Joanna arrived in the office the following morning. When he did reappear an hour later, she pounced on him immediately. 'Tom, I've found something on—'

Tom stopped her and held up his hands. 'Deal's off, I'm afraid. You're being moved to Pets and Gardening.'

Joanna stared at him. 'Pardon?'

Tom shrugged. 'Nothing to do with me. The whole point in the first couple of years here is that you work on every section of the paper. Your time on the newsdesk has ended forthwith. You no longer belong to me, Jo, love. Sorry, but there it is.'

'I . . . but I've only been on the section for a couple of months. Besides, this story, I can't just let it go. I . . .' She was so shocked she couldn't take it in. 'Pets and bloody Gardening?! Jesus! Why, Tom, why?'

'Look, don't ask me. I just work here. Go and see the Ed if you want. It was him who suggested a move round.'

Joanna glanced down the corridor at the threadbare carpet in front of the glass-panelled office, which had been worn down by nervous hacks facing a demolition job from their boss. Joanna swallowed hard. She did not want to cry in front of Tom, or anyone else in the office for that matter.

'Did he say why?'

'Nope.' Tom sat down behind his computer screen.

'Does he not like my work? Me? My perfume? Everybody knows that dog shit and mulch is the armpit of the newspaper for aspiring young journalists. I'm being buried alive.'

'Joanna, Joanna, it'll probably only be for a few weeks. If it makes you feel any better I did stand up for you, but it was no-go, I'm afraid.'

Joanna watched as Tom typed something on the screen. She leaned forward. 'You don't think . . .'

He looked up at her. 'No. Absolutely not. Just type up that frigging piece about the memorial fund, then you'll have to clear your desk. Mighty Mike is doing a direct swap with you.'

'Mighty Mike? On news?'

Mike O'Driscoll was the butt of many office jokes. He had the physique of an undernourished gnome and suffered from severe sincerity overkill. Tom only offered her a shrug. Joanna stomped back to her desk and sat down.

'Problems?' asked Alice.

'You could say that. I'm being swapped with Mighty Mike, on to Pets and Gardens.'

'Blimey, give the *Express* details of a scoop, did you?'

'I've done absolutely bugger all,' moaned Joanna, folding her arms and putting her head on her desk. 'I just can't bear it.'

'You think you've got problems. I've got Mighty

Mike moving in next door now,' groaned Alice. 'Oh well, no more freezing your tits off on someone's doorstep, just gentle little articles on canine psychology and what time of year to plant your begonias. I wouldn't mind a rest like that.'

'Nor would I when I'm sixty-five with a great career as a journalist behind me.' Joanna sat upright. 'I suppose I'd better finish this bloody piece.'

She typed aggressively, too upset to really concentrate. Ten minutes later, there was a tap on her shoulder and a huge bouquet of red roses were pressed into her hand by Tom.

'They should cheer you up.'

'Tom, I didn't know you cared,' she quipped sarcastically as he returned to his desk.

'Blimey!' Alice looked at her with envy. 'Who're they from?'

'A sympathizer, probably,' Joanna muttered as she tore off the small white envelope and opened it.

Despite her depression, Joanna could not help but smile at Marcus's note. 'These are to say good morning. I'll call you later, yours ever, M.'

'Come on then, spill the beans? Who is it?' Alice studied her. 'It's not, is it?'

Joanna blushed.

'It bloody well is! You didn't, did you?'

'No I didn't! Now will you just shut up!'

*

Joanna finished her particularly uninspired article on Marcus and the memorial fund, feeling guilty because of the flowers and how good he'd been to her. But her brain just wasn't up for it. She cleared her desk during lunch and sadly traipsed her belongings to the other side of the office.

Mighty Mike was virtually hopping up and down with excitement, which made the whole thing even worse. It transpired that it wasn't the newsdesk he was looking forward to, but the prospect of sitting next to Alice, whom he'd apparently had a crush on for years.

At least that'll pay her back a little, thought Joanna bitchily, as she sat down at Mighty Mike's recently vacated chair and studied the photos of cute pooches he'd pinned on the cork board by his desk.

That night, the thought of going home alone to an empty flat was too much, so she broke her firm habit of not joining the gossipmongers in the pub and went with Alice to drown her sorrows in a few gin and tonics.

Joanna knew she was getting reasonably sloshed and when she saw Tom come in, she left Alice and made a beeline for him, the alcohol giving her Dutch courage. She perched on the bar stool next to him as he ordered his whisky.

'Don't fuckin' start, Jo. It's been a hell of a day.'

'Tom, answer me one question: am I a good reporter?'

'You were shaping up very nicely, yes.'

'Okay.' Joanna nodded, trying to collect her thoughts through her fuzzed brain. 'How long exactly does a junior stay on your section before being moved on?'

'Joanna . . .' he groaned.

'*Please*, Tom! I have to know.'

'Okay, about six months minimum, unless I want to get rid of them faster.'

'But you just said I was shaping up very nicely, so you didn't want to get rid of me, did you?'

'No.' Tom gulped down his whisky.

'Therefore, I must deduce that my sudden and hurried demotion has nothing to do with my work, but with something else that I might have stumbled over. Yes?'

He sighed, then nodded. 'I tell you, Haslam, if you ever say it was me who tipped you the wink, it won't be shit and mulch, it'll be the fuckin' dole queue for you, okay?'

'I swear, I won't.' Joanna nodded, indicating her empty glass and Tom's to the barman.

'If I were you, I'd keep your head down, your nose clean and this whole thing'll soon be forgotten about.'

Joanna handed Tom his whisky, anything to keep him there for a few more minutes. 'Look, the thing is, I discovered something more at the weekend. I wouldn't put it on state-secret level, but it is interesting.'

He looked at her, sympathy in his eyes. 'Sweetheart, I've been in this game a long time. And from the way them up there are acting, what you're on to might just well be state-secret level. I've not seen the Ed so jumpy since Di's Gilbey tapes. I'm telling you, leave it be.'

Joanna sipped her gin and tonic and studied Tom, his greasy grey hair that stuck up in tufts from his constant running of hands through it, his unfit, overweight torso and his whisky-sodden eyes.

'Tell me something,' she spoke quietly so Tom had

to lean in to hear her, 'if you were me, just at the start of your career, and you had totally by coincidence stumbled on something that was obviously so hot even the editor of one of the bestselling dailies in the country had been warned off, would you "leave it be"?'

He thought for a minute, then looked up and smiled at her. ''Course I fuckin' wouldn't.'

She patted his hand. 'I thought not.' She slipped off the bar stool. 'Thanks, Tom.'

'Don't say I didn't bloody warn you, and trust no fucker!' he called as she crossed the bar to retrieve her coat.

Alice was being chatted up by a photographer.

'You off?'

'Yes. I'd better go and do my homework on how best to prevent snails eating one's pansies,' she quipped.

'Never mind, you've always got Marcus to console you.'

'Yeah.' Joanna nodded, too tired to argue. 'Bye, Alice.'

Joanna caught a taxi to Simon's flat, wishing she'd not had so many gin and tonics. On arrival she made a large mug of strong coffee, then checked the answering machine for messages.

'Hi, Jo, it's Simon. I should be back by ten tonight. Hope all's well. Bye.'

'Hi, Simon, Ian here. Thought you'd be home by now, but would you give me a call when you get in? Something's come up. Okay bye.'

Joanna wrote the message down on the pad with the pen that she'd found on the floor of her bedroom. She looked underneath the telephone, where she'd put the card Simon had given her with his friend's number on. Taking a deep breath, she calmly studied the initials on the Cross pen.

I. C. S.

Then she looked at the card.

IAN C. SIMPSON

'trust no bugger . . .' Tom's basic but meaningful words floated into her head. Was it the alcohol and the awful day she'd had that was making her paranoid? There had to be a lot of people whose initials were I. C. S. On the other hand, how many robbers really did carry an initialled gold fountain pen when they were trashing a joint? And the letter . . . she'd never even paused to consider Simon's offer might be anything other than a genuinely helpful one . . . He'd been so insistent, now she thought about it. And what did he do exactly as a 'civil servant'? This was a man who'd got a first at Trinity College, Cambridge, a brain hardly likely to be processing parking tickets, and certainly not with 'mates' in the forensic lab . . .

'Fuck!'

Joanna checked her watch. It was ten to ten. He'd be home any minute.

'Oh Simon,' she groaned.

*

Twenty minutes later, Joanna heard the key turn in the lock.

'Hi, how are you?' Simon put down his holdall and kissed the top of Joanna's head.

'Fine, yes fine.' Joanna feigned a yawn and uncurled her legs from under her. 'I must have dozed off. I had a few drinks at the pub after work.'

'That good a day?'

'Yeah. That good.' Joanna nodded. 'How was your trip?'

'Hard work.' Simon shrugged, going into the kitchen and switching on the kettle. 'Want a coffee?'

'Go on then. Oh, by the way,' Joanna added casually, 'there was a message from Ian for you on the answering machine when I got home. Can you call him?'

'Sure.' Simon made two cups of coffee and came to sit down opposite her. 'So, how've you been?'

'Good, good.' Joanna nodded. 'My flat's almost back to normal. I've got a new bed and the sofa's arriving tomorrow. So I'll ship out of here now you're back.'

'Take your time. There's no rush, Jo.'

'I know, but I think I'd like to get home.'

'Of course.' Simon nodded and took another sip of his coffee. 'So, any more progress on strange little old ladies and their correspondence?'

'No. I told you I wasn't going to pursue it, unless your forensic friend came up with anything.' She looked at him. 'Did he?'

Simon put his coffee down on to the table and shook his head. 'No nothing. I popped into the office on the way home and there was a letter on my desk from my mate.'

Joanna shrugged. 'Oh well. Do you have the letter? I'd like to keep it at least.'

'No, I'm afraid I don't. Apparently it disintegrated during the chemical process. My mate did say he thought it was over seventy years old. Sorry about that, Jo.'

She shrugged. 'Oh well, it was probably of no importance anyway. Never mind. Thanks for trying, Simon.'

'Blimey, I thought you'd go berserk.' Simon studied her in surprise. 'I was dreading telling you what had happened.'

'Well, it seems like I have more pressing problems of my own to attend to, rather than flying off on some wild-goose chase. My dear and beloved editor has decided, for reasons best known to himself, to transfer me from the newsdesk to Pets and Gardens. I have to plot and plan how to make my stay there as short as possible.'

'I'm sorry to hear that. He didn't give you a reason?'

'Nope. Anyway, at least I don't have to doorstep anymore, just wander round the Chelsea Flower Show in a floaty dress and a pair of gloves.' Joanna grinned at Simon wryly.

'You seem to be taking it very well. I would have thought you'd be fuming.'

'What's the point? There's bugger all I can do about it. And as I said, I've had a few gins to take away the pain. You should have heard me in the pub earlier.' Joanna giggled. 'Anyway, if you don't mind, I'll take a shower and then hit the sack. The shock's worn me out.'

'You poor old thing, you. Don't worry, one day you'll be the Ed and can get your own back.'

'Maybe.' Joanna stood up. 'I'll see you tomorrow.'

'Yes, night, Jo.' Simon kissed her on the cheek, picked up his holdall and went into his bedroom. He dumped the holdall on the floor, took out his mobile phone and dialled a number.

'Simon here.'

'Hi, Simon. Good gig?'

'It went okay. What's up?'

'Phone Jenkins at home. He'll tell you.'

'Okay. See you tomorrow.'

'Night, Si.'

Simon dialled the number from memory.

'Sir, it's Warburton.'

'Thank you for calling. Did you tell her as planned?'

'Yes.'

'Did she take the news well?'

'Surprisingly so.'

'Good. Listen, Simon, you're to report to Whitehall at nine tomorrow morning. There's someone who wants to meet you.'

'Right, sir.'

'I've recommended you for this, Warburton. Don't let me down, will you?'

'No, sir.'

'Goodnight, Warburton.'

'Goodnight.'

*

The following morning at a quarter to eight, Simon tiptoed through the darkened sitting room to reach the shower and realized Joanna had already gone.

Simon picked up the note she'd left attached by a magnet to his fridge.

'Went home to get some clean clothes before work. Thanks for having me. See you soon, Jo.'

To the uninitiated eye there was nothing wrong with the note, but the matter-of-fact tone, compared to Joanna's jokey correspondence of the past struck a chord.

And last night, she'd been far too calm about the letter disappearing. As Simon showered, he became more and more convinced that Joanna was most definitely up to something. And he'd bet his life she was still foolishly on the trail of her little old lady.

chapter eighteen

As filming in Norfolk continued, Zoe became more and more immersed in the character of Tess, the woman who had thrown tradition to one side and become an outcast in her village for having an illegitimate child. Zoe could not help but draw parallels between her own life and that of her character's. She only hoped she didn't come to such a tragic end.

Tim, the director, was thrilled with her performance so far. 'Keep it up, Zoe, and you'll be heading for a BAFTA.' He smiled as they drove back to the inn after watching the rushes one night. 'And Ade says you're positively glowing for the camera. Bed early tonight for you, sweetheart,' he said as they collected their keys from the tiny reception in one corner of the oak-beamed bar.

Zoe walked up the steep, creaking stairs to her room. Her mobile rang from inside her handbag as she opened her door. Reaching for it hurriedly, she closed the door behind her and answered.

'It's me.'

'Hello me,' she answered affectionately. 'How are you?'

'Oh, hectic, missing you, darling. Dreadfully.'

Zoe sank on to the bed, cradling the phone to her ear as she drank in his voice.

'And I miss you too.'

'Can you make it to Sandringham this weekend?'

'I think so. Tim says he wants to do some early-morning mist shots but I should be ready by lunchtime. I'll probably fall asleep by seven though. I'll have been up since four.'

'As long as it's in my arms, I don't care.' There was a pause on the line. Then, 'Oh Zoe. Dammit! I wish I was anyone else.'

'I don't. I'm glad you're you,' she soothed. 'Only a couple more days and we'll be together. Are you sure it's safe?'

'Absolutely. Those who have to know are aware of the delicacy of the situation. It's more than their job's worth. Discretion *is* their job, in fact. Darling, don't worry, please.'

'It's not for myself. It's Jamie I'm concerned for.'

'Yes. And that's understandable. But trust me, will you? I'll have my driver wait for you outside the inn from one onwards on Saturday. I've got the lodge for the night, told the rest of the family I want some privacy. They understand. They won't disturb us.'

'Okay.' Zoe nodded. 'I'll see you on Saturday, then.'

'Darling, I'm counting the hours. Goodbye.'

'Bye.'

Zoe clicked the phone off and lay on the bed staring at the ceiling. She smiled. A whole twenty-four hours with Pip was more than she'd ever enjoyed before.

And even for Jamie's sake, she could not refuse.

*

Later, having taken a long hot bath, Zoe went down-stairs for supper. Most of the others had driven to nearby King's Lynn to try an excellent Chinese res-taurant. Zoe had chosen to stay at the inn and have an early night. The small restaurant, with its dark var-nished cottage-style table and chairs, was empty. Zoe sat down in the corner near the fire and ordered from the young waitress who had scurried in from the kitchen holding a photocopied menu.

Just as she was about to begin her melon balls, William Fielding the old but sprightly actor playing her father appeared, swaying slightly, at the entrance to the restaurant.

'Hello, m'dear. All alone?' He smiled.

'Yes.' Zoe smiled back, then, a trifle reluctantly, said, 'Why don't you join me?'

'I'd like that very much indeed.' William walked towards her, pulled out a chair and eased himself into it. 'This darned arthritis is eating away at me bones. Bloody thing it is, bloody.' He smiled at her then leaned so near that Zoe could smell the alcohol on his breath. 'Still, should be happy I'm working and playing a man a good few years younger than meself. I look like your grandfather, not your dad, m'dear.'

'Nonsense. Age is how you feel inside, and you skipped up those stairs like a spring chicken during filming today,' Zoe soothed.

'Yes and it nearly bloody well killed me. Still, can't let our revered director think I'm past it, now, can I?'

The waitress was hovering by the table with a menu.

'Thank you, m'dear.' William put on his glasses. 'Now what do we have here?' He perused it. 'One soup, the roast of the day and a double whisky on the rocks to wash it down.'

'Yes, sir.'

'Would have a nice glass of claret, but the stuff they serve here is no better than vinegar,' William remarked as he removed his glasses. 'Enjoying the grub though. Location catering is always one of the treats, don't you think?'

'Absolutely,' agreed Zoe. 'I've put on almost four pounds since the beginning of the shoot.'

'Looks like you could do with it too, if you don't mind me saying. Suppose you're still getting over the death of Sir James. '

'Actually, I don't think I'll ever really get over it. He was more of a father to me than my real dad. I miss him every day and the pain doesn't seem to get any less.'

'It will, m'dear. I can say that because I'm old and I know. Ah, thank you.' William took the whisky from the waitress and took a large gulp. 'I lost my wife five years ago to cancer. Didn't think I could live without her. But I'm still here, surviving. I still miss her, but at least I've accepted that she's gone now.' William took another swig of his whisky. 'Lonely old life though now. Don't know what I'd do if I didn't have the work.'

'A lot of actors seem to live to grand old ages. I've often wondered if that's because they never really retire, just carry on until they—' Zoe blushed.

'Drop down dead. Yes, quite.' William nodded, drained his whisky and signalled for another. 'Your grandfather lived until ninety-five, didn't he? A good innings if I may say so. It inspires me to think I could have another fifteen years or so still to go.'

'Are you really eighty?' Zoe said with genuine surprise.

'This year, to you, my dear. To the rest of the business, I hover around sixty-six.' William put a finger to his lips. 'I only ever remembered exactly how old I was because I knew Sir James was exactly fifteen years older, to the day. We shared a birth date. Once celebrated it together, many, many years ago. Aha! Soup, and it smells delicious. Excuse me while I plunder my bowl.'

'Not at all.' Zoe watched as William rather messily slurped his soup.

'Did you know my grandfather well?' she asked when William had pushed the bowl away and ordered another whisky.

'As I said, many, many years ago, before he became, and I mean quite literally, James Harrison.'

'What do you mean, "quite literally"?'

'Well, I'm sure you know James Harrison was his stage name. When I met him, he was as "Oirish" as they come. Hailed from Cork somewhere, called Michael O'Connell when I first knew him.' He pulled out an untipped cigarette.

Zoe regarded him in astonishment. 'William, are you sure you're thinking of the same actor? I know he was fond of Ireland, talked about it being a beautiful place, especially towards the end of his life, but I had no idea he actually was Irish. And it's never mentioned in any of his biographies. They all say the same, that he was born in Maidstone.'

William shrugged. 'He obviously had his reasons for changing the facts. Surprised you didn't know though, being family. Without a doubt, you're descended from Irish blood.'

'Thank you.' Zoe leaned back as the waitress brought her chicken supreme and cleared away the soup bowl. 'So tell me, where did you first meet my grandfather?'

'At the Hackney Empire, or was it the Players?' William scratched his head. 'One or t'other, anyway. I was only seven at the time. Michael was twenty-two. In his first job.'

'Seven?' marvelled Zoe.

'Yes, born in a prop basket, that's me. My mama was in variety and seemed to have mislaid my daddy. So she took me to the theatre when she worked and I'd sleep in a drawer in her dressing room. When I got bigger I used to do odd jobs for everyone, bring in food, take messages and generally fetch and carry for a few bob. And that's how I met Michael, except I used to call him Siam. His first job was playing a strongman in the Empire pantomime. He had his head shaved and darkened his skin. I thought he looked like the pictures I'd seen of the King Of Siam, with his bracelets and earring. The nickname stuck, as I'm sure you know.'

'Yes.' Zoe nodded.

'Of course, he wanted to get into proper theatre, but we all have to start somewhere. He was trying very hard to get rid of that Irish accent. Any serious actor worth their salt in those days had to speak with a plum in their mouth. But even in those days he had charisma.

All the young dancing girls used to queue up to go out with him. Must have been that Irish charm.'

Zoe watched William carefully as he drained another glass. He'd had four double whiskies since he joined her. Besides, he was remembering back over seventy years. There was every chance he had James confused with someone else. She picked at her overcooked chicken as his roast pork arrived. 'Got some apple sauce for me, darling?' he asked the waitress. 'Thank you.'

'So are you saying he was a bit of a boy?'

William chuckled. 'I suppose he was. But he always dumped them with such charm they ended up loving him anyway. Then one day, m'dear, halfway through the season, he upped and left. Disappeared off the face of the earth. When he didn't appear for the performance I was sent round to his lodgings to find out if he was ill or on the juice. All his belongings were still there but, m'dear, your grandfather was not.'

'Really? Did he return?'

'Yes, six months later. I popped round quite a bit to his lodgings to see if he'd come back. Then one day, my knock was answered. He opened the door with a smart new haircut and expensive suit to boot. Told me it was from Savile Row. I remember him showing me the label. He looked like a real gentleman and the Irish accent had disappeared completely.'

Zoe shrugged. 'Blimey, this is some story.' She ordered another drink for both of them. 'Did you ask him where he'd been?'

'Of course I did. I was fascinated. Your grandfather told me he'd been doing some lucrative acting work and that's all he'd say. Then he said he was coming back to the Empire to continue his act, that it had all been arranged. And when he did, the management didn't bat an eyelid. It was like he'd never been away.'

'Have you ever told anyone else about this?' Zoe asked him.

'Absolutely not, m'dear. He warned me not to. Michael was my friend. He trusted me, helped me get started when I became an actor myself, treated me like a son. Anyway, I haven't got to the most interesting bit yet.' William's eyes were alight with the thrill of his captive audience. 'Shall we order coffee and wander through to the bar and the comfy seats? My backside has gone positively numb.'

Zoe agreed and the two of them found a comfortable banquette in the corner of the bar. William lit up a cigarette.

'Anyway, one day, a couple of weeks after he's come back, he calls me into his dressing room. He hands me two shillings and a letter and asks me if I'd run an errand for him. So he sent me off to stand in front of Swan and Edgars, tells me to wait there until a pretty young woman comes along and asks me if I had the time.'

'And did you?'

'Of course.' William chuckled. 'In those days, for two shillings, I'd have run to the moon.'

'And the woman came?'

'Oh yes.' William smiled. 'In her lovely clothes, with her posh English accent. I knew she was a lady, and I mean a *lady*.'

'Was it just the once?'

'Oh no. Over the space of those few months, I met her fifteen, maybe twenty times.'

'And what did she give you?'

'Well, one week she'd collect the letter Michael had given me, and then the next week she'd give me a small, square package, wrapped in brown paper.' William flicked his ash into the ashtray.

'Really? And what do you think was inside?'

William shrugged. 'I have no idea. Not that I didn't try to guess.' He smiled.

Zoe bit her lip. 'Do you think he was involved in something bad?'

'Could have been, but Michael never struck me as the kind of man to be mixed up in anything criminal. He was such a gentle man.'

'So what do you think it was all about?'

'I suppose I always thought it was some kind of a secret love affair.'

'Between who? Michael and the woman you met?'

'Perhaps. But I think she was an emissary, just as I was.'

Zoe studied him. 'You didn't look?'

'Not once, although I could have done. No, I was a loyal bod, and your grandfather was so generous to me I couldn't betray his trust.'

Zoe sipped her coffee, feeling weary but fascinated, whether the tale was truth, fiction or a little of both embellished by the passage of time.

'Then the next thing that happens is Michael calls me round to his lodgings and says he's got to go away again. This time, he says, for a long time. He gives me enough money to make sure I'd eat well for a good five years and suggests that I forget what has taken place in the past few months, for my own sake. If anyone was to ask me, especially those in authority, I don't know him. I mean, only to talk to.' William stubbed out his cigarette. 'And it's bon voyage Michael O'Connell.'

'You have no idea where he went?'

'None.' William shrugged. 'Then blow me down, the next time I see Michael O'Connell, a good twelve months later, his picture is staring down at me from a theatre in the avenue under the name 'James Harrison'. He'd dyed his hair black, and was sporting a moustache, but I'd have known those blue eyes anywhere.'

Zoe looked at William in amazement. 'So you're saying he disappeared *again*, then resurfaced with dark hair, a moustache and under another name? William, I have to tell you I'm finding most of this hard to believe.'

'Well.' William burped. 'I swear it's all true, m'dear. Of course, having seen his picture outside the theatre and knowing it was him, even with an assumed name, I go to the stage door and ask for him. When he saw it was me, he swiped me into his dressing room tout de suite and closed the door. He told me it would be much, much better for my general well being if I stayed away from him, that he was someone else now without the past I knew of, that it was extremely dangerous for me. So,' William shrugged, 'I took him at his word.'

'Did you ever see him again?'

'Only from the stalls, m'dear. I wrote a couple of times but the letters were never answered. Got an envelope sent to me on every birthday, full of money. No note, but I knew it was from him.'

'Well, well.' Zoe drained her coffee cup.

'So, there you are. The strange tale of your beloved granddad in his early years, never before repeated by these lips. Now the old boy is dead, I hardly think it matters any more. And you may well be able to investigate further, if it pleases you to do so.' William scratched his head. 'I'm trying to remember the name of the young lady I met all those times in front of Swan and Edgars. She told me once. Daisy . . .? No. Violet . . . I'm sure it was a flower . . .'

'Rose?' suggested Zoe.

William stared at her, a smile crossing his face. 'By golly, you're right! It was Rose!'

'And you have absolutely no idea who she was?'

William touched his nose. 'Can't betray all his secrets, y'know. I had an idea all right, but maybe it's best it goes to the grave with him.'

'Well, I think I'm going to have to go to the attic where James kept all his memorabilia and sift through it. See if I can find anything relating to what you've told me.'

'I doubt you will, m'dear. If it's been covered up for this long, strikes me we'll never know the truth. Still, makes for an interesting evening's chat.'

'Yes.' Zoe looked at her watch. 'William, I think I must go to bed. I've an early call tomorrow. Thank you so much for telling me all this. I'll let you know if I turn anything up.'

'You do that, Zoe.' William watched her as she stood. He caught her hand and squeezed it. 'You're so like him when he was young, m'dear. I was watching you this afternoon and you have the same gift. You're going to be very, very famous one day, and make your grandfather proud.'

Tears came to Zoe's eyes. 'Thanks, William,' she muttered and walked away in the direction of the stairs.

chapter nineteen

Joanna had spent a miserable three days on Pets and Gardens, and an uncomfortable two nights sleeping on the floor of her bedroom, because, of course, she'd lied to Simon about her bed arriving to give her an excuse to leave his flat and go home. The furniture store had promised delivery of both bed and sofa this coming Friday. Tonight, she was meeting Marcus for dinner. Just the thought of having a soft comfortable mattress beneath her might be enough to tempt her into staying with him for the night, she thought ruefully as she pulled on a short black lycra dress and teemed it with a cardigan and slip-on shoes, rather than her favourite pair of Doc Martens. She added some mascara to her lashes, a little blusher and some lipstick, and with her long hair still damp from the shower, set off for the bus stop.

As the bus trundled its way into central London, Joanna mused on the evening ahead. She'd missed Marcus in the past few days and hated herself for being so excited at the prospect of seeing him. She'd also spent the last few days pondering whether she should take Marcus into her confidence and tell him what she had discovered about his grandfather. With Simon so obviously untrustworthy and possibly in the enemy camp, and with Tom to all intents and purposes relinquishing his support, it seemed to her she needed an ally to help her if she was to make further progress.

*

Marcus was waiting for her in the bar at Kettner's when she arrived.

'Darling, how are you?' He kissed her warmly on the lips.

'Fine, just fine.' She smiled, climbing up on to the stool next to him.

'You look . . . good enough to eat.' Marcus's eyes travelled up and down her body. 'Champagne?'

'Go on then, you've forced me into it. Is it a special occasion?'

'Of course. We're having dinner together. That's special enough for me.' He grinned. 'Good week?' he asked.

'No, shitty. Apart from the fact I've been demoted at work, my new furniture hasn't arrived.' Joanna sighed.

'Poor you. I thought you were staying with a friend until it did.'

'I was, but it got a bit . . . crowded,' she informed him. 'Simon came back and the flat's too small for both of us.'

'Try and jump you, did he?'

'God no!' Joanna looked horrified. 'He's my oldest friend. We've known each other for years.'

'Fall out, did we?'

'No, not really. It's . . . well,' Joanna took a deep

breath, 'it's a long story, vaguely connected with you, actually.'

'He heard I was after his "best friend" and threw a loop?'

'No, nothing like that.'

'Well, tell me all over supper. Let's take the champagne with us. I'm starving.'

Once they had ordered food and further champagne, Marcus looked at Joanna quizzically across the table.

'Go on then.'

'Go on what?'

'Tell me all.'

'Oh Christ, Marcus, I really don't know whether I should.'

'That big a deal?'

'That's the thing, it may be something or nothing.'

Marcus reached across the table and held Joanna's fingers in his own. 'Sweetheart, if you want this to go no further than this table, I swear it won't. Strikes me you need to talk to someone about it.'

'I do, I do. Okay. But I'm warning you, it's bizarre and complicated. Right. It all started when I turned up at your grandfather's memorial service . . .'

*

It took the starters, main course and dessert before Joanna had brought Marcus up to date. Marcus lit a cigarette and blew out the smoke slowly. He stared at her steadily. 'So that whole piece about me and the memorial fund was a cover up so you could procure information from me about my grandfather and his dodgy past?'

'Well, I suppose so, yes,' Joanna admitted. 'Although it is going to be used in the paper.'

'I admit to feeling just a little used, Jo.'

'I'm sorry.' She shrugged.

'So tell me bluntly, are you having dinner with me tonight to see what else you can extract, or did you want to see me?'

'I wanted to see you.'

'Really?'

'Really.' She nodded, taken aback by his obvious hurt.

'So, apart from the other thing, you like me a little?'

'Yes, Marcus, of course I do.'

'Okay.' His face cleared. 'So, let's go over the facts again. Strange old woman at Sir Jim's funeral, letter, programme, your flat gets trashed, you give said letter to so-called friend who now tells you it's disintegrated—'

'I can't believe it did. I mean, think of letters from hundreds of years ago that are still in existence but would have been chemically processed to determine their age.' Joanna shook her head. 'But Simon never lies to me. He really is my best friend.'

'I think you're right to be highly suspicious of him, Jo. Then you tell your boss, who tells you to follow it up, then does a quick about-turn a few days later and has you moved to an innocuous section of the paper where you can cause no harm.' Marcus rubbed his chin. 'Joanna, whatever it is you're on to, it's something. The point is, where do you go from here?'

Joanna rifled through her bag for the appropriate envelope. 'This is the photo I borrowed to dress up the article. And this is the programme.' She laid the programme by the side of the photo. 'See? It's him, isn't it? Even with blonde hair.'

Marcus studied both pictures. 'Sure looks like him, yes. Well, if anyone knows about this it's my sister Zoe. Except she's in Norfolk at the moment. They were thick as thieves, Sir Jim and her.'

'All I know is that I have to be very careful from now on, look as though I've dropped the whole thing. But I'd love to speak to Zoe.' Joanna smiled. 'Could you arrange it?'

'Maybe, but it'll cost you.'

'What?'

He grinned. 'A brandy back at my place.'

*

Joanna sat in Marcus's living room watching the flames in the gas fire leap. She felt calm, a little drowsy, and comforted that she had shared her secret with someone else.

'There you are.' Marcus handed her a brandy glass and sat down next to her. 'So, Miss Haslam, where do we go from here?'

'Well, you try and arrange for me to see Zoe and . . .'

He put a finger to her lips. 'No, I wasn't talking about that. I was talking about us.' He ran his finger up her cheek and caught a lock of her hair. 'You see, I really don't want to be your "best friend".' He took her glass away from her before she had even taken a sip, then leaned towards her. 'Let me kiss you, Joanna, please. You can tell me to stop at any time if you want to, and I promise I will.'

Marcus put his lips to hers. Joanna closed her eyes as she felt his tongue enter her mouth. His arms closed around her shoulders and he pulled her towards him. She relaxed into him as sense and right and wrong vanished in a haze of longing. Then, suddenly, he abruptly pulled away.

'What?' she asked him.

'Just making sure you don't want me to stop.'

'No, I don't,' she answered.

'Thank God for that,' he whispered and pulled her back towards him. 'You're so bloody sexy. How I stopped myself in Kent I'll never know. Joanna, Joanna, God, you're gorgeous.'

He kissed her thoroughly and passionately, and his hands began to search for the flesh underneath her dress. He cupped a hand to her left breast and Joanna moaned in pleasure. She could feel his erection against her left thigh as he rolled her off the sofa and on to the floor beneath him. In one swift movement her dress was over her head, then her underwear discarded. She watched as Marcus removed his clothes and felt an unladylike surge of raw lust as she studied his broad shoulders and his erection rising from beneath his boxer shorts. Thanking God she'd stayed on the pill since Matthew had left, she moaned as he kissed her stomach, running his hands over her breasts, then moving his lips to take first one, then the other nipple in his mouth. Joanna reached for his hardness, massaging him, wanting him inside her. She squirmed in pleasure as his fingers caressed her groin, teasing her, resisting the temptation to go within her. As his lips covered her own once more, she sighed in relief as his fingers entered her, discovering the extent of her own arousal. A thumb rubbed against her clitoris and she came, suddenly, sharply.

'Joanna, I knew you wanted me, I knew it.' His fingers slipped away from her and he rose above her, enabling her to take him in her mouth. She sucked on him, gently at first, then harder, until he abruptly pulled out.

'Oh God, I'll come, I'll come.' He sighed as he kissed her again, then guided himself into her, her hips rising to meet his.

His hands kneaded her breasts and she threw her head back, longing for another release. His hand grasped her neck and brought her face to his. He kissed her thoroughly, panting. 'Joanna, I think I love you, I think . . . I . . . love . . . you . . . Go . . . d.'

She felt him explode inside her, triggering her own orgasm. She sank on to him, too out of breath to talk. His arms wrapped around her shoulders and she drank in the smell of his fresh, clean hair and the faint smell of aftershave still on his neck.

'You okay?' She heard him whisper.

'Yes.'

He rolled her to the side of him and propped himself up on his elbow.

'I meant what I said, you know. I think I'm falling in love with you.'

'Bet you say that to all the girls,' Joanna replied coyly.

'Before maybe, but never after.' He grinned, then sat up and fumbled in his trouser pocket for his Marlboros. 'Want one?'

'Go on then.'

Marcus lit up two cigarettes. They sat on the floor cross-legged, smoking.

'That was really enjoyable.'

'The sex?'

'No, the ciggie.' Joanna stubbed hers out in the ashtray.

'Come here.' Marcus reached for her again and kissed her. 'You know, you really have done something to me.'

'Yes, and don't my knees know it.' She grimaced.

'Jo, I'm being serious. Ever since that first lunch I've thought about you constantly. I just have to know, is there a future for the two of us?'

'Oh, Marcus, I don't know. I told you before I had a long-standing relationship with an awful ending. I'm still very vulnerable and scared of getting hurt. And as your reputation goes before you, I've . . .'

'What do you mean?'

'Come off it. My friend Alice told me what a Lothario you've been.'

'Okay, okay, I've been a bit of a lad, I'll admit. But I swear I've never felt like this before.' Marcus stroked her hair. 'And I promise I'd never do anything to hurt you. Please give me a chance, Jo. We can take it as slowly as you like.'

'Marcus, that was not very slowly,' she quipped.

'Why are you so flippant every time I try and talk to you seriously?'

'Because' – Joanna rubbed her nose – 'I'm covering up how scared I really am.'

'Well, look at it this way, I've had you, notched up another nail on my bedpost, and the worst that can happen is that you never hear from me again. I have to say your fear is rather like shutting the gate after the horse has bolted.'

'Yes, I suppose you're right.' Joanna yawned. 'I'm exhausted.'

'And now you're going to ask me if you can stay tonight, seeing as you haven't a bed of your own to go to.'

'I've been perfectly okay on the floor for the past few days.'

'Joanna, don't be so defensive. I was joking. There is nothing I would like more than to wake up next to you tomorrow morning.'

'Really?'

'Yes, really.'

'Okay. Sorry, Marcus.'

He stood up and offered her his hand to pull her to standing. He led her out of the sitting room and into the bedroom, then threw back the duvet.

'Ahh, a bed. Heaven.' Joanna climbed in and snuggled down contentedly as Marcus slid in beside her and turned off the light.

'Jo?'

'Yes?'

'Do we really have to go to sleep straight away?'

*

The following morning, Joanna was awoken by something hard pressing into her back. Still half asleep, she came to as Marcus gently caressed her, then slowly made love to her yet again.

'Oh my God! Look at the time. It's twenty past nine! I'm going to be horrifically late!' Joanna sprang from the bed, and ran into the sitting room to search for her clothes. Marcus followed her.

'Don't go, Jo. Stay here with me. We could spend the day in bed.'

'I wish. I'm holding on to my job by a whisker as it is,' she said as she hopped around the room trying to put her tights on.

'Come back tonight, then?'

'No, I have to go home and unwrap my sofa and my bed. At least I hope I do.' Joanna threw her dress over her head.

'I could come and help you unwrap them,' he said hopefully.

'Tell you what, I'll give you a ring from work.' Joanna put on her jacket and picked up her rucksack. She kissed him. 'Thanks for last night.'

'And this morning.' He grinned.

'Yes.' Joanna walked into the hall with Marcus following her. She opened the front door. 'By the way, would you call Zoe for me?'

He kissed her on the nose. 'Leave it with me, ma'am.'

*

Marcus spent some of the morning sleeping and the rest of it in a hot bath thinking about Joanna.

The telephone rang about two o'clock. He ran for it, hoping it was her.

'Marcus?'

'Yes?'

'You may not remember me. We used to go to school together many years ago. My name's Ian, Ian Simpson.'

'Yeah, I think I do remember you. How you doing?'

'Fine, just fine. Listen, how do you fancy getting together for a drink? Discuss old times, etcetera, etcetera.'

'Er, well, why not? When were you thinking of?'

'Tonight actually. Why don't you meet me at the St James Club.'

'Not tonight. I'm already booked, I'm afraid,' Marcus answered.

'Could you cancel, by any chance? There's something we should talk about, which might be to your financial benefit.'

'Really? Well, I suppose I could make it around seven, as long as you don't mind me shooting off.'

'Not at all. The St James at seven, then. Look forward to it.'

'And me. Bye.' Marcus put the telephone down, shrugged in puzzlement, then picked it up again and dialled Joanna.

'Hello, sweetheart, did your bed arrive?'

'Yes, thank God. The woman upstairs only just caught them as they were about to proceed off again with the booty. I *told* the delivery people to ring the upstairs bell. Oh well, at least they're in situ at long last.'

'Want me to help unpack them? Test out the new bed?'

'Would you mind if I declined, Marcus? This afternoon I've got to go visit three celebrities' houses to have their pooches test out some new kind of organic dog food. I'll not be back until after nine and I'm exhausted.'

'Now why would that be?'

'You know why.' There was a smile in her voice.

'Okay, have a nice rest. I shall be round to exhaust you again sometime over the weekend.'

'Bye, Marcus.'

'Bye, darling.'

*

Marcus recognized Ian Simpson instantly. The man had not changed in the slightest since his schooldays.

'Marcus, good to see you old chap.' Ian shook his hand heartily. 'Do sit down. Drink?'

'A G&T would do wonders.'

'Super.' Ian signalled for a waiter and ordered two gin and tonics. He leaned forwards, his elbows resting on his skinny knees, his hands clasped together. 'So, how've you been?'

'Er, since leaving school? Fine.' Marcus nodded.

'And what line of work are you into now?'

'Films,' nodded Marcus noncommittally.

'How glamorous. I'm just a poor old Civil Service bod, earning enough to bake my daily bread. But then, I suppose with your background, there was a natural progression.'

'Sort of, although I haven't been helped by my

family. One could actually say it's been a hindrance, in fact.'

'Really? You surprise me.'

'Yes, it surprises most people,' Marcus agreed morosely. 'At the moment I'm starting up a fund in memory of my grandfather, Sir James Harrison.'

'Really?' Ian said yet again. 'Well now, what a coincidence, as that's just what I wanted to talk to you about. Thank you.' The waiter put their drinks on the table.

Marcus eyed Ian suspiciously. Would there ever be a time when someone was interested in meeting him for himself, rather than his family?

'Cheers.'

'Yes, cheers.' Marcus took a healthy slug of gin. 'So, what's this about my grandfather?'

'Well now, it's all a bit hush-hush and you have to understand that we're really taking you into our confidence by telling you this. You see, the situation is thus: apparently your grandad was a bit of a boy, had a ding-dong with a certain lady who was very much in the public eye. And apparently, she wrote him some rather steamy letters. Your grandad returned nearly all of them and always promised to will the last and most, shall we say, compromising one to this lady's family on his death.' Ian picked up his glass and sipped from it. 'But it seems he changed his mind.'

'Mmm, can't say I remember anything of that nature being in the will,' murmured Marcus innocently.

'Quite. Well now, the family concerned have contacted us to see if we can retrieve this particular letter.

I mean, it could all be very embarrassing if it fell into the wrong hands.'

'I see. Is there any point in asking who the family might be?'

'No, but I can tell you they're rich enough to offer a substantial reward to anyone who might come across it. And I mean substantial.'

Marcus lit up a cigarette and studied Ian. 'And how far have you got with your enquiries?'

'Well, at one point we thought it had been found. Unfortunately, it was the wrong one.'

The letter Joanna had been sent by the old woman, deduced Marcus. He waited for Ian to mention her and sure enough, he did.

'We hear tell that you are friendly with a young journalist.'

'Joanna Haslam?'

'Yes. Have you an idea how much she knows?'

'Not really. We haven't discussed it much, although I did know she'd been sent a letter, presumably the one that found its way to you.'

'Quite. Er, look, Marcus, to put it bluntly you don't by any chance think that Miss Haslam is encouraging your friendship because she thinks you might lead her to further information, do you?'

Marcus shrugged. 'Well, I suppose it is a possibility, especially after what I've just heard.'

'Well, forewarned is forearmed as they say. And obviously this conversation is completely between our-selves. The British government is relying on your discretion in this matter.'

'Cut the crap, Ian, and tell me exactly what you want me to do.'

'You have access to your grandfather's houses, both in London and in Kent. We've looked, I admit, and found nothing. However, there may be places we are unaware of, trusted friends of your grandfather who might have been given the letter for safe keeping. The situation is so . . . delicate that we have to keep the net tight. It's literally on a need-to-know basis. We've chosen you because we know you are a man of discretion, with perfect and innocent access to places and people we cannot touch without arousing deep suspicion. And as I stressed before, you'll be well rewarded for your troubles.'

'Even if I don't find it?'

Ian reached in his pocket and pulled out an envelope. He put it on the table. 'There's a small retainer to cover any expenses. Why not take the lovely Joanna off for a weekend away, wine her and dine her and find out how far she's got in her search? Gently, gently, catchee monkey, as the saying goes.'

'Yes, I get your drift, Ian.'

'Good. And if the Golden Fleece is discovered by you, what's in that envelope will seem like small change. I must go. My card's in that envelope. Call me anytime of the day or night if you have news.' He stood up and held out his hand. 'Goodbye, Marcus. Oh, and by the way, not wishing to be overdramatic but I should warn you, the stakes are high. Any leaks to the wrong drain and you could find yourself next to it in the gutter. Goodnight.'

Marcus watched Ian leave the room. He sat down

abruptly and ordered another gin, his fingers itching to find out exactly how much was in the envelope. He felt confused and slightly euphoric all at the same time. Was this his moment when he might actually reap the benefit of having a famous family? What if he could find that letter? Pass it into the right hands, having struck an appropriate amount of compensation for its loss – and from what Ian had hinted, he could virtually name his price – then ride off into the sunset with Joanna by his side. With enough money to turn his dream into reality.

Marcus wondered, despite what Ian had said about 'leaks down the wrong drain', whether he should come clean with her and tell her about the past half-hour's conversation. Then they could work together, no secrets from the start. But what if the grey suits found out? Ian had underlined the danger and he didn't want to put Joanna at risk. Maybe it was best he didn't tell her. What she didn't know couldn't hurt her.

Marcus drained his glass, offered to pay the bill but discovered the amount was already covered, picked up the envelope and went downstairs to the Gents toilet. Locking himself in a cubicle, he opened the envelope. He whistled. Three thousand pounds in twenties and fifties. Not bad to be paid for the pleasure of taking a woman he adored away to Chewton Glen or maybe Le Manoir Aux Quatre Saisons . . .

Marcus went back up the stairs and out of the front door, whistling to himself. Of course, the next step was to see Zoe, no longer just for Joanna but for himself and his future too . . .

*

On Saturday lunchtime in Norfolk, Zoe arrived back at the inn from the shoot and ran up to her room to collect her holdall. Heart banging against her chest, she delivered her keys to reception.

'Someone's waiting in the bar for you, Miss Harrison.'

'Thanks.' Zoe walked through to the main body of the pub full of local Saturday lunchtime drinkers. Before her eyes could scour the place, a man was by her side.

'Miss Harrison?'

'Yes.' She had to crane her neck to look at his face. He was extremely attractive; tall, well built, with sandy hair and very blue eyes. He looked out of place in his immaculate grey suit, shirt and tie.

'I'm your chauffeur. Can I take your bag?' His face crinkled into a warm smile.

'Thank you.'

They walked outside and Zoe followed him into the car park where a black Jaguar with dark tinted windows was waiting. He opened one of the back doors.

'There you are. Climb in.'

Zoe did so. She watched as he pressed a button on his key fob and the boot opened. Stowing her bag inside, he closed it and climbed in behind the wheel.

'Were you waiting long?' she asked.

'No, only about twenty minutes.' He started the engine and reversed out of the car park.

Zoe settled back on to the soft, fawn-coloured leather as the Jaguar purred along the country roads.

'How far is it?'

'Oh, half an hour or so,' the chauffeur replied.

Zoe suddenly felt extremely uncomfortable, embarrassed in front of this handsome, polite man. After all, he knew he was driving her to an assignation with his employer. Zoe couldn't help but wonder how many times he'd done this kind of thing for Pip before.

'Have you been working for, er, Prince George for long?'

'No, this is a new duty for me. You'll have to give me marks out of ten.' He smiled at her in the rear-view mirror.

'Oh no, I couldn't . . . I mean, this is my first time too . . . er. I mean . . . going to Sandringham to see him.'

'Well then, we're both beginners in the royal enclave.'

'Yes.'

'I'm not even sure whether I should be speaking to you. I suppose I'm lucky they let me keep my tongue and my ba . . . Yes, well, you know what I mean.'

Zoe giggled as the back of his neck turned slightly pink. 'Well, I won't tell if you won't,' she added, feeling much more comfortable.

They drove the rest of the way in companionable silence.

Shortly, her driver picked up a mobile and dialled a number. 'Arriving with PG's visitor.' He signalled right and drove through a pair of heavy, wrought-iron gates. Zoe looked back as they closed silently behind the car.

'Almost there,' he said as he drove along a wide, smooth road. Swathes of mist covered the open parkland making it impossible to see too much. The car turned right again and down a narrow lane lined with bushes on either side, then came to a stop.

'Here we are. He knows you're arriving.' The driver stepped out of the car and opened her door for her.

Zoe barely had time to take in the elegant Victorian residence nestling in amongst tall trees before Pip came out of the front door. 'Zoe! How lovely to see you.' He kissed her warmly but slightly formally on both cheeks.

'There you go, sir, madam. Shall I take the bag inside?' the driver asked.

'No, I'll take it, thank you.'

Simon watched a trifle wistfully as Pip put a protective arm round Zoe Harrison's shoulders and led her inside the lodge. He'd rather been expecting an arrogant, vain celebrity with delusions of grandeur. What he'd found was an extremely beautiful, sweet and terribly nervous young woman. He walked back to the car and climbed inside. He dialled a number and said, 'Package delivered to PG.'

'Okay. He's insisting on privacy, wants the area kept clear. We'll cover from here. Report at eleven hundred hours tomorrow. Night, Warburton.'

'Night, sir.'

chapter twenty

'Darling Zoe, it's been wonderful.' Pip kissed her on the lips as they stood in the hall. 'So, you'll be staying in London?'

'Yes, just for the next three days. I'm back in Norfolk on Thursday.'

'I'll call you, but it might be that I can pop round. I'm going back to town later tonight.'

'Okay, ring me. And thank you for a lovely time.'

They walked out to the waiting Jaguar together. The driver had already stowed her holdall in the boot. He opened the door for her.

'Take care.' Pip waved as the driver started the engine. Zoe watched as he receded into the black of night and the car passed through the gates of the estate.

'I'm taking you to Welbeck Street, is that correct?'

'Yes, thank you.'

Zoe stared unseeingly out of the window. The past twenty-four hours had left her emotionally and physically shattered. They'd done little more than drink, eat and make love. The intensity of his presence near her for so long had exhausted her. Zoe closed her eyes and tried to doze. Thank God she had three days off to recover, to *think*. Pip had mentioned plots and plans he'd dreamed up to let them spend time together alone. He wanted to tell his family of their love, and then, perhaps the country ... She sighed heavily. Fine thoughts, but how could there ever be a future? The effect of the attention Jamie would subsequently receive could be catastrophic.

'Are you too warm, Miss Harrison? Let me know and I'll turn the heating down.'

'No, I'm fine, thank you,' she answered. 'Did you have a nice weekend?'

'Yes, it was pleasant enough, thank you. Yourself?'

'Pleasant, yes.' She nodded in the gloom of the car.

The driver remained silent for the rest of the journey. She was grateful that he sensed she was not in the mood for small talk.

They arrived in Welbeck Street at just after seven o'clock. The driver carried her holdall up the steps as she unlocked the front door.

'Thank you.' She gave him a sweet smile. 'What's your name, by the way?'

'I'm Simon, Simon Warburton.'

'Night then, Simon.'

'Night.'

Simon got back into the car and watched as Zoe shut the front door behind her. He radioed in that she had been delivered safely and headed back to the car pool to hand in the Jag and pick up his own vehicle.

To say he had lied to Zoe when she'd asked him if he'd had a good weekend was an understatement. When he'd arrived back at his flat yesterday afternoon for the first time in five days, he'd spotted the letter from Australia immediately. As he read it, Simon had realized that somewhere deep inside he'd never really expected Theresa to come back to him. But the actuality of it happening was no less devastating. She'd met someone else, she'd explained. She loved him, and Australia, and was going to marry him as soon as she could and stay there.

Simon had cried very few times in his life. Last night had been one of them. After waiting for her all this time, stalwartly resisting other offers, the bitterness he felt that she should leave it until just before she was due to return ate into him. The one person he wanted to comfort him, just as he'd comforted her, was either out or not answering the telephone. And to cap it all, he'd had to spend his Sunday chauffeuring a lovesick female back to London.

What on earth he was doing being a bloody driver after his years of special training, he really did not know. When they briefed him at Whitehall that morning he had been told he was 'helping out' while they were understaffed at the Palace garages, but it really didn't wash with him. If he was minding one of the royals, that would have been different, but to draft him in just to chauffeur the pretty actress mistress of the Prince seemed most odd.

Simon handed over the Jaguar, the driving of which had been the one pleasure of the past two days, and climbed back into his own car. He only hoped that he was now 'relieved' of his special duty and could get back to the real meat of his job.

Simon drove up to north London wishing he was not arriving home to an empty flat. On impulse he drove past Joanna's flat and saw the lights were on.

Parking his car outside, he got out and went to ring the bell.

Joanna peered out of the window, saw it was him and came to open the front door.

'Hello.'

He noticed she did not look pleased to see him. 'Have I called at a bad time?'

'Er, yes, a bit. I'm just writing up an article for tomorrow.' She hung about in the doorway, obviously reluctant to invite him in.

'Okay. I was only passing.' He shrugged.

'You look tired,' said Joanna, torn between asking him why he looked so miserable, then subsequently having to ask him in. At present, she wanted to maintain a safe distance.

'I am. I've had a busy weekend.'

'Join the club.' Joanna smiled. 'Everything okay?'

Simon shrugged. 'Yes, everything's fine. I'll be better after a good night's sleep, methinks. Give me a ring and come round to supper sometime. We've got some things to catch up on.'

'Yes.' She nodded, knowing something was wrong and feeling horribly guilty at her refusal to become involved. 'I will.'

'Bye then.' He nodded, stuffed his hands in his pockets and walked off down the path.

*

Zoe was just relaxing in a hot bath when she heard the doorbell ring.

'Oh fuck,' she swore uncharacteristically. She lay there hoping the caller would go away. It wasn't Pip.

He was still travelling back from Sandringham and she'd spoken to Jamie at school earlier.

The doorbell rang again. Giving up, she grabbed a towel and dripped down the stairs.

'Who is it?' she called through the door.

'Your darling brother, sweetheart.'

'Oh. Okay.' Zoe opened the door. 'Hi. Come in. I'm going to get my robe, then I'll be down.' She flew back up the stairs and Marcus wandered into the sitting room.

Zoe followed him in five minutes later. She leaned down and kissed her brother. 'You look well. Plus, you haven't got a drink and you've been here all of five minutes.'

'The love of a good woman, that's what it is.'

'I see, who is she?'

'Tell you in a bit. How's filming going?'

'Well. I'm enjoying it.'

'You look radiant, Zo.'

'Do I? I feel exhausted.'

'The love of a good man, maybe?'

'No. You know me, wedded to my art and my child.' Zoe smiled. 'So, tell me who this woman is who has put you on the path to sobriety.'

'I wouldn't go that far. But, Zoe, I really think I'm in love. How do you fancy meeting for dinner tomorrow night at the bistro round the corner from me? My treat. Then you can take a dekko at her. You know I've always trusted your opinion.'

'Okay.' Zoe nodded.

The sound of a mobile emanated from somewhere in the room. Zoe stood up and began searching for her handbag. She located it by the doorway, pulled it out and spoke. 'Hello?'

Marcus watched her face soften and dissolve into a smile.

'Yes, I did thanks. Did you? Me too. Okay, bye.'

'And who was that?' Marcus raised an eyebrow. 'Father Christmas?'

'Just a friend.'

'Yeah, yeah, sure.' He studied her as she tried to tuck away her dreamy expression with her mobile phone. 'Come on, Zo, you've met someone, haven't you?'

'No . . . yes . . . sort of.'

'Who is he? Do I know him? Do you want to bring him to supper tomorrow night?'

'I wish.' She sighed. 'It's all a bit complicated.'

'Married is he?'

'Yes, I suppose you could say he is. Look, Marcus, I really can't say anymore. I'll see you tomorrow night, at about eight if that's okay.'

'Sure.' Marcus stood up. 'Her name's Joanna by the way.' He walked to the front door. 'Be nice to her, won't you, sis?'

'Of course I will.' She kissed him. 'Night night.'

'Night, sis.'

*

Joanna felt more than a little apprehensive about meeting Zoe Harrison.

'For God's sake, just don't ask who Jamie's father is, darling. She's paranoid enough and when she hears you're a journalist she'll be uneasy anyway.' Marcus ordered a bottle of wine and lit a cigarette.

'She might calm down when I tell her I'm only interested in what type of begonias she plants in her garden,' sighed Joanna. 'Really, I don't know how much longer I can stand it at work.'

Marcus wrapped an arm round Joanna's shoulders. 'You'll be back in pole position sooner than you know it, especially if you uncover the great mystery of Sir Jim.'

'I doubt it. From the sound of things, my editor wouldn't print it anyway.'

'Ah, but there'll always be some scandal rag that will, sweetheart.' He kissed her. 'Here's Zoe.'

Joanna stood and saw a woman dressed in a pair of jeans and a lambswool sweater. Her blonde hair was coiled into a topknot, her face was devoid of make-up. She looked ravishing.

'Joanna, I'm Zoe. It's lovely to meet you.'

The two women shook hands. Joanna, always aware of her height, realized she towered over the diminutive, dainty Zoe.

'Red or white, Zo?' Marcus asked as the waiter opened the wine.

'Whatever.' Zoe sat down in between them. 'So where did you meet my brother?'

'Er . . . I . . .'

'Joanna is a journalist for a national newspaper. She interviewed me about the memorial fund. By the way, when is that piece going in, darling?'

'Oh, any time in the next week or so.' Joanna was

watching Zoe's face. A flicker of fear had just passed across it.

Marcus handed Zoe and Joanna a glass of wine each.

'Cheers. Here's to having the two most fragrant ladies in London in my captivity.'

'Yes, cheers.' Zoe lifted her glass and took a sip. 'What kind of stuff do you write about, Joanna?'

'Everything and anything. I'm on Pets and Gardens at the moment.'

Relief crossed Zoe's face.

'But not for long, sweetheart, eh? I'm hoping this woman will become successful enough to keep me in my old age.'

'She'll need to,' drawled Zoe. 'Not exactly a candidate for chairman of the Bank of England are we, Marcus?'

'Don't mind her,' said Marcus, shooting Zoe a warning glance. 'We spend most of our lives bitching at each other.'

'Yes, we certainly do,' nodded Zoe. 'But it's best you see Marcus as he really is. We don't want any shocks or surprises along the way, do we now?'

'No, sis, we certainly don't. Now how about we choose our food.'

The waiter having taken their order, Marcus left the Bistro to run next door for a packet of cigarettes.

'I hear you're down in Norfolk shooting *Tess*,' said Joanna.

'Yes.'

'Are you enjoying it?'

'Very much,' nodded Zoe.

'I've always loved Hardy's books, especially *Far From the Madding Crowd*. I studied it for O level and they made us watch the video of the film every time it was too wet to play netball. I wanted to be Julie Christie desperately so I could kiss Terence Stamp in his soldier's uniform!'

Zoe giggled. 'So did I! There's something about a man in uniform when you're fifteen.'

'Maybe it was all those shiny buttons,' mused Joanna.

'No, it was definitely the sideboards that nailed me,' grinned Zoe. 'God, you think back to some of the people you fancied then and shudder. Simon Le Bon was another one I used to dream of at night.'

'Well at least he was good looking. No, no, mine was much worse.'

'Who?' Zoe asked. 'Go on.'

'Boy George from Culture Club.' Joanna looked at her toes.

'But he's—'

'I *know*!'

When Marcus came back in with his cigarettes, the two women were wiping the tears from their eyes.

'Was Zoe telling you some hilarious titbit from my infancy?'

Zoe tutted. 'Why is it that men immediately presume that we are talking about them?'

'Well, we were, sort of.'

'I wouldn't call one of those men!'

'No, you're right,' said Joanna.

'Well, could you both control yourselves enough to tuck into the starter?' Marcus said sulkily as the waiter arrived at their table.

*

Three bottles of wine later, Marcus was feeling like the odd one out. Although it pleased him to see the way the two women had hit it off, he'd spent the evening feeling a tad left out. He'd felt he was eavesdropping on a girlie evening, sharing stories from their past that he really didn't think were that funny. Besides, it wasn't getting them anywhere in terms of what he needed to know. Zoe was in full flight about a prank at boarding school, involving a hated teacher and a durex full of water.

'Thanks, Marcus.' Joanna nodded as he poured more wine into her glass.

'That's okay, ma'am. I aim to please,' he muttered.

'Marcus! Stop sulking immediately,' said Zoe. She leaned across the table conspiratorially. 'A tip from one who knows him: if his lips pucker and he goes slightly cross-eyed, it's a sign he's throwing a moody.'

Joanna winked. 'Message received and understood.'

Zoe diplomatically turned the conversation to Marcus. 'So, how's the memorial fund going?'

'Oh, you know. I'm plodding along. I'm getting an audition panel together at the moment. I thought it should consist of one head of a drama school, one director, one well-known actor and one actress. I was wondering if you wanted to be the actress, Zo, seeing as it's Sir James's fund.'

'Yes. I think I'd like that. Lots of young eighteen-

year-old males who I'll have to wine and dine to make
sure if they're the right calibre . . .'

'Can I have the ones you don't want?'

'Joanna!' said Marcus.

'A sort of alternative Miss World.'

'You should have them in their swimming trunks,'
nodded Joanna.

'Whilst reciting a speech from *Henry V* . . .'

Marcus shook his head in despair as the two women
giggled hysterically.

'Sorry, sorry, Marcus,' Zoe said as she wiped her
eyes on her serviette. 'Seriously, I'd be honoured to be
on the panel. Oh, talking of which, I had a fascinating
conversation with the actor playing my father in *Tess*.
Apparently he knew James way back.'

'Really?' Marcus replied casually.

'Yes.' Zoe took a gulp of her wine. 'He told me
some outrageous yarn about James not being James at
all when he first met him. No, apparently he was Irish,
from Cork, and called Michael O'Connell. He was
doing some music-hall show at the Hackney Empire
and suddenly disappeared. Oh, and William also mentioned something about letters that were written, some
kind of tryst James was having with a woman.'

Joanna was listening in amazement. It confirmed
absolutely that her theory on the two men being one
and the same was correct. A shudder of excitement
crackled up her spine.

'How would he know about that?' asked Marcus as
calmly as he could.

'Because he was Michael O'Connell's messenger.
He had to stand in front of Swan and Edgars waiting

for someone called Rose.' Zoe rolled her eyes. 'I ask you. William's a dear old boy, certainly, but senile, definitely.'

Joanna's heart was thumping against her chest but she kept silent, praying Marcus would ask the right questions.

'It might be true, Zo.'

'Some of it, maybe, yes. I'm sure William did know him years ago, but I think the passage of time has clouded his memory and he's got James confused with someone else. Although, admittedly, he seemed very definite about the details.'

'You've never heard anything about this before?' asked Joanna, unable to stop herself.

'Never.' Zoe shook her head. 'And to be honest, if there was a story to tell, I'm sure James would have told me before he died. We kept few secrets from each other. Granted, towards the end he did mutter on about Ireland, something about a house in a place that began with an R. I can't remember the name exactly.'

'As a matter of fact,' Joanna said, 'I've read one of your grandfather's biographies. I'm surprised nothing was mentioned in there.'

'I know. That's why I find it all so hard to believe. William said it was all hush-hush, that he himself was warned off by James, told it was better if they went their separate ways. My explanation for that would be that maybe William was a hanger-on James couldn't get rid of, so he paid him off with some cock-and-bull story.'

'Surely it would be worth investigating?' said Marcus.

'Oh I will, when I have time. That attic in Kent needs sorting out anyway. When I've finished filming I'll go and spend a weekend there and see what turns up.'

'Unless you want me to do it, Zo.'

'Marcus, I can hardly see you trundling through boxes of dusty old letters and newspaper cuttings. You'd get fed up after the first one and dump the lot on a bonfire.'

'No I wouldn't! Don't be so damning. I'd quite enjoy it actually. Besides I had an idea the other day.'

'What?'

'Well, to be truthful, it was Joanna's. I was telling her about all the stuff in Kent and she came up with the idea of either auctioning it to raise funds for the memorial scholarship or handing it over to the Theatre Museum. But that means the whole lot will have to be sifted through and catalogued.'

Zoe shrugged. 'I'm not sure whether I want to let it go.'

'Zo, sweetheart, it's rotting away up there. If you don't do something with it soon there'll be nothing worth holding on to anyway.'

'I suppose you're right. Well, what about if we make a joint effort? Plan to spend the first weekend I'm back down in Kent. Joanna could come and help us, couldn't you? As long as you swear not to splash any juicy secrets we might uncover on the front of your newspaper.'

'I think I could just about manage to guarantee that.' Joanna smiled.

'By the way, was the actor you were talking about William Fielding?' asked Marcus.

'And the lady whom he met was definitely called Rose?' added Joanna.

'Yes. To both of you.' Zoe looked at her watch. 'Sorry to spoil the party, chaps, but I need my beauty sleep.' She stood up. 'The food was fab, and the company even better. Do you want me to take you to that designer seconds place, Joanna?'

'I'd love you to.'

'Okay. Any excuse to shop.' Zoe picked up her jacket from the chair and put it on. 'How about next Saturday? Oh, except Jamie's home for half-term. I tell you what, you and Marcus come to my house on Saturday morning. Marcus can babysit his favourite nephew while you and I go out shopping.'

'Hold on a minute . . . I . . .'

Zoe kissed him on the cheek. 'You owe me, Marcus. Night, Joanna.' She waved and disappeared smartly out of the bistro.

Marcus scratched his head in amazement. 'Well, what an evening. You scored a hit with madam. I've rarely seen her so relaxed.'

Joanna was too shell-shocked to reply. Marcus squeezed her hand. 'Come on, let's go back to my place. We can have a brandy and discuss what Zoe said.'

They left the bistro and walked the five minutes back to Marcus's flat. Joanna sat on the sofa as Marcus poured her a brandy then sat down next to her.

'So it seems you were right about Michael

O'Connell and Sir Jim being one and the same person,' Marcus mused.

'Yes.'

'William Fielding knew James all those years ago, under a different name, leading a different life, and never said a word. That's loyalty for you.'

'It might also have been fear,' added Joanna. 'If he was delivering and receiving letters for James, and those letters contained sensitive information, it was surely imperative he keep his mouth shut.'

'Yes. I wonder why he suddenly told Zoe after all this time?'

'Oh, perhaps because James was dead, because seventy years is a long time . . .' Joanna yawned. 'I'm so tired of trying to think what any of it means.'

Marcus gave her a cuddle. 'Then think some more in the morning. Come to bed and sleep on it.'

'Yes. I will.'

He kissed her, then pulled her up to standing.

Joanna smiled at him. 'Thanks for supper. I thought Zoe was lovely, by the way. Not at all how you'd described her.'

'Mmm.' Marcus rubbed his chin. 'We weren't trying a bit *too* hard for our own selfish reasons, were we? It'd be very convenient for your investigation to get pally with Zoe.'

Furious, she disentangled herself from his grasp. 'Marcus! How dare you! Christ! I make an effort to get on with your sister, mostly for your sake, find I genuinely like her and you accuse me of that! Jesus! You really don't know me very well, do you?'

He was taken aback by her sudden anger. 'Simmer down, Jo. I was joking. It was great to see the two of you getting on. Zoe could do with a female friend. She never opens up to anyone.'

Joanna eyed him. 'I hope you mean that.'

'I do, I do. And let's face it, we didn't exactly have to torture her to spill any beans. She did it without any prompting whatsoever.'

'Yes.' Joanna walked towards the hall. Marcus followed her.

'Where are you going?'

'Home. I'm too cross to stay.'

'Joanna, please don't go. I've said I'm sorry. I . . .'

She opened the door and sighed. 'Look, I just think we're going too fast, Marcus. I need some breathing space. Thanks for dinner. Night.'

Marcus closed the door behind her miserably, pondering the complexity of the female, then poured himself a brandy and sat down to work out how he could interrogate William Fielding further without arousing his sister's suspicion.

chapter twenty-one

William Fielding sat beside his old gas fire in his favourite armchair. His bones ached and he felt weary. He knew his days left as a working actor were numbered, before he had to give in and turn himself over to some ghastly home for the ancient and bewildered. Once he stopped working, he doubted whether he'd last too long.

Talking to Zoe Harrison had been one of the pleasures of making *Tess*. And it had sent his brain skittering back rather unwillingly into the past.

William looked down at the thick gold signet ring clasped in the palm of his gnarled hand. Even now he blushed to think of it. After all the kindness Michael had shown him, he'd been low enough to steal from him. Just the once, when he and his mama had been desperate. She had said it was a bad stomach bug that rendered her unable to work. But in retrospect William rather suspected an assignation with a back-street butcher and a knitting needle.

Michael had sent him back to his lodgings to pick up a pot of glue for his moustache. William had let himself in, and there, sitting on the washbasin by the pot of glue, had been the ring. He'd taken it straight to the pawnbroker's and got enough to keep himself and his mum out of penury for a good three months. Only she'd died a couple of weeks later. The odd thing was that Michael had never questioned him about the missing ring, even though he was the obvious candidate to have stolen it. Six months later, having saved hard, William had gone to the pawnbroker's and bought it back. But by then, Michael had vanished again.

He was going to give the ring to Zoe tomorrow when he saw her down in Norfolk. He knew she thought him an old codger and a storyteller, and who could blame her? But it felt right that she should have it. As William lay in bed that night, the ring on his own finger so he would not forget it in the morning, he pondered whether he should also tell her the secret he'd kept to himself for seventy years, believing James absolutely when he'd warned him of the danger. For he had discovered who Rose had been . . .

*

'Hi, Simon, having a good week?' Ian clapped him on the shoulder.

For want of anything better to do, Simon had joined the boys in the pub down the road.

'So, so. I got dumped by my girlfriend and I'm still on standby as an upmarket taxi-driver,' he replied.

'Ah well, you know better than to question the workings of them upstairs. Drink?'

'Go on then. I'll have a pint.'

'You should buy me one, actually. It's my birthday. And I intend to get absolutely pissed,' nodded Ian. 'A pint for the young man,' he shouted at the barman.

By the look of Ian, Simon reckoned he'd already achieved his objective.

'So, in search of new tottie then?' Ian came and sat down opposite him.

'I think I'll let the dust settle before I walk back into the Lion's den.' Simon took a gulp of his pint. 'I have this unerring urge to grab any female I see and put my hands round their neck as punishment to their sex for making me so bloody miserable. I'll get over it, I'm sure.'

'That's the spirit. Anyway,' Ian burped, 'I hope it's taught you a lesson.' He wagged his finger at Simon. 'My motto is, don't get under the thumb, get your leg over.'

'Mmm. Not really my style, womanizing.'

'Well, you'd better start making it your style. It might shrivel up and drop off if it's not put to use soon. Talking of womanizers, I met an old friend the other night. Now he could teach us all a thing or two. And Christ, what a prat! Yet bint after bint falls at his feet.' Ian shook his head.

'Do I hear the ring of jealousy?' Simon teased.

'Jealous of Marcus Harrison? Jesus, no! He's a complete waster. Never done a decent day's work in his life. As I said to Jenkins when he asked me to encourage him to help us with an inquiry, offer him a few pound notes and he's yours for the taking. Of course, I was right. We've paid the bastard to spy on his girlfriend. And from the gist of the conversation last night, he's not even realized his flat has been bugged.'

'Ian, you're talking too much.' Simon shot him a warning glance.

'Christ, Simon! Virtually every single person in this boozer is from our place. I'm hardly giving away state secrets, am I? Stop being so tight-arsed and buy your mate a drink.'

Simon wandered off to the bar, thinking it wasn't the first time he'd seen Ian like this. Whether it was his birthday or not, Ian had been hitting the booze hard for the past few months. He was sure it wouldn't be long before a warning shot was passed across his bow. It was drummed into you time and time again during your training. Just one slip of the tongue, a single careless comment could spell disaster, and even possible death.

Simon paid for the two beers and took them back to the table.

'Happy Birthday.'

'Thanks. Will you come on with us? We're going for a curry then to some seedy disco that Jack says does a great line in busty teenagers. Could be just what you need, Si.'

'I think I'll pass, but thanks anyway.'

'Look, I'm sorry if I'm out of it tonight, but I had a particularly nasty little job to organize this morning.' Ian swept a hand through his hair. 'Poor old bloke. He actually shat in his pants, he was so terrified.'

'Ian, sorry, I don't want to hear this.'

He shook his head. 'No, no, I'm sure you don't. It's just, jeez, Si, does the strain never get to you? Being unable to share details of your daily existence with your friends and family?'

'Yes, of course it does. Look, why don't you go and

talk to someone about it? Maybe you need a break, a holiday.'

'You know as well as I do that if you show any signs of cracking, bingo! You're out on your arse pen-pushing for the local fucking council. No.' Ian shook his head. 'I'll be fine. It was just a hell of a way to spend a birthday.'

Simon drained his pint glass and clapped Ian on the shoulder as he stood up. 'Don't let it get to you. Have a good night.'

'Yeah, sure.' Ian feigned a smile and waved an arm as Simon left the pub.

*

'Zoe? It's Tim here.'

'Hi, Tim. How's things down in Norfolk?'

'We have a bit of a problem actually. William Fielding was attacked in his home yesterday by a gang of thugs. He's on the critical list and they're not sure if he's going to make it.'

'Oh God! How awful.'

'I know. You really do start to wonder what the world is coming to. Apparently they burst into his house yesterday morning, stole God knows what paltry possessions he owned and left him for dead.'

'The poor, poor man.' Zoe choked back a sob.

'As you can imagine, it's messed up our schedule for this week. By the sound of things, even if he does make it, he'll be in no fit state to continue with the film. We're looking through now to see what we have and haven't got. With some careful editing we reckon we're just about there. Anyway, until we've sorted that out, filming's on hold.'

'Of course.' Zoe bit her lip. 'Listen, Tim, do you happen to know which hospital William's in? If I'm going to be in London for the next few days I'd like to go and see him.'

'That's sweet of you, Zoe. He's in St Thomas's. Don't know whether you'll find him compos mentis or not. If he is, send our love from everyone in Norfolk.'

'Of course. Okay, Tim, thanks for calling.'

Zoe put the telephone down, berating herself for making derogatory comments about William to Joanna and Marcus on Monday night. Now she was in London for a week unexpectedly because of poor old William's bad luck. Rather guiltily, she realized it might give her a chance to see Pip. Unable to settle to anything at home and surprised at just how upset she was, Zoe set off later that day for St Thomas's.

With her unimaginative bunch of flowers, grapes and fruit juice, Zoe was directed to intensive care. 'I'm here to see William Fielding,' she informed a burly nurse.

'He's too ill to see any visitors other than close family. Are you close family?'

'Er, yes, his daughter, actually.' On celluloid, anyway, Zoe thought to herself.

The nurse took Zoe to a corner of the room, pulled back a curtain and there was William, his head swathed in bandages, his face covered in lurid yellow and purple bruises.

Tears came to Zoe's eyes.

'He's slipping in and out of consciousness. Very poorly, I'm afraid. Now you've turned up I'll get the doctor along to talk to you about his condition and take some details. We weren't aware he had any children. I'll leave you with him for a while.'

Zoe nodded silently, then, when the nurse left, put her bag down and took William's hand in hers. 'William, can you hear me? It's Zoe, Zoe Harrison.'

There was no response. William's eyes remained closed, his hand limp inside hers. Zoe sat down and stroked his hand.

'All the cast and film crew down in Norfolk send their love. They hope to see you back down there soon,' she whispered. 'Oh William, what a terrible thing to happen. I'm so sorry, I really am.' Whether it was that this was reminiscent of sitting by James's bedside so recently and watching him slip away, Zoe didn't know, but tears began to plop down her cheeks. 'I'm so sorry we didn't have a chance to talk more about when you knew my grandfather. It was fascinating, it really was. Some of the things you were telling me; well, he must have really trusted you all those years ago.'

Zoe felt one of William's fingers twitch inside her palm. She saw his eyelids flickering too.

'William, can you hear me?'

One of his fingers was moving so strongly that Zoe had to let go of his hand. His index finger lay on the sheet, enclosed by a large signet ring, twitching violently.

'What is it? Is the ring hurting you?' Zoe noticed William's fingers did look swollen. 'Do you want me to take it off?'

The finger waggled again.

'Okay.' Zoe struggled to remove the ring, which seemed far too tight a fit.

'I'll put it in your locker for safekeeping.'

Then she noticed his head was shaking, only very slightly and slowly from side to side. His index finger was pointing at her.

'You want me to look after it for you?'

His thumb managed a rather pathetic thumbs-up.

'Okay, of course I will.' Zoe stowed the ring away in her pocket. 'William, do you know who did this to you?'

He nodded, slowly but definitely.

'Can you tell me?'

Again, a nod.

Zoe put her ear close to his lips as he struggled to form a word.

The first attempt came out as a hoarse, unrecognizable whisper.

'Oh William, can you try again?' she urged.

'Ask . . . Rose.'

'You said Rose, is that right?'

He squeezed her fingers, then spoke again.

'Lady in . . .'

'Lady in where?' urged Zoe, hearing William's breathing becoming more ragged.

'Wait . . .'

'I'm here, William, I'm going nowhere.'

'. . . Waiting . . .!'

'I will wait, I promise.'

Zoe watched as William sighed, then slipped away into unconsciousness. She sat there for another forty minutes stroking his hand, hoping he'd return to her, but he did not. In the end, she stood up and walked out of the ward, passing quickly by the nurses' station before the nurse accosted her and asked her for details she could not give.

She hailed a taxi outside the hospital and sat in the back staring blankly out of the window. Deciding she really didn't want to go home, she leaned forward and tapped on the glass.

'Change of plan. Can you take me to Holland Park?'

*

Marcus was still in his dressing gown when he answered the door.

'Hi, sis. You look shitty. What's wrong?'

She followed him inside. 'You remember I was telling you about that actor, William Fielding?'

'Yes?'

'He was brutally attacked yesterday. I've just been to see him and I reckon it'll be a miracle if he makes it through tonight.' Zoe sat down on the sofa and started to sob. 'It's just upset me so much.'

Not half as much as it's upsetting me, grimaced Marcus. He went to sit beside her and gave her a hug. 'Come on, sweetheart, he wasn't family, was he?'

'No, I know. Have you got a cigarette?'

'Sure.' Marcus found a packet and lit one up for her. 'Was he able to talk?'

'No, not really. When I asked him if he knew who had done this he whispered something about Rose, and a lady in somewhere and waiting for him.' Zoe blew her nose. 'I think he was rambling. And only the other night I called him senile.'

Only the other night . . . Was it coincidence? But how could they have known? Unless . . . Marcus swallowed hard. Shit. He grabbed a pen and a piece of paper. 'Did you write down what he said?'

'No.' Zoe shrugged. 'Should I have done?'

'Yes. It might help the police with their enquiries.' He handed her the sheet of paper. 'Put down exactly what he said.'

'Should I take it to the police?' she asked as she finished scribbling.

'Tell you what, seeing as you're so upset, I'll do it for you.'

Zoe nodded gratefully and handed the paper to him. 'Okay, Marcus. Thanks.' Zoe's mobile rang. 'Hello? Yes, Michelle, Tim called me this morning. I know, wasn't it? I went to see him and . . .'

Realizing it was Zoe's agent, Marcus whispered he was going to get dressed and left the room. He was back five minutes later, just as Zoe had finished talking. She put the mobile down on the sofa.

'Listen, Marcus, thanks. I'll just use your loo and be off.'

'Okay.'

A few minutes later, Zoe had left and Marcus was pondering whether it was possible that someone had bugged his flat. It was a common enough phenomenon these days. If they were paying him to find out what he could, then surely they'd want to be the first to know. It was the only way he could think of that others could have known about William Fielding and his association with James Harrison so quickly. If the letter, whatever it contained, was important enough to have a man left for dead, he knew the reward for finding it could be massive.

A telephone rang while Marcus was in the kitchen. Puzzled, as it was not the sound of his own phone, he went into the sitting room and saw Zoe's mobile lying in a corner of the sofa. He picked it up and clicked it on.

'Zoe? It's me.' The voice sounded very familiar.

'Er, Zoe's not here. Can I take a message?'

The line immediately went dead at the other end. Marcus immediately pressed 'recall'. The line rang and a voice answered. In shock, Marcus cut the connection. And realized who the caller had been.

chapter twenty-two

'Come in, Simpson, and take a pew.'

Ian's head throbbed. He only hoped he wouldn't throw up in front of his boss's expensive, leather-bound desk.

'Can you explain to me why the job was not completed?'

'Sorry?'

He leaned forward. 'He's still hanging on. He's likely to die, but not before Zoe Harrison managed to get in to see him. God only knows what he told her. The doctor in charge had been called away and a nurse let her in. Bloody hell! Simpson. You've messed up good and proper on this one.'

'Sorry, sir. I took a pulse and listened and I was convinced he was dead.'

He drummed his fingers on the desk. 'Well, you obviously didn't listen hard enough. I'm warning you, one more slip-up like that and you're out. Do you understand me?'

'Yes, sir.' Ian's woolly head was spinning. He wondered if he might pass out.

'Send Warburton in. And damn well get your act together, do you hear?'

'Yes, sir. Sorry, sir.' Ian stood up and walked as carefully as he could to the door.

'Bloody hell. You look green!' Simon was sitting in a chair outside.

'I feel it.' Ian felt in his pocket for a handkerchief. 'Excuse me. I have to dash. You're in.'

Shaking his head, Simon stood up and knocked on the door.

'Come.'

Jenkins smiled at Simon. 'Sit down, will you, Warburton?'

'Thank you, sir.'

'Firstly, I want to ask you, without compromising any loyalty and friendship you may have struck up, whether you think Simpson is feeling the pressure, whether he could do with . . . a break.'

'It was his birthday yesterday.'

'Mmm. Hardly an excuse under the circumstances, but still . . . I've told him to shape up. Keep an eye out will you? He's a good member of the team but I've seen countless others go in a similar direction. Anyway, let me get to the point. There's a car taking you to Whitehall in ten minutes.'

'Really, sir?'

Jenkins leaned across the desk. 'I have personally recommended you for this assignment. It's of the utmost delicacy, Warburton. Don't let me down, will you?'

'I'll do my best not to.'

Jenkins nodded. 'That's all. Wait downstairs for the car.'

*

Half an hour later, Simon was being ushered along the thickly carpeted corridor of an upper floor in Whitehall. The woman tapped on a thick oak-panelled door.

'Come!' barked a voice from inside. The woman pushed the door open.

'Warburton to see you, sir.'

'Thank you.'

Simon walked towards the desk, noting the huge chandelier that lit the vast room, the heavy velvet curtains that hung at either side of the tall windows. The grand setting was in stark contrast to the diminutive, ancient figure sitting behind the desk in a wheelchair. Yet his presence dominated the room.

'Sit.'

Simon did so, into a comfortable, high-backed leather chair.

The gimlet eyes surveyed him. 'Your boss tells me good things about you.'

'That's gratifying to hear, sir.'

'I've read your file and I was impressed. Like to sit where I'm sitting one day, Warburton?'

Simon presumed he meant this in the context of the room, rather than the wheelchair. 'I would, sir.'

'Do a good job for me and I can guarantee immediate promotion. We're putting you on the Royal Protection Squad from tomorrow.'

Simon's heart sank in disappointment. From the fuss that was being made, he'd been imagining a much more glamorous, meaty assignment. 'May I ask why, sir?'

'We think you are the most suited for the task. I believe you've already met Zoe Harrison. As I'm sure

you have gathered, she and Prince George are involved.
You will be assigned to her.'

'I see. Sir, may I ask why you feel it necessary to
place an MI5 agent such as myself as a bodyguard? Not
wishing to sound churlish, but the position is hardly
what I've been trained for.'

He stared at Simon, a glimmer of a smile hovering
on his lips. 'As it happens, I rather think it is.' He
pushed an envelope towards Simon. 'I must leave for a
meeting. You will stay here, read this dossier and have
it memorized by the time I return. You will be locked
in while you read it.'

'Of course, sir.'

'You will understand exactly why I want you to be
close to Miss Harrison. The situation suits our purposes
well.'

'Yes, sir.' Simon took the thick file.

He wheeled himself round his desk and across the
carpet. 'We can discuss things further when you've
absorbed the information.'

Simon stood up, walked to the door and opened it
to allow his wheelchair to pass through.

'Thank you, Warburton.' He nodded and left the
room.

Simon closed the door behind him, then heard the
key turn in the lock. He went back to his chair and
studied the file. The red stamp on the front told him
he was about to read the highest category of classified
information. Few pairs of eyes would have glanced at it
previously. He opened the dossier and began to read.

*

At two minutes past four, the door opened.

'Have you read and understood, Warburton?'

Simon's brain was still reeling from shock.

'Yes.'

'Are you aware of why we think you would be suitable to act as Zoe Harrison's bodyguard for the foreseeable future?'

'I believe so, sir.'

'I've chosen you because your discretion and capabilities are highly regarded by both myself and my colleagues. You are also a personable young man who is quite capable of befriending a female such as Miss Harrison. She will be informed by the Palace that you are to move into her house from the weekend and accompany her wherever she goes.'

'Yes, sir.'

'This should give you ample opportunity to discover what she knows. If he has told anyone of the letter's whereabouts, it's her. You will also have unlimited access to both houses. Your directive is to find and retrieve the letter.'

'Yes, sir.'

'Warburton, I need hardly tell you that what I have entrusted you with is of the utmost delicacy. Others, such as Simpson, are on a need-to-know basis only. The subject matter must not under *any* circumstances be discussed outside this room. If there are leaks, it will be you whom I will blame. However, if the situation is brought to a satisfying conclusion, I can guarantee you'll be rewarded.'

'Thank you, sir.'

'When you leave you will be issued with a telephone

number. You will use it only to report directly to me at four o'clock each afternoon. Otherwise, in your role as bodyguard, you will report to the Palace security office.' He gestured to an envelope on the table, which Simon picked up. 'Your orders are in there. Prince George wishes to see you in his rooms at the Palace in an hour. I'm relying on you, Warburton. Good luck.'

Simon stood up, shook the proffered hand and left the room.

*

Zoe gazed out of the window, admiring the statue that stood in front of the Palace from a different and very privileged angle.

'Come away, darling. You never know who's hovering up a tree with a telephoto lens these days.' Pip closed the thick damask curtain tightly and led her back to the sofa.

They were in Pip's sitting room, on the third floor of the Palace. Adjoining this was his bedroom, bathroom and study. Zoe snuggled into Pip's arms and he handed her a glass of wine.

'Here's to us, darling,' he toasted.

'Yes.' She raised her glass to his.

'By the way, did you retrieve your mobile phone?'

'Oh God, yes. Marcus called to say I'd left it at his flat. Why? Did you speak to him?'

'No. As soon as I realized, I rang off. I was only calling to ask you to bring a nice snapshot of yourself so I could put it in a frame and admire you when I'm away from you.'

'Christ, I hope Marcus didn't recognize your voice,' Zoe worried.

'I doubt it. I only said three words.'

'Well, he didn't mention you'd called me, anyway. Hopefully he's forgotten all about it.'

'Zoe, sweetheart.' Pip took a lock of her hair and wound it round his finger. 'You do realize, if we continue to see one another, that someone will find out.'

'Why should they? I mean look at your brother, having an affair for all these years. They managed to keep that well hidden.'

'That was slightly different, Zoe. He was married. The trouble is, part of me would love to go public. Then I could take you everywhere with me. We could face the world together, defy them.'

'No, Pip! Please! I just can't even contemplate it, for Jamie's sake. After all these years of keeping him out of the limelight, his life would be made a misery.'

'Of course he'd be the subject of intense media interest to begin with, but they're not too bad with children. They've left my nephews alone for most of the time.'

'But can you imagine the speculation? There'd be a witch hunt to find the father. Besides, I hardly think an unmarried mother is a suitable and acceptable consort for a prince now, anymore than she was ten years ago.'

Pip stood up and paced the room. 'If you're referring to the little meeting that took place while I was suddenly whisked off to Canada, to find your "Dear John" letter when I returned, I know all about that.'

'Do you?'

'Oh yes. I'd always suspected you were put under pressure to write it, to tell me it was over. I had a showdown yesterday morning with my mother and father and one of their senior advisers. They admitted that they'd had you called in and told the relationship had to end.'

Zoe put her head in her hands. 'I can hardly bear to think about it, even after all these years.'

'Well, I hadn't helped matters by telling the family I'd met the girl I wanted to marry. At the age of twenty, while still at university, and you being only just eighteen. I insisted I wanted our engagement announced as soon as possible.' Pip shook his head. 'I panicked them into taking action, like any parent would pall at what they saw as some kind of illogical infatuation. Except, of course, my situation was magnified by ten thousand.'

Zoe watched him silently, amazed at his revelations. 'I had no idea you'd told them that,' she said quietly.

'I feel completely responsible for what subsequently happened. If I hadn't rushed in like a bull at a gate, but calmly and sanely courted you for another few years, things could have been very, very different. And I'll regret what I did until the day I die. It put you through hell.'

'Yes,' Zoe agreed. 'It did. Of course, I didn't tell them about the baby. But even if I had, I knew they'd suggest I got rid of it.' Zoe shrugged. 'I've often wondered whether they were shocked when they read about the birth of my baby in the newspaper. But they treated me like a common whore when I came for the meeting. I suppose they assumed you were one of many.'

Pip took her in his arms. 'Darling, if only I'd have known all this then.'

'Well, it wouldn't have made any difference, would it?' Zoe sighed.

'I suppose not.' Pip led her to the sofa and sat her down. 'That's all in the past now. As far as our future goes, myself and my parents have reached a truce. They know how I feel about you; they could hardly discard the feelings of a thirty-year-old man the way they did a twenty-year-old, and they're aware that my intentions are serious.'

Zoe was cringing. 'And what did they say? Are they going to sling me back into the gutter from whence I crawled?'

Pip smiled wryly. 'No. I told them that if they were unprepared to accept you, I was equally prepared to abdicate my right to the throne. I mean, it's hardly a big deal, is it? I'm the second spare, hardly likely to get a crack of the whip anyway.'

Zoe gazed at Pip in amazement. 'You'd do that for me?' she whispered.

'Yes. Absolutely yes. My life is a sham, anyway. I have no particular role to play, and as I said to my parents the public in particular have been up in arms about the cushy number the junior royals have got. Of course they don't reckon that serving in the navy for nine years was anything like hard work. They're convinced that I got special feather-filled pillows on my bunk and a down duvet with a crest on it while everyone else was sleeping on rocks under a hair blanket . . .' Pip sighed. 'The point is, they can't have it both ways. If I'm to fulfil their wish to be a "normal" person, then equally they must respect the fact that I have fallen in love with a woman who already has a child. Which, in the times we live in, is hardly something unusual.'

Zoe took a large gulp of her wine. 'Sure, it sounds okay in practice, but I just can't see it happening. So how did the meeting conclude?'

'Oh, Dad ranted and raved, Mother was calmer.' Pip shrugged. 'I do think their attitude has softened in the past few years, what with all the divorces and whatnot. We agreed that you and I would continue to see each other as discreetly as possible whenever we wanted. That you could come here, and stay as often as you liked. That within the family and its advisers, you would be an open secret.'

'And if the secret got out?'

Pip shrugged. 'Nobody quite knows how the public will react. We all suspect a mixture; some saying how outrageous our liaison is, others agreeing with the more modern approach to a royal relationship. I guess it's a suck it and see situation.'

Zoe shuddered. 'I'm sorry, Pip, but I am totally terrified of anyone discovering us.'

He knelt in front of her and held her hands. 'Darling, I really do understand.' He sighed. 'What can I say? Trust me. I'll do all I can to protect you and Jamie. There is one more thing we ought to discuss.'

'What's that?'

'I'm afraid the one thing the powers that be, and myself to be honest, must insist on is that we install a bodyguard.'

'What?' Zoe was outraged. 'In my house?'

'Darling, darling, calm down. You're the one who says she wants this to remain our secret for as long as possible. A bodyguard is also responsible for being the forward defence. He can be useful in making sure that there is no one lurking outside, listening to your calls, bugging your house. Besides which, the minute you become entangled with the member of the firm, you become a target.'

'Oh,' nodded Zoe, 'and what do I tell Jamie? Do you not think he might find it odd when he comes home from school to find a strange man sleeping in the spare room?'

'If you're really not ready to tell him about us, then I'm sure we can concoct some story for him. The chap whom we've chosen you've met already: Simon War-burton, the driver who took and collected you from Sandringham. Nice chap, and highly trained too. I had a chat with him this afternoon and he understands the situation.'

It was Zoe's turn to get up and pace.

Pip went to her and took her in his arms. 'Please, let's at least try it. Surely, after all this time, all you've suffered, we owe it to each other. And I promise I'll completely understand if you find it all too much and take the decision to end it.'

Zoe leaned on his shoulder as he stroked her hair.

'I know what you're thinking: is he really worth it?'

Zoe smiled sadly. 'I guess I am.'

'And am I?' He took her gently by the shoulders and forced her to look at him.

She nodded. 'God help me. I guess you are.'

chapter twenty-three

Joanna stared at her computer screen, then ran through her thesaurus to try and find new and inspiring ways of describing the bliss on a particular spaniel's face as he noisily ate his way through the bowl of dog food he was testing. She also had toothache. And after lunch it had been grim enough for her to ask Alice for the number of a dentist where she could get an emergency appointment.

Her extension rang and she picked up the phone. 'Joanna Haslam.'

'It's Marcus, darling.'

'Hi,' she answered casually.

'Ready to forgive me yet? I'm bankrupting myself with all these bouquets, you know.'

Joanna glanced at the three vases full of blooms that had arrived over the past couple of days. 'I might be.'

'Good, because I have something for you, something that Zoe told me.'

'What is it?'

'Give me your fax number. Given the circumstances, it's safer if I send it on paper. See if you come to the same conclusion I did.'

'Okay.' Joanna gave him the number. 'Send it now.

I'm about to leave for the dentist. I'll go and stand by the machine.'

'Ring me straight back when you've read it. We need to see each other and talk, but maybe not over the telephone.'

'Okay, speak in five minutes. Bye.' Joanna put down the receiver and ambled across to the fax machine. While she waited for the message to come through, she pondered her feelings for Marcus. He was a very different personality to the rather serious Matthew. Joanna had begun to think that Marcus Harrison, with all his faults, was actually just what she needed. Last night, as she'd lain in her new bed, missing his arms around her, she had decided she'd trust him, take him on face value when he said he loved her, and sod the consequences. Protecting herself and her heart from further upsets was safe, but was 'safe' living?

The fax machine activated and Marcus's message started to come through.

'*Hi, darling. Speak to me immediately. I miss you, Marcus.*'

'How's the toothache?'

Joanna jumped and saw Alice behind her trying to read the fax. She pulled the message out of the machine and folded it.

'Dreadful.' Joanna walked back to her desk, eager to lose Alice and read the fax.

Alice propped herself on Joanna's desk and folded her arms. 'Oh Miss Haslam, I see danger ahead.'

'So? You face danger every time you eat a piece of chicken, beef or, apparently now, even lamb,' snapped Joanna.

'So, you become a vegetarian.'

Joanna rubbed her nose. 'Trouble is, I've always been a terrible carnivore. And I'd hate to deprive myself.'

'Oh God, bring back the days when women such as us were married, barefoot and pregnant in the kitchen by the age of twenty-one. At least we didn't have to worry about waging psychological warfare with the opposite sex. They courted, they kissed and then they had to marry us if they wanted a poke.'

'Oh please, Alice! I for one am glad Mrs Pankhurst chained herself to the railings.'

'Yeah, it's allowed you to spend your days becoming a dog-food expert, and your nights either alone or in bed with someone whom you're not sure will still be there the following night.'

'That's rather a cynical view, if I might say so.'

'Maybe it is.' Alice shrugged. 'But do you know many of your single girlfriends over the age of twenty-five who are actually happy?'

'Yes, lots,' affirmed Joanna.

'Okay, but when are they *most* happy?'

'When they've had a good day at work or met a—' Joanna stopped herself.

'An elephant? A canary? Their grandmother?' Alice shrugged. 'See? I rest my case.'

'At least we have the choice.'

'Too much choice, if you ask me. We're all too fussy. If we don't like his brand of aftershave, or his oh-so-irritating habit of channel hopping when we're trying to watch the latest BBC costume drama, we toss him aside and go off in search of fresh flesh.' Alice sighed. 'We seek perfection and, of course, it doesn't exist.'

'No, maybe not,' agreed Joanna.

'So then what happens? We get over thirty, realize our biological clocks are ticking and we're in danger of becoming the family's next-generation maiden, so we rush into the arms of the first man who'll have us and live unhappily ever after.'

Joanna shook her head. 'Alice! That's so—'

'True!'

'I was going to say depressing.'

'Yeah, that as well.' Alice slid off Joanna's desk. 'Anyway, all I was trying to say is that if Marcus Harrison gets down on one knee at any point in the near future grab him with both arms. If he messes you around afterwards, at least you'll have half a nice house and money to fall back on, which is more than you get when you break up with some rat with whom you've had a "modern" non-committal relationship. Night, Jo. Hope my dentist sorts you out.' She waved and walked off across the office.

Joanna sighed and wondered which 'rat' had just dumped Alice. She unfolded the fax from Marcus and read it.

'Ask Rose.' 'Lady in . . .' 'Wait . . .' 'Waiting.'

Rose. Lady-in-waiting. It had to be. She dialled Marcus's number.

'Figure it out?'

'I think so.'

'Let's meet up tonight. Discuss it.'

'I'd love to, but I really can't tonight. I've got awful toothache and I must go to the dentist.'

'Afterwards, then? There's something I really need to tell you and not over the telephone.'

'I'll see how I feel. I might not be able to talk. But definitely tomorrow, okay?'

'Okay. I'll give you a call in the morning.'

'Fine.'

'Do you miss me? Just a little?'

Joanna smiled. 'Yes. Night, night.'

Tucking the fax into her jeans pocket, she switched her computer off, grabbed her coat and headed for the door. Tom was behind his desk, hiding from her as usual. She did a U-turn and went to stand behind him.

'When's my piece about Marcus Harrison and his memorial fund going in? He keeps asking me and it's getting very embarrassing.'

Tom shrugged. 'Ask Features. It's their shout.'

'Okay, I . . .' Joanna glanced at Tom's screen and recognized the name at the top of it. 'William Fielding. Why are you writing about him?'

'Because he's dead. Any more questions?'

Joanna gulped. Maybe that was what Marcus had wanted to tell her. 'Where? When? How?'

'Got beaten up a couple of days ago. Died this morning in hospital. The Ed's launching a campaign on the strength of it, trying to pressure the government into providing free security equipment for the old and infirm, and tougher penalties for the yobs that perpetrate the crimes.'

Joanna sat down abruptly in the seat next to Tom.

'What's up? You've turned pale.'

'Oh God, Tom. Oh God.'

Tom looked nervously in the direction of the Ed's office. 'What, Jo?'

She tried to clear her thoughts. 'He . . . William, knew things about Sir James Harrison. He knew Rose, my old lady, remember? Fucking hell, Tom! This wasn't an accident! It was planned, it must have been, just like Rose's death.'

'Jo, I'm warning you, I don't want to hear. You're talking crap anyway. They've arrested someone for it.'

'Poor sod. I tell you now, he or she didn't do it.'

Tom stared at her wearily. 'You can't know that, Jo.'

'I can, Tom. Listen, do you want to hear or not?'

Tom couldn't resist. 'Okay, shoot, quickly.'

Tom folded his arms when Jo finished. 'Okay, so say you're right and his death was arranged. How did they find out so quickly?'

Joanna shrugged. 'I don't really know. Unless . . . unless Marcus's flat has been bugged. He faxed me a few minutes ago, said it wasn't safe to speak.' Joanna pulled the fax out of her pocket and laid it on his desk. 'He said William had spoken these words to Zoe. Maybe she went to the hospital to see him before he died.'

He read the fax, then looked at Joanna. 'You've worked it out, I presume?'

'Yes. William was trying to say Rose was a lady-in-waiting.'

'Yes, I'd deduce that too.'

'Tom, this is getting out of hand. I'm getting scared, I really am.'

'Then for fuck's sake, leave well alone.'

'I have been trying to, but it keeps following me around.' Joanna shook her head. 'I don't know what to do, really. Sorry, Tom. I'm aware you don't want to hear.' She stood up and began to walk towards the door. 'Oh, by the way, you were right. I never did get that letter back. Night.'

Tom watched her leave. He lit up a Rothman's and stared at the screen. He had less than two years before he collected his pension and ended a fine career as a respected member of the media. He shouldn't do anything to rock the boat. But fuck it! He knew he'd regret it every day for the rest of his life if he let this one go. Tom stood up and went down to the library to gather as many cuttings as he could on Sir James Harrison, and to try to dig something out on a lady-in-waiting called Rose.

*

Joanna came out of the front door of the Harley Street dentist. Her head was throbbing from the drill and half her mouth was numb from Novocaine. She walked slowly down the steps and along the street, feeling decidedly woozy. A woman brushed past behind her and Joanna jumped. She felt her heart beating far too hard against her chest.

Had they been listening that night at Marcus's flat? Were they watching her now? Joanna broke out in a muck sweat and purple patches appeared before her eyes. She dropped on to her haunches, her head down between her legs and tried to take long, deep breaths to slow her breathing.

She leaned back against the railings of a building and looked up at the clear night sky.

'Oh fuck.' She groaned quietly, wishing a taxi would arrive inches away from her and carry her off home. Staggering upright, Joanna decided buses and tubes were a non-starter with her in this state. She set off along the street once more, hoping she'd find a taxi in the maze of roads behind Oxford Street. She walked along Harley Street, constantly sticking out her arm to full taxis, turned the corner and found herself in Welbeck Street. Where Zoe lived: number fifteen, she remembered. Zoe had written the address down for her after supper.

Joanna paused on the street, realizing she was standing almost directly opposite number fifteen. Another wave of faintness overtook her and she dropped down on to her haunches once more, wondering if it would seem impertinent to knock on Zoe's door and ask for a cup of hot sweet tea to help her on her way. The lights were on inside the house anyway. Joanna decided that as soon as she felt strong enough, she'd cross the road and throw herself at Zoe's mercy.

Joanna rifled in her rucksack for a furry polo. She felt rather like a vagrant, crouched between the wrought-iron railings in the entrance to someone's basement flat.

Just as she was trying to stagger to her feet, she saw Zoe's front door open. Zoe appeared, and from Joanna's perfect vantage point, she saw her walk on to the first step, sweep her eyes up and down the road, then turn back inside the house. Another figure became visible, a figure that Zoe kissed hurriedly. The figure grasped her hand, then walked swiftly down the steps and opened the back door of a car parked directly outside. As soon as the door was shut, the car indicated and moved off along the road.

Joanna knew her mouth had dropped open. She was gawping like an idiot. Either she was much sicker than she'd thought, and was suffering from delusions that should send her running to the local psychiatric unit for help, or she had just seen George Philip Edward, more commonly known to his family as 'Pip', royal prince and third in line to the throne, walk out of Zoe Harrison's front door.

*

Joanna soaked in a deep bath, the water tepid just in case she had another fainting fit. She took a sip of the brandy she'd poured to help with her toothache and stared at the magnolia ceiling for inspiration. Forget letters from strange old ladies-in-waiting, deaths of ageing actors, plots and conspiracies . . . Unless she was imagining things, Joanna had just seen some kind of tryst between one of the world's most eligible and, let's face it she thought, newsworthy bachelors and a young and very beautiful actress.

Who had a child.

A shudder of excitement went up Joanna's spine. If she had caught that kiss on camera, by now she could have probably netted a couple of hundred thousand from whichever British newspaper took her fancy. Zoe Harrison and Prince George. Joanna shook her head. What a story! Tomorrow she must do some research, find out whether the two of them had any past, whether she should write off what she'd seen as the meeting of two 'old friends'. She was seeing Zoe on Saturday. Maybe it might be possible to extract some information subtly. There was no doubt that a scoop like this would have her off Pets and Gardens faster than you could say 'manure'.

Joanna groaned and put a flannel over her face. She shook her head. How could she even *think* of blowing the whistle? She was going out with Zoe's brother. Besides which Zoe and she had got on well enough to think there might be the basis for a strong future friendship there. And especially after her initial conversation with Marcus, when she'd told him how ethical she intended to be, how she hated the way the press tore into and revealed the private lives of the rich and famous.

The sad thing was that if Prince George and Zoe were having some kind of relationship, whether she spilled the beans or not, the story would be broken in the very near future. Newshounds were like leeches, they could sniff out scandal before the two people concerned had barely consummated the relationship.

Joanna put on her pyjamas, made herself a cup of cocoa and climbed into her comfortable new bed. She pondered whether Marcus knew. Somehow, she doubted it. From what she had witnessed over dinner, brother and sister were not particularly close.

Joanna finished her cocoa, turned off her light, and dozed off dreaming wistfully of 'Joanna Haslam, journalist and friend of Zoe Harrison, gives an exclusive and revealing insight into the life and feelings of the new love in Prince George's life'.

*

Simon knocked on the front door of number fifteen, Welbeck Street.

Zoe opened it. 'Hello,' she said.

'Hello, Miss Harrison.'

'I suppose you'd better come in.' Reluctantly, Zoe indicated he should enter.

'Thank you.'

Zoe shut the door behind him and they stood in the hall.

'Er, I've given you a room at the top of the house. It's not very big, but it has its own shower.' She nodded.

'Thank you. I shall do my best not to intrude. Sorry, and all that.' He smiled at her.

Zoe realized Simon was as uncomfortable about the situation as she was. Her face softened. 'Look, why don't you go and put your stuff upstairs, then come down for a coffee. It's the door on the left, right at the top of the stairs.'

'Okay, thanks.' She watched Simon mount the stairs and went into the kitchen to put on the kettle. She checked her watch. She was due to pick up Jamie at four and she knew how bad the traffic could be on a Friday evening.

'Black or white? Sugared or not?' she asked as Simon wandered into the kitchen.

'Black, one sugar,' answered Simon.

'There, please sit down.' Zoe indicated the table.

'It's a beautiful old house this, Miss Harrison,' he said as he sat down and Zoe put the coffee in front of him.

'Thank you. And please, if we're to live together, I mean, under the same roof, I think you'd better call me Zoe.'

'Thanks.' Simon sipped the coffee. 'I'm sure having me here is the last thing you want. I promise I'll be as unobtrusive as possible. I'm afraid I will have to accompany you on all your journeys, either behind you while you drive your car or, if you'd prefer, I'll chauffeur you.'

'Yes, well, I have to go and pick up my son Jamie from school this afternoon.' Zoe sighed. 'I'm not quite sure how to explain your presence to him when we get home.'

'Maybe you should say I'm an old friend of the family, a cousin perhaps, who's over in London from abroad, and I'm staying with you for a while until I find a place of my own.'

'Jamie's very bright. I can't fob him off.' Zoe sighed. 'Okay, we'll try that, and see if it washes with him. He'll want to know on exactly which side of the family, mind you. You'd better say you're a great nephew of Kitty, my grandfather's dead wife.'

'Fine.' Simon nodded. 'It might be easier if I drive you to the school this afternoon. I think your son might think it a bit strange if he notices me following on behind.'

'Yes. And the other thing is, I don't want any members of my family to know either. It's not that I don't trust them, but . . .'

'You don't trust them!'

Zoe smiled. 'Exactly. Oh dear, this is going to be so difficult. My friend and I are going shopping tomorrow. Do you have to come along with us on that too?'

'Afraid so, but at a polite distance, I promise.'

Zoe sipped her coffee. 'I've suddenly started to have much more sympathy for the royal family and those connected with them. It must be ghastly feeling as though you have no privacy in your own home.'

'I suppose they've grown up with it, accepted it as part of their lives.'

'It can't be much fun for you either. I mean, what about your home life? Do you have a wife, a family who misses you when you're away?'

'No,' answered Simon. 'A lot of the chaps tend to be single.'

'My, what dedication to duty,' smiled Zoe. 'And I'm sorry you've got such a boring posting. I can hardly see the IRA having my name on the hit list. I mean, nobody knows about Pip and me.'

'Yet.'

Zoe's face darkened. 'Yes, well, it'll stay that way for as long as I can make it.' She stood up. 'If you'll excuse me, I need to go and get ready to pick up my son.'

chapter twenty-four

'Hi, Marcus. Hi, Joanna. Come in.' Zoe led the two of them inside the Welbeck Street house. 'Shall we go straight off? I'm tingling to get to the shops.' Zoe smiled.

'Whenever,' Joanna replied as Zoe ushered them through to the kitchen.

'You're not going to be too long, are you, sis? I mean, like, a couple of hours or something,' Marcus asked uncomfortably.

Zoe winked at Joanna. 'Oh, definitely no more than a couple of hours, Marcus, darling. Your charge is upstairs in his room, playing with his computer. Should keep him happy for ages. I'll just nip upstairs and get my coat and we'll be off.'

Marcus lit up a cigarette. 'Don't be too long, Jo. I can think of better ways to spend a Saturday than babysitting my precocious nephew.'

'And I can't think of a better way to spend my Saturday than shopping!' Joanna gave Marcus an affectionate kiss. Marcus pulled her to him and kissed her properly.

'You owe me for this, madam.'

'Zoe, I . . .'

Joanna heard a familiar voice behind her. She

turned round and saw Simon staring at her from the hall, the shock in his eyes mirroring her own.

'I . . .'

Zoe stood behind him in her coat.

'Did I mention Simon was coming to stay, Marcus?'

Joanna stared at Simon as Marcus unwound his arms from her body.

'Simon who?' Marcus asked.

'Warburton. He's Kitty's great-nephew. He wrote and said he was coming to the UK and could he stay with me for a while. So,' shrugged Zoe, 'here he is.'

Joanna's eyes were getting rounder. She watched Marcus shake hands with Simon.

'Good to meet you, Simon. So, we're distantly related?'

'Yes, it seems so.' Simon had recovered his cool.

'Here for long?'

'A while, yes.'

'Good. Well, we must meet up for a beer at some point. I'll show you the hippest places in town.'

'I look forward to it.' Simon nodded coolly.

'Come on then, Jo, let's hit the road. Jo?'

Joanna was still staring at Simon. Zoe watched her nervously.

'Yes, yes, of course. Right. Bye, Simon. Bye, Marcus.' Joanna turned and followed Zoe out of the front door.

Simon shrugged on the jacket he'd been holding. 'I'm off too. I thought I might take in some sights. Good to meet you, Marcus.' He smiled as he turned and walked towards the front door.

*

Zoe and Joanna spent the morning on the King's Road, then caught a bus to Knightsbridge. They wandered round Harvey Nichols until their feet ached, then took refuge in the restaurant on the top floor.

'It's on me, by the way,' said Zoe, as the waiter passed them a menu. 'Any woman who is as nice and intelligent as you are and prepared to take on my brother deserves at least one free lunch!'

'Thanks, I think,' laughed Joanna, as Zoe ordered food and a bottle of white wine.

'You're just so good for Marcus. He needs a steadying influence. If he asks you, marry him, please, and then we can do this kind of thing regularly.'

Joanna was touched at how eager Zoe was to make friends. She felt horribly guilty for any thoughts she'd had of shopping Zoe to her newspaper. They ate lunch and discussed whether Zoe should go back for an outfit she'd tried on in Nicole Farhi.

'Wasn't it tragic about William Fielding?' Joanna mentioned as she sipped her wine.

'Dreadful. I went to see him, you know, the day before he died.'

'Yes, Marcus mentioned it.'

'He was in a terrible state. It really upset me, especially as we'd had that chat about my grandfather only a few days before.'

'He gave me a beautiful signet ring, presumably for safekeeping. I brought it to show you.' Zoe fumbled in the zip pocket of her handbag, produced the ring and handed it to Joanna.

'It's so heavy.' Joanna turned the ring round in the palm of her hand. 'What are you going to do with it?'

'Take it to the funeral next week and see if any of William's relatives turn up, I suppose.' Zoe tucked the ring safely back in her handbag.

'What about the film?'

'They reckon they've got enough in the can to work around him. I'm back to Norfolk on Wednesday.'

'How long is your, er, friend Simon staying for?'

'I'm not sure. He's in London for a while and I've said he can stay as long as he wants. The house is so big there's ample room for the two of us.'

'Oh.' Joanna didn't know what else to say.

Zoe stared at her. 'I watched your face when you saw him at the house. You almost looked as though you recognized him. Do you know him?' she challenged.

'I . . .' Joanna blushed and said, 'Yes.'

Zoe visibly crumpled. 'I knew you did. Where from?'

'I've known Simon for most of my life. We virtually grew up together.'

Zoe silently poured the last of the wine into their glasses. She took a gulp. 'So,' she said slowly, 'I suppose you're aware that he is not in any way related to me?'

'Yes.'

She eyed Joanna uncertainly, as if trying to come to a decision. 'Are you aware of what he does for a living?'

'He's always said he worked for the Civil Service pen-pushing, which I suppose I never quite believed. He got a first from Cambridge and is very, very clever. Really, Zoe, you don't have to explain. It's obvious you have your reasons for making up some story about Simon for me and Marcus. I suppose it was just unfortunate that I happened to know him. I won't say anything, I promise.'

'Oh Joanna, I'm so scared to trust anyone at the moment. And you less than most being a journalist. Yet I feel I want to tell you. If I don't talk to someone, I think I shall go mad.'

'Zoe, if it's any help, I think I know,' Joanna said quietly.

'You do? How? Nobody knows.'

Joanna sighed. 'Pure coincidence.' She looked at Zoe. 'I saw a . . . a man come out of your house on Thursday evening.'

'How come? Were you spying on me?'

'No.' Joanna shook her head wearily. 'I went to the dentist in Harley Street, felt awfully faint and found myself in Welbeck Street while I was looking for a taxi. I was just about to come in and ask for a cup of tea and a sit down when your front door opened.'

Zoe eyed her suspiciously. 'Are you sure? Please don't lie, Joanna, I couldn't take it. Are you sure someone at your newspaper hadn't tipped you off?'

'No!' Joanna laughed. 'If there was a tip-off, they wouldn't give it to a junior reporter on Pets and Gardens.'

'No.' Zoe fiddled with her napkin. 'I suppose they wouldn't. Oh Christ, Jo. I'm so scared.' She looked straight at her. 'Did you see who the man was?'

Joanna nodded.

'So, I suppose you sort of guessed why Simon is living in my house.'

'Vaguely. Some kind of protection, I presume?'

'Yes. They . . . he, insisted on it.'

'Well, you couldn't ask for anyone better to look after you. Simon is quite the nicest man I know.'

A glimmer of a smile crossed Zoe's face. 'Like that, is it? Should I tell Marcus he has a rival?'

'No, it isn't. We've never been out together. We really are just good friends.'

'Talking of Marcus, you haven't said anything to him about what you saw on Thursday night?'

'No. I'm actually very good at keeping secrets. Tell me if you don't want to talk about it, but are the two of you . . . I mean, is it serious?'

Zoe's blue eyes filled with tears. 'Very. Unfortunately.'

'Why "unfortunately"?'

'Because I want Pip to be an accountant in Guildford, a married man even, but not who he is.'

'You can't help falling in love, Zoe.'

'No, but can you imagine how it'll affect my son if the story leaks?'

Joanna sighed. 'Yes. But I was only thinking the other day that it will leak at some point, especially if you're both serious about each other.'

'I know.' Zoe shook her head. 'The worst thing is, I just can't stop myself. Pip and I . . . well, it's always been this way.'

'You've known each other for a long time?'

'Yes. Years. I swear Joanna, if I ever read about this conversation in your newspaper, I couldn't be held responsible for my actions,' she said fiercely.

'Zoe, I admit I would *love* to be the person to hand this scoop to my editor, but I'm a Yorkshire girl and up there, a person's word is her bond. I won't, okay?'

'Okay. God, I need another drink.' She signalled to the waiter and asked him to bring another bottle of white wine. 'As you seem to know most of it, and as I'm desperate to talk to someone, I might as well tell you the whole story.'

*

Seeing the two girls were still deep in conversation, Simon took the opportunity to go to the men's room. Closing the toilet door and checking it was four o'clock, he dialled a number on his mobile.

'It's Warburton, sir.'

'Yes.'

'A problem this morning. I'm afraid Haslam arrived unexpectedly at Miss Harrison's house. Obviously, she recognized me.'

'I would think that was more of a problem for Miss Harrison, wishing to keep her liaison secret, than it is for you.'

'If she questions me, what do I tell her?'

'That you are a member of the Royal Protection Squad. Which, to all intents and purposes, you are. What other news?'

'Nothing, sir. So far I've been unable to search the house as Miss Harrison's son is home from school and her brother is there too. I'll try tomorrow.'

'All right, Warburton. Good afternoon.'

*

Marcus was watching a Wales vs. Ireland rugby match on the box and working his way through Zoe's supply of beer. He glanced at his watch. It was a quarter past four and still the girls were not back. They were taking the piss. Thankfully, Jamie was still ensconced in his room, playing some nerdy computer game. Marcus reckoned he got more obnoxious each time he saw him.

'Hi, Uncle Marcus.' Jamie poked his head around the door. 'Can I come in?'

'It's your house,' shrugged Marcus reluctantly.

Jamie walked uncertainly into the room, standing with his hands in his pockets facing the television.

'Can you move, Jamie? I can't see.'

'Sorry.' Jamie stepped aside. 'Who's winning?'

'Ireland. Wales are getting hammered,' replied Marcus abruptly.

'Great-James once told me a story about Ireland.'

'Did he?'

'Yes. He said he'd been to stay there once, in a place by the sea.'

'Yeah, well, a lot of Ireland's by the sea.'

Jamie went to the window and tweaked the net curtains to see if there was any sign of his mother returning. 'He told me where he went, showed me on the big atlas. There was this big house, he said, surrounded by water, like it was marooned in the middle of the sea. And then he told me a lovely story about how a young man fell in love with a beautiful Irish girl. I remember the story had a sad ending. He loved her and she loved him, but even though he wrote to her, she didn't get his letters and thought he didn't love her anymore. I said to Great-James it sounded as if it would make a good film.'

Marcus's ears had pricked up. He watched Jamie,

who was still staring out of the window. 'When did he tell you this?'

Jamie turned his blue eyes, so like Zoe's, on to Marcus. 'Just before he died.'

Marcus stood up and went to the bookcase. His eyes ran along the titles until he found a world atlas. Turning the pages until he found Ireland, he laid the book on the coffee table. He beckoned Jamie to him.

'Where did Great-James say this place was?'

Jamie's finger went immediately to the bottom left-hand corner of the map. 'There. The house is in the bay. He said I should visit it some day. That it was an enchanted place.'

'Mmm.' Marcus closed the atlas and looked at Jamie. 'Want something to eat?'

'No, Mumma said she'd cook me something when she got back. She's been a long time.'

'Yes. Hasn't she.'

'Mumma said the lady she's gone with is your girlfriend.'

'She is.'

'Will you marry her?'

'Maybe.'

'Then I'll have an aunt. That'll be fun.' Jamie nodded at Marcus. 'I'll go back to my room now.'

'Sure.'

*

Zoe and Joanna rolled in at half past five with numerous shopping bags.

'Had a good couple of hours, ladies?' Marcus asked as he met them in the hallway.

'Great.' Zoe nodded.

'So great we thought we'd do it again tomorrow. We didn't quite finish everything.' Joanna smiled.

'It's Sunday tomorrow, darling.'

'Yes, and these days all the shops are open, darling.' Marcus looked horrified.

'We're joking, brother dear. I'll have to give my credit card a two-week rest at a health spa after the abuse it's taken today,' smiled Zoe.

The door opened again and there was Simon. 'Hi, chaps,' he said.

'Hello. See the sights?' asked Marcus.

'Yes.'

'Which sights were those, Simon?' Joanna could not resist it.

'Oh, you know, the Tower, St Paul's, Trafalgar Square.' Simon looked squarely back at her. 'I'll see you later.' He nodded at them, then began to mount the stairs to his room.

'Where's Jamie?' asked Zoe.

'His room.'

'Marcus, you've not let him sit on that computer all day, have you?' admonished Zoe.

'Sorry. I did my best. Come on, Jo, don't bother taking your coat off. Let's scoot.'

'Oh, okay.'

Zoe kissed Joanna, then Marcus. 'See you guys soon. And thanks for a fun day, Jo.'

'Not at all. I'll ring you in the week.'

They exchanged a small, secret smile as Marcus ushered Joanna out of the door.

Zoe went upstairs to see Jamie and discover whether supper should be spaghetti bolognese or cottage pie. Jamie went for the former and followed his mother downstairs to chat to her while she cooked.

'I don't think Uncle Marcus likes me all that much.'

'Jamie, of course he does!'

'No he doesn't. I'm not stupid, Mumma.' Jamie shrugged. 'It's cool. You can't expect everyone in the world to love you.'

'No, but you are wrong about Marcus. Did he say anything to you today when he was here?'

'No, nothing. That's the whole point. I always feel like he doesn't even want to be in the same room with me.'

Zoe stopped stirring the mince and went to put her arms round Jamie's shoulders. 'Well, I'm Marcus's sister and he's always been aloof, ever since he was a boy of your age. When we lost our mum so young I think it made both of us a bit funny in the emotional department.'

'Sure. Maybe his new girlfriend will make him feel better. Uncle Marcus said he might like to marry her.'

'Really?'

'Yes. Have you got a boyfriend, Mumma?'

'I . . . well, there's a man I really like, yes.'

'Is it Simon?'

'Lord, no!' Zoe giggled.

'I like Simon. He seems nice. Is he coming down for supper?'

'I . . . well, I thought you and I could have supper together and a nice chat.'

'It's a bit awful not to ask him, isn't it? I mean, he is our guest.'

'I suppose so. Go on then,' Zoe weakened, 'see if he wants to join us.'

*

Jamie dragged Simon down the stairs and along the hall into the kitchen. Simon looked vaguely embarrassed.

'Are you sure it's okay? I can easily get a pizza.'

'My son insists on your presence,' smiled Zoe, 'so sit yourself down.'

Zoe did her best to keep a straight face through supper as Simon regaled Jamie with stories, all gleaned from Theresa's letters, of the Australian sheep farm he lived on back home.

'Oh Mumma! One day, can we go and visit Simon? It sounds cool!'

'I should think so, yes.'

'Simon, do you want to come and see the new computer game Mumma got me? It's fantastic, but much better when there's someone else to play against.'

'Jamie, poor Simon,' sighed Zoe.

'It's fine. I'd love to play, as long as you don't mind, Zoe.'

'Course Mumma doesn't mind. Come on.' Jamie stood up and indicated Simon should do the same. With a shrug, Simon followed Jamie out of the kitchen and upstairs.

An hour later, Zoe went upstairs to the sound of

screams of excitement emanating from both her son and Simon.

'Oh Mumma! You've not come up to tell me it's time for bed! It's Saturday and we've nearly got to level three *and* I'm winning.'

'You can win again tomorrow then. It's gone half past nine, Jamie.'

'Mum!'

'Sorry, Jamie. Your mum's right. We'll play again tomorrow, I promise. Night.'

'Night, Simon,' Jamie called as he left the room.

Zoe tidied up Jamie's room while she waited for him to come back from the bathroom. She tucked him in. 'Anything you'd like to do tomorrow?'

'Finish the game.'

'Apart from that?'

'No, not really. Watch loads of TV, drink gallons of coke, stay in bed late, all the things I can't do at school.'

'Okay. We'll decide in the morning.' Zoe kissed him. 'Night.'

'Night, Mumma.'

Simon was pouring himself a glass of water from the kitchen tap when Zoe arrived downstairs.

'Sorry. All that excitement made me thirsty.' He smiled. 'I'll clear out of your way.'

'I think you deserve a proper nightcap after that masterpiece of imagination at the supper table. Are you sure you didn't train as an actor?' She eyed him with mock suspicion.

'As it happens I do feel I know Oz rather well. My girl . . . I mean, my ex-girlfriend, has spent the past year out there.'

'Ex?'

'Yeah. She loves it so much she's staying.'

'Would you like a brandy? Whisky? Drambuie?'

'I . . .' Simon shrugged. 'As long as I'm not in your way?'

'No. You Know Who's Off Somewhere Else.' Zoe sighed. 'The drinks' cabinet's in the sitting room. I'll put the fire on. It's turned nippy.'

Simon sat in an armchair while Zoe stretched out on the sofa.

'Well you've certainly made a hit with my son.'

'He's a bright kid. You must be proud of him.'

'Yep. Excruciatingly so,' she agreed. 'You don't think I protect him too much, do you? Marcus is always saying he's in danger of becoming a nancy, the way I mollycoddle him.'

'Not at all. I think he's an extremely well-adjusted and normal young boy.'

'Yes, you *can* have another brandy, Simon.' Zoe grinned. 'Oh, by the way, Joanna sent you a message. She wants you to ring her.'

Simon sighed. 'I see.'

Zoe sipped her Drambuie. 'She told me she's known you for years. She won't let on about you to Marcus, will she?'

'Absolutely not. I'd trust Jo, and have done in fact, with my deepest secrets.'

'Good. Because today I trusted her with mine.'

'You told her about Prince George?'

'Well, what with you being here and something else she'd seen, she'd virtually guessed anyway.'

'She was very good this morning when she saw me.

I was waiting for her to give me a hug and say "Hello, Simon."'

'So you think even though she's a journalist, she wouldn't spill the beans?'

'Never.'

'I do hope she and Marcus stay together. She's a good influence on him.'

Simon nodded silently. He took a sip of his brandy. 'I bet you miss your grandfather.'

'I do, very much.'

'Were you close?'

'Extremely. Jamie misses him as well. He was the man of the house, his father figure. Mind you, I don't think he told me everything. I suppose when you've been alive that long, you forget sections of your life. William Fielding was telling me only last week my grandfather originally hailed from Ireland.'

'Really? And you didn't know?'

'No. In fact he told me all sorts of strange things.' Zoe shrugged. 'Whether they were true or not, who knows? Fact gets mixed with fiction when you go back eighty-odd years.'

'Did he tell you stories of the old days? I'll bet he knew the good and the great.'

'He did.'

'Did you keep all his letters? Bits and pieces?'

'Oh yes. They're all festering away in the attic in the house in Kent.'

'Love letters?' Simon raised an eyebrow.

'Not that I've found, although I am going to go through them all thoroughly at some point.' Zoe yawned.

'You look tired.' Simon drained his brandy glass and put it down on the coffee table. He stood up. 'Thanks for the drink.'

'No problem. Thanks for amusing my son. Night.'

'Night, Zoe.'

As Simon climbed the stairs to his room, he was as convinced as he'd ever been that Zoe Harrison had no more idea about her grandfather's amazing past than Joanna did. And he hoped, for both their sake's, it stayed that way.

*

Marcus switched on the clock radio. Music blared out of the small speaker.

'What the hell have you put that racket on for?'

He pulled both of them under the duvet and whispered, 'William Fielding's murder wasn't coincidence, was it?'

'I don't think so, no.'

'How do you think they found out he knew something?'

'I'm not sure, but I reckon this flat is bugged.'

'I thought of that too. I've looked everywhere and I can't find anything. But that means nothing.'

'No.' She sighed. 'Where do we go from here?'

'Well, darling, how do you fancy spending the weekend after next in a luxury country hotel in Ireland?'

'Sounds good, but why?'

'Because I've never been there, because it's meant to be beautiful, and because I think I've pinpointed the place where dear old Sir Jim may have hailed from.'

'Really?' Joanna sat upright, the duvet falling away

to reveal her naked breasts. Marcus eyed them with lust.

'God, you're beautiful.' He stroked a nipple. 'Okay. Me and Jamie had a chat,' Marcus whispered. 'He told me how Sir Jim had spun him some tale about this magical place in Ireland where a man and a woman had fallen in love, then he mentioned letters which were written and never received. He showed me the place on the map.'

Joanna removed Marcus's hand from her breast so she could concentrate. 'And where was it?' she whispered.

'He pointed to Rosscarbery, a small village in West Cork. Apparently this house stands right out in the bay. I'll call the tourist board on Monday, get them to recommend a first-class hotel. Even if it turns out to be a red herring, it's a great excuse for a holiday. It'd be even better if you could take an extra day off, then it wouldn't be such a rush to get there and back.'

'I'll see what I can do about the extra day.' Joanna yawned, pulling the duvet back over her. 'Can we turn off that racket now? I'm pooped.' She snuggled down under the duvet as Marcus turned off the radio and the light.

'Joanna?'

'Yes?'

'I love having you here.'

'Thanks. Night.'

'Night.'

Marcus lay next to Joanna thinking. He was much less concerned now about finding the letter than he'd been a few days ago. It looked as if he might have another income stream to sort out his immediate *distrait*. The fight with his conscience had been fairly swift. Sure it had been a rotten thing to do, especially to his sister, but Marcus knew if he hadn't taken advantage of the situation then someone far less deserving would have done eventually. If he was right, then a large cheque would be winging its way to him sometime in the next week or so. If he was wrong, then there was no harm done. And it was impossible for Zoe to ever find out who it was. Marcus turned on his side, closed his eyes and slept the sleep of an innocent baby.

*

Outside number fifteen, Welbeck Street, the photographer waited patiently.

chapter twenty-five

'I've had a call from the Palace. I'm picking the Prince up at eight tonight.'

'Yes.' Zoe nodded, still looking back at the receding figure of Jamie standing on the steps of his school. She sat in the front of the Jaguar, formality dispensed with. 'You know, I think Jamie was more sorry to say goodbye to you than he was to me.'

'I don't think that's true, but we did have fun. There are some bright spots to this job after all.' Simon turned the car to the right and headed in the direction of London. 'Zoe?'

'Yes.'

'Far be it from me to comment but do you not think it might be safer for you to go to Pip at the Palace rather than him coming to Welbeck Street? It's so much more secure.'

'I know. But I feel so unrelaxed there, Simon. I just feel as though someone might be listening at the door.'

He shrugged. 'The price you pay, I'm afraid. I'll make myself scarce tonight, obviously.'

'Thanks. Er, Simon, when I go down to Norfolk this week to start filming again, how will you explain your presence there?'

'Oh, I'll check in, hang out in the bar, be a groupie on the film set . . .' Simon shrugged. 'I can be pretty invisible when I want to.'

'I'll take your word for it.' She smiled.

*

Simon pulled the car to a halt outside Welbeck Street.

'Don't bother opening the door. I'll hop straight out.'

'All right, sir.'

The prince got out of the car and Simon watched as he made his way up the steps.

An infra-red light on the other side of the road signalled that the act had been recorded.

Simon sighed and looked at his watch. The two of them could be hours. Simon took a thriller out of the glove box, switched on the spotlight above him and began to read. His mobile rang at ten to eleven.

'I'm coming out in five minutes.'

'Right, sir.'

Simon put his book away and turned the engine on. Exactly five minutes later, the front door opened. Zoe appeared, looked both ways, then beckoned to Pip. In the hallway he gave her a quick peck on the cheek and ran out to the car.

The infra-red light flashed again.

'Okay, Warburton, home sweet home.'

'Yes, sir.'

*

There was a sombre mood the first morning back on the set of *Tess*. Everyone was shocked by William's death and it had broken the jovial, pleasant atmosphere that had reigned previously.

'Thank God it's only one more week,' said the actress playing Tess's mother. 'It feels like a grave here too. That your new boyfriend?' she asked in the same breath.

'No, he's a journalist sent down to cover me for a week.'

This was the story Zoe and Simon had concocted to tell the rest of the cast and crew. Although he was never in her face, as it were, Zoe found Simon's presence somewhat unsettling. But, due to the heavy workload, she was crawling upstairs to bed soon after she arrived back from the set and seeing little of him.

On Thursday morning, her mobile phone rang.

'It's me.'

'Hi, I'm in make-up.'

'Then listen and I'll talk. How do you fancy going away for a few days?'

'Er, where to? I'll have to be back on Monday. I'm post-synching in London in the afternoon.'

'Hampshire. Warburton can drive us down on Friday night. I've some friends who have a nice house to lend us. We'll get you back home on Monday morning.'

'Okay. That sounds good.'

'How's work?'

'Sad, without William here.'

'I can imagine. Still I'll cheer you up at the weekend, darling.'

'Yes.'

'I miss you, Zoe.'

'And I miss you.'

Zoe switched the line off and it rang again immediately.

'Hi, sis, it's me. How're you getting on?'

'Fine, Marcus.'

'Are you coming home at the weekend? Only I thought it was about time we went down to Kent and made a start on the attic.'

'No, I'm not. I'm going away actually.'

'I see. Anywhere nice?'

'Just a house party with some friends.'

'Well would you mind if Jo and I went down to Kent and made a start on the boxes in the attic?'

'I don't see why not. Just don't throw anything away until I've seen it. Okay?'

'Sure. I'll divide it into "worth it" and "worthless" piles.'

'Yes. All right, Marcus. I'll speak to you soon. Love to Jo. Bye.' Zoe briefly wondered whether it was sensible to let her brother loose in Kent, then got on with the business of learning her lines.

*

Marcus put down the receiver, then picked it up and redialled.

'It's me.'

'Hi.'

'Any luck so far?'

'No, the photos were just too blurred.'

'I'd watch her this weekend. She's off somewhere and my bet is with him.'

'Right. He's not turned up here to see her yet.'

'He might on Friday.'

'Sure. We'll be in touch. Bye.'

Joanna had just emerged from the shower.

'Zoe's given the okay to go down to Kent and have another rifle through all that stuff in the attic.'

'Oh Marcus, I can't this weekend. I'm working on Saturday.'

'Then unwork.'

'That's impossible. Some of us really do have a job to do.' Joanna sat on the sofa and combed through her long wet hair. 'I'd have no flat and nothing to eat if I lost my job.'

'You can come and stay here.'

'Thanks, but from what I've seen, you don't seem to be generating much income either.'

'Some of us have private means, darling.'

'Then some of us are lucky.'

'I'm going to go down to Kent.' Marcus pouted.

'Fine.' She shrugged. 'You do that.'

*

When the car reached the front entrance of the imposing Georgian House, Simon helped both Zoe and the Prince out, then removed their luggage from the boot.

'Thanks, Warburton. Why don't you take the weekend off? My man is here. Any trouble and we'll call you.'

'Thank you, sir.'

'See you on Monday, Simon.' Zoe smiled sweetly and let her prince lead her inside.

Simon arrived back at his flat in Highgate two hours later with a sigh of relief. It was over a week since he'd been home and had some time to himself. He listened to his messages; four of them were from Ian sounding drunker and less intelligible each time. He dialled Joanna's number and left a message suggesting she come round for supper tomorrow night so they could have a chat. Probably in that arsehole Marcus's bed, thought Simon, as he switched on some jazz and took a bottle of beer from the fridge. He had a lot of faith in Jo and her instinct for others, but Marcus Harrison was obviously hiding qualities that Simon just could not see. Still, it was horses for courses, as they said.

Simon showered, cooked himself spaghetti carbonara and sat down to blear at the late night film. The telephone rang the minute his backside had reached the sofa.

'Simon? You're home.' It was Joanna.

'I am.'

'I thought you might be off back to Oz for some sheep-shearing.'

'Under the circumstances, that's not funny. Are you free tomorrow night?'

'No.'

'A hot date with Marcus?'

'No, a hot date at some agricultural event in Rotherham. Apparently there's some new form of revolutionary weedkiller being premièred. I'm not going to be back until late. But I can do Sunday lunch.'

'Fine, although I'm working in the afternoon, so come early and I'll do brunch.'

'Okay. Yours at twelve then?'

'Fine. See you then.'

Simon put the telephone down. Either it was his imagination or there had been a cool breeze blowing through the calm paradise of their relationship. Ever since, he admitted to himself, he'd failed to return the letter to her. There was no doubt that Joanna was highly suspicious of him, especially now she knew he did not spend his days pen-pushing for the civil service.

He would have to tread carefully, interrogate her subtly to see how much more she might have discovered. Now he understood the incredible delicacy of the situation, it was imperative Joanna steer clear. Or she might find herself in the kind of danger even he couldn't save her from.

The front doorbell rang. Simon sighed heavily then went to the intercom.

'Hello?'

'It's me.'

Ian Simpson was the last person Simon needed on his first night off in ages.

'Hi. I was just hitting the sack.'

'Can I come up. Please?'

Unwillingly, Simon pressed the buzzer.

Two minutes later, Ian stumbled through the door. He looked ghastly. His face was red and bloated, his eyes bloodshot pinpricks. Always known for his zippy collection of Paul Smith and Armani suits, tonight, Ian resembled a vagrant with his dirty mac and plastic carrier, from which he retrieved a half-empty bottle of whisky.

''Lo, Simon.' He slumped in a chair.

'What's up?'

'The bastards have put me on *compassionate* leave.

For a month. I have to go and see the quack twice a week, like I'm some kind of fuckin' loony, basket case . . .'

'What happened?' Simon perched on the edge of the sofa.

'Oh, I blew a job last week. Went to the pub for a few jars, lost track of time, lost the target.'

'I see.'

'You know, it's not exactly a fun job, Si, is it? Why do I always get to set up the nasty ones?'

'Because they trust you.'

'Did trust me.' Ian burped.

'Well, you've got a paid holiday. I'd enjoy it if I were you.'

Ian raised his eyes to Simon's face. 'You think I'll be allowed back? No fuckin' way. It's over, Simon, all those years, all that work . . .' He began to cry.

'Come on, Ian, you don't know that. They won't want to lose you. You've always been one of the best. If you get your act together, prove that this was a blip that will never occur again, I'm sure you'll get another chance.'

Ian hung his head and shook it from side to side. 'Nope, Si. It's parking tickets for me, if I'm lucky. I'm scared, I really am. I'm a loose cannon, aren't I? Drunk in charge of all those secrets. What if they . . .?'

'Course they won't.' Simon hoped he sounded convincing.

'So, you think there's a special rest home for burnt out intelligence officers? Do you think *The Prisoner* was based on fact after all?' Ian started to laugh. 'And it was that fucking programme made me want to go into the Service in the first place. I used to look at those gorgeous women and think, if they're all like that in the service, then that's the job for me.'

Simon remained silent. He really didn't know what to say.

'So,' Ian sighed, 'this is it. The end. And what do I have to show for my years of faithful service? A bedsit in Clapham and an enlarged liver.'

'Come on, mate. I know things look bleak now, but I'm sure if you stay off the juice for a while, things'll get better.'

'Christ, Simon! The booze is the only way I can make it through. Anyway,' Ian stood up, 'sorry to disturb you.'

'You don't have to leave,' Simon offered rather half-heartedly.

'Yes I do. They're probably tailing me now. I wouldn't want to see you tainted by association.' He staggered towards the door, then wagged his finger at Simon. 'You're going to go far. But just watch your back, and tell that journo girlie of yours to fuck off out of Marcus Harrison's bed. It's dangerous and besides, from what I've heard, he's a crap lover.' Ian managed a small smile, then disappeared out of the front door.

Simon sat staring into space, pondering the conversation. There was no doubt that Ian, however drunk, had made some salient points. Was it worthwhile? He could have been a banker, a lawyer; well paid, respected, with a family and a social life . . . He checked himself. That kind of thinking was negative and pointless. For his own sanity, he had to forget what Ian had said and get on with his job.

*

On Sunday morning, Simon woke abruptly from the kind of restful sleep that can only be found in one's own bed with one's own things around. His clock read ten fifty-two, far past his usual immaculate seven o'clock mental alarm call. He must have been more tired than he'd realized. Switching on Radio Four and leaving the coffee to brew, Simon went to shower. He was just slipping into a tracksuit, ready for a relaxed jog down to the paper shop when the telephone rang. 'Yes?'

'There's trouble. You're to report directly to Welbeck Street. I'll be calling to let you know further plans.'

'I see. Why the change?'

'Read the papers. You'll find out. Goodbye.'

Simon sank back on to his pillows. 'Oh, fucking hell. Poor Zoe.'

*

He was almost ready to leave when his doorbell rang. Trying to control his anger, everyone was guilty until proven innocent, Simon pressed the button that would allow Joanna upstairs.

'Hello,' she said breezily as she walked in, kissed him on the cheek and handed him a bottle of wine.

He handed the paper to her. 'Seen this?'

'No, I knew you'd have the Sundays, so I didn't bother buying them. I . . . Oh, shit. Poor Zoe.'

'Yes, poor Zoe,' mimicked Simon.

Joanna studied the photograph of Prince George, his arm looped round her shoulder, and another of him kissing her on top of her head. They could have been any pair of young lovers taking a stroll in the countryside. Except, they were not.

'Prince George and his new love, Zoe Harrison, enjoying a weekend together at the house of the Hon. Richard Bartlett and his wife, Cliona,' Joanna read out. 'Weren't you there?'

'Yes. I dropped them down on Friday. And I have to go now.'

'Oh, so lunch is off?'

'Yes, it's off.' He stared at her. 'Joanna?'

'Yes?'

'Have you seen which newspaper is covering the story?'

'Of course. Mine.'

'Yes, yours,' he said pointedly.

The penny suddenly dropped as she studied Simon's red, angry expression.

'I hope you're not thinking what I *think* you're thinking.'

He did not remove his gaze from her face. 'There's every chance I am, yes.'

Joanna blushed red, not from guilt, but from indignation. 'God, Simon, how could you even suggest it? Who the hell do you think I am?'

'An incredibly ambitious journalist who saw the opportunity of the scoop of the year dangled before her.'

'How dare you! Zoe's my friend. Besides, you're presuming she's told me.'

'Zoe said she had. I've been with her almost twenty-four hours a day. I just can't see how anyone else could have found out. Perhaps you didn't mean it, but you just couldn't resist and . . .'

'Don't patronize me, Simon. I'm terribly fond of Zoe. Okay, I admit I thought about it . . .'

'See?'

'But of course I couldn't betray her.'

'It's *your* paper, Jo. Christ! Zoe asked me whether she should trust you and I gave you an all-round recommendation in discretion. I wish to God I hadn't now!'

Joanna was so angry and so shocked that she had to sit down. 'Simon, please, I swear I didn't leak the story.'

'Zoe told me no one else knew. Only you.'

'I know it looks suspicious, but . . .'

'Damned right it does! That poor girl. She's got a son she's trying to protect who's now going to be hounded. She's going to be in bits and . . .'

Joanna stared at Simon and shook her head in astonishment and hurt. 'Jesus, Simon, are you in love with her, or what? You're her paid protector, or so I gather. It's Prince George's job to comfort her, not yours.'

'Don't be ridiculous! Besides, you're one to talk. Hanging around with that prick Marcus just to garner further information about that love letter, thinking you're some kind of vigilante Sherlock Holmes—'

'Fuck off! I'm terribly fond of Marcus. In fact I might even be in love with him, not that it's any of your bloody business who I spend my time with and—'

'How could you have deceived her so cold-heartedly?'

'I bloody didn't, Simon, and if you don't know me well enough to realize I could never do a thing like that – betray my friend – then I wonder what these years of our relationship have been all about. Besides, you're not so lily white! You gave me all that shit about the letter I trusted you with disintegrating, when I bloody well know you used our friendship to retrieve it for your fucking bosses!'

Simon stared at her silently.

'You did, didn't you?'

He shook his head. 'I'm leaving.'

He picked up his holdall and walked to the door, shaking with anger and guilt.

'I hope this is on your conscience for the rest of your life. And I suppose it's my duty to warn you that Marcus Harrison is being paid by my "fucking bosses" to fuck you. Ask Ian Simpson. Let yourself out, Joanna.' The door slammed behind him.

Joanna sat there in shocked silence. She could hardly believe that the past ten minutes had been a dialogue between her and Simon, oldest friends and confidantes. In all the years they'd known each other, Joanna could rarely remember a cross word being exchanged.

She put her head in her hands, feeling a lump in her throat. If that was Simon's reaction, a man who had known her for all these years, then she held out no hope for Zoe believing her. And what was all that rubbish Simon had spouted about Marcus being paid? Surely not? Marcus had seemed to know nothing about the Rose business when she'd originally told him.

Joanna let out a small shriek of frustration. The fabric of her world seemed to be slowly disintegrating. She rifled in her rucksack and drew out her wallet. She pulled out Ian Simpson's card, thought for a moment, then went to Simon's telephone and picked up the receiver. Not quite sure what she would say, but knowing she had to speak to him, she dialled the number.

It rang for ages before it was finally picked up.

' 'Lo?' A sleepy voice answered.

'Er, is that Ian Simpson?'

'Who wants to know?'

'This is Joanna Haslam, a friend of Simon Warburton.'

'Hi, Joanna.' Rather than sleepy, she realized the voice sounded slurry.

'Look, I know this may sound ridiculous, and I don't want to drop Simon in it or anything, but he mentioned that apparently my, er, boyfriend, Marcus Harrison, might ... umm ... be in the employ of someone you work for?'

There was silence on the other end of the line.

'Maybe you could just answer yes or no and leave it at that.'

'Yes.'

'Thank you, Ian. I'm sorry to bother you.'

Joanna put the receiver down, her bottom lip quivering. She sank on to the floor and burst into tears.

*

Simon had driven off at top speed, then realizing he was far too upset and angry to drive without being a hazard he pulled over and switched the engine off while he calmed down.

'Shit!' He banged the steering wheel with the palms of his hands. It was the first time in his adult life he could ever remember completely losing his cool. Joanna was his oldest friend. He'd not even given her a chance. He'd found her guilty before she'd even opened her mouth. As he became more rational, he knew he had totally overreacted.

Why?

Was it Ian Simpson's visit unsettling him? Or was it, Simon blushed at the way Joanna had managed to hit the nail on the head, because he was becoming far fonder of Zoe Harrison than he should be? It wasn't love. How could it be? He'd only known her for a couple of weeks, and most of those at a distance. Yet there was something about her that touched him, a vulnerability that made him want to protect her. And not . . . he admitted, in a purely professional sense. That would explain his irrational dislike of Prince George. The man was decent enough, but Simon found him rather spineless, rather wet, and was more than a little surprised that the capable, intelligent and warm Zoe could find herself in love with him. However, he was a prince. Simon supposed that made up for rather a lot.

He groaned as he thought of the final exchange between himself and Joanna. He'd completely breached the rules of his organization when he'd told her about Marcus being paid, but he'd been on the defensive, striking out in reaction to Joanna's accusation about his behaviour over the letter. Having said that, Simon rather thought he'd done Joanna a favour. He hoped, for her own sake, that she'd now disentangle herself from him, see him for what he was. And leave the entire situation be.

Calmer now, Simon switched on the engine and prepared to do his job.

*

He arrived at Welbeck Street to find a posse of photographers, camera crews and journalists camped outside on the doorstep. Fighting his way through them, he pulled out his key and let himself inside. Slamming the door behind him, he put on every lock and bolt the door had to offer.

'Zoe? Zoe?' he called.

There was no reply. Maybe she hadn't made it back yet. Checking the sitting room, he saw a camera pointing in through a crack in the net curtains and ran to pull the heavy damask curtains shut. He walked into the dining room, the study and then the kitchen, finding no sign of Zoe. He walked upstairs, checked the main bedroom, Jamie's room, the guest room and bathroom.

'Zoe?' he called again.

He mounted the stairs to the two small attic rooms. His own was empty. He pushed open the door to the room across the narrow landing. It was filled with discarded furniture and some of Jamie's baby toys. There, huddled on the floor in a corner, between an old wardrobe and an armchair, and hugging an ancient teddy to her, was Zoe. Her tear-stained face devoid of make-up, her hair swept back harshly in a ponytail and wearing an ancient sweatshirt and jogging bottoms, she looked not much older than her son.

'Oh Simon, oh Simon, thank God you're here, thank God you're here.' She reached out her arms to him, like a child reaching out to a father. Simon knelt down and took her in his arms. She laid her head against his chest and sobbed.

Simon remained silent, stroking her hair, willing himself to ignore the less than fatherly physical feelings that were paralysing his body.

Eventually she looked up at him. 'Are they still there?'

Simon nodded.

'One of them had a ladder. He was look . . . looking into Jamie's room, trying to take a photograph. I . . . Oh God, I want Jamie here, I want Jamie, I want my son. What have I done? What have I done?'

Zoe sobbed afresh. Simon offered her his hanky and she mopped her face.

'I'm sorry. It's just that it was all such a shock.'

'Nothing to apologize for. Where's the Prince?'

'Back at the Palace, I suppose.' Zoe shrugged. 'They woke us up at five o'clock, said we had to leave. Pip went off in one car and I went in the other. I arrived at seven and they were already here. I thought you'd never come.'

'Zoe, I'm sorry. They didn't call me until half past ten this morning. Have you heard from him since you arrived back?'

Zoe indicated the mobile phone on the floor next to her. 'No, not a word.'

'Well, I'm sure he'll ring, and the Palace will make sure you're safe and looked after.'

'You think so?'

'Of course. They won't just leave you stranded here. In fact, why don't I go and call in now?'

'Okay.' Zoe nodded. 'I'm sure I'll feel better when I've spoken to him. There was no time to discuss anything this morning.'

'Do you want to come down? I've shut all the curtains. Nobody will see you.'

Zoe shook her head. 'Not just yet. I'll calm down a little first.'

'Then I'll bring you a coffee. White, no sugar, isn't it?'

Zoe smiled. 'Yes. Thanks, Simon.'

He went downstairs to the kitchen, switched on the kettle, then called the Palace security office. 'It's Warburton. I'm at Welbeck Street and the place is besieged. What is the directive?'

'At present, none. Stay where you are.'

'I see. Understandably, Miss Harrison's in a dreadful state. Is there a more secure address being arranged?'

'Not that I know of.'

'It might be better if she was at the Palace.'

'I don't think that's a possibility.'

'I see. What about her son? She's obviously very concerned about the effect this will have on him.'

'Then she'd better talk to the headmaster, see what he can arrange in terms of extra security. Is that all?'

Simon looked skyward, trying to control his anger. 'Yes.'

'Right. Goodbye, Warburton.'

He made another call, then mounted the stairs with two cups of coffee and a plate of biscuits.

'Did you speak to them?'

'Yes.' Simon handed Zoe the coffee, then knelt down next to her. 'Jammy Dodger?'

'No thanks. What did they say?'

'That we're to hold tight here. They're arranging something at the moment. Pip sends his love.'

Zoe's face lit up. 'Does he? And Jamie?'

'I've spoken to the headmaster and they're aware of the situation. The media isn't down there yet but they'll take extra precautions as necessary. The headmaster said Jamie's fine. They don't have that "rag" as he put it, in the school anyway.'

'Thank goodness.' Zoe reached for a Jammy Dodger and bit into it. She shook her head and looked up at Simon. 'What on earth am I going to say to him? How do I explain all this?'

'Zoe, give Jamie a little more credit. He's a bright boy. To a certain extent he's always grown up in the spotlight, what with your grandfather and yourself. He'll cope.' Simon sighed. 'You haven't committed a crime, you know, just fallen in love.'

'Yes, I suppose you're right.' Zoe nodded. 'Was it Joanna who leaked the story, do you think?' she asked slowly.

Simon shrugged. 'I don't know. I saw her this

morning before we came here. We had a massive argument in which I admit I accused her of the dirty deed. She flatly denies it.' Simon shrugged. 'I accept it would be totally out of character, but . . .'

'It is a coincidence.'

'Yes.'

'She was the only one that knew?'

'Yes.'

Zoe looked at him miserably. 'It's my own stupid fault. I was so desperate to talk to someone. It all sort of spilled out. I can see how stupid I was now. I mean, I hardly know her and she *is* a journalist, but I just had this funny feeling I could trust her.'

'I'm sorry I assured you you could.'

Zoe sighed. 'So we're stuck here until they tell us what to do.'

'Looks like it.'

She nodded, then sipped her coffee, then looked up at him and smiled. 'Simon?'

'Yes, Zoe?'

'I'm awfully glad you're here.'

chapter twenty-six

As dusk fell on fifteen Welbeck Street, still there was
no word from either Pip or the Palace. Eventually, Zoe
came out of hiding upstairs in the attic and sat instead
in the darkened sitting room, still holding on to Jamie's
teddy and staring into space.

Simon prowled around the house, for want of
anything better to do, methodically checking each
window for cracks in the curtains, signs of chisels under
sash windows and wished with all his heart that they'd
hurry up and decide what they were going to do with
Zoe. At present she was a virtual prisoner, and he with
her, marooned in a house from which they could not
escape. He walked slowly down the hall, hearing the
buzz of voices outside. He stood in the entrance to the
sitting room where Zoe was still sat, unmoving.

'Cup of tea? Coffee? Something stronger?' suggested
Simon.

Zoe looked up at him and shook her head. 'Thanks,
but I'm feeling very queasy. What time is it?'

'Five to five.'

She nodded. 'I must go and call Jamie.' She bit her
lip. 'What on earth do I say?'

'Speak to the headmaster first, take his advice. If

Jamie knows nothing at the moment then maybe it's best it stays that way.'

Zoe nodded slowly. 'Yes, you're right.' She climbed off the sofa and picked her mobile, which was on recharge, off the floor.

Simon left the room and went to the kitchen to make himself his tenth cup of coffee. He just couldn't understand why the Prince had not rung. If he professed to love her, as Zoe assured Simon he did, then surely a brief, sympathetic and reassuring chat would be uppermost in Pip's mind? Simon sighed. And admitted he was running out of optimism. Was it possible that Pip and the Palace would not come to Zoe's rescue and leave her here to face the music alone? And if they did, where would that leave him?

'He sounds fine.' Zoe's relieved voice broke into his thoughts.

Simon turned and smiled at her. 'Good.'

The headmaster said there are a couple of journalists hanging about outside the school gates, but he's informed the local constabulary and they're keeping an eye out. Jamie wanted to know what sort of a week I'd had and I said it had been fairly non-eventful.' Zoe chuckled.

'Well, that's great,' Simon agreed.

'Of course, I'm not stupid enough to think it'll be long before he does hear a whisper . . . you really think it best not to say anything?'

'Absolutely,' confirmed Simon.

Zoe sat down at the kitchen table and rested her head on her arms. 'Ring, Pip, please ring.'

Simon patted one of her shoulders gently. 'He will, Zoe, you'll see.'

At eight o'clock that evening, Simon set up the portable TV from Zoe's bedroom in the study. It was in the middle of the house, without windows, and Zoe said she felt safer there. He'd tried to tempt her to eat something, but she'd refused. He could see she was becoming more and more distressed.

'Look, why don't you call Pip? You have his mobile number, don't you?'

Zoe rounded on Simon. 'Don't you think I already have? Like, a hundred times so far today? "The voda-phone number you are calling has been switched off. Please try later,"' Zoe repeated in a sing-song voice.

'Okay, I'm sorry.'

Zoe sighed heavily. 'And so am I. None of this is your fault. I don't want to take it out on you.'

'You're not. And if you are, it's understandable.'

Zoe paced the room. 'Why hasn't Marcus called me? Surely he must have seen the news? He was down in Kent over the weekend but he must be back by now. I'll try him.' Zoe dialled Marcus's London number but only got the answering machine. She didn't leave a message. 'Thanks for the brotherly support, Marcus dear,' she hissed at the phone. 'Christ, I . . .'

'*Today it was reported that Prince George, third in line to the throne, has a new lady love. Zoe Harrison, actress and granddaughter of the late Sir James Harrison, was seen walking with the Prince in the grounds of a friend's stately home in Hampshire.*'

Zoe and Simon stared in silence as the Welbeck

Street house, with its posse of photographers overflowing messily from the steps on to the pavement and on to the other side of the street came on the screen.

'*Miss Harrison arrived at her house in London early this morning and has so far avoided speaking to the media who are at present camped on her doorstep. If Miss Harrison is romantically involved with the Prince it would cause a dilemma for the Palace. Miss Harrison is an unmarried mother, with a young son of nine. She has never revealed who the father is. Whether the Palace will give its blessing to such a controversial relationship remains to be seen. A spokesman for Buckingham Palace issued a short statement this morning, confirming Prince George and Miss Harrison were together in Hampshire attending a house party but that their relationship was no more than good friends.*'

Simon scanned Zoe's face for a reaction. There was none. Zoe's eyes were glassy. She shuddered suddenly, violently and uncontrollably.

'Zoe, I . . .'

She shook her head, then stood up. 'I should have known how it would be.' She shrugged as she walked to the door. 'You see, Simon, I've been there before.'

*

The following morning, Simon called in yet again to the security office.

'Any directive?'

'Not at present. Stay where you are.'

'Miss Harrison has to go out today, to a studio in London to do some post-synching. How exactly do I extricate her without causing a riot in a central London street?'

There was a pause on the other end of the line. 'You use the years of training that the British government paid for you to receive. Goodbye, Warburton.'

'Fuck you!' Simon swore uncharacteristically into the receiver.

It was now becoming patently obvious that the Palace had no intention of supporting or helping Zoe out.

'Who was that?' Zoe was stood at the kitchen door. She looked ghastly; pale and wan. Her eyes darted around like a frightened rabbit.

'My boss.'

'What did he say?'

Simon took a deep breath. It was pointless lying to her. 'Nothing.'

Zoe nodded slowly. 'I see. So, we're on our own?'

'Yes.'

'Fine.' She turned in the doorway. 'I'm going to go and write a letter to Pip.'

Zoe went into the study to her grandfather's fine antique desk. She pulled open one of the small drawers which still contained a beautiful gold ink pen. She pulled off the top and scrawled on the blotting paper. The pen was empty. She rifled through another drawer. Finding the ink, and some cream vellum paper, she filled the pen. The television was standing on top of the desk. She knelt down between the sides of the desk and reached to the wall behind to unplug it. As she did so, she noticed that above her, neatly set under the polished lip at the front of the desk, was a shallow but wide drawer she'd never noticed before. Placing her hand on the bottom of the drawer, she slid it forward. It opened with ease.

Kneeling upright, Zoe glanced in at the contents of the drawer. Disappointingly, it resembled every other drawer in the desk; more letters. She perused them, then placed them on the floor, some envelopes, further bills. She checked each one, with 'Paid' and the date, written across them in her grandfather's distinctive flowing hand. The last one she looked at in surprise.

Regan Private Investigation Services Ltd.
Final Bill Due.
Total = £8,600

James had scrawled 'Paid' across that too, and the date '19/11/95' underneath it. Zoe chewed her lip, wondering why on earth her grandfather would need to hire the services of a private detective agency, especially so near to the end of his life. From the amount he'd paid, they'd done some kind of major investigating.

'You okay?'

Zoe, deep in thought, jumped at the sound of Simon's voice. He stood in the doorway, looking down at her.

'Yes, fine.' She stuffed the letters and bills back into the drawer and slid it back into position. 'Could you put the TV on the floor so I can use the desk?'

'Sure.' Simon did as he was asked.

'Thanks.' Zoe settled herself into the comfortable, curved chair.

'Er, Zoe, what time do you need to be at the studio?'

'Two o'clock.'

'Right. Well, we should leave around one. I'm going to go out now. I want to move the car, position it better for a hasty getaway.'

'Am I going to have to face that barrage out there?'

'Not if you're prepared to wear a silly hat and do some breaking and entering.' He grinned at her lopsidedly. 'Sit tight, I'll see you in a few minutes.'

Zoe returned her thoughts to the letter.

'*Dear Pip*,' she wrote, the awful task made slightly more pleasurable by the exquisite writing instrument she was using. '*Firstly, I just want to say that I understand the dreadful position this whole situation has put you in. I feel . . .*'

Zoe's mobile rang, breaking her flow.

'Yes? Oh hello, Michelle.' It was her theatrical agent. She listened while the woman spoke. 'No, I don't want to go on GMTV, or give an interview to the *Mail*, the *Express*, *The Times*, or the bloody *Toytown Gazette* . . . I'm sorry they're hassling you. What can I say apart from the fact I have *nothing* to say. No comment . . . All right. I will. Bye.' Zoe ground her teeth. The telephone rang again. 'What?!' she barked.

'It's me.'

'Pip! Oh God, I'm sorry. I thought you'd never call!' Zoe gave a small sob of relief.

'I'm sorry, darling. All hell's let loose here, as you can imagine.'

'It's not exactly comfortable at this end either.'

'No. I'm so sorry, Zoe, really. Look, we need to talk.'

'Where?'

'Where indeed? Is Warburton there with you?'

'Yes, I mean, not at this minute. He's gone out to move the car. It's like some kind of siege here, Pip. I feel like a caged animal.' Zoe willed herself not to cry.

'It must be ghastly, darling. Really, I completely understand. What about your house in Kent? Could you slip out and get there by tonight?'

'Probably. Could you?'

'I can certainly do my best.'

'Please, please try, Pip.'

'Of course. Just remember I love you.'

'I will. I love you too.'

'I have to go. I'll see you later. Bye, darling.'

'Bye.'

Zoe felt the tension, and her resolve, flood away from her. Just hearing his voice had given her courage. She looked at the letter she had begun, shook her head and tore it up. He still loved her. Maybe there *was* a way . . . She had to think positive.

The front door opened and Zoe heard the voices of the media hurling questions at Simon. The voices receded as he slammed the door. She went into the hall to greet him.

'They're like a pack of baying wolves. No doubt I'll now end up on the front page of some rag being suggested as Jamie's father . . .'

Zoe's face darkened.

'Sorry, that was highly insensitive of me, Zoe.'

'But accurate.' Zoe nodded.

'You look better. Get some things off your chest?'

'No. Pip rang. He suggested I go down to the house in Kent tonight. He's going to try and join me there later. So we absolutely have to get out of this house with no one spotting us. I'm going to go upstairs, shower and pack.'

'Fine. But travel light.' Simon winked. 'I 'ave ze mean und cunning plan.'

He watched her make her way up the stairs, then, when he heard the bathroom door lock, he went into the study and opened the drawer he'd seen Zoe close earlier. He ran as quickly as he could through its contents. Finding the invoice that Zoe had been so engrossed in, he folded it up and stuck it in his trouser pocket. Closing the drawer carefully, Simon left the room and headed up the stairs to pack his own bag.

*

The two of them stood by the kitchen door.

'Okay. I'm going to give you a leg-up over that wall. There's a ledge about four feet down on the other side which you can step on to. Then we go over the next wall and the next. I'm hoping the antique furniture shop four doors down has a back door to its basement like this. We break in, find our way on to the shop floor and walk out the other side as if we're customers.'

'Won't the back door be alarmed?'

'Bound to be, but we'll cross that bridge when we come to it. Right. Let's go.'

With both of their hearts pounding, the two of them made their way over the walls separating the back of each building along the street. Finally, they stood in front of a grilled rear door. A small red light was flashing above it.

'Shit.' Simon inspected the door. 'It's deadlocked from the inside.' He walked to the small window, which also had a grille over it. Taking out a pair of wire-cutters from his pocket, Simon worked away until the bottom part of the wire broke free. He lifted it up, revealing an old sash window. There was a gap of maybe half an inch between the window and the frame.

'I don't know whether this is alarmed too, so get ready to leg it back over the wall if I set it off.'

Zoe stood in an agony of suspense as Simon turned red from exertion. Finally, the window gave a small groan of dissent and slid up grudgingly. The alarm did not go off.

Simon tutted as he beckoned Zoe over. 'People really should be more careful. No wonder there are so many burglaries. Hop in.' He indicated Zoe should squeeze through the one and a half foot gap. Sixty seconds later, both she and Simon were standing on the other side. They were in some kind of storeroom.

'Beret on,' he ordered.

Zoe pulled the beret out of her pocket, stuffed her long hair inside it and smiled at Simon.

'How do I look?'

'Adorable,' whispered Simon. 'Now, follow me.'

He led her through a maze of broken chairs, tables and general tatty objets d'art. There was a door at the other end of the room. Simon opened it and indicated a flight of stairs.

'Okay, this must take us up into the showroom. Nearly there, now.'

Simon mounted the stairs with Zoe behind him. He turned the handle of the door at the top and peeped through it. He nodded, opened it further and crept through, signalling Zoe to do the same. Immediately they were through the door, Simon headed for a long, ornate chaise longue. An ageing assistant appeared from round the corner.

'Sorry, sir, I didn't hear the front bell ring.'

'Not to worry. Er, my wife and I were interested in this. Can you tell me a little bit about it?'

*

Five minutes later, after promising to come back, having measured the wall in the sitting room along which the chaise longue would reside, Zoe and Simon stepped into the bright sunshine of a spring-like February day.

'Don't look behind you, Zoe, just keep walking,' Simon muttered as he marched swiftly to his car, parked a few yards up the street.

Once inside the Jaguar, Simon indicated into the flow of traffic. Zoe turned back and saw the huddle of media less than twenty yards away. Just as they turned the corner, she stuck two fingers up at them.

'Do you know, I really enjoyed that.' She smiled. 'And the thought that all those vultures are sat waiting outside a deserted house has cheered me up no end.' She reached for Simon's hand, resting on the gear-stick, and squeezed it. 'Thanks, Simon.'

'We aim to please, madam.' He nodded as Zoe's light touch on his hand played havoc with his concentration. 'Don't be lulled into a false sense of security.

Sooner or later someone'll twig you're no longer at home.'

'I know.' Zoe nodded soberly. 'Let's just hope it's not before tonight.'

While Zoe scurried into the recording studio, Simon phoned in on his mobile.

'Sorry to ring earlier than usual, sir, but it might be hard to do so later.'

'Understood.'

'I've found something. It may be nothing, but . . .' He read out the details on the invoice he had retrieved from the drawer in the desk.

'I'll get on to it, Warburton. I hear you're having a busy time.'

'Yes. I'm driving Miss Harrison down to Kent.'

'Keep talking to her, Warburton. Sooner or later, something will slip out.'

'I will, sir. Goodbye.'

Simon hung up, drove off and managed to find a parking space in the NCP in Brewer Street. Feeling suddenly hungry, he took himself off for a Mac-Donalds. He eyed the pub across the road, longing for a pint, but knowing a drink was completely out of the question. He chomped his way through the tasteless hamburger and chips and tried to concentrate on his book. Visions of Zoe kept filling his brain as he recalled the touch of her hand on his. Get a grip, Warburton, he lectured himself. First rule of operation: never become emotionally involved. But he knew in his heart he'd already passed the point of no return. There was nothing he could do save execute a damage-limitation programme: eg, expect to suffer horribly when his services were no longer necessary and Zoe and he went their separate ways.

At twenty to five, his mobile rang.

'Hi, Simon. I'll be out of the studio in ten minutes.'

'I'll be waiting.'

*

As Zoe got into the car, he noticed she'd added make-up to her face. He rather preferred her without. She was so incredibly beautiful that she didn't need it. Stop it, Warburton, he chastized himself as he headed towards the South Circular.

'Have a good post-thingy?' he asked.

'Fine. Of course, everyone was far more interested in Pip and me than anything else.' Zoe brushed a hand through her long hair. 'The director was very sweet, mind you. He has a flat in the south of France. He said anytime I wanted to use it, to give him a call.'

'I suppose he's also thinking how having the new girlfriend of Prince George starring in his up-and-coming film might boost ticket sales.'

'That's awfully cynical, but you're probably right.' Zoe sighed as she looked out at the water running underneath Battersea Bridge.

'Anyway, you seem much happier.'

'Of course I am.' She looked at him, her eyes full of warmth. 'I'm seeing Pip in a few hours time.'

*

The Kent house was, as always, freezing. And spread all over the sitting room were the higgledy-piggledy contents of ten boxes from the attic.

'Damn you, Marcus!' Zoe cried as Simon attempted to light the fire and she began to heap the piles of old paper back into the crates. 'I *knew* you'd get bored halfway through and give up. Now it's even worse than it was before.'

'Oh well, if we're stuck down here for a while, I suppose it'll give you something to do.'

'I'm hoping Pip might have other plans. Maybe he'll suggest we should go abroad for a while, but then what about Jamie? Oh God, I don't know. I'll just have to wait 'til Pip gets here.' Zoe spoke her thoughts out loud. 'Can you help me take these back upstairs to the attic?'

The sitting room cleared, the fire lit and the Aga coaxed into action, Zoe set about storing the food Simon had purchased in a supermarket on the journey down.

'Will he have eaten, do you think? Should I make something? Maybe put a casserole in the Aga so it won't matter what time he arrives.'

Simon fielded her questions as best he could, feeling her tension, wishing the Prince would arrive as soon as possible and Zoe subsequently calm down.

While she went upstairs to change and air the beds, Simon went outside to survey the lie of the land. His heart sank as he saw two cars parked beyond the gate, a ladder being lengthened and balanced precariously against the hedge surrounding the house. How did these people do it? he wondered, as he went inside to inform Zoe. Fifteen minutes later, she was standing in the kitchen, a look of desolation on her face.

'Zoe, sweetheart, you *have* to warn him they're down here.'

'Why? Oh damn it!' She thumped the old oak table. 'Don't answer that. I know why. Why can't they leave us alone? Why? Why? Why?' She thumped the table, harder each time.

'Look, I'll ring if you'd like.'

She slumped into a chair. 'Yes, whatever, whatever.'

Simon duly delivered the message and was assured it would be passed on. He went back into the kitchen, where Zoe was sitting smoking a Marlboro.

'Didn't know you were an addict to the evil weed.'

'Marcus must have left them here. If there was ecstasy, heroine, Prozac in the house, I'd take them tonight.' She looked up at him. 'He won't come now, will he?'

'No.'

She nodded and continued to smoke.

'Look, why don't I knock up a little something for supper? I haven't seen you eat a thing since I arrived yesterday morning.'

'It's kind of you, but I just couldn't force it down.'

'Fine. Then I'll cook it for me.'

Zoe shrugged, then stood up. 'There should be enough hot water for the bath. I'm going to take one.' She ambled disconsolately out of the room.

Simon set about gathering ingredients from the larder to see what he could cobble together for supper.

*

When Zoe arrived back downstairs in her grandfather's ancient but cosy paisley dressing-gown, there was an enticing smell emanating from the kitchen.

'Mmm. What is it?' She peered over Simon's shoulder at the pot he was stirring.

'Does it matter? You don't want any, remember.' He indicated an open bottle of red wine on the table. 'Help yourself. I opened it for culinary purposes only.'

Zoe poured herself a glass, sat down and watched Simon at work.

'Is this part of your training?'

'No. I love cooking,' he answered simply. 'I'm ready to serve. Want some?'

'Oh, go on then, as you've worked so hard.'

Simon filled two plates and put one in front of Zoe. 'It's spicy beef with lentils. I should have marinated it for a few hours first, of course, but it should be edible.' He sat down opposite her.

Zoe forked up a mouthful. 'That is really good, Simon.'

He shook his head. 'Why is it that women always sound as if they're patronizing men when they compliment them on their cooking? Most of the great chefs in the world are male.'

'Sorry,' Zoe apologized hurriedly. 'I didn't mean it. This is wonderful. You're wasting your talents. You should open a restaurant.'

'That's what Joanna always says.'

'She's right.' Zoe continued to eat. 'Were you and Joanna ever, you know?'

'Lovers?'

'Yes.'

'Never. I thought of her as my sister. Somehow it would have seemed . . . incestuous. Although . . .'

'Yes?'

'Oh, it was nothing really. A few weeks ago, she was staying with me and we kissed.' Simon shrugged. 'Her boyfriend had just dumped her, but I still thought my relationship with my lady love was intact. So I stopped it.' Simon paused with a forkful of food halfway between his mouth and his plate. 'If I'd known then about Theresa, I wonder if I'd have reacted differently.'

Zoe's plate was empty.

'Would you like some more? There's plenty.' Simon's eyes twinkled.

'I'd *love* some more.' She smiled. She watched him as he picked up their plates and refilled them. 'Thanks. Will you do this for ever?'

'What's that?'

'Be a bodyguard. Subjugate your own life to the pursuit of the safety of others?'

Simon shrugged. 'Who knows?'

'I just think you're wasted. It's a bit of a dead-end job, isn't it?'

'I suppose.'

'Well.' Zoe raised her glass. 'To both of us finding our true paths.'

Simon raised his glass of water. 'To us.'

At that moment, Zoe's mobile rang.

'Excuse me.' She hurried out of the kitchen to take the call.

Simon duly cleared the plates away and began to do the washing up.

Ten minutes later, Zoe was back in the kitchen, a

smile lighting up her face. 'Oh Simon!' She came over to him and gave him a hug. 'It's all going to be okay.'

'Is it? Good.'

'That was Pip. He's arranged for us to go abroad. An industrialist friend of his has offered his private jet and his summer house to us. Apparently it has the most sophisticated security. We can relax and talk about the future in complete peace with not a prying eye in sight.'

'I see. When do you leave?'

'Tomorrow morning. I have to be at Heathrow for nine o'clock. We're meeting in the VIP suite at Terminal Four.'

'Right,' nodded Simon.

'And then, you'll be glad to hear, you'll be free of me. Pip's taking his own people to look after us while we're there.'

'Yes. Coffee?'

'Love some. Let's take it into the sitting room by the fire. Oh God, Simon, I've got absolutely nothing to wear. All my clothes are in London. I . . .'

Simon followed Zoe into the sitting room with the coffee as Zoe chirped on.

'. . . and it'll be so fabulous not to have anyone spying on us. We so desperately need time to talk. Thanks.' Zoe settled herself down cross-legged by the fire.

Simon sat on the sofa and sipped his coffee slowly. 'So, if he asks, will you marry him?'

'Do you think he will ask? Could he, with the situation being such as it is?'

'Okay, let me put it another way; do you *want* to marry him?'

Zoe's eyes shone. 'Oh God, yes. I've wanted it every single day for the past ten years.'

'*Ten* years? Blimey, I was wrong. The story did take a long time to leak.'

'No,' she shook her head, 'I first met him ten years ago. We had a fling, which was short-lived, but,' Zoe shrugged, 'I was never able to get him out of my mind. By the same token, I'm not so naive as to think it'll all be plain sailing. His family may have vetoed me, just like they did ten years ago. I may be flying to Spain for Pip to tell me as nicely as he can that it's no-go.'

Simon did not mention the discussion he'd heard on Radio Five Live as to whether the royal family was ready for an unmarried mother to join the clan. The opinion polls rather suggested not.

'There is one thing I was going to ask you.' She looked up at him.

'Fire away.'

'Well, I'm not sure how long I'll be away. I was wondering . . . well . . .'

'Spit it out, Zoe.'

'If you'd go and visit Jamie for me at school next weekend. I promised to go down, and obviously I'm not going to make it. He seemed so fond of you and . . .'

'Of course I will. Consider it done.'

'I'll let the school know where I'll be. Maybe I'll suggest they tell Jamie I'm shooting a . . . a commercial in Spain, or something.'

Simon nodded, thinking how exquisite she looked in the firelight. He stood up, not wishing to prolong the agony any longer. 'I'm going to turn in. We've an early start. We may have to do some extravagant driving to lose those outside that are sure to be immediately on our tail.'

'Yes.' Zoe stood up too, walked towards him, stood on tiptoe and planted a kiss on his cheek. 'Thank you, Simon. I'll never forget what you've done for me in the past two days. You've kept me sane.'

He nodded. 'Night then,' he muttered and left the room.

*

'Pip!' Zoe left Simon's side and ran into his arms. Simon thought he noticed a slight reluctance on the Prince's part to return the loving hug Zoe was embracing him with.

'Hello, Zoe.' Pip kissed her on the top of her head. 'Right, we'll be off. Thanks, Warburton, for all your help.' He nodded at Simon perfunctorily.

'Yes, bye, Simon.' Zoe smiled at him as Pip led her out of the VIP room. A small posse of security men followed after the couple.

Simon made his way back through the maze of corridors that took him back land-side. His mobile phone rang.

'Warburton.'

'Yes, sir?'

'You're relieved of duty for the next seven days, until Miss Harrison returns. I'll call you if you're needed.'

'Right, sir. Thank you, sir.'

Simon drove the Jaguar back into central London, handed over the keys and headed for the pub, where he treated himself to a perfect foaming pint of Tetley's, in which he could try to drown his sorrows.

chapter twenty-seven

Joanna sat dejectedly typing at her desk. She felt numb, empty, used and confused. On the verge of giving it all up and returning to Yorkshire to milk cows for the rest of her days. Marcus had called her last night at her flat. Joanna had pretended she was out. She was out to Marcus for the rest of her life. She was counting the minutes until it was half past five and time to switch off her screen, though why she wanted to go home to an empty flat with no boyfriend and no Simon, she didn't know. It didn't help that the whole office was buzzing with the news of Zoe Harrison and the Prince. Or that this morning, Marian, the features editor, had called her into her domain.

'You wrote the piece on the Harrison family.'

'Yes,' Joanna had replied sullenly.

'And word has it that you're screwing Zoe's brother.' Marian never minced her verbs.

'I was, but I'm not now.'

'As of when?'

'As of yesterday.'

'What a shame. I was going to suggest sending you to try and get an interview from her, seeing as you're almost family.'

'Impossible, I'm afraid.'

'Pity. It could have got you off Pets and Gardens.' Marian chewed her biro as she studied Joanna.

'Okay, Jo, it's your call. If you won't do it, then someone else will. You trying to protect her?'

'No.'

'Fine. Because if you are, the best thing you could do is to get her to agree to talk to you. At least that way she'll get a sympathetic hearing.' Marian had waved at her dismissively and Joanna had slunk back to her lowly desk.

At long last it was twenty-nine minutes and fifty-five seconds past five. With a sigh of relief, Joanna switched off her computer and headed swiftly for the door. She was waiting for the lift when Tom came up to her.

'Hi, Jo. You okay?'

'No.'

'I want a word, but not here. I'll meet you in the French House in Soho at seven.' Tom turned on his heel and went back into the office.

Joanna spent an hour wandering aimlessly around Leicester Square and the Trocadero. Tom was already on a stool when she arrived in the crowded bar.

'G&T?'

'Yep,' nodded Jo, pulling up the bar stool next to him.

'Hear it's not been a good day.'

'Nope,' agreed Joanna.

'Marian wanted you to do that interview. Then you could have used it as a lever to come back to me.'

'It would have been a pointless exercise, Tom. Zoe

thinks I was the one who spilled the beans in the first place. She'd prefer to pose semi-naked for the *News of the Screws* rather than talk to me.'

Tom's mouth dropped open. 'You knew about her and the Prince?'

'Yes. She'd told me all about it. Thanks.' Joanna took a healthy slug of her gin. 'In quite some detail, I might add.'

Tom groaned. 'So, you could have broken the story?'

'Oh yes. To be honest, I wish I bloody well had as I seem to have got the blame.'

'Fuck, Jo! You really are going to have to learn to toughen up. Breaking a story like that could have given your career a lifetime boost.'

Joanna shook her head. 'No. I spent most of last night thinking that maybe this game isn't for me. I don't have the necessary lack of moral fibre. I have this awful, unjournalistic quality of being able to keep a secret.' She finished off her gin. 'Can I have another?'

'Well, at least you're beginning to drink like a hack.' Tom grinned as he signalled same again to the barman. 'C'mon, you'll cheer up after another gin and the news I've got for you.'

'Am I being reinstated?'

'No.'

Joanna slumped forwards and put her head on her arms. 'Then nothing you say can cheer me up.'

'Even if I was to tell you I've found out some juicy info on your little old lady?' Tom eyed her as he lit up a Rothman's.

'Nope. I've given up on that one. That bloody letter's ruined everything and I've had enough.'

'Fine.' Tom took a drag of his cigarette. 'Then I won't tell you I'm pretty sure I know who she was. That, just before she arrived in England, she'd been living in France for the past sixty years.'

Joanna lifted her head slightly, looked at Tom, then shook it. 'No, I still don't want to know.'

'Or that James Harrison managed to purchase fifteen Welbeck Street outright in 1928. It was owned by a senior politician who had been in Lloyd George's cabinet prior to that. Seems strange a penniless actor could afford a big house like that, doesn't it? Unless, of course, he'd just come in to a large sum of money.'

Joanna sat up and took a swig of her fresh gin. She took a deep breath and shook her head. 'Sorry, Tom, I'm still not there.'

'So finally, I won't tell you, then, that there was a Rose Alice Bethan Fitzgerald, working as a lady-in-waiting in a certain royal household in the 1920s.'

Joanna stared at him. She nodded slowly. 'Fuck it! Get me another gin.'

*

'So what you're saying is that Rose and Michael O'Connell were in cahoots, blackmailing someone, probably in the royal household?'

The two of them had adjourned to a recently vacated corner table.

'It's what I've surmised, yes. And I think the letter that you found was actually a love letter from Rose

herself to James, aka Siam, which had nothing whatsoever to do with the real plot.'

'But why does Rose talk about not being able to see
him in the letter?'

'Because Rose Fitzgerald was a lady-in-waiting. She
came from an excellent Scottish family. I hardly think
a penniless Irish actor would have made a good match.
So I'm sure they had to keep their liaison secret.'

'Christ! Why have I had so many gins? My head's
foggy. I can't think straight.'

'Then I'll think for you. Put simply, I reckon James
and Rose—'

'Michael, in those days,' corrected Joanna.

'Okay, Michael and Rose were lovers. Rose had
discovered something juicy whilst going about her duty,
told Michael, aka James, who then blackmailed the
person concerned. The parcels you say William Fielding
used to collect for James, well it was obvious they
contained money. Michael then does a disappearing
act, possibly flees the country, dumping poor old Rose
along the way. A few months later, he arrives back,
dons a new persona, buys his pile in Welbeck Street,
marries Kitty and all is tickety boo.'

'Okay. Let's work on your premise. Let's face it, it's
as good as any I've come up with so far and it does all
seem to fit. Why the sudden mass panic when James
Harrison dies?'

'Well now, let's try some lateral thinking. We know
Rose had arrived back in the country after being abroad
for many years. Then, suddenly, Sir James pops his
clogs and goes to the great stage in the sky. Is it possible
that Rose planned to reveal all after Sir James's death?

Maybe blacken his name, pay him back for dumping her all those years ago?'

'Then why hadn't she done it before?'

'Maybe she was frightened. Maybe James had something on her, had threatened her . . . I dunno, Jo, I'm surmising here.' Tom ground out a cigarette in the ashtray and lit another.

'All I know is it's something very, very big,' breathed Joanna. 'Big enough to persuade Marcus Harrison to wine, dine and bed me to see what I knew.'

'Who told you that?'

'My friend Simon.'

'You sure about that?'

'Oh yes. Someone else confirmed it.'

'Shit, Jo! What is all this?'

She shrugged. 'If we follow your idea, then obviously whatever it was Rose and Michael had discovered was major. Two people have already died in odd circumstances . . .' Joanna shuddered. 'I don't want to be the third.'

'No, I can see your point.'

'Tom, why this sudden interest after freezing me out?'

Tom sighed. 'Because this just won't seem to go away, will it? Strikes me you need some help. Everyone else seems to have fucked you over. I may be an unlikely knight in shining armour, but I'll have to do.'

'*If* I decide to continue investigating.'

'Yeah. What next? If you do decide to continue?'

'Marcus and I were going on a foray to Ireland next week. William Fielding had indicated an Irish connection and Marcus seems to have managed to pinpoint where, if anywhere, Michael O'Connell might have hailed from.'

'How?'

'Zoe's son Jamie mentioned a place in Ireland that his grandfather had talked about before he died. He might have got it wrong, but . . .'

'Never dismiss child-talk, Jo. I've coerced some of my best scoops out of nippers.'

'You are quite without scruples, Tom.'

'But loveable with it.' He checked his watch. 'I gotta go. We never had this conversation, of course. And I shall not advise you to go to Ireland and sit in the local bar where any amount of gossip can be garnered, nor shall I suggest you do it tout de suite before Marcus, or perhaps someone else, gets there. And I shall certainly not mention that you do not look at all well tonight and there's every possibility you'll be too sick to make it into work tomorrow. Or that Aer Lingus operates a commuter flight to Cork which leaves Heathrow at ten to ten every morning.' Tom stuffed his cigarettes into his pocket. 'Night, Jo. Call me if there's shit.'

'Night, Tom.'

She watched him leave the bar. Despite herself, she smiled. If nothing else, Tom, or the gin, or a mixture of both, had managed to lift the blues. Hailing a taxi, Joanna decided she'd sleep on it, digest the information and think about it in the morning.

There were eight messages from Marcus on her machine when she got home. That was added to the seven on her mobile answering service, plus numerous calls she had asked the receptionist to bar at work.

'They must have paid you one hell of a lot of money, you slimy, double-crossing, arrogant fuckwit of a rancid, decomposed little toad,' she said to the machine as she headed for the bathroom and a shower.

The bell was ringing when she came out. Peeping through the curtains, Joanna saw that the slimy, double-crossing, arrogant fuckwit of a rancid, decomposed little toad was standing on her doorstep.

'Oh *Christ!*' she cried, switched the TV on and prepared to ignore it for as long as it took.

'Joanna,' he was shouting through the letter box. 'It's me, Marcus. I know you're in. I saw you behind the curtains. Joanna, let me in. What have I done wrong? *Joanna!*'

'Fuck! Fuck! Fuck!' Joanna growled as she stood up and headed for the front door. Marcus was going to wake up half the neighbourhood if he didn't shut up. She saw his eyes peering through the letter box at her.

'Hi. Let me in, Jo.'

'Piss off.'

'Charmed, I'm sure. Can you let me know exactly what I'm supposed to have done?'

'If you don't know, then I'm not bloody telling you. Just get out of my life and stay out, for ever.'

'Joanna, I love you. More than I have ever loved anyone. And if you don't let me in to discuss whatever crime it is I'm meant to have committed, then I shall have to stay out here all night and . . . *sing* my love to you.'

'Marcus, if you don't get off my doorstep in the next five seconds, I'm calling the police. They'll arrest you for harassment.'

'Okay. I don't mind. Of course, we'll probably make the front page of tomorrow's newspaper, with my new-found celebrity status as brother of Prince Philip's new shag, but I'm sure that won't worry you . . . I . . .'

Marcus almost toppled through the front door as Joanna opened it.

'Okay. You win.' She was quivering with anger.

Marcus went to touch her. She flinched and backed away. 'Don't come near me. I mean it.'

'Okay, okay,' he said hurriedly. 'Tell me then, what is it I've done?'

Joanna crossed her arms and stared at him. 'I have to say I thought it was odd that you were so caring, so prolific in your affections. I mean, I'd already been told what a rotten, stinking rat you were. And silly me, I decided to take you on face value, thought that maybe you felt differently about me than the rest of most of the female population of London.'

'I do, really, Jo. I—'

'Shut up, Marcus. I'm talking. Then, I discover that your feelings for me didn't even come into it. It was your wallet that was enjoying my company.'

'I . . .' Marcus looked confused. 'Spit it out, Jo.'

'I was told that you were being paid to court me, and bed me for that matter.' She stared at him and saw the hectic red blush rise up into his cheeks.

He shook his head. 'No. Whoever said that has got it totally wrong. I mean, I was given some money, but not to court you. It was to try to find the letter. I swear I didn't know anything about Rose when you told me, or on the first night we went to bed. It happened a couple of days later. I thought of telling you, then knew you wouldn't believe me, and you don't and I don't blame you and . . .'

'Would you?'

'No, of course I wouldn't. But . . .' Marcus looked as if he was about to burst into tears. 'Please, you have to believe I love you. I've never felt like this before, never. It had nothing to do with money, apart from the fact I thought that if we pooled our resources and our knowledge, the result might set us up for the rest of our lives. I . . . shit!' Marcus wiped away tears from his eyes.

Joanna had to admit she was surprised by his reaction. She'd expected him to tough it out, deny it, or callously confirm it when he knew he'd lost. Instead, she seemed to be witnessing the genuine confusion and grief of a ten-year-old boy. However, she'd had enough. After Matthew, Simon and now Marcus, men were firmly off the agenda. And before her resolve broke, she wanted Marcus out.

'Marcus. Your five minutes are up. I want you to leave.'

Marcus nodded. 'Sure. I understand.' He shook his head. 'Well, I've really blown it this time, haven't I?'

'Looks like it, yes.'

'You can't give me the benefit of the doubt? One last chance?'

'Absolutely not. Even if you're telling the truth, you're still admitting you lied to me. And what kind of basis is that for a relationship?'

Marcus hung his head, turned and walked to the door. 'Bye, Jo.'

'Yes, bye.'

He stood on the doorstep, and looked at her, tears flowing unchecked down his cheeks. 'I'm not lying when I say I love you. It's my own fucking stupid, pathetic fault I've lost you.' He shrugged. 'I've really got my come-uppance this time. I'm going to regret it for the rest of my life.'

'Night, Marcus.' Joanna closed the door before he saw the tears in her own eyes. It was tiredness, emotion and tension, that was all. He was a newly acquired habit she could break, Joanna assured herself as she headed for the cupboard in which she kept her rather pathetic collection of alcoholic beverages. Taking a swig of some ancient cooking sherry, Joanna turned off the lights and climbed into bed. She lay there, her head throbbing. Her brain was like a newborn hare, jumping from one fresh fact to the next. Eventually, she gave up trying to sleep, switched on the kettle and took all her Rose information from her rucksack and spread it on the bed. Making herself a nice, strong cup of tea and sitting on the bed cross-legged, Joanna studied the facts, then wrote herself a precise 'map' of exactly what had happened and facts she had gathered so far.

Joanna drained her cup and put it on the bedside table. She shook her head. Should she give it one more try? Ireland was meant to be extremely beautiful. As Marcus had pointed out, at the very least she could use the trip as a much needed break from London and all that had happened since Christmas.

'Sod it!' she breathed. She owed it to herself to take one step further down the line. Otherwise she might spend the rest of her life wondering. She seemed to have nothing left to lose . . . except her life . . . Telling herself to stop being overdramatic, that she was just preparing to go on an impromptu break for restorative purposes, Joanna decided she'd leave for Ireland at the weekend. Relieved to have made the decision, Joanna climbed back into bed and fell into an exhausted sleep.

*

On Friday morning, having checked in on the Aer Lingus flight to Cork, Joanna took out her mobile as she walked towards the departure gate.

'Hello?'

'Tom?'

'Yeah?'

'It's me. Can you tell the Ed I've got the most dreadful flu. So bad, in fact, I might not be feeling better until the middle of next week.'

'Mmm. Air tickets are cheaper when they include a Saturday night stopover.'

'Yes. Bye then.'

'Bye, Jo. Good luck. And watch your back, darlin'. You know where I am.'

'Thanks, Tom. Bye.'

It was only once she was in the air and on the way to her destination across the Irish sea that she mentally breathed out.

chapter twenty-eight

Marcus was still in bed, even though it was half past three in the afternoon. He wasn't asleep; he was just lying there, because he couldn't see much point in getting up. This had been pretty much the pattern for the past few days, since he'd been booted out of Joanna's flat. Although he'd called everywhere imaginable to locate her, even managed to track down her parents' house in Yorkshire, Joanna had disappeared off the face of the earth.

With the morning post had come a cheque for the substantial sum of twenty thousand pounds. Added to his ten from Sir Jim's will, plus the thirty he'd received from Zoe, he was solvent again. With enough of a deposit, perhaps, to raise a little more and begin the process of putting his film into production. Six weeks ago, he would have felt triumphant. From a seemingly hopeless situation, he'd achieved, with the minimum of hard graft, the impossible. But suddenly, it all seemed very pointless. And there was no one to blame but himself. He had let down Joanna and his sister, who, for all her patronizing, had always tried to help him. He had betrayed them both.

As he'd lain there in his bed, Marcus had taken

a retrospective on his life. It had been the most unpleasant seven and a half hours he'd ever spent. Every unpalatable situation he'd found himself in previously had a scapegoat, another person whose fault it was that Marcus had landed arse-up. But now he could see that *he'd* been the instigator; a selfish, juvenile, arrogant pillock who had always tried to pin the blame on someone else when all along it had been his own shortcomings that had landed him in the situation in the first place.

The cheque lay in a drawer by his bed: blood money. He had sold his own sister and her son. In a drawer in the cabinet opposite him lay the remnants of what he'd been paid to keep tabs on Joanna . . .

Christ he was a shit!

Tears of self-loathing dripped down Marcus's face. As he closed his eyes, he saw Joanna's face appear in front of him, as it had done a hundred times since he'd woken that morning. He knew the reason for the sudden, clear insight into what a cunt he really was. He'd fallen in love properly for the first time in his life.

*

At eight that evening, Marcus was contemplating getting up, but thinking it rather pointless as it was only a few hours until bedtime.

The bell rang.

Marcus jumped up, and, like a rabbit free of a trap, sprang to the front door.

His hopes high after the mea culpa session he'd raged with his conscience, he opened the door expecting to see Joanna standing there, sent to him by a forgiving

God. Instead, the tall, thin frame of Ian Simpson stood on his doorstep.

'Hello,' he managed, his heart sinking to his feet.

Ian stepped inside without even asking politely.

'Er, what can I do for you, Ian?' he asked as Ian marched into the living room.

'Where's Joanna Haslam?' Ian asked, his eyes darting around the room.

'Not here, that's for sure.' Marcus shrugged.

'Then where?' Ian walked towards Marcus, in a less than friendly manner.

'I really don't know. As a matter of fact, I've been looking for her myself. She's not answering the telephone at home, she's not at work and her mobile is switched off.'

Ian stood in front of him, so close that Marcus could hear his rather uneven breathing. He swore he could smell alcohol on Ian's breath.

'We were paying you to keep tabs on her, remember?'

'Yes. Well, maybe she found out and that's why I've not seen hide nor hair of her since.'

This seemed to unsettle Ian. His eyes wandered for a few seconds, as if he were remembering something unpleasant. Then he grabbed Marcus by the collar of his dressing-gown. 'You know where she is, don't you, you little shit!'

'I really don't. I . . .' Close up, Marcus could see that Ian's eyes were bloodshot. The man was drunk, there was no doubt about it. 'Look, can you let me go and we can talk about this rationally?'

A punch in the stomach sent Marcus reeling

towards the sofa. Marcus's head hit the back of it and he saw stars.

'Steady on, mate. We're on the same side, remember?'

Ian laughed. 'I hardly think so.'

Clutching his head, Marcus sat upright and watched as Ian paced around the room. 'She's gone somewhere, hasn't she? She's on the trail.'

'What trail? I—'

Ian advanced towards him and landed another kick in Marcus's groin, which sent him off the sofa and on to the floor, howling in pain.

'It would be a good idea if you told me. I know you're covering up for her, protecting her.'

'No! Really. I—'

A kick in the kidneys from Ian's foot produced further howls of pain.

'What were you planning? Tell me?'

'Nothing. I . . .' A brainwave came into Marcus's head which he hoped would make the man refrain from kicking him to death and subsequently leave.

'We were going to Ireland this weekend. It seems my grandfather might have hailed from that part of the world.'

'Where in Ireland?'

'County Cork . . .'

'What part?'

'I . . .' Marcus struggled to remember. 'Rosscarbery. It's a village on the west coast. If she can't be found anywhere else, I suppose she may have gone there.'

Ian looked down at him silently. Marcus prayed he'd given the man enough to satisfy him.

'I'll make some calls. If I find out you're lying, I'll be back, do you understand?'

'Yes, but look, it's only a thought. If you find her, please let me know. I'm worried.'

Ian made a snorting sound that could have been laughter, pity, or a mixture of both. 'You were always an arsehole at school. You haven't changed, Marcus, have you?' Ian aimed the tip of his toe at Marcus's nose. Marcus cringed as the toe swung wide and hit a cheek. 'Be seeing you.'

Marcus listened for the door to close behind him. Breathing a sigh of relief, he rolled on to his knees, moving his jaw from side to side and cursing in pain. He managed to get on to the sofa and sat staring into space, his face, his balls and his stomach throbbing. He'd have taken Ian Simpson for many things, but not a bully. He'd always been so calm, so controlled, even at school extracting what he wanted through mental rather than physical pressure. Tonight, the man had seemed quite deranged.

Thank God he'd managed to come up with the Ireland line. Of course, Marcus supposed he'd be back when he discovered Joanna wasn't there, but at least he'd be prepared. A sudden surge of fear settled round Marcus's already painful chest. What if she *was* there? No . . . Marcus shook his head. Why would she be? On the other hand . . .

'Christ!'

Had he just thrown Joanna to an extremely unstable and drunken lion? Yet again, to save his own skin?

*

Simon whistled along to Ella Fitzgerald as he drove down the motorway towards Berkshire and Jamie's school. The week he had taken off had been long overdue. He felt rested and calmer than he had done for a while. Even if the spare time had given him the opportunity to think. On the upside, Simon knew that the spectre of Theresa had been washed away. On the downside, he knew the feelings had been transferred and magnified thousands of times over. The fact that he was seeing Zoe's son in half an hour's time filled him with a kind of illicit pleasure.

*

Jamie was quieter than he had been at home in London. As Simon drove them towards the town and a hotel that purported to serve excellent Sunday lunches, Simon struggled to engage the boy in conversation.

'I'll have the beef, I think.' Simon perused the menu and looked at Jamie. 'You?'

'The lamb, thanks.'

Simon ordered and purchased a pint for himself and a coke for Jamie.

'So, how's your week been?' Simon couldn't help noticing how similar Jamie was to his mother. The same big blue eyes, thick blond hair and delicate features.

'Fine.' Jamie nodded uncertainly. 'How long is Mumma away for, Simon?'

Simon shrugged. 'I don't know exactly. I think she'll probably be back sometime next week.'

'Oh.' Jamie nodded. 'What kind of work is it?'

'Some advert, I think. I'm not sure.'

Jamie took a sip of his coke. 'Are you staying at the house in London?'

'Well, tomorrow I've decided to go do a bit of touring. Scotland, maybe Ireland,' Simon answered. 'So how's the last week been at school?'

'Okay. You know, the same.'

'Right.'

Simon was grateful when their food arrived. Jamie picked at his lamb, answering most of Simon's attempts at conversation in monosyllables. He refused pudding, even though there was chocolate gateau and trifle on the menu.

'I remember always yumming everything up when my parents came to take me out for lunch from school. You sure you're okay, old chap?'

'Yes. Do they have boarding schools in Australia?'

'I . . . yes, of course they do. If you're miles away from anything in the outback, you have to board in the city,' Simon invented. 'Sure I can't tempt you to some ice-cream?'

'Positive.'

Simon was relieved when it was time to take Jamie back to school. Jamie sat in the car staring out of the window, humming to himself.

'What's that you're humming?'

Jamie turned and looked at Simon. 'A nursery rhyme, "Ring A Ring O'Roses". Great-James used to sing it to me all the time. When I got older, he told me it was all about people dying of the Black Death.'

'Do you miss him, Jamie?'

'Yes. But I know he's still looking after me from heaven.'

'I'm sure he is.'

'And I still have his roses to mind me on the earth.'

'Roses?'

'Yes. Great-James loved roses.' The car came to a halt and Jamie opened the door and climbed out. He held out his hand across the gear-stick. 'Thanks for taking me out, Simon. Safe journey back to London.'

Simon watched as the door slammed and Jamie raced up the steps and inside the school. Sighing, he drove the car back along the gravel path and out of the school. When he arrived back at his flat, there was a message on his answering machine.

'Report to me at O eight hundred tomorrow.'

Knowing his short sabbatical was well and truly nearing its end, Simon cooked himself some pasta, showered and took himself off to bed.

*

Simon sat in the same, leather-bound chair.

'Mr Simpson has gone AWOL.'

'I see.' Simon nodded.

'And your friend, Miss Haslam.'

Simon wanted to quip that maybe they'd eloped, but he thought it unwise.

'Could it be a coincidence, sir?'

'I somehow doubt it under the circumstances. We've just had the evaluation of Mr Simpson's psychological report. The psychologist was concerned enough to recommend he receives urgent and immediate treatment.' He wheeled his chair round the desk and studied Simon. 'He knows too much. I want you to find him,

Warburton, and fast. My instincts tell me he may have followed Miss Haslam wherever she has roamed.'

'I thought her flat was bugged? And Marcus Harrison's? Did they not give you an indication of where she might be?'

'Jenkins informed me the entire computer system has been malfunctioning for the last week. That's modern technology for you. I've always thought it was being relied on too heavily. In my day, agents used their ears, their eyes and their brains. By the time all was well again, Miss Haslam and Simpson had vanished.'

'And no one has any idea where either of them might have gone?'

'You've read the file, Warburton.' He replied irritably. 'If you were Haslam, wishing to ferret out further information about our man, where would you go?' He wheeled himself back behind his desk. 'If Haslam or Simpson get there before we do, you know what it would mean.'

'Yes, sir.'

'Mr Harrison is still in residence. Maybe you should have a word with him, as you are his Australian and extremely distant cousin.' He raised an eyebrow.

'Yes, sir.'

'I see you went to visit young Jamie Harrison yesterday?'

'Yes.'

'Business or pleasure?'

'I did it as a favour for Zoe Harrison, sir. She's away at present.'

'I am aware of that, Warburton.' He eyed Simon. 'You know the rules.'

'Of course, sir.'

'Righto. Let me know when there's news.'

'I will.'

Simon rose from his chair and left the room, praying the old man hadn't seen the blush he could feel heating his face. His mind and his body could be trained and disciplined. It was obvious his heart could not.

chapter twenty-nine

On arriving at Cork airport, Joanna went to the car-hire desk and rented herself a car. Having furnished herself with a map and some Irish money, she headed towards her bright red Fiesta. Expecting to drive out on to some kind of dual carriageway, she was surprised when the main road from the airport resembled a by-road from her native Yorkshire. The March day was sunny and as she drove Joanna appreciated the lush greenness of the rolling fields on either side of her.

An hour later, Joanna found herself driving down a steep hill into Rosscarbery village. To her left, a deep estuary surrounded by a low wall stretched into the sea far away. Houses, cottages and bungalows were dotted on either side of it. When she reached the bottom of the hill, Joanna stopped the car to take a better look. The tide was out and all manner of bird life was swooping down on to the sand, swans were floating gracefully in a large pool of water left behind when the tide went out.

Getting out of the car, Joanna leaned against the low wall, breathing in deeply. The air smelled so different from that of London; clean, fresh, with a hint of salt that indicated the Atlantic was less than a mile away. It was then she saw the house. It stuck right out into the estuary, built on a bed of rock with water surrounding it on three sides. It was large, covered in grey slate, a weathervane on the chimney spinning slightly in the breeze. From the description Marcus had given her of a house 'out in the bay', surely this had to be it? Joanna felt suddenly faint. Why did she feel she'd seen the house before? She'd never been here in her life.

A cloud suddenly effaced the sun, casting a shadow across the bay and on to the house. Joanna turned hurriedly, got into her car, started the engine and drove off.

*

Four hours later Joanna was installed in the cosy bar of the local hotel, sipping a hot port by the fire. The sudden and irrational fear that had gripped her earlier had gone. Due possibly to a nap of two and a half hours on the big old double bed in the room the friendly landlord had indicated was hers.

It was years since she'd slept in the afternoon. She'd only laid down to study the map of Rosscarbery, to try and form some kind of plan of action and then, the next thing she knew, it was six o'clock and the room was in darkness.

'Will ye be wanting to take your supper in the dining room or will ye have it here by the fire?'

It was Margaret, wife of Willie, owner and landlord.

'Here will do just fine.' Joanna smiled.

She sat in her corner of the bar eating her bacon, cabbage and potatoes and watched as a trail of locals came through the door. Young and old, they all knew each other and seemed to be on intimate terms with the minutiae of each other's lives. Feeling relaxed and sated after her filling supper, Joanna sauntered towards the bar and ordered a final pre-bedtime hot port.

'So, yer here for a holiday?' a middle-aged man in overalls and wellingtons asked her from his perch at the corner of the bar.

'Partly.' Joanna nodded. 'I'm also looking for some-one. A relative of mine.'

'Sure, there's always people coming over here look-ing for a relative. It might be said our blessed country managed to germinate half the Western hemisphere.'

This elicited laughter from the other drinkers in the bar.

'So what would your relative be called then?' asked the man.

'Michael O'Connell. I'd reckon he was born here around the turn of the century.'

The man rubbed his chin. 'There's bound to be a few of those, being as it is such a common name in Ireland.'

'Have you any idea where I could check?'

'The register of births and deaths, next door to the chemist in the square, the churches, of course. Or you could go into Clonakilty where yer man has started up a business tracing yer Irish heritage.' The man finished his beer. 'He's bound to find an O'Connell that's related to you on his computer, long as you've paid him his fee.'

The man winked at his neighbour on the bar stool next to him. 'Strange really, how times change. Sixty years ago we were bogmen who'd crawled out from under a stone. Nobody wanted to exchange the time of day with us. Now, even the president of the United States wants to be related to us.'

'True, true,' nodded his neighbour.

'Do you by any chance know who owns the house sticking out into the estuary? The grey stone one, with the weathervane?' Joanna asked tentatively.

An old woman dressed in an ancient anorak, a scarf tied tightly round her jaw, studied Joanna from her seat in the corner with sudden interest.

'Ah, jaysus, that old wreck? It's been empty as long as I've been living here. You'd have to be asking Jim Mulcahy, the local historian, maybe. T'was owned by the British once long ago. They used it as a coastguards' outpost, but since then . . .' The man shrugged. 'I'd say there's a lot of property lying about these parts without an owner to tend to it.'

'Thanks anyway.' Joanna took the hot port from the bar. 'Goodnight.'

'Night, missus. Hope you find yer roots.'

The old woman in the corner stood up soon after Joanna had left the bar. She headed for the door.

The man at the bar nudged his neighbour. 'Should have sent her down to mad Ciara Deasy. She'd be sure to spin her a tale or two of the O'Connells of Rosscarbery.'

Both men laughed heartily and ordered another round on the strength of the joke.

*

Joanna dreamed that night. She was racing across the sand towards the house in the bay, hearing the terrified screams of a woman locked inside. As she ran towards it, two arms grabbed her from behind and dragged her back into the estuary. 'Please, no!' she shouted as he forced her face under the water, the iron grip on her arms making it impossible for her to struggle up above the water and fill her lungs with the air she so desperately needed. 'Please! Help me! Help me . . .'

Joanna woke up with a start, hearing the words coming out of her mouth. She was sweating, shaking, her breathing coming in short, sharp gasps.

'Oh God,' she groaned, putting her head in her hands, wishing she was back in London, safely ensconced in Marcus's arms, instead of here, alone, feeling suddenly so very vulnerable.

*

The next morning, a fine Irish breakfast filled her stomach and calmed her nerves. The weather was filthy outside; the spring of yesterday forestalled by a grim grey rain that shrouded the bay below her in mist.

She spent the morning wandering round the fine Protestant Cathedral and spoke to the friendly dean who willingly let her look through the records of baptisms and marriages. 'It's more likely you'll find your fella registered in St Mary's, the Catholic church down the road. Us Protestants always have been a minority around here.' He smiled ruefully.

At St Mary's the priest finished hearing confession, then unlocked the cupboard where the register books were kept. 'If your man was born here, he'll be registered. There wasn't a baby round these parts that wasn't baptized here in those days. Now, it's 1900 we're after, isn't it?'

'Yes.'

Joanna spent the next half an hour looking through the names of those baptized. There was not a single baby O'Connell in the year. Or the years before or after.

'Are you sure you have the right name? I mean, if it was O'Connor then we'd be in business.'

Joanna shrugged. She wasn't sure about anything. She was over here on the words of an old man, and the throwaway comment of a young boy. Freezing cold by now, Joanna wandered across the square and back to her hotel for a bowl of soup to warm her up.

'Any luck?' asked Margaret.

'Nothing,' shrugged Joanna.

'You should maybe ask some of the old ones in town. They might remember the name. Or Jim Mulcahy, as Jamsie suggested last night. He teaches history up at the boys school. He usually pops by at half past five for a jar. I'm sure he'd know more about that old coastguard's house.'

Joanna nodded. That afternoon, having discovered the register of Births, Marriages and Deaths only opened on a Friday, she borrowed a bicycle from Margaret's daughter and set off from the village and along the estuary. The narrow path wound round for a good mile before the coastguard's house came into view. She stopped her bicycle by its wall, her nerves tingling. She could see there were holes in the slate roof, a window pane missing.

Joanna took a tentative step towards the rusting gate. It creaked open. She climbed the steps up to the front door and wiped some grime away from one of the windows and peered in. It was too dark to see anything. She tried the front door. The old lock may have been rusty, but it still knew how to keep out uninvited visitors.

The window pane that had broken was one that overlooked the estuary. The only way to get to it was to walk down into the estuary and climb up the wall behind the house. Luckily, being mid-afternoon, the tide was out. Joanna went out of the gate and round and down on to the sand. The wall stood about six feet high, protecting the house from flooding. Although Joanna could see that the estuary was so sheltered by hills on either side it was doubtful there had ever been much risk.

She clambered up the wall and on to a thin ledge of about two feet. Above her was the broken window. She peered inside. Even though there was little wind outside the house, she could hear the soft cry of it inside. The room she was looking into had obviously once been a kitchen. There was still an old black range, heavy with dust, in one corner and a sink with an old-fashioned water pump over it. Joanna looked down and saw a dead rat in the middle of the slated floor.

A door banged suddenly somewhere inside the house. Joanna jumped and fell backwards off the ledge, landing in the soft wet sand below. The fall winded her, but otherwise she was unhurt. Dusting the sand from her jeans, Joanna scurried back to her bicycle and pedalled as fast as she could away from the house.

*

Ciara Deasy watched the girl from the window of her cottage just across the bay. She'd always known that one day, someone would come and she'd be able to tell her story at long last.

*

'This is yer man, Jim Mulcahy,' announced Margaret, guiding Joanna over to the bar.

'Hello.' Joanna smiled, trying to keep the surprise out of her voice. For some reason she'd expected Jim Mulcahy to be an extremely old, fusty-dusty professor type person with a white straggly beard. In fact, Jim Mulcahy was probably not much older than her and was dressed very pleasantly in a pair of jeans and a fisherman's jumper. He had thick black hair, blue eyes and instantly reminded Joanna of Marcus. He stood up and Joanna saw he was much taller than her erstwhile ex-boyfriend, with a far leaner frame.

'Good to be meeting you, Joanna. I hear you've lost a relative.' He smiled back.

'Yes.'

Jim tapped the bar stool next to him. 'Take a pew, we'll have a glass and you can tell me all about it. A glass and pint, Margaret, please.'

Joanna, who had never tasted stout in her life, found the creamy, irony taste of the Murphy's very palatable indeed.

'Now then, what's the name of this relative of yours?'

'Michael O'Connell.'

'You've tried the churches, I suppose.'

'Yes. He wasn't mentioned. I would have tried the registrar's office but—'

'It only opens on a Friday. I know. Well, I can sort

that. The registrar just happens to be my father.' Jim smiled and dangled a key in front of her. 'And they live above the shop.'

'Thanks.' Joanna nodded, sipping her Murphy's.

'And I hear you're interested in the coastguard's house?'

'Er, yes. Although I'm not sure it has anything to do with my missing relative.'

'A grand old house, it was once,' nodded Jim. 'My dad's got photos of it somewhere. Sad it's been left to rack and ruin, but of course none in the village would touch it.'

'Why's that?'

Jim sipped at his fresh pint. 'Oh, you know how it is in small places. Myths and legends grow out of a small grain of truth and some mighty gossip. No, I'd reckon it'll be some rich American or German who'll come along and steal the place for nothing.'

'What was the legend, Mr Mulcahy?'

'Come now, call me Jim.' He shook his head. 'I'm a historian. I deal with facts, not fantasy, so I've never believed a word of it.' His eyes twinkled. 'Except you wouldn't find me down there around midnight on the eve of a full moon.'

Joanna watched him, waiting for him to expound his knowledge.

'It is said that seventy years ago or so, a young woman from the village, Niamh Deasy, got herself in trouble with a man who was staying at the coastguard's house. The man left to return to his homeland in England, leaving the girl with child. She went stone mad with grief, so they say, gave birth to the baby in the house before dying soon after. There are those in the village believe the house is haunted, that Niamh's cries of pain and fear can still be heard echoing from the house on a clear night. Some have even spoken of seeing her face at the window, her hands covered with her blood.'

Joanna's own blood had run cold. She shook her head to help the flow of oxygen to her brain.

'Are you all right, Joanna?' Jim was staring at her with concern. ''Tis only a story. I didn't mean to upset you.'

'No.' Joanna shook her head. 'You haven't, really. It's fascinating.' She took a sip of her Murphy's. 'Seventy years ago,' she mused, 'there must have been people around who are still living today.'

'There are, there are indeed. The girl's sister, Ciara, still lives in the family homestead. Don't try talking to her, mind. She's always been short of a few pence, stone mad since she was a child. She believes every word of the story, and adds her own finishing touches to it, I can tell you.'

'Wh ... what about the baby?' asked Joanna tentatively.

'I don't know,' shrugged Jim. 'Some say it didn't survive, others that the girl's father murdered it. I've even heard tell that the baby was taken off by the fairies ...' He smiled and shook his head. 'Try and envisage a time, not so long ago, without electricity, when the only form of sport was to gather together to drink and swap stories, true or otherwise. News has always been a little like Chinese whispers in Ireland, each man vying with the other to make his news bigger and better. In this case, mind, 'tis true the girl died. But in that house, mad from thwarted love?' Jim shook his head. 'I doubt it.'

'Where does this Ciara live?'

'Down in the pink cottage overlooking the bay. 'Tis almost opposite coastguard's house. A bird's-eye view, you might say.'

'Mmm.'

'Well now, would you like to pop along the road and have a look through the records my father has?'

'Yes, if it's convenient for you.'

''Tis fine. No rush.' Jim indicated Joanna's stout. 'We'll go when you're ready.'

*

The small office that had recorded every birth and death in the village of Rosscarbery for the past one hundred and fifty years did not seem to have changed much in that time, apart from the harsh strip light illuminating the bog-oak desk.

Jim busied himself in the back room, looking out the records for the turn of the century. 'Right now, you take the births, I'll take the deaths.'

'Okay.'

They sat on each side of the table, silently going through each entry. Joanna found a Fionnuala and a Kathleen O'Connell, but not a single boy born of that surname between 1897 and 1905.

'Anything?' she asked.

'No, not a thing. I have found Niamh O'Sullivan though. She was registered as dead on the second of March 1927. But there's no note that her baby died with her. Let's see if someone registered the baby's birth.'

Jim went to fetch another ancient, leather-bound book. They both pored over the yellowing pages.

'No, nothing.' Jim shut the book and a fug of dust flew into the air, making Joanna sneeze violently. 'Maybe the baby was a myth after all. Are you sure now that Michael O'Connell was born here in Rosscarbery? Each townland or district kept their own records, you see. He could have been born a few miles up the road, in Clonakilty for example, and his birth would be registered there.'

Joanna rubbed her forehead. 'To be honest, Jim, I know so little.'

'Well now, it might be worth checking the church records in Clon. I'll just close up here, then I'll walk you back to the pub.'

The bar was fuller than it had been the previous night. Another Murphy's arrived in front of Joanna and she was drawn into a group that Jim was talking to.

'Go and see Ciara Deasy, just for the craic!' laughed a young woman, hearing of Joanna's fascination with the coastguard's house. 'She terrified all of us with her talk. I'd say she was a witch.'

'Stop that now, Eileen. We're no longer peasants believing in such fantasy,' admonished Jim.

'Doesn't every land have its fables?' Eileen asked, fluttering her eyes at Jim. 'And its eccentrics? Even the EU can't ban those, you know.'

There then ensued a heated debate between the pro- and anti-EU supporters.

Joanna yawned surreptitiously. 'It's great to meet you all. I'm going to go to bed now.' She nodded.

'A young London thing like you? I thought t'was dawn before ye all crawled to your beds,' said one of the men.

'It's all your clean fresh air. My lungs can't get over the shock. Night, everyone.' She headed off in the direction of the stairs but was halted by a tap on the shoulder.

'I have tomorrow morning until twelve free. I could take you to the public records office in Clonakilty. They'll have a record of who owns the coastguard's house. We could pop into the church as well, see if that throws anything up for ye.'

Joanna smiled at Jim. 'Yes, thank you. That would be great. Night.'

*

Joanna sat in bed, propped up by her pillows. She was ashamed of the fact that she didn't dare turn off the light, that the nightmare might come if she slept. She tossed up going back to England tomorrow. This was meant to be a relaxing break away from the tension of the past few weeks in London. Yet, so far, it had only filled her with some strange sense of impending doom.

*

At ten the next morning, after a sleepless night, Jim was waiting for her in the deserted bar.

'There you go.' He handed Joanna a crash helmet.

'Jim, I have a car outside.'

He studied her. 'Where's your sense of adventure, girl?'

She handed him back the helmet. 'Gone away in the night with the fairies. We'll take the car.'

Fifteen minutes later they were in a large, newly built council office. Jim seemed to know a girl behind the counter. Jim indicated Joanna should follow him and the girl into a storeroom.

'Right, that's Rosscarbery plans, all along the shelf over there.' The girl pointed to a shelf loaded with files. She walked to the door. 'If you need anything else, Jim, just you call me, okay?'

'Sure, Ginny. Thanks.'

As Joanna followed Jim over to the shelf, she got the feeling that this young man was the stuff of every local girl's dreams.

'Right. You take that pile, I'll take this. The house is bound to be here somewhere.'

For an hour they trolled through pages of yellowing, dusty files, until at last Jim gave a whoop of triumph. 'Got the bugger! Come here and look.'

Inside the file was the plan of the coastguard's house, Rosscarbery.

'Drawn for a Mr H. O. Bentinck, Lisselan House, Rosscarbery, 1869,' Jim read out. That was a local Englishman living here at the time. He left during the troubles. A lot of the Brits did.'

'But surely that doesn't mean he still owns it? I mean, it's over one hundred and twenty years ago.'

'Well his great-granddaughter, Emily, still lives at Lisselan, just behind the estuary. She's turned the estate into a business venture. She trains racehorses up there.

Maybe you should go and ask her, so you should.' Jim was looking at his watch. 'I'll have to go in half an hour. Let's get these photocopied and run to the church, okay?'

Once Jim had greeted the priest and done some fast talking, the old records of baptism were unlocked from their cupboard and opened for them.

Joanna scanned her finger quickly down the register. 'Look here!' Joanna's eyes lit up with excitement. 'Michael James O'Connell. Baptized the tenth of April 1901. It has to be him!'

'There you go now, Joanna,' said Jim, smiling at her. He looked at his watch. 'Would you mind spinning me back to Ross now? I can't be late for my class. I'll show you where the Bentinck estate is on the way.'

'So, where do you go from here, now you've found your man?' Jim asked as Joanna drove out of Clonakilty towards Rosscarbery.

'I don't know.' She sighed. 'But at least I feel I haven't been on a completely wild goose chase.'

Having dropped Jim at his school, Joanna proceeded back up the hill from which she had first seen Rosscarbery, to the gate Jim had said led to Emily Bentinck's house. The gates were open as Joanna turned into them. She drove for a mile or so before a large house appeared in front of her. She could see that behind the house was a stunning view of both the estuary and the Atlantic stretching out into the far distance.

Getting out of the car, Joanna began to hunt for a sign of life. The front door to the house was open. 'Hello?' she called, her voice echoing round the huge hallway. Going back out of the house, Joanna walked round to the back where she saw a stable block. A woman in an ancient anorak and a pair of old jodhpurs was grooming a horse.

'Hello, sorry to bother you but I'm looking for Emily Bentinck.'

'You found her.' The woman who had a clipped English accent nodded. 'Can I help you?'

'Yes. I was wondering whether you could tell me if your family still owns the coastguard's house down in Rosscarbery.'

'Interested in buying it, are you?'

'No, not really. More in the history of it.'

'I see.' Emily continued to groom her horse. 'Don't really know that much about it, apart from the fact my great-great-grandfather commissioned its building in the mid-nineteen hundreds. The English wanted an outpost in the bay to try and stem the smuggling that was going on down there. Don't think the family ever actually owned it, though.'

'I see. Do you know how I might be able to find out about it?'

'There you go, Sargeant, good boy.' Emily patted the horse on its rump and led it back into one of the stables. She came out and looked at her watch. 'Come inside and have a cup of tea. I was just going to brew up anyway.'

Joanna sat in the huge, untidy kitchen. Every available wall was covered with rosettes won from hundreds of competitions both in Ireland and abroad.

'Must admit I've been a little tardy in tracing the family history over here. So damned busy with the nags outside and putting this place back on its feet.' Emily poured Joanna a cup of tea from a large stainless-steel pot. 'Granny lived here until her death, using just two rooms downstairs. The place was going to rack and ruin when I came here ten years ago. Some things are lost for ever. The dampness in the air rots everything it gets into.'

'It's a beautiful old house, though.'

'Oh yes. In its heyday it was extremely well regarded. The balls, parties and hunts were legendary. My great-grandfather entertained the great and the good from all over Europe in this house, including English royalty. Apparently we even had the Prince of Wales having a tryst with his Irish mistress. It was a perfect hideaway. The cotton boats used to sail regularly from Clonakilty to England and you could pop on a boat from there and sail round the coast with no one knowing of your arrival.'

'Are you restoring it?'

Emily nodded. 'Trying to. Need the horses to come back with a few wins at Cheltenham next week and that'll help us on our way. The house is too big for the four of us. When more of it's habitable I intend to make it pay its own way and open it to tourists as an up-market B&B. Could be way past the millennium before that happens, mind you. So,' Emily's bright eyes studied Joanna, 'what are you doing over here?'

'I'm a journalist, actually, but I'm not on company business here. I'm looking for a relative. Before he died, he mentioned Rosscarbery and a house that stuck out into the bay.'

'Was he Irish?'

'Yes. I found a record of his baptism in the church at Clonakilty.'

'What was his name?'

'Michael O'Connell.'

'Where are you staying?'

'The Ross Hotel.'

'Well, I'll have a hunt through the old deeds and documents in the library later tonight and see if I can dig anything up for you on the place.'

'Thank you very much.' Joanna drained her teacup and stood up. They walked out of the kitchen together.

'Do you ride?'

'Oh yes. I was brought up in Yorkshire and I had four legs under me for most of my childhood.'

'If you want a mount while you're staying here, you're welcome to one. Bye now.'

*

Later that evening, Joanna was in her usual place in the bar by the fire, when the landlord called to her.

'Telephone for you, Joanna. It's a Mrs Bentinck.'

'Thanks.' She stood up and walked round the bar to take the receiver.

'Hello?'

'Emily here. I dug up some very interesting stuff while I was in the process of looking for your information. Seems our neighbour has managed to siphon off at least ten acres and fence them with trees while dear old granny wasn't looking.'

'Oh dear, I'm sorry. Can you get them back?'

'No. Round here, after seven years of fencing them and if no one has claimed the land back, it's yours.

Explains why our next-door neighbour runs away in fright every time I approach him, mind you.'

'Oh dear. Did you manage to find any documents relating to the coastguard's house?'

'No, I'm afraid not. I found a couple of title deeds to hovels that probably are no more than ruins now, but none relating to the coastguard's house. I think the best thing would be for you to get hold of an ordnance map showing where it's positioned and send it to a law searcher. He'll look up the title deeds at the Land Registry Office in Dublin.'

'How long does that take?'

'Oh a week, two weeks maybe.'

'Could I do it myself?'

'I suppose so, yes, as long as you took a map with you. It's a bit of a hack to Dublin, though. A good five hours by car, three by train.'

'I might go tomorrow. I've never been to Dublin and I'd like to see it. Thanks for your help anyway, Emily. I do appreciate it.'

'Hold your horses, Joanna. I said I didn't find any title deeds, but I did find a couple of other things you might be interested in. Firstly, and it might be coincidence, I found an old ledger, used to keep a record of staff wages in 1919. A man by the name of Michael O'Connell is listed there.'

'I see. So he may have worked at the house?'

'Yes, it would seem so.'

'Doing what?'

'The ledger doesn't say, I'm afraid. But in 1923 his name vanishes from the list, so I presume he must have left.'

'Thank you, Emily. That's really helpful.'

Secondly, I found a letter. It was written to my great-grandfather in 1926. Do you want to pop over tomorrow and see it?'

'Could you read it to me now?'

'Of course.'

Joanna stuck a finger in her ear to try to drown out the noise of the bar.

'Righto, here goes. It's dated the eleventh of November 1926.

' "Dear Stanley," that's my great-grandfather, "I hope this letter finds you well. I am asked by Lord Ashley to write to inform you of the arrival to your shores of a gentleman, guest of HM government. He will be staying for the present at the coastguard's house. Your new neighbour will be taking up residence on the second of January 1926. If possible, we would like you to meet him off the boat which will dock in Clonakilty harbour at approximately O one hundred hours and see him safely to his new abode. Would you arrange, please, for a woman to come in from the village and clean the house up before his arrival. Such a woman might wish to work for the gentleman on a regular basis, keeping house and cooking for him, as he is of single status at present.

' "The situation with this gentleman is highly delicate. We would prefer his presence at the coastguard's house to be kept quiet. Lord Ashley has indicated he will be in touch with further details regarding this. Love to Amelia and the children. I am, yours very faithfully, Lt. John Moore." There you go, dear. Get all that?'

'Yes. I suppose you didn't find any correspondence indicating who this gentleman might be?'

'None, I'm afraid, but that's not to say there isn't any. I have boxes and boxes to sort through. Anyway, hope it helps you on your way. Good luck in Dublin. Night, Joanna.'

chapter thirty

Marcus went to answer the doorbell.

'Hello, cousin Simon. And what are you doing in this neck of the woods?'

'Can I come in?'

'Sure, feel free.' Marcus shrugged.

Simon looked about him. The sitting room was a tip. Old dinner plates, cans of beer and newspapers were everywhere. Marcus himself didn't look much better, he was unshaven, with at least a week's growth of stubble on his chin.

'Sorry.' Marcus shrugged, waving his arms round the room. 'Been a bit preoccupied one way and another. Want a drink?'

'Coffee would be nice.'

'You'll have to take it black. I don't have any milk, or if I do, it's cheese.'

Simon followed Marcus through to the kitchen, which smelled of rotting food.

Marcus switched the kettle on. Simon leaned against a worktop and watched him light a cigarette.

'How's Joanna?' he asked.

Marcus looked as if he was about to burst into tears. 'Gone. Left me high and dry.'

'Sorry to hear that.'

'Don't be. I deserved it.' Marcus took a drag of his cigarette. 'Bloody miss her though.' He shrugged. 'I really thought this was it.'

'She might come back.'

Marcus shook his head. 'Nope, she won't.'

'Have you tried talking to her?'

'I would if I knew where she was. She's not at home or at work.'

'And you've no idea where she is?'

'None at all.' Marcus sluiced out a mug, put in a teaspoon of coffee and added some water. 'There you go.'

'Thanks.' Simon followed Marcus back into the living room and made a space for himself on the sofa.

'To be honest, I'm getting worried about her. It's not just me she's been avoiding. Other people seem to have mislaid her too,' Marcus said mournfully.

'Well, I suppose it's not surprising if she's not been seen at home or at work.'

'I was thinking of calling the police, actually. Getting her registered as a missing person.'

'No need to do that.' Simon took a sip of his coffee, which was disgusting. 'Look, Marcus, I'm going to have to come clean with you. I am not really your long-lost cousin from Oz. Zoe preferred that I tell people I was because of her ... delicate situation. While I was staying with Zoe I was acting as her bodyguard, fairly standard practice when someone becomes closely connected with a royal.'

'I guessed as much,' he replied. 'I'm not quite as stupid as I may look.'

'You knew about her relationship, then?'

'I . . . no.' Marcus blushed. 'Well, I thought something was going on, anyway.'

Looking at the man's guilty face, it suddenly dawned on Simon that Marcus was a far more likely candidate for telling the newspapers than Joanna had been. Simon's dislike for him increased. It was a low-down thing to do to an enemy, let alone a sibling.

'Well, that's old news now. The world has heard, thanks to some filthy purveyor of gossip . . .' Marcus's blush increased and Simon was convinced he'd hit the nail on the head. 'That is not the reason why I'm here. The point is, one of my colleagues, Ian Simpson, has gone AWOL.'

The colour drained immediately from Marcus's face. 'What do you mean, AWOL?'

'He's been taken off his duties and given sick leave. I know he had had some contact with you previously, and my superiors were just wondering whether he'd been in touch since.'

Marcus nodded. 'Yes . . .' He cleared his throat. 'Yes. He came round on Saturday and virtually beat me up. I've got a nice yellow bruise on my cheek thanks to his big left foot.'

'Was he, by any chance, asking after Joanna's whereabouts too?'

'Yes. As a matter of fact he was. I tell you, he didn't look too well, either. I think he was pissed.'

'Yes, more than likely. Were you able to give him any ideas as to where Joanna might be?'

'No, not really. I did mention we were due to go to Ireland this weekend, down to West Cork for a break.'

'Look, the thing is,' Simon continued, 'that Ian was very involved in this case. A couple of weeks ago he had a minor breakdown, due to the stressful nature of his job. He's obviously concerned that he convinces his superiors that he is well enough to continue. Therefore, the theory is that he may have gone after Joanna to see if she can lead him to this letter and therefore cover himself in glory before his bosses.'

'Shit!' Marcus looked at Simon in panic. 'You don't think Joanna's gone to Ireland, do you?'

'I can soon find out. Why?'

'I told Ian Simpson Joanna might have headed for Ireland to prevent him from killing me. It was the first thing that came into my head.'

'I see.' Simon stood up and pulled his mobile out of his pocket. 'When was the last time you saw Joanna?'

'Er, Monday. I went round to her flat and she chucked me out.'

Simon did his best to suppress a grin. He dialled a number.

'Can you check all flights from the UK into Cork and, I suppose, Shannon airport, any date after last Wednesday? See if either a J. Haslam, Miss, or our friend, under a codename or his real name, were on any of the passenger lists. Thanks. Yes, I am.'

'If she has gone to Ireland, and Ian has followed her, surely there's no danger to Joanna, is there?'

Simon paced the room, waiting for his colleague to call him back.

'Sane, Ian's no more danger to anyone than your average old-aged pensioner, but the way he is at the moment . . . well . . .' Simon's mobile rang. 'Hello?

Right, Okay, thanks. Tell Jenkins to call me. We need to alert the Irish intelligence forces too. Give a description. I'll be back in about twenty minutes.' Simon clicked off his mobile and stared at Marcus. 'You were right. Joanna left Heathrow last Friday morning headed for Cork. There's no record of Ian or one of his codenames being on the passenger list then or during the next two days, but that means nothing. I've got to go, Marcus.'

'Christ, is Joanna really in danger?'

Simon's face answered Marcus's question for him.

'What can I do?'

'Stay here and for God's sake, if Joanna rings warn her and tell her to get on a plane and fly straight home.'

'I will.' Marcus followed Simon feebly to the door. 'Sorry if I've caused any of this.'

Simon turned and stared at him. 'What you do with your private life is no concern of mine. As for your sister, well, that's between you and your conscience, isn't it? Goodbye now.'

The door slammed in Marcus's face.

*

Zoe opened the shutters and walked out on to the balcony. The Mediterranean sea sparkled beneath her. The sky was a cloudless blue, the sun already beating down. It could have been a July day in England; even the maid had commented how unusually hot it was for February, even in Menorca.

The villa she and Pip were staying in was superb. Owned by one of the King of Spain's brothers, its whitewashed, turreted outer shell nestled in forty acres of gardens. It was built high up, overlooking the sea. Unless the paparazzi were prepared to scale sixty feet of rock face, or dodge the Rottweilers that patrolled the high walls with their lethal electrified wire on the top, Zoe and Pip had the comfort of knowing they could enjoy each other's company undisturbed.

Zoe sat down in a lounger and gazed into the distance. Pip was still asleep and she had no wish to wake him. The past week had, to all intents and purposes, been blissful. For the first time there was nothing and no one to drag them apart. The world was going on somewhere else, managing to turn without either of them.

Night and day, Pip had sworn undying love to her, promised that he'd let nothing stand in his way. He loved her, he wanted to be with her, and if others would not accept it, then he was prepared to take drastic action.

It was a scenario she'd dreamed of for years. And Zoe could not understand why she didn't feel ecstatic with happiness.

Maybe it was the stress of the past few weeks catching up with her; people often said that their honeymoons were less than perfect, the reality being less than the expectation. Or just maybe Zoe had come to realize that she and Pip hardly knew each other as people on a day-to-day basis. Their brief affair ten years ago had been as teenagers, immature and vulnerable humanbeings still working their way blindly towards adulthood. The past few weeks they'd spent no more than three or four days together, and still fewer nights.

Zoe thought back to yesterday evening, when the friendly Spanish maid had cooked a special and wonderful paella as a surprise. When it was served, Pip had pouted and suggested next time that the maid consult him on the menu before she presented it to them. Apparently, he loathed shellfish of any kind. Zoe had hoovered up the paella and praised the maid fulsomely on her recipe, which had sent Pip into a sulk, and he'd accused her of being 'too friendly' with the staff.

There had been numerous other, small things over the past few days that had irritated rather than angered Zoe. It seemed they both always did what *he* wanted, not that he wouldn't ask her opinion first, but then he would talk her out of the idea and she'd end up agreeing for the sake of a quiet life. She'd also discovered that they had very little in common, which was not surprising, given that their worlds had been so vastly different. For all Pip's fine public school and university education, his broad cultural knowledge and his grasp of politics, he seemed to have little idea of the kind of staples that filled the average person's day.

Zoe sighed. She was sure most of these differences were discovered by every couple who began living together twenty-four hours a day, having only ever been out on dates previously. It would work itself out, settle down and Pip and she could return to the magical romance that they'd shared up to now.

The problem was exacerbated, of course, by the fact they were held captive in the most luxurious prison imaginable. Zoe looked beneath her and thought how much she'd like to leave the house and go for a long walk on the beach alone. But that would entail alerting Dennis, the bodyguard, who would then tail her in the car so that the whole point of going and being solitary for a little while was lost. For some reason, she'd not objected to Simon being around her.

Zoe stood up and leaned her elbows on the balcony, remembering the evening they'd spent together at the house in Kent. The way he'd cared for her, cooked for her, soothed her when she needed comfort. She'd felt like herself then, like Zoe. Comfortable enough to be who she was.

Was she herself with Pip?

Zoe shook her head.

She didn't know.

'Morning, darling.' The voice called her from the bed as she tiptoed across the room to the bathroom.

'Morning,' Zoe replied brightly.

'Come here.' Pip's arms stretched towards her.

Zoe did a U-turn and walked towards the bed. Pip encircled her and kissed her on the lips.

'Another fucking day in paradise,' he joked, tickling her. 'I'm famished. Have you ordered breakfast?'

'No, not yet.'

'Why don't you go see Maria and have her bring us some fresh orange juice, croissants, and some kippers. She said she could have them flown in yesterday and my tastebuds are tingling for them.' Pip rolled Zoe away from him and got out of bed. 'While you do that I'll take a shower. I'll see you on the terrace downstairs.'

'Oh, but Pip, I was going to take a . . .'

'What, darling?'

Zoe looked at him striding across to the bathroom and shrugged. 'Nothing. I'll see you downstairs.'

*

They spent the rest of the morning sunbathing by the pool, Zoe reading a novel, Pip scanning the English newspapers.

'Listen to this, darling. Headline: should the son of a monarch be allowed to marry an unmarried mother?'

'Really, Pip, I don't want to know.'

'Yes you *do*. The newspaper had a phone poll, and twenty-five thousand of their readers called to register their opinion. Eighteen thousand of them said yes. That's over two thirds. I wonder if Mater and Pater have read it.'

'Would it make any difference if they had?'

'Of course. They're terribly sensitive to public opinion, especially at the moment. Look, there's even an archbishop in *The Times* who's come out in support. He's saying single mothers are part of modern society and that if the monarchy is going to last into the new millennium, it has to throw off its shackles and show it can adapt too.'

'I'll bet there's some whinging moralist in the *Telegraph* who's saying it's the duty of public figures to set an example, not use the sloppy sexual behaviour of the general public as a get-out,' returned Zoe.

'Of course there is. But look, darling.' Pip climbed off his chair and knelt beside her. He took her hand in his and kissed it. 'I love you. Jamie is my flesh and blood anyway. From whichever moral standpoint you look at it, our marriage is the right thing to happen—'

'But no one can ever know that, can they, Pip? That's the point.' Zoe climbed off her lounger and leaned over the balcony. 'I just don't know how I'm ever going to tell Jamie about us.'

Pip followed her and put his arms round her shoulders. 'Darling, you've given up the past nine years of your life for Jamie. He was a mistake that—'

Zoe swung round, her eyes blazing. 'Don't you *dare* call Jamie a mistake!'

'I didn't mean it like that, darling, really. All I'm saying is that he's growing up now, forging a life of his own. Surely this is about you and me, and our chance for happiness before it's too late?'

'We're not talking about an adult here, Pip! Nowhere near. Jamie's a nine-year-old boy. And you make it sound like a sacrifice that I brought Jamie up. It wasn't like that at all. He's the centre of my world. I'd do it all over again.'

'I know, I know. I'm sorry. Seem to be getting it all wrong this morning.' Pip sighed. 'Anyway, I've got some good news. I've arranged for a boat to come and collect us this afternoon. We're going to sail over to Majorca and pick up Prince Antonio and his wife in the harbour. Then we're going to sail the high seas for a couple of days. You'll love them, and they're very sympathetic to our predicament.' He stoked her hair. 'Come on darling, cheer up.'

*

Just after lunch, as the maid was packing Zoe's clothes to place on the boat, her mobile telephone rang.

'Hello?' she said tentatively, still scared stiff it might be a journalist that had her number.

'Miss Harrison? It's Dr West, headmaster at your son's school.'

'Hello, Dr West. Is everything all right?'

'No, I'm afraid not. Jamie has gone missing. He disappeared this morning, just after breakfast. We've searched the school and grounds thoroughly and there's no sign of him.'

'Oh God!' Zoe could hear the blood pumping round her body. She sat down before she crumpled to the floor. 'I . . . has he taken anything? Clothes? Money?'

'No clothes, although it was pocket-money day yesterday, so he might well have that. Miss Harrison, I am concerned, under the circumstances, that Jamie may have been abducted.'

Zoe put her hand to her mouth. 'Oh my God, oh God. Have you called the police?'

'Well, that's obviously why I'm calling you. I wanted to ask your permission to do so.'

'Yes, oh yes! Do it immediately. I'll fly home as soon as possible. Please, Dr West, ring me immediately if there's any news.'

'Of course. Try not to panic, Miss Harrison. Under usual circumstances, I'd tell you that this kind of thing is reasonably common; a spat with a friend, a telling off from a master . . . The boy is usually back within a few hours. And it may just be that simple. I'm going to interview all the boys in his class now, see if they can shed any light on his disappearance.'

'Yes, thank you. G . . . goodbye, Dr West.'

Zoe sat, her entire body shaking, small, high-pitched noises emanating from her. 'P . . . P . . . Please G . . . God . . . anything, I'll give anything, just let him be okay, let him be okay.'

'Signorina? Are you all right?'

Maria received no response.

'I go get 'is Royal Highness, okay?'

*

'Darling, whatever is it?'

'Pip.' She looked at him with agonized eyes. 'Jamie. Jamie's gone.'

'Gone where?'

'He's missing fr . . . fr . . . from school. Dr West thinks he might have been abducted!' Zoe slid her palms roughly up and down her face. 'If anything has happened to him because of my selfishness, I . . .'

'Hold on now, Zoe. I want you to calm down and listen to me. All boys run away from school. Even I did it once, sent my detectives into a spin, and . . .'

'Yes, but you had detectives, didn't you?! I asked you if Jamie was going to get some protection but you said it wasn't necessary, now look what's happened!'

'Zoe, listen to me. There is absolutely no reason to suspect foul play. I'm sure Jamie is fine and will arrive back at the school as right as rain in time for supper, so—'

'If there was no reason to suspect foul play then why on earth did you give *me* a bodyguard and not your own *son*? Your own son, who is far more vulnerable than I am. Oh God! Oh God!' Zoe was pounding the bed with her fists hysterically.

'*Zoe!* Will you calm down. You're blowing this all out of proportion.'

'What?! My son goes missing and you accuse me of being overdramatic! Get me on a plane home, *now*, Pip!'

Zoe began throwing things on top of the neatly packed suitcase.

'Now you really are being silly. Sure, if he hasn't turned up by tomorrow morning, then we'll get you home, but for tonight, come on the boat, enjoy supper with Antonio and Magda. They're so looking forward to meeting you. It'll help take your mind off it.'

Zoe threw a shoe at him in frustration. 'Take my mind off it! Jesus Christ! It's my son we're talking about, not some damned family pet that's gone off for a wander! Jamie is missing! I can't float round the Med enjoying myself while my child, my baby' – Zoe gave a huge sob – 'might be in danger.'

Pip's lips pursed together in irritation. 'Zoe, you're going completely over the top. Besides, I doubt we can get you home tonight. You'll have to fly out of Majorca in the morning.'

Zoe was beside herself with fear and anger. 'Yes, you can, Pip. You're a prince, remember? Your wish is everyone else's command. Get a plane, here, now, to take me home, or I'll find one myself!' She was shouting now, past caring what he thought of her.

He put his hands out as he backed away towards the door. 'Okay, okay. I'll see what I can do.'

*

Three hours later, Zoe was standing in the small VIP room at Mahon airport. She was travelling home via private plane to Barcelona, and then from there on a late BA flight to Heathrow.

Pip had not accompanied her to the airport. He had to board the boat to set sail for Majorca. They had said a terse goodbye as Zoe had climbed into the car, kissing each other politely on the cheek.

Zoe fumbled in her handbag for her mobile. It would be the early hours of tomorrow before she stepped on to British soil to search for her son. And in the meantime, there was only one person she could trust completely to help her find him.

Zoe dialled his number, praying he'd answer.

'Hello?'

'Simon? It's Zoe Harrison.'

chapter thirty-one

Joanna sat on the Cork-Dublin express staring at the rivulets of water streaming down the other side of the glass. It had not stopped raining since last night. The pitter-patter of the raindrops had kept her awake, like some kind of hypnotic torture the faint noise of which had grown inside her head to become pounding hailstones. Not that she'd wanted to sleep anyway. She'd been far too uptight, had spent most of the night staring into space, trying to work out where the new information left her.

'*The situation with this gentleman is highly delicate . . .*' What did that mean? What did anything mean at the moment, Joanna thought wearily. She crossed her arms and closed her eyes to see if she could doze away the remaining hours.

'Is this seat taken?'

The voice was male and American. She opened her eyes to see a tall man dressed in a check shirt and jeans.

'No.' She shook her head.

'Great. It's so unusual to find a smoking carriage on a train. We don't have those anymore back home.'

Joanna was faintly surprised that she had sat in a

smokers' carriage. She wouldn't have done normally. But then normally she wasn't as tired or confused.

The man sat down across the table from her and lit up a cigarette. 'Want one?' he asked.

'No thanks. I don't,' she replied, praying this man was not going to keep her talking for the next two hours and forty minutes.

'Want me to stub it out?'

'No, you're fine.'

He took another drag as he studied her. 'You English?'

'Yes.'

'I was there myself before I came over here. I stayed in London. I loved it.'

'Good,' said Joanna abruptly.

'But I just love Ireland. You on holiday here?'

'I suppose so. A working holiday.'

'You a travel writer or something?'

'No, a journalist, actually.'

The man studied the ordnance map on the table in front of Joanna. 'Thinkin' of buying some property?'

'No. I'm just investigating the history of a house I'm interested in.'

'Family connections?'

'Yes,' she agreed, thinking it was the simplest option.

The tea trolley was beginning its progress through the carriage.

'Jeez, I'm starving. Must be all this good ol' fresh air. I'll take a coffee, and one of those pastries, ma'am, and a packet of tuna sandwiches. Want anything . . . er . . .?'

'Joanna, Joanna Haslam. I'll take a coffee, please,' she said to the young girl in charge of the trolley. She reached into her rucksack to take out her purse, but the man waved it away.

'Hey, I can just about run to a cup of coffee.' He presented it to her and smiled. 'Kurt Hoffman. No relation to Dustin, ma'am, before you ask.'

'Thanks for the coffee, Kurt.' She nodded.

'No problem.' He unwrapped the plastic from his pastry and took a large bite. 'So, you think you got some heritage over here in Ireland?'

'Possibly, yes.' Joanna sat up, realizing she could forget about dozing for as long as Kurt was on the train.

'Me too. Down in a li'l ol' village on the coast in West Cork. It seems my great-great-great-great-grand-father hailed from Clonakilty.'

'That's the next town to where I've been staying, in Rosscarbery.'

'Really?' Kurt's face lit up like a child's, happy with the relatively small coincidence. 'I was only there the day before yesterday, in that great cathedral. I had the best pint of stout I've had so far afterwards in that hotel in town—'

'The Ross? That's where I'm staying.'

'So, you off to Dublin?'

'Yes.'

'Been before?'

'No. I have some business to do, some more research, then I thought I'd take a potter around the city. Have you been before?'

'No, ma'am, my first time too.' He eyed her. 'Maybe we should join forces.'

'No. I've got to go to the Land Registry. It might take hours to find out what I need to know.'

'Is that where they keep title deeds to homesteads?' enquired Kurt, tucking in with relish to a tuna sandwich.

'Yes.'

'You tryin' to find out whether you have an inheritance?'

'Sort of. There's a house in Rosscarbery. No one seems to know who owns it.'

'It is a bit more casual here than at home. I mean,' Kurt rolled his eyes, 'no one has alarms on their cars, or locks their front doors. I was in a restaurant in town yesterday when the owner said she had to go off on business and would I put my plate in the sink and shut the door behind me! It sure is a different way of life. So,' Kurt indicated the map, 'show me the house.'

Despite her initial misgivings, the journey to Dublin passed pleasantly enough. Kurt was good company and entertained her with stories about his native Chicago. As the train pulled in to Heuston Station, Kurt pulled out a small notebook and a gold pen from his pocket.

'Give me your number in Rosscarbery. Maybe we could get together for a drink.'

Joanna pulled out a box of matches with the number of her hotel on it. He stood up and pulled on his jacket. 'Well, it sure has whiled away a journey talkin' to you, Miss Haslam. When do you travel back to West Cork?'

'Oh, either later tonight or tomorrow. I'm leaving it flexible.' She held out her hand as the train came to a halt. 'Good to meet you, Kurt.'

'And you, Joanna. Maybe see you again soon.'

'Maybe. Goodbye.' She smiled at him, stood up and followed the other passengers out of the train.

*

After a lot of form-filling, Joanna went up to the desk and was handed a file.

'There's a free desk over there if you want to study the deeds,' said the young girl.

'Thanks.' Joanna made her way towards the desk and sat down. Disappointment filled her when she saw that the coastguard's house had been handed over from HM government on 27th June 1928 'to become the property of the Free State of Ireland'. Taking a photocopy of the deeds and the plans, Joanna handed the file back, thanked the girl and left the Land Registry Office.

Outside it was pouring with rain. Feeling deflated, Joanna walked until she reached Grafton Street, and the myriad of small lanes off it with enticing-looking pubs. Choosing the nearest, she went inside and ordered a glass of Guinness, wanting to compare it with Murphy's. She took off her jacket, which, although waterproof, seemed to belie its name, and brushed a hand through her damp hair.

'Fine, soft day out, isn't it?' said the barman.

'Does it ever stop raining here?' she asked.

'Not often, no,' said the barman without irony. 'And they all wonder why so many of us end up alcoholics.'

Joanna was just about to order a cheese bap, when a figure she recognized hurried through the door.

He looked at her in delight. 'Jo! Hi there.'

Kurt came to sit next to her at the bar, the water on his jacket making a puddle on the floor below him. 'I'll have a Guinness please, and another for the lady.' He indicated to the barman.

Joanna was still gazing at him in disbelief.

'Hey, it's not really so weird. You are in one of the most famous pubs in Dublin. McDaid's is on every tourist's "must go" list.'

'Really? I didn't notice the name. I ran in here to get out of the wet.'

'So, how did your research go?'

'Nowhere.' She sighed, reaching for her Guinness.

'Yeah well, I've had a morning pretty like that. It's so darned wet out there you need a set of windscreen wipers to see anything. I've decided to give up, spend the evening drinking and the night in the lap of luxury. I booked myself a room at the Shelbourne, supposedly the best hotel in town.'

'I'll have a cheese bap, please.' Joanna indicated to the barman. 'Well, I think I'm going to go and find myself a bed for the night in town. I'm too exhausted to face the train back, plus the drive at the other end.'

'Say, why don't you come have dinner with me tonight at the Shelbourne. My treat, to cheer you up.'

'Thanks for the offer, but . . .'

Kurt held up his hands. 'Ma'am, I swear, no funny business. Just strikes me you're alone, I'm alone and maybe we'd enjoy the night better if we kept each other company.'

'Kurt, I've come as I am. I doubt they'll let me in in jeans to dine at the Shelbourne.'

'If they won't, we'll go elsewhere. Please, Jo. I sure enjoyed your company on the train this morning.' Kurt's earnest face begged her to acquiesce.

'Oh, all right then,' smiled Joanna, realizing any diversion from her own thoughts was a positive one.

'Great.' Kurt finished his pint. 'I gotta few things to do, like write some postcards back home, let Mom know I'm still alive. I'm thirty years of age and she still treats me like a kid. I'll see you at the Shelbourne at eight? Would that suit?'

'Yes.'

'See you then. Bye, Jo.' Kurt climbed down from his stool and left the bar.

'Sure, your young man there must be worth a bob or two. That Shelbourne's the kinda place where they put a cocktail cherry in yer Guinness,' the barman commented as he put a rather dry-looking cheese bap in front of her. 'I'd say some folk have all the luck, wouldn't you?'

*

'Sign there,' Margaret indicated to the young man.

'Thanks.' He looked up at her. 'By any chance, has a young Englishwoman called Joanna Haslam crossed your path in the last few days?'

'And who'd be wanting to know?'

'Oh, I'm her boyfriend.' He smiled.

'Well, yes, there has been a girl by that name staying here. She's gone today though. Back tonight or tomorrow.'

'Great. I don't want her to know I'm here. It's her . . . birthday tomorrow and I thought I'd surprise her.' He put a finger to his lips. 'Mum's the word, eh?'

'Sure, Mum's the word, so.'

Margaret handed the young man his key and watched as he went upstairs. Oh to be young again, she thought fondly, before going back to the cellar to change the barrel.

chapter thirty-two

'Hello, Zoe.' Simon had been so startled by her voice that he had to pull over and park, which had proved very difficult on the Hammersmith flyover. 'Where are you?'

'At Mahon airport. Oh Simon.'

He heard her choke back a sob.

'What is it? What's the matter?'

'It's Jamie. He's gone missing. He might have been kidnapped or abducted. God, Simon, he might be dead. I—'

'Hold on a minute, Zoe. Tell me calmly and carefully what's happened.'

She did her best to do so.

'Has the headmaster called the police?'

'Yes. But Pip wants it to be as low-key as possible. He says he doesn't want the media involved unless absolutely necessary, because of—'

'Putting him, you and Jamie back in the spotlight,' Simon finished for her. 'Well he might have to suffer it. At the end of the day, it's more important that Jamie is found and members of the public being alerted to a missing child can always be helpful.'

'I know, Simon, but what can I do? How did Jamie seem when you went to see him?'

'A little quiet, admittedly, but okay.'

'He didn't say he was worried about anything to you, did he?'

'No, but I got the feeling that maybe he was, which also tells me Jamie is probably all right. Maybe he just needed some time alone. He's a sensible kid, Zoe. Try and keep calm.'

'Simon, I'm not going to be back for hours. Would you do me a favour?'

'What?'

'Would you go to the house in London? You still have the key, don't you? If he's not there, try Kent. The key's under the water barrel round the back to the left-hand side.'

'Surely the police—'

'Simon, he knows you. He trusts you. *Please*. I . . .' Zoe's voice disappeared.

'Zoe? Zoe? Are you there?'

Simon knew he was talking to thin air.

'Fuck!' He hit the steering wheel with his fists. He was on his way to Heathrow airport, and Joanna, across the sea in Cork. Someone else who didn't realize she was vulnerable, someone who needed him too. Besides, it was his job. Where did his loyalty lie?

Practically, there was no contest. It lay with his oldest friend, and his allegiance to the government he served. Emotionally, with a woman who was so very publicly involved with another man and a child whom he'd known for no more than a few weeks. Simon agonized for a couple of minutes, then indicated out into the flow of traffic. As soon as he could safely do so, Simon swung his car round and headed back for central London.

*

Joanna looked up at the high ceiling of the bedroom. She'd half known that it would happen as soon as she'd walked into the restaurant. Although not a handsome man, Kurt had looked so safe in his jacket and tie; so solid and apple-pie wholesome. She turned a little and saw he was asleep beside her, breathing steadily. Naked, he was much thinner than she'd imagined him to be, with a short torso in contrast to his long legs.

The sex had been pleasant, that was all. A small price to pay for a night next to a warm human being. It was the first one-night stand she'd ever had in her life. Two months ago, she'd never have believed she could have done it. But life was different, *she* was different. Joanna reached for the light and switched it off, begging for a dreamless, restful sleep.

*

The London house was in blackness, and there seemed to be no sign of anyone outside. Simon had half expected the media still to be there, waiting for a spectre that had long since left. He turned the key in the lock, then switched on the light. He checked all the rooms downstairs, knowing from his trained instincts the search was fruitless. The house *felt* empty.

Simon climbed the stairs, checked in Zoe's room, then Jamie's. He sat down on Jamie's bed, staring round the room, its mixture of teddies and remote-control cars a testament to the betwixt-and-between age Jamie was at. His walls were covered with a variety of nursery prints; on the back of the door hung a Power Rangers poster. Simon sat staring into space, staring blankly at a small but intricate sampler which hung above Jamie's bed.

'Where are you, old chap?' he asked the air. Receiving no reply, Simon sighed and wandered out of the room to investigate the top floor of the house.

Closing the front door behind him, Simon was aware of a Panda car drawing up in front of the house.

'Sir, are you a resident of this establishment?' enquired the detective.

'No.' Simon wearily produced his identification.

'Right, Mr Warburton. I presume you're looking for the young man who's done a bunk, are you?'

'Yes.'

'All got to be kept hush-hush for now, apparently. Them up high don't want his disappearance getting to the newspapers, because of his mum and her ... boyfriend.'

'Quite.' Simon nodded. 'Well, I've checked the house and he's not there. Are you going to stay here, just in case he should make an appearance?'

The man shook his head. 'No, I've been asked to check the place, that's all, but I can leave someone here.'

'I think it would be advisable. It's likely, if he's free to do so, he'll head for home.'

*

An hour and a half later, Simon pulled up in front of the oast house. He checked his watch. It was just after eleven. He retrieved his torch from the glovebox, climbed out of the car and set off in search of the water barrel and its hidden key. Finding it with a shiver of disappointment, he trudged round to the front of the house and opened the heavy front door.

Switching on the lights, Simon went from room to room, seeing the pans still sat on the drainer from the supper he'd cooked Zoe, her bed upstairs still unmade from the morning they'd left so early.

Nothing. The house was empty.

Simon went back downstairs and called the detective to find out if Jamie had returned to Welbeck Street. He hadn't. Informing him that Jamie had obviously not set foot down in Kent either, Simon went into the kitchen and switched on the kettle to make himself a cup of black coffee. He sat down at the table and rubbed his hands harshly through his hair, trying to think. If Jamie hadn't made an appearance by tomorrow morning, then the Palace be damned. They'd have to go public on this. He stood up and spooned some powdered coffee into a mug and added boiling water, playing over and over in his head the conversation he'd had with the boy last Sunday.

After his third mug of coffee, which made him feel liverish and slightly sick, Simon stood up and prowled round the house once more. He turned on the floodlights outside and opened the kitchen door to the back garden. The garden was large and well stocked, although its seasonal condition was that of a sketch waiting to be painted. Simon disconsolately shone his torch into the hedge which fringed the garden. In one corner of the house, presumably positioned to catch the best of the sun, was a small pergola. Inside it, a bench made of stone. Simon sat on it. The pergola was covered in some kind of creeping plant – Simon leaned forward and gave a small cry when a vicious thorn pricked his finger.

Roses, he thought. How beautiful this would look in the height of summer.

Roses . . .

'*Great-James always loved roses . . .*'

Simon jumped up and ran to the back door to make a phone call.

*

The cemetery was only a quarter of a mile down the road from the oast house, behind the church. Simon parked his car outside the iron gate. Discovering it was padlocked, he swung himself over the top of it and began to walk through the graves, shining a light on each name. Despite himself, Simon shuddered. A half-moon appeared from behind a cloud, bathing the cemetery in a ghostly, silvery light. The church clock struck midnight, the bell clanging slowly and mournfully, as if in remembrance to the dead souls that lay all around his feet.

Finally, Simon reached the seventies and then the eighties. Right at the back of the cemetery, Simon espied a gravestone that had 1991 chiselled into it. Very slowly, he walked past the headstones, watching the dates become more and more recent. He was almost at the edge of the cemetery now, only one last grave remaining. Set by itself, with a small bush planted below the headstone.

SIR JAMES HARRISON,

ACTOR.

1901–1995

'Goodnight, sweet prince,
and flights of angels sing
thee to thy rest.'

And there, lying huddled on top of the grave, was Jamie.

Simon approached the boy silently. He could tell from the way Jamie was breathing that he was fast asleep. He knelt down next to him and angled the torch so he could see the boy's face, yet at the same time not disturb him. Apart from smudges of mud on his cheek and forehead, Jamie seemed unharmed. Simon felt for his hand. It was cold, but not danger-ously so. Simon stroked his blonde hair gently.

'Mumma . . .?' Jamie stirred. Simon continued to stroke his hair.

'No, it's Simon, and you're perfectly well and perfectly safe, old chap.'

Jamie shot up from his prone position, his eyes wide and terrified.

'What . . .? Where am I?' He looked around him, then began to shiver.

Instinctively Simon pulled the boy to him, cradling him in his arms.

'Jamie, you're fine. Simon's here. Now, I'm going to pick you up, put you in my car and drive you down the road to home. We're going to make a big fire in the sitting room and, over a hot cup of tea, you can tell me what happened. Okay?'

Jamie looked up at him, his eyes at first fearful, then trusting. 'Okay.'

When they reached the house, Simon found an eiderdown from Zoe's bed and tucked the shivering boy on to the sofa. He lit a fire as Jamie stared silently into the distance. Having made a cup of tea for both of them and alerted the London detective to Jamie's safe return, Simon sat down at the other end of the sofa.

'Drink it, Jamie. It'll warm you up.'

The boy sipped at the hot liquid, his small hands clasped round the mug. 'Are you cross with me?'

'No, of course not. Worried that you were okay, yes, but not cross.'

'Mumma will be furious when she finds out.'

'She already knows you've disappeared. She's on her way home, should be landing at any minute. I'm sure she'll ring when she lands at Heathrow and you can speak to her and let her know you're safe.'

Jamie sipped some more tea. 'She wasn't filming in Spain, was she?' he said slowly. 'She was with him, wasn't she?'

'Him?'

'Her boyfriend, the Prince. Prince George.'

'Yes.' Simon studied the boy. 'How did you know?'

'One of the older boys put a photo from a newspaper in my locker.'

Simon sighed. 'I see.'

'Then Dickie Sisman, who's always hated me

because I made the first eleven and he didn't, kept calling Mu . . . Mumma a prince's wh . . . whore.'

Simon winced, but said nothing, just waited silently.

'Then he asked who my father w . . . was. I said Great-James, and Dickie and the others laughed at me, said he couldn't be my dad because he was my great-grandfather and I was stupid. I knew that he wasn't my father really, b . . . bu . . . but he *was*, Simon, in every other way. Great-James was my dad and now he's g . . . gone.'

Simon watched Jamie's shoulders heave with sobs. He shook his head and wiped a hand across his face. 'He said he'd never leave me, that he'd always be there when I needed him, that all I had to do was call and he'd answer, b . . . but he didn't, be . . . because he's dead!' Jamie cried as if his heart might break. Simon gently took the tea mug from his small hands, then pulled Jamie into his arms.

'I . . . did . . . didn't think he'd gone, not really. I me . . . mean I knew he wasn't there in person, he'd said he wouldn't be, but he'd always be somewhere, but when I needed him he was nowhere!'

More pitiful sobs emanated from Jamie's chest. 'And then Mumma was gone too. And there was nobody. I couldn't stand it at school anymore. I had to just get out, so I we . . . went to Great-James.'

'I thought you might,' said Simon quietly.

'Bu . . . but . . . worst of all, Mumma lied to me!'

'Not on purpose, Jamie. She did it to protect you.'

'She's always told me everything before. We didn't have secrets. If I'd have known, then I could have defended myself when the boys were so horrid to me.'

'Well, sometimes adults misjudge situations. I think that's what has happened with your mother.'

'No.' He shook his head wearily. 'It's because I'm not number one anymore. Prince George is. She loves him more than she loves me.'

'Oh Jamie. That could not be further from the truth. Your mother adores you. Believe me, she was frantic when she heard the news. She moved heaven and earth to get on a plane and come back to find you.'

'Did she?' Jamie wiped his nose morosely. 'Simon?'

'Yes?'

'Will I have to move into the Palace?'

'I don't know, Jamie. I think that kind of decision is a long way off.'

'I heard one of the masters laughing in his study with the games teacher. He said that it wouldn't be the first time a bastard has moved into the p . . . Palace.'

Simon cursed the cruelty of human nature under his breath. 'Jamie, your mum is going to be in England very soon. I happen to know that you are the most important thing in her life. I want you to promise me you'll tell her everything you've told me, so there'll be no misunderstandings in future.'

Jamie looked up at him. 'Have you met the Prince?'

'Yes.'

'What's he like?'

'Nice. He's a nice man. You'll like him, I'm sure.'

Jamie shrugged. 'I don't think I will. Do princes play football?'

Simon laughed. 'Yes.'

'And eat pizza and baked beans?'

'I'm sure they do.'

'Will Mumma marry him, Simon?'

He kissed the top of Jamie's head. 'I think that is something only your mother can tell you.'

His mobile rang in his pocket. 'Hello? Yes, he's safe and absolutely fine. We're down in Kent. Want a word?'

Simon passed the phone to Jamie. 'Mumma? . . . I know, I'm sorry . . . Yes, see you in a while. Bye.'

A little colour was returning to Jamie's cheeks. 'Will she be very angry with me?'

'Did she sound angry?'

'No,' Jamie admitted. 'She sounded very happy.'

'There you go then.'

Jamie snuggled down on to Simon's knee and yawned. 'Wish you were the Prince, Simon,' he said drowsily.

So do I, he thought, but did not say.

Jamie lifted his head and smiled at Simon. 'Thanks for knowing where to look.'

'Anytime, old chap, anytime.'

*

Zoe paid the taxi-driver and opened the front door. All was silent. She went first to the kitchen, then into the sitting room. Jamie was curled up with his head on Simon's knee, fast asleep. Simon was resting against the back of the sofa, his eyes closed too. Tears came to her eyes at the sight of her son, obviously unscarred by his escapade. And Simon, who had so generously helped when it seemed no one else would.

Simon opened his eyes and saw her. Very carefully, he extracted himself from beneath Jamie, substituting a cushion for his lap and indicating they should leave the room.

They walked silently into the kitchen. Simon closed the door behind him.

'Is he okay? Really?'

'He is absolutely fine.'

Zoe sat down in a chair and put her head in her hands. 'Thank God, thank God. You can't imagine what was going through my mind on that interminable flight.'

'No.' Simon walked to the kettle. 'Tea?'

'No, a brandy, I think. There's some in the cupboard over there. Where did you find him?'

'Asleep on your grandfather's grave.'

Zoe clapped a hand to her mouth. 'Oh Simon! I . . .'

'Don't blame yourself, Zoe, really. I think what happened to Jamie was an unfortunate combination of some unkind but natural teasing at school, delayed grief and . . .'

'The fact that I wasn't there either.'

'Yes. There you go.' He put the brandy in front of her.

'So he knows about Pip from the other boys?'

'I'm afraid so.'

'Dammit! I should have told him. Why do adults always underestimate children?'

'We all make mistakes, but this is something that can easily be rectified.'

Zoe took a sip of her brandy. 'I knew he was too calm after James died. I should have seen it coming.'

'Well, I think it hit Jamie yesterday for the first

time that the man he adored, his father figure, really had gone for good. But he's a child, he'll cope. Besides, it may well be that he'll be replaced by someone else.' Simon looked at her questioningly.

'Yes.' Zoe rubbed a hand up and down her brow.

'Look, now you're here, I'm afraid I have to go.'

Zoe looked startled. 'Where?'

'Duty calls.' Simon tiptoed back into the sitting room to collect his jacket. 'Jamie's still sleeping soundly. I think a dollop of TLC from his beloved mum is the only medicine he needs.'

'Yes. Boy, have we got some talking to do.' Zoe followed him to the front door. 'Simon, how can I ever thank you?'

'Really, don't worry about it.' He shrugged. 'Take care of both of you, and send my love to Jamie, say I'm sorry I had to leave before I said goodbye.'

'Of course.' Zoe nodded wistfully. 'Simon?'

He turned and looked at her. 'Yes?'

She paused, then shook her head. 'Nothing. Bye.'

'Goodbye, Zoe.'

chapter thirty-three

Joanna pulled her Fiesta into the kerb and switched off the engine. She sat there, staring out at the rain pelting down on the picturesque square. She not only felt exhausted, but rather ashamed of her sluttish behaviour last night. She had no problem with women exercising their right to sexual liberation, no big moral dilemma with the actual *act* itself. The point was, it was just not the way *she* did things. Which only served to underline how screwed up emotionally she obviously was, how the control she'd always had over her actions seemed to have vanished. Undermined by a set of circumstances that had been sparked by a coincidental meeting, which had somehow managed to impinge on every area of her life.

The Joanna of last year would have enjoyed Kurt's company, acknowledged he was an attractive and likeable man, but after dinner taken herself off home to the bed and breakfast accommodation she had found herself in Ballsbridge. Instead of which Joanna had woken up in the luxurious hotel room and shared a good Irish breakfast with him.

'Last night was real special. I'll be coming back down to Clonakilty later today. Can we meet up?' he'd asked as she'd stood by the door, ready to leave.

'I'm sure we can.' Joanna had nodded, kissed him goodbye and shot off to collect her holdall from the bed and breakfast. On the train home, Joanna had decided she did not intend to be there when Kurt arrived back down in West Cork.

Enough was enough. She was going home, consigning the past two months to a strange, dreamlike phase in her life and forgetting about all of it. She decided that she would post all the information she had gathered to Simon. It was obvious now that he pursued a much more high-flying and glamorous career than she'd previously thought. She'd guessed he worked for the British intelligence services, which would suit his quick-witted, clever brain. She also reckoned he'd been planted in Zoe Harrison's house to discover the whereabouts of the letter. Well, he could have everything she had. And that was an end to it.

Joanna opened the door to the car, retrieved her holdall from the boot and walked into the front entrance of the hotel.

'Hello there. Did you have a good trip?' enquired Margaret, appearing behind the bar.

'Yes. It was pleasant, thanks.'

'Grand.'

'I'm going to check out, Margaret, fly back to England if I can get a seat on a flight this evening from Cork.'

'Right then.' One of Margaret's eyebrows raised slightly. 'Someone brought an envelope for you while you were away.' She turned and stuck her hand into Joanna's pigeonhole. 'There.'

'Thanks,' Joanna answered as Margaret handed her the white envelope.

''Twill be a birthday card, no doubt?'

'No, my birthday's not until August. Thanks anyway.'

Margaret watched her mount the stairs. She thought for a moment, then placed a call to Sean at the local Garda station. 'You know you were after asking me about that young man, the one who checked in yesterday, Sean? Well, maybe he's not who he seems after all. He's gone out, said he'd be away until sixish. I think you'd better, so. Grand.'

*

Joanna unlocked the door to her room, put down her holdall and tore open the letter. She skimmed through the couple of lines once, then sank on to the bed. It took her some time to decipher the terrible spelling and pidgin English.

Deer miss,
   I hurd in bar you talk abut costgard house. I no about it you talk to me will sea troot. Pink cotag is wear I will bee.
   miss ciara deasy

Ciara . . . The name rang a bell. Joanna surfed her memory bank to try to remember who it was that had spoken the name. It had been Jim Mulcahy, the schoolteacher. Joanna shook her head. She seemed to recall he'd said Ciara was mad. Besides, what was the point in going? It would only lead to another wild-goose chase, half-remembered facts that had little bearing on a situation which Joanna had labelled as 'filed'.

Look at the trouble half-crazy little old ladies had got her into in the first place.

No.

Joanna firmly screwed the letter up into a ball and tossed it into the wastepaper basket. She picked up the telephone, dialled 9 for an outside line and spoke to Aer Lingus reservations. They could get her a seat on the half past seven plane out of Cork. Joanna paid by Barclaycard and began to put all her things into her holdall. Then she picked up the telephone again and dialled Tom at the newspaper.

'It's me.'

'Fuck, Joanna! I thought you might have called me before now.'

'Sorry. Time disappears here without you realizing it.'

'Yeah, well, the Ed's haunted me every day, wanting to know where you were calling from, where the doctor's certificate has got to. He sent someone round to your flat and they know you've not been there. I did my best, but he told me to tell you if you did call that you're fired.'

Joanna sank on to the bed, a lump in her throat. 'Oh God, Tom!'

'Sorry, sweetheart. I don't know whether he's being leaned on to discover your whereabouts, but that's how it is.'

Joanna sat there silently, willing the tears back inside her eye sockets.

'Jo, you still there?'

'Yes. I'd just decided to give up on the whole bloody mess. I'm flying back to London tonight. If I come and see the Ed tomorrow, prostrate myself at his feet, apologize profusely for my tardiness and offer to make the tea for free until he forgives me, do you think I stand a chance?'

'Nope.'

'No, I didn't think so.' Joanna stared miserably at the old patterned paper adorning the walls.

'So, from what you're saying, you've found out nothing?'

'Virtually nothing. Only that a Michael James O'Connell was born five miles down the coast from here, and possibly spent his early years working for the great-grandfather of someone I spoke to. Oh, and an old letter from a British official, confirming that a gentleman shipped over to the house James mentioned to his grandson to stay as a guest of His Majesty's government in 1926.'

'Who?'

'I dunno.'

'Don't you think you should find out?'

'No, I don't. I'm in over my head. I want,' Joanna bit her lip, 'I want to come back home and have my life back like it was before.'

'Well, seeing as that's an impossibility, have you anything to lose by investigating further?'

'I can't hack it, Tom, I really can't.'

'Come on, Jo. As I see it, the only way you can relaunch your career is by getting a cracking story and flogging it to the highest bidder. You now have no allegiance to this newspaper. And if others won't publish here, they'll publish abroad. I have a feeling you're very close to some answers. Don't fall at the final hurdle, Jo.'

'What "answers"? None of it makes sense anyway.' She shrugged.

'Someone will know. They always do. But watch your back. It won't be long before they track you down.'

'I'm going, Tom. I'll call you when I get back to London.'

'Okay, Jo. Make sure you do. Take care now.'

*

'You off, so?'

'Yes.' Joanna handed Margaret her credit card. 'Thanks for making my stay so pleasant.'

'Not at all. Hope you'll be back to see us again soon.'

Joanna signed the slip Margaret handed her.

'There you go. Bye, Margaret and thanks.' She picked up her holdall and walked to the door.

'Joanna, you weren't expecting anyone to come visit you here, were you?'

'Why? Did somebody call me?'

'No.' Margaret shook her head. 'I was just thinking about the card, that's all. Safe journey home, mind yourself.'

'I will.'

Joanna stowed the holdall in the boot of the Fiesta, sat behind the wheel and turned the engine on. She drove out of the square and down towards the estuary. As she indicated left and waited for a car to pass, she noticed the small, single-storey pink cottage, situated on its own on the opposite side of the estuary to the coastguard's house. The two dwellings were no more than fifty yards apart across the sandbanks.

Joanna hesitated for a moment, shook her head in resignation, then indicated right. The car that had been behind her also changed direction and followed some distance behind as the Fiesta drove down the narrow road along the side of the estuary.

*

'Come in.'

The door was ajar. Joanna hadn't even announced her presence. She did as she'd been bid. The small room was rustic, reminiscent of another, much earlier era. A healthy fire burned in the large grate, a black kettle hung above it on a chain. The sparse furniture was wooden and shabby, the only adornments on the walls were a large crucifix and a yellowing print of the Madonna and child.

Ciara Deasy was sitting in a wooden chair on one side of the fire. She was of indeterminate age; anywhere between sixty and eighty, guessed Joanna. Her white hair was cut into a savage short back and sides, her green eyes twinkled and as she stood to greet Joanna, her legs did not betray a whisper of unsteadiness.

'The lady from the hotel?' Ciara shook Joanna's hand firmly.

'Joanna Haslam,' she confirmed.

'Sit down,' Ciara ordered imperiously, indicating an identical wooden chair to her own on the other side of the fireplace.

'Now, tell me, why would ye be wanting to know about coastguard's house?'

'Miss Deasy, it's a long story.'

'They're my favourite kind. And call me Ciara, now, will you? "Miss Deasy" makes me sound like an old maid. Which of course I am, there's no denying it.'

'Well, to cut a long story short, I'm a journalist and I'm here investigating someone called Michael O'Connell. It just might be that when he returned to England, he was known as someone completely different.'

Ciara looked at Joanna. 'I knew he went by the name of Michael, but I never knew his second name. But aye, you're not wrong about him changing his name.' She nodded.

'You knew he used a different identity?'

'Joanna, I've known since I was eight years old. Sixty-nine years is a long time to be called a liar, an inventor of fairy stories. The village has thought I'm stone mad since, but of course I wasn't. Never have been, so. I'm as sane as you.'

'And do you by any chance know if he has any association with the coastguard's house?'

'He stayed there, while he was sick. They wanted him hidden away 'til he was better.' Ciara nodded.

'You met him?'

'I wouldn't say I was formally introduced, no, but I went there to the house often with Niamh, God rest her soul.' The old woman crossed herself.

'Niamh?'

'My sister. Beautiful, she was, so beautiful, with her

long dark hair . . .' Ciara stared off into the distance. 'Any man would have fallen for her, and he did.'

'Michael?'

'That's the name he used, yes, but we know different, don't we?'

'Yes, yes we do. Ciara, why don't you tell me the story from the very beginning?'

'I'll try, so, I will. 'Tis a long time since I've spoken these words.'

*

Joanna listened as the woman spoke lyrically of her beautiful older sister, and the money she was offered by Stanley Bentinck, Emily Bentinck's great-grandfather, to keep house for the stranger who had come to live on the other side of the estuary.

'Of course, I was only a girleen at the time, not old enough to understand what was happening between them. I caught them once, in the kitchen, embracing, but I knew nothing of love, or physical matters at that age. Then he went, disappeared that night out to sea, before they came to get him—'

'They?' interrupted Joanna.

'Them as was after him. She'd warned him, see, even though she knew she'd lose him, that he'd have to go for the sake of his life. But she was convinced he'd send for her when he got back to London. Looking back now, there was no hope, but she didn't know that.'

'Who was it that was after him, Ciara?' Joanna asked again.

'I'll be telling you when I've finished. After he'd gone, Niamh and my daddy had a fierce fight. She was screaming mad, he was shouting back at her. Then, the next morning, she disappeared too.'

'I see. Do you know where she went?'

'I don't. Not for the next few months, anyway. Some from the village said they'd seen her with the gypsies up at the Ballybunnion Fair, others that she'd been spotted in Bandon.'

'Why did she leave?'

'Now, Joanna, you'll stop asking questions and you'll hear the answers. About six months after she'd disappeared, Mammy and Daddy had gone to Mass with my sisters, but I'd stayed home, having a bad cold. Mammy didn't want me to cough all through the preaching. 'Twas as I lay in bed I heard the noise. A terrible noise it was, like an animal in its final death throes. I went to that front door' – Ciara indicated it with her hand – 'in my nightshirt, and listened. And I knew it was coming from the house. So I walked across the sandbanks, the tide was after being out, with that awful sound ringing in my ears.'

'Weren't you frightened?'

'Terrified altogether, but it was as if I was drawn to it, like my body was not my own.' Ciara looked across the bay. 'The front door was open. I went inside and found her upstairs, lying on his bed, her legs covered with blood . . .' Ciara covered her face with her small hands. 'I can still see her face now, clear as day. The agony on it has haunted me for the whole of my life.'

Cold fingers were walking up Joanna's spine. 'It was your sister, Niamh?'

'Yes. And lying between her legs, still attached to her, was a newborn baby.'

Joanna swallowed and stared at Ciara silently while she composed herself.

'I . . . I thought 'twas dead, for it was blue and it didn't cry. I picked it up and used my teeth to cut the cord, like I'd seen Daddy do with the animals. I wrapped it in my arms, trying to give it what little warmth my body afforded and it gave a small whimper.'

There were tears in Joanna's eyes. 'It was alive?'

'Yes, just. So I moved up to Niamh, who had stopped screaming by now. She was lying still, her eyes closed, and I could see the blood still seeping out of her. I tried to stir her, to hand her baby to her, but she didn't move.' Ciara's eyes were wide and haunted, her mind having crossed the years, reliving the dreadful scene with little lessening of the pain.

'So I sat on the bed, nursing the babe, trying to wake my sister. Finally, her eyes did open. I said to her, "Niamh, you have a babe. Will you hold it?" She could hardly shake her head, she was so weak, but she beckoned me to come to her, put my ear to her mouth so she could whisper.'

'What did she say?'

'That there was a letter, in her skirt pocket, for the baby's daddy in London. That the baby should go to him.' Tears were dripping down Ciara's cheeks now. She wiped them harshly away. 'Then she raised her head a little, kissed the babe on its brow, gave a sigh and spoke no more.'

Joanna watched as Ciara tried to compose herself. She reached for a tissue and blew her nose hard.

'How terrible for you to witness that so young,' Joanna whispered. 'What did you do?'

'I wrapped the babe in a covering from the bed. It was wet from blood but better than nothing. Then I reached in Niamh's pocket and took out the letter. I knew I must run for the doctor with the babe and, not having a pocket in my nightshirt and in fear of losing it, I took up a floorboard and stowed the letter away beneath it to collect later. I stood up and crossed Niamh's hands over her breast, like I'd seen the undertaker doing for my granny. Then I gathered up the babe and ran for help.'

The two women both turned in unison to stare out of the small window, at the house across the bay: the house that had inextricably affected them both, haunting their dreams and changing their lives.

'What happened to the baby?' asked Joanna slowly.

'Well now, this is where I become confused. I'm told they found me, standing in the middle of the estuary, screaming that Niamh was dead in the house. Joanna, I was a sick girl after that for many months. Stanley Bentinck paid to have me taken above to hospital in Cork. I had pneumonia and my mind was wandering so much that they put me in the madhouse once I was better. Mammy and Daddy told me all I'd seen had been a dream, brought on by the fever, that Niamh had not come back, that there'd been no baby.' Ciara shrugged. 'I tried for weeks telling them that she was still dead in the house and asking after the babe and was he all right, but the more I talked about it, the more they shook their heads and left me in that terrible place for another month.'

Joanna clapped a hand to her mouth. 'How could they? They must have taken the baby out of your arms.'

'Yes. I knew what I'd seen was real, but I was beginning to know that if I continued, I'd be spending the rest of my life with the other mad people. So, the next time Daddy came up to see me, I pretended I was out of my fit, that I'd never seen anything, that the fever had made me hallucinate.' Ciara gave a wry smile. 'He brought me back home that very day. Of course, from that moment on, everyone in town saw me as stone mad. The other children would laugh at me, call me names.' She shrugged. 'I got used to it, played their game and frightened them with strange talk to get my own back.'

'And what you saw was never mentioned again by your parents?'

'Never. You know what I did, though, Joanna, don't you?'

'You went back to the house to check whether the letter was still there?'

'I did, I did. I had to know I was right and they were wrong.'

'And was it there?'

'Yes.'

'Did you read the letter?'

'Not then. I couldn't, I didn't know how. But later, when I'd learned, I did, most definitely.'

She took a deep breath. 'Ciara, what did the letter say?'

Ciara stared off into space. 'I might be telling you that in a while. Listen to me, I haven't finished.'

Joanna stared at her. Was the woman telling the

truth? Or was she, as the other inhabitants of the town seemed to think, as mad as a hatter?

' 'Twas a good few years until it all made sense. I was eighteen when I discovered why. Why they'd kept it quiet, why 'twas something so important they'd been prepared to lock their daughter away and call her mental for saying what she'd seen . . .'

'Go on,' urged Joanna.

'I was in Cork city, buying some linen for new sheets with Mammy. And I saw a newspaper, the *Irish Times*. There was a face on the front I knew.'

'Who was it?'

Ciara Deasy told her.

chapter thirty-four

He climbed the stairs to his hotel room, and discovered the room was unlocked. Shrugging at the slapdash behaviour of the chambermaid, who must have forgotten to lock it when they came in to make his bed, he opened the door.

Three uniformed officers were standing in his bedroom.

'Hi. Can I help you?'

'Would you be Ian C. Simpson, by any chance?'

'No, I would not,' he answered.

'Then would you be telling us why you have a pen with his initials on it by your bed?' asked another, older officer.

'Of course. There's a simple explanation.'

'Grand. Ye be telling us then. Down at the station might be more comfortable.'

'What? Why? I'm not Ian Simpson and I've done nothing wrong.'

'Grand, sir. Then if you'll accompany us, I'm sure we can sort this out.'

'I will not! This is ridiculous! I'm a guest in your country. Excuse me, but I'm leaving.' He turned and headed for the door. Two of the officers made a grab for him and held him by his arms. Instinctively, he struggled.

'Let me go! What the fuck is going on here? Look in my wallet, I can prove that I'm not Ian Simpson!'

'All in good time, sir. Now, would you be coming quietly? I don't want to upset Maggie and her regulars downstairs.'

He sighed and surrendered himself to the officers' vice-like grip. They marched him off down the corridor. 'I'll be contacting the British embassy about this. You can't just march into someone's bedroom, accuse them of being someone they're not and cart them off to jail. I want a lawyer, I want a . . .' His voice receded as they took him downstairs and out into the waiting Garda car.

*

Simon arrived at Cork airport at twenty past three that afternoon. He'd been on the wrong end of a bollocking from Whitehall for failing to get on the flight last night. Emerging from arrivals, Simon headed for a telephone.

'Glad you've made it, at long last,' Jenkins said sarcastically.

'Any news?'

'Yes. The Irish police think they've located Simpson. He was holed up at the same hotel as Haslam. They've taken him to the local station as we requested and are waiting for you to arrive to give a positive identification.'

'Good.'

'He is unarmed at present and they didn't find a

weapon in his room, but I think we should send a couple of our people over to help you escort him back.'

'Sure. And Joanna?'

'Our Irish colleagues tell us she's checked out. Seems she's headed back for London. Her name's on the passenger list for the half past seven flight this evening. As Simpson is under lock and key for the present, I want you to wait at the airport for her arrival. Find out what she's discovered, if anything. Call me for further instructions later.'

'Right, sir.' Simon sighed heavily, not relishing another three-hour stint at an airport or the subsequent conversation with Joanna. He sauntered over to the newsagents, bought a paper and settled down on a seat which gave him a clear view of both entrances.

*

Three hours and fifty minutes later, the final call for Heathrow was being broadcast over the tannoy. Having already confirmed with the check-in desk that J. Haslam was a no-show and scouring the passenger lounge thoroughly, Simon was aware that Joanna was not coming. He sat and watched the final passenger rush through the boarding gate and down the stairs to the waiting plane.

'That's it, sir. We're closing the flight,' said the young Irish girl on the desk.

Simon strode to the large window and watched the stairs slide silently away from the plane and the door shut. He sighed in resignation. It had all seemed too easy. Twenty minutes later, Simon was in a rented car, haring down the N71 towards West Cork.

*

The sitting room was lit only by the flames from the fire, casting ghostly, flickering shadows on the walls. The two women sat in silence, hardly noticing the night that had descended on them, too lost in their own thoughts.

'You believe me, don't you?' Ciara was almost childlike in her need for reassurance. After sixty-nine years of being labelled insane, Joanna knew it was hardly surprising. She herself was stunned; shocked, almost to the point of catatonia. She seemed unable to move, her brain unwilling to function in a logical and rational way.

Joanna raised her head and looked at Ciara. 'Yes, I do.' She put her hand to her temples. 'I . . . can't think straight at the moment. There are so many things I want to ask you.'

'There's time, Joanna, tomorrow maybe. You have a rest, collect your thoughts, then come back and see me.'

'Yes.' She nodded slowly. 'Maybe that's best. But I must ask you one thing. Have you kept the letter?'

'No.'

Joanna's body visibly slumped in disappointment. 'Then there's no way of proving what you've told me.'

'The house has.'

'Sorry?'

Ciara gave a small, subdued sigh. 'I left it there,

under the floorboards. I'd a feeling 'twas the safest thing.'

'Would the damp not have got to it by now?' asked Joanna.

'No. That house might be old, but it's dry. It was built to withstand the worst of weather.'

'Can I go and get it? If I'm going to finally prove that both of us are not mad, I need it.'

''Tis not my right to bar you.' Ciara shuddered suddenly. 'But be careful, Joanna. That house, it holds bad spirits. I still hear her crying, sometimes, the sound echoing across the bay . . .'

It was Joanna's turn to shudder. 'Shall I fetch the letter and bring it to you tomorrow morning?'

'Yes.' Ciara nodded. She glanced out of the window. 'There's a storm brewing. The estuary'll be swollen by the morn . . .'

Joanna stood up, the darkness and talk of storms and ghosts galvanizing her into action.

Ciara stood too. She reached up and kissed Joanna on her cheek. 'I knew you would come.'

'Did you?'

'Yes.' She gazed at Joanna. 'Do you know how like her you are? The living image. When I first saw you, I thought it.' She squeezed Joanna's hand. 'May God go with you.'

'I'll be back here tomorrow.'

Ciara nodded, the uncertainty in her eyes evident.

'Thank you, Ciara.' Impulsively Joanna returned the kiss. 'And may God go with you too.'

Outside, the wind was howling across the estuary,

the rain skudding fast at an angle. Joanna shivered
uncontrollably as she saw the big, black mass of the
coastguard's house outlined against the ebony sky. She
struggled in the darkness to fit the keys in the lock of
the car, panic besetting her. She eventually unlocked
the door and climbed inside, closing the door against
the gale. She switched the engine on to stem the noise
outside, and drove off up towards the village. A hot
port and a warm by the fire would comfort her frayed
nerves, give her a chance to sort out her thoughts. She
was just switching off the engine, ready to go back into
the hotel and tell Margaret she was staying for an extra
night, when a face she knew extremely well emerged
from the front door of the hotel.

For a few seconds, she stared at him, then instinctively ducked down as he stepped out on to the
pavement.

'Please God, don't let him see me,' she breathed.
The blood pumped in her ears, deafening her. A pair
of headlights bathed the car in light for an agonizing
split second, then there was darkness once more. She
sat up, put her head back and breathed again.

What did it mean, Simon being here?

Joanna closed her eyes and shook her head. It meant
they knew, that they were on to her. It meant she had
very little time left. And it also meant that she must go
now, to the coastguard's house, and retrieve the letter
before someone else did.

*

There was a tap on her window. Joanna nearly jumped
out of her skin. She opened her eyes slowly and saw a

familiar face smiling at her through the glass. She sighed in relief as he opened the door.

'Hi, Jo.' Kurt leaned in and kissed her on the cheek.

'Hi, Kurt,' she said wearily. 'How are you?'

'Fine, just fine. I thought I'd missed you. I dropped by the hotel and they said you'd gone back to London. I was just on my way back to my hotel in Clonakilty when I saw you sat out here in the car.' He studied her. 'You look awful pale. Anything wrong?'

Joanna let out a small sigh. 'Kurt, it's a very long story and I don't have that long.'

'You going somewhere?'

'Yes, yes I am. Look, why don't I give you a call at your hotel tomorrow?'

'Sure.' He shrugged. 'You positive you're okay?'

'I'm fine.' She nodded. 'Bye, Kurt.'

'Yeah, bye.' He slammed the door and gave a small wave as she turned the key and started off up the road.

*

Simon drove through the lashing rain towards the Garda station at the other end of the village. He'd stopped off at the hotel to quickly check out Ian's room before going to identify Ian. Margaret, the woman in charge, had told him that the room had already been cleared by the guards and everything taken down to the station half an hour ago. As for Joanna, Margaret had not seen her since she left for the airport at five o'clock that afternoon.

Simon pulled up in front of what could only be described as a doll's house, its Garda sign outside the one indication that this was a police station. The reception was deserted. He rang a bell and eventually an elderly man came through a door.

'Good evening to you, sir. Terrible weather we're cursed with, isn't it?'

'My name's Simon Warburton. I've come to ident-ify Ian Simpson.' Simon flashed his identification card and the guard nodded.

'I'm Sean Ryan and I'm glad to be seeing you. Your man's given us trouble ever since he arrived. He's not happy to be here. Not that any of them are.' He smiled.

'Is he sober?'

'I'd say that he was, yes.'

'Right, let's go and take a look at him then.'

Simon followed Sean down a short narrow corridor. 'I had to lock him in, Simon, he was acting up so.'

'Okay, open the door.'

Sean did so, then stepped aside to let Simon enter first. A figure was slumped over the desk, his head resting on his arms, a Marlboro burning to its filter in the ashtray. The figure looked up and let out a sigh of relief.

'Simon, thank God! Maybe you can tell this ignor-ant bunch of Paddies that I'm not Ian fucking Simpson!'

Simon's heart sank. He smiled wanly. 'Hello, Marcus.'

*

Joanna parked the car on a grass verge just opposite the house. She reached for the torch she had just purchased from the petrol station cum Spar situated opposite the

entrance to Emily Bentinck's house. She was sweating
and shivering in turn. The thought of getting out of
the car, crossing the road and going inside – alone, at
night, in a storm – was enough to make her usually
strong, obedient body metamorphose into a quivering,
indignant mess.

Galvanizing every ounce of strength she possessed,
she opened the car door, switched on the torch and
crossed the road. She shone the torch down on to the
sandbanks and saw the tide had come in, filling the
estuary with water. The only way inside was to wade
through it, climb up the wall and slip in through the
kitchen window.

The water was freezing, reaching up to her knees,
the rain soaking the top of her body. Feeling her way
round the wall by using her hands, she shone the torch
upwards to locate the kitchen window. A few more
steps and she was just beneath it. She reached up to
grab the top of the wall with her fingertips, then pulled
her body upwards, her muscles straining with the effort.
She gave a cry of anguish as she lost her grip and nearly
toppled over backwards into the water. Another three
tries and her foot managed to find an indent in the
brick, which she used as a lever to haul herself up.

She lay flat on top of the wall, panting and shivering. Pulling herself to stand on the ledge, Joanna
shone the torch and located the broken window pane.
The space was not large enough to allow her to enter.
Pulling down the sleeve of her jacket, and covering
her hand with it, Joanna punched at the bottom corner of the remaining glass, until there was enough

room to haul herself in. Clearing the remnants of the glass from the frame, she launched herself inside, head first.

The beam of the torch showed her the floor of the kitchen was three feet below her. She reached down, her legs still hanging out of the window, and her fingertips touched the damp floor beneath her. She cried out as she lost her balance and went tumbling through the window, landing with a thump on the hard floor. She lay there for a few seconds feeling something furry tickling the side of her face. Joanna sprang up, shone the torch down and saw the dead rat on the floor.

'Oh God, Oh God!' she panted, her chest heaving in shock and disgust, her shoulder aching from taking the brunt of the fall.

As she stood there, the atmosphere of the house curled around her. Every nerve ending in her body sensed the danger, the fear and the death that seeped out of the walls. They begged, pleaded with her to follow their instructions and get out, run before it was too late.

'No, no,' she panted. 'All I must do is climb the stairs and get the letter. Nearly there now, nearly there.'

Her hands shaking so much, the beam of the torch wavered erratically in front of her, Joanna located the door that would lead her into the rest of the house and left the kitchen.

The stairs were before her. She mounted them slowly, hearing the storm reach its zenith outside – inside – she wasn't sure anymore. Each stair creaked beneath her, groaning at the sudden intrusion. At the top, Joanna paused, her sense of direction paralysed by fear, uncertain of which way to turn.

'Think Joanna, think . . . she said the room directly overlooking the cottage,' she panted. Getting her bearings, Joanna turned left and walked down the corridor. There was a door right at the end of the passage. It was closed.

For some reason, she crossed herself.

Then she walked down the corridor and opened the door.

*

'Fucking hell, Simon! Can you tell me what the hell is going on?' Marcus followed him to his car, parked outside.

'No, not really, other than the fact that we thought Ian Simpson had come across here after Joanna.'

'But Joanna's gone home. Margaret told me.'

'Not from Cork airport she hasn't. I waited for her there and she didn't show up for her flight. Look, I'll drive you back to the hotel. I want to check Joanna's room anyway.'

'I'm out of this godforsaken country tomorrow morning.' Marcus shook his head. 'Those idiots had an entire cache of credit cards with my bloody name on it and they still wouldn't believe I was me.'

'You also had Ian Simpson's pen with his initials engraved on it by your bed.'

'Yeah, well, not my fault if Jo had left the pen at my flat and I'd picked it up, was it?'

'I'm sorry for the misunderstanding, Marcus. The most important thing now is to locate the real Ian Simpson, and Joanna.'

Marcus sighed as Simon parked in front of the hotel. 'Christ knows where she is.'

The two men entered the hotel. Fear crossed Margaret's face as she saw Marcus. 'Is he . . . safe?'

'Perfectly.' Simon nodded. 'A case of mistaken identity, nothing more. Could I have the keys to Miss Haslam's room? We're concerned for her. She didn't get on the flight at the airport this evening.'

'I haven't touched it, so. It's been too busy in here.' Margaret handed Simon the key.

'Thanks.'

'A double brandy, please, Margaret,' said Marcus autocratically. 'Want one, Simon?'

'No thanks. I'll be down in a jiffy.'

He climbed the stairs two at a time and let himself into Joanna's room. He checked the usual places and found nothing of interest. He sat on the bed and put his head in his hands. 'Come on, Jo, help me here. Where are you?'

His eyes caught the wastepaper basket, containing its normal mixture of discarded tissues and crumpled paper. Simon sprang from the bed and emptied the contents on to the floor. He unscrewed a tightly balled piece of paper and tried to decipher what it said. A few seconds later, Simon was down in the bar. He had a word with Margaret, then went over to Marcus, who was on his second double brandy.

'Got to go. You stay here, keep out of trouble and I'll see you later.'

'Where . . .' Before Marcus could finish, Simon was through the door and gone.

*

Simon drove down to the estuary as Margaret had told him to. The small cottage was unmissable, standing as it did alone overlooking the sandbanks. Simon jumped out of the car and walked towards the door.

chapter thirty-five

Joanna stood in the room, as still as the inanimate walls around her. The room was bare, stripped by unknown hands of anything it had ever contained.

She shone the torch on to the ground, looking at the thick wooden floorboards. How was she to know which one was hiding the key to a long-ago mystery? She crouched down, pulling at a floorboard with her hands. It crunched, then came free. Joanna gulped as she heard a sudden scratching, a patter of small paws scurrying away.

Starting in one corner of the room, Joanna worked methodically, her fingers numb with cold. The rotten boards put up little resistance but refused to reveal her quarry.

Then she heard the footsteps outside the door. They were slow and measured, as if the owner of the feet was commanding them to step forward as quietly as they could. Joanna switched off her torch, and stayed where she was, knowing there was nowhere to hide, nowhere to run to. Her breath came in short, sharp gasps as she heard the door creak open.

*

The sitting room was warm and inviting, if basic. The fire's power had died, leaving only a warm mass of glowing embers. Simon opened the latch door into the kitchen. There was an enamel sink with a pump above it and a pantry containing a collection of tinned vegetables, half a loaf of soda bread, some butter and cheese.

The back door took him outside to a lavatory. Simon went back inside, walked through the sitting room and began to mount the stairs. The door at the top was shut. He tapped on it gently, fearful of frightening the old lady out of her wits if she was asleep. He tapped louder, considering she might be deaf. Still there was no reply. Simon pulled up the latch and opened the door. The room was in darkness.

'Miss Deasy?'

Still there was no reply. He felt for the small torch in his pocket and switched its delicate beam on. He saw there was a shape in the bed. The woman was obviously fast asleep. Simon walked towards the bed, leaned over and shone the torch on her chin. He saw her mouth was open and slack. He shone the beam upwards and jumped instinctively as a pair of green eyes stared unblinkingly back at him.

Simon found a light switch and turned it on, his heart heavy with dread. There was no sign on the body of bruising or a wound, but the terror in the green eyes told Simon their own story. This was not death by natural causes, but the work of an expert.

*

Joanna heard the feet enter the room. It was so dark, she did not know whether they carried a human form above them. The beam shone suddenly and brightly into her eyes. She covered her face with her arms, shielding herself against any oncoming physical attack.

'Jo? Joanna?'

The feet walked towards her, the light in her eyes burning her pupils. Arms encircled her and she struggled against them.

'Please! Stop! Stop!'

'Joanna, it's me, it's Kurt. Calm down, I won't hurt you, ma'am, honest.'

It took a while for her brain to break through the paralysing fear and recognize that, yes, this was a voice she knew, a voice that held the promise of safety. Her hands shaking violently, she lifted her own torch and shone the light in his eyes.

'Wh . . . what are you doing . . . he . . . here?' She was shivering, her teeth chattering from the combination of fear and cold.

'I'm sorry to have startled you, honey. I was just a little concerned about you, that's all. So I followed you down here to make sure you were okay.'

'Oh.'

'Jeez, Jo, you're soaked. You're gonna catch your death. Here.' Kurt reached into a pocket and took out a flask. 'Here, drink some of this.' He put the flask to her lips.

Joanna almost gagged as the strange tasting liquid was poured down her throat. 'Yeuch! What was that?!'

'Around here, they call it poteen.' Kurt replaced the top and put the liquid back in his pocket. 'Better?'

'A little.' She nodded without much conviction.

'Tell me, Jo, if it's not a silly question, just what are you doing in an empty house in the middle of the night?'

She shook her head, and brushed her wet hair back from her face. 'I told you, Kurt, it's a long story.'

He regarded her silently. 'Okay. Then I'll have to deduce for myself. You're searching for something you think is here, right?'

Joanna nodded wearily. Kurt shone his torch across the part-uprooted floorboards. 'And, presumably, you've been tipped off the buried treasure lies somewhere underneath these?'

'Not buried treasure exactly.'

'A document of some kind, maybe?'

'Yes. A letter.'

'Appertaining to the lost relative?'

'Possibly.'

'Fine, then why don't I help you find it and then we're out of here and back to the nearest fire before you catch your death.'

She shrugged. 'Okay.'

'Right, you start that end, I'll start this end. We'll meet in the goddamn middle.' He smiled, helping her to her feet.

Slowly, with fingers and thumbs that ached from the effort, Joanna moved towards the middle of the room.

'Anything yet?' she shouted to Kurt, trying to make herself heard above the howling wind. The house itself seemed to be visibly shaking at the battering it was taking.

'No, sweet FA so far. You?' he shouted back.

'No, and we're running out of floorboards. Maybe we're in the wrong room.'

'Jeez, Jo, are you telling me we might have to take up the entire top floor of this house?'

'No,' she said. 'Hold on a minute . . .' Rather than feeling the dusty, scratchy surface beneath the boards, Joanna's hand had touched on something smooth.

'You got something?' Kurt was by her side in a second.

'Possibly.' Joanna's scratched, bloody fingers fumbled to find the edge of the rectangle. Slowly, not wishing after all this to damage it, she pulled it from beneath the floor.

Kurt shone his torch on the fragile, yellowed envelope. Faint traces of a name written in ink could be seen but not deciphered.

'Open it, Jo. See what it says,' he urged.

'Later. Let's get out of here now.' She gave her strangely woozy head a slight shake. 'I'm feeling a little tired and . . .' Jo's voice trailed off as her vision became blurred and Kurt's hand reached out to take the letter from her.

'I'll keep it safe for you, Jo.'

'No, I . . . I should keep it.' She ordered her fingers to hold their grasp around the envelope, but they did not obey. She watched as Kurt tucked the letter into the zip pocket of his waterproof.

'Come on, I'll help you.' He reached forward to take her hands and pull her up. Joanna's legs buckled beneath her and Kurt placed an arm round her waist and took her weight.

'Feeling sleepy?'

'Yes, I don't know why ... I ...' Her head was spinning now and her own voice belonged to someone else, someone in the distance. Kurt hauled her out of the room and along the corridor. The door banged loudly behind them as they headed for the stairs. Suddenly, the torch that had lit their way to the top of the stairs went out and the heavy blackness of the house surrounded them.

'Shit. Hold there a minute while I find another battery.' Kurt's hand fell from her waist and she tee-tered at the top of the stairs trying to keep her balance. A hard shove from behind sent her toppling down into the blackness below.

*

Simon stood outside the cottage, still nauseated from what he'd discovered upstairs. The wind was wailing like a banshee in his ears, the rain driving into his face as he tried to collect his thoughts.

'Joanna, for God's sake, where are you?' he cried out.

Then, above the wailing of the wind came another sound. A woman was screaming, howling in terror or agony, he couldn't decipher which. As the moon appeared from behind a fast scudding cloud, Simon saw the big house on the other side of the bay. He'd seen a photograph of that house in the file. And was certain the voice came from there. He checked over the wall and saw the water in the estuary was too deep to wade across. Simon sprang into his car and turned on the engine.

*

Joanna woke with a moan of pain, the rain splattering on her face acting as a reviver. Her brain felt as though it was wrapped in thick fog. As she gazed up, her vision still blurred, she saw the moon, rising just above the chimney of the house. She raised herself up from her prone position and saw she was lying outside the front door. Joanna gave a strangled sob of desolation and lay back down on the rough gravel as another dizzy spell threatened to rob her of consciousness. A pair of hands grabbed her shoulders roughly and began to drag her towards the steps that led down to the water.

'What are you doing? Stop, please.'

'You stupid little bitch. Thought you were so damned clever didn't you?!'

Joanna was confused. This was a voice she recognized, but it wasn't Kurt's. She tried to galvanize her muscles into action as she was bumped unceremoniously down the steps. The iron grip on her shoulders was unbreakable.

'Who are you? Please, let me go!' Joanna struggled pathetically. The hands left her shoulders and grabbed her forearms, rolling her over until they were behind her back and she was staring into the blackness of the water below.

'Do you know how much trouble you've caused everyone? Do you?' he asked as he yanked her head upwards by her hair until she felt her neck might break.

'Stop it! *Please!*' Joanna began to weep. He let go of her hair abruptly and instead pushed it down. She managed to snatch in a breath before her face was submerged in the icy cold water. In her fuddled brain, she tried to think of a prayer, something that people said at the end of their lives. Her lungs had nothing left, they would burst, explode. She was going to die, just like in the nightmare . . .

The grip on her head was removed abruptly. Joanna came up for air, gasping and spluttering as she rolled away unhindered from the water's edge. As she thankfully sucked in air, in the left-hand corner of her vision, she saw Kurt staring up at the house behind them as if in a trance.

'Who is it?' he shouted. 'Who's there?'

Joanna could hear nothing but her own ragged breathing and the water swirling in the gale.

Kurt put his hands to his ears and began shaking his head. 'Stop it! For fuck's sake, stop it!' He keeled over to one side, screaming in some kind of invisible agony, his hands still over his ears.

Joanna knew that whatever was happening to him, this was her chance for escape. But the letter . . . Leave it, her head told her, leave it and run before it's too late.

Staggering upright on the wet, slippery stone, Joanna realized her path to safety was blocked by Kurt, still curled in a foetal ball, a high keening sound emanating from his lips. To escape without risk of him seeing her, she'd have to wade through the water, make her way to the estuary wall and climb over it. Her head still feeling like a block of stone, her lungs still painfully grabbing for oxygen, she plunged into the icy-cold water. Although it only came up just beyond her waist, the swell from the wind made the current extremely strong. That, coupled with her poor physical condition, made the fifty yards or so across to the wall seem like an impossible task.

'Come on, Jo, come on, you can do it,' she told herself as dizziness and nausea heralded a blackout. She turned round to check whether Kurt had noticed her leaving, and it was then she saw the figure, in the upstairs bedroom of the house, arms outstretched, as if beckoning Joanna to her. She blinked and shook her head, sure it was just another trick her oxygen-starved brain was playing on her. But the figure was still there when she opened her eyes. Joanna watched as the figure nodded, then turned and receded from the window.

She was suddenly aware that the storm's earlier ferocity had died down. Even the water around her had calmed and the wind no longer howled. The sudden silence was deafening. Joanna turned and headed for safety. She was just nearing the wall when two large hands grabbed her shoulders from behind, pushed her forwards and under the water. This time, there had been no split second to take a breath and her tired lungs protested immediately at the deprivation. Joanna contented herself with the image of the figure in the window and prepared to do as she had seemed to be asking and join Niamh Deasy.

*

Simon too noticed the stillness as he jumped out of his car and headed for the house. As he approached the front door he heard a splash from the water behind him and a howl of anger. Then the sound of gunfire.

'Shit!' Shining his torch in the direction of the noise, Simon saw two men struggling in the water.

There was another shot and one of the men fell backwards and disappeared under. Jumping in, Simon waded as fast as he could across to them.

'Don't come any nearer, Warburton. I've got a gun and I'll blast you where you stand.'

'Ian, for Christ's sake! What are you doing? Who just got hurt?' Simon shone the torch on to the water and saw two bodies floating face down.

'Your girlfriend led me straight to it, just like I knew she would.'

'Where is she?'

Ian nodded at one of the bodies. 'Bloody awful swimmer.' He chuckled. 'But I got it. Reckon I'll have my old job back next week, don't you? This'll show them I can still cut it, won't it?'

'Course it will.' Simon nodded, wading towards him. He lunged for Joanna and picked her up out of the water before he felt the press of cold steel poking under his ribs.

'Sorry and all that, but can't have you stealing my thunder, Warburton.'

Simon heard the safety catch open. He raised the arm that held his torch and smacked Ian across the face with it, sending him backwards into the water, his gun falling out of his hand as he did so. Swiftly, Simon carried Joanna out of the water and rolled her over the estuary wall. Ian was coming back for him, the fury of madness evident on his face in the torchlight.

'Come on, old chap. Let's get the other gentleman to safety and then we can talk about this.' He was scanning the water for the other body he'd seen floating, but it had disappeared.

'Don't think so, Warburton. I want to be the only one to cover myself in glory.' He patted his pocket. 'I found the letter, after all.'

'Yes, you did, and you should get all the credit, of course.'

'Rest assured I will.' Ian lunged for Simon, insanity giving him superhuman strength. Simon went down under the water, the grasp on his neck unbreakable. Legs kicking out, hands flailing, Simon realized he stood no chance. Concentrating his energy on removing his own gun from his inside jacket pocket, using every iota of strength he possessed and the last of the oxygen from his lungs, Simon pushed upwards in order to free himself. His attempt failed, the iron grip managing to hold his head under water.

'I'm sorry, Joanna, so sorry,' he thought as the salty sea water began to invade his lungs.

From somewhere above him was a muffled bang. The iron grip was relinquished and Simon sprang up from beneath the water coughing and choking. A cloud shifted from in front of a full moon to replace Simon's lost torch. Ian was lying face down in the water next to him. A figure standing behind the wall was holding a gun. Simon dived back into the water to make himself a less easy target, then he heard a voice calling his name.

'You okay, Simon?'

'Yes. Who is that?'

'Marcus. Bloody hell, have I killed him?'

'I'm not sure. I'll take a look. Thanks, Marcus, you just saved my life, mate.' Simon began wading towards him. 'How's Joanna? Is she . . .?'

'She's breathing, it's okay. I gave her a very unpro-
fessional kiss of life,' Marcus muttered. 'Seemed to do
the trick anyway. I laid her in what I think is the
recovery position.'

Simon was by Joanna's side, checking her painfully
slow pulse, the greyness of her skin.

'We've got to get her some immediate attention.
Can you help me to the car? I'll give you my telephone
and you could drive her up to the hotel. They'll know
the nearest doctor and hospital.'

'Er, don't think I can drive. I've got a bloody great
hole in my arm that your mate Ian gave me.'

Simon saw that Marcus was not exaggerating. His
left arm was a mass of blood.

'Christ, you need that looked at too. Stay with Jo,
I'll fish out Ian and then we'll move.'

Marcus, now the adrenalin had stopped pumping
and his arm had started hurting, began to shiver. He
went and sat beside Jo, stroking her cheek with a
quivering hand.

'So sorry, darling. I do love you, Jo, you'll be okay.'

Simon laid Ian out on the steps, knowing it was
pointless finding him immediate medical attention.
Carefully removing the letter from his waterproof
pocket, he ran back to Marcus and ordered him to
head for the car. He picked up Joanna in his arms and
carried her. Her eyes flickered open for a second and
she gave him a watery smile.

'Simon,' she whispered, 'I've got a really great
scoop.'

chapter thirty-six

The horse's hooves thundered over the rough grass, his mane flying, his back covered in damp sweat. As he reached the top of the hillock, he was drawn to a halt. The rider climbed down from his back and tethered him to the nearest rock.

Joanna flung herself down on to the coarse grass, panting hard. She looked up at the Yorkshire sky and knew she had, at best, half an hour before the blue above her made way for the grey clouds coming in from the west. She sat up, her hands round her knees and tried to still her breathing. Her chest was still tight, still sore, and her shoulder ached, but the doctor had assured her that as long as she took care of herself, she would make a full recovery.

It was two weeks since she'd been let out of hospital. The hours after the terrible night she had nearly drowned were a blur, full of pain and tubes and nightmares. She'd woken properly a couple of days later to find herself in a hospital in Leeds, with little idea of how she'd got there.

Her mother had been by her bed, the look of concern replaced with a smile as Joanna had opened her eyes. Joanna had soon cottoned on when her mother had told her what a godsend it was that Simon had been on holiday in Ireland with her and able to rescue her when she'd fallen into the water. Simon, clever chap that he was, had also managed to organize an RAF jet to bring them and the other gentleman that had been injured that night back to England.

At the time, she'd been too ill to think about anything. She'd had a collapsed lung, a fractured shoulder and a huge lump on her temple, which, despite being the least physically serious of her injuries, throbbed day and night.

Two weeks later, the hospital had released her to the care of her mother, who had taken her home to their moorland farm, fed her endless home-made soups, helped her wash, dress, and generally enjoyed nurturing her like a baby once more.

It was now over a month since that night had passed, the night she had so very nearly lost her life. And it was only in the last few days she'd really had the strength to contemplate what had happened. She had so many unanswered questions, memories that had come filtering back in a disorderly fashion. She was no longer sure what was real and what she had dreamed.

Maybe tomorrow, finally, some of those questions would be answered. Simon had called her to say he was coming up to stay with his parents for a few days and would pop round to see her. He'd been away on leave, apparently, which was why he hadn't been up to Yorkshire before. Joanna stared down at the woolly dots on the hillside. It was lambing season and the hillside resembled an overcrowded maternity ward.

The problem was, would she get the truth from Simon?

*

'Jo! How are you?' A tanned and healthy looking Simon shot through the kitchen door on Wednesday lunchtime like an eager puppy.

'I'm okay.' She nodded, suddenly feeling shy.

'Good. And you, Mrs Haslam?'

'Same as always, Simon. Nothing much changes up here, as you know.'

'Hoorah for that. Things move too fast in London, don't they, Jo?'

She nodded.

'Tea? Coffee? A slice of cake?'

'Later maybe, thanks, Mrs Haslam. I thought I'd take Jo out for a pub lunch, treat myself to a pint of good old Yorkshire bitter. That be okay with you, Jo?'

They drove across the moors to Haworth and opted for The Black Bull, an old haunt of theirs when they'd been teenagers.

Simon put a pint and a gin and tonic down on the table, then lit a cigar.

'Cheers, Jo. Glad to see you so much better.'

'Thanks.'

'Take it slowly though. You really did have a very near miss.'

'I know. Please, can you talk me through exactly what happened? My mind's so foggy about that night . . . I . . . Who was Kurt?'

'Look, before I do, I want to say something to you. I'm really sorry that I accused you of blowing the whistle on Zoe. I know it wasn't you and I feel like a real shit for ever thinking it might be.'

Joanna shrugged. 'That's okay.'

'And I'm sorry I lied to you about that love letter disintegrating. I was being leaned on, hard. I did it for your own safety, really, Jo. You'd got yourself into something way over your head.'

'Water, mainly.' She smiled wryly. 'Never mind, it's all under the bridge now.'

'Thanks for taking it like this.'

'Well, if I remember rightly, you managed to save my life. I have to show a bit of gratitude.'

'Can't really take all the credit for that one. Marcus Harrison played his part too.'

'Blimey, are you sure it wasn't another case of mistaken identity? Marcus is hardly the kind of man who's into heroics of any kind.'

'Love does funny things to people. Brings out the best, and the worst for that matter.' Simon sipped his pint ruefully. 'I admit to thinking he was a prat. He did some very stupid things, but I'd say that night he rather redeemed himself.'

'And is he okay?'

'He's got an arm that, even after surgery, is never going to work as well as it used to, but he'll live. I visited him a few days ago in London. He said to send his love to you.'

Joanna nodded. 'Now tell me, Simon, please, because it's been driving me mad ever since I woke up at the hospital, who was Kurt?'

'You remember my colleague, Ian Simpson?'

'Yes.'

'It was him.'

Joanna nodded. 'He turned over my flat originally, didn't he?'

'He was there, yes, just in case.'

'In case of what?'

Simon sighed. 'Look, sweetheart, I understand how you feel, you want to know and understand everything, but sometimes, as you've found out, it's better to leave it be.'

'No!' Joanna's eyes blazed. 'I know he was working for your lot, trying to stop me getting to the truth. And then, when I did, he wanted me dead.'

'For starters, Ian was not working for "our lot" when he tried to murder you. He had been placed on sick leave because of his associated mental problems, exacerbated by drink. He was a loose cannon who wanted to cover himself in glory and get his job back.'

'Where is he now?'

'He died, Jo.'

The colour drained from her face. 'That night?'

'Yes.'

'How?'

'He was shot.'

'Who by?'

'Me,' Simon lied smoothly.

Joanna covered her face in her hands. 'Oh God.' She suppressed a sob. 'Is that what you do for a living?'

'No, but these things happen in the course of duty, just like the police. Better him than you.'

Joanna was silent, thinking in horror of that night she'd slept with him in Dublin.

'He must have drugged me, put something in the poteen. I can hardly remember anything after that.'

'I'll get us both another drink.'

She watched as Simon headed to the bar and came back with another round. She sipped her gin and stared at him.

'I know what it was all about, Simon.'

'Do you?'

'Yes. Not that it means anything. The letter I discovered is presumably at the bottom of the ocean with Ian. And if it isn't, then it's gone to a place where I will never be able to find it.' She eyed him.

'I retrieved the letter, Jo, for what use it was. A soggy, pulpy mess.'

Joanna nodded. 'Is this Simon, Jo's oldest friend speaking, or Simon, crack secret-service man employed by the government?'

'Both.' Simon fished in his pocket and drew out a plastic envelope. 'I knew you'd ask so I brought the remains for you to see.'

Joanna took the envelope and looked at the bits of browning, watermarked paper it contained.

'Take a look,' Simon urged. 'It's important you believe it.'

A thin, smudged ink line on one of the pieces convinced her it was genuine. She waved the envelope at Simon. 'So, all the fuss, for this?'

He nodded. 'Ridiculous, isn't it? Want some grub? I'm starving.'

He ordered them both a beef hotpot. Simon hoovered his up while Jo picked.

'Not hungry?'

'No. Let's go for a walk. I want to know once and for all if I've got my facts right. Then, maybe, I can finally forget about the whole thing and start putting my life back on track.

They walked past Haworth Church and up on to the moors behind, towards Top Farm where Emily Brontë had set *Wuthering Heights*.

They settled themselves down on a rock.

'Okay, shoot,' said Simon.

'Well, there's still a lot that doesn't fit, but I reckon I've got most of the gist.' Joanna took a deep breath. 'My little old woman with the tea chests was in the employ of the royal household. She was a lady-in-waiting, who had met and fallen in love with an Irish actor called Michael O'Connell.'

'How do you know that?'

'William Fielding told Zoe he used to meet a lady called Rose to exchange letters. The one I discovered was one of those which were passed between Rose and Michael O'Connell. Their relationship was clandestine, because of her high birth.'

'Yes.'

'That was the Red Herring, if you like. It certainly wasn't the letter you lot were after, was it?'

Simon grinned. 'No.'

'At first I thought Rose had happened on some kind of a scandal, but in fact it wasn't that way round at all.' Joanna shook her head. 'Although she had told Michael that her employer's husband was being sent away to Ireland to stay in a place he knew very well.'

'How did he know it?'

'Because he'd been born not far from there. And worked for a family who resided just across the bay from the coastguard's house.'

'Right.'

'William Fielding told Zoe that during 1926, Michael O'Connell kept disappearing. What if he'd gone home to Ireland, innocently at first, to visit his relatives, and while he was there, heard some chat in the local pub about the English stranger who was staying in the coastguard's house?'

'Do continue, Jo.' Simon was intrigued.

'What if he'd heard gossip that the stranger was having a love affair with a girl from the village? The girl who kept house for him? Ciara Deasy's sister, Niamh.'

Simon nodded.

'Of course, Michael must have been fascinated by this, because he knew the identity of the stranger. Rose had told him. I'd bet Michael became even more interested when rumours circulated that Niamh was pregnant by him.'

'And who was the stranger, Joanna?'

'Ciara told me. She'd seen his photograph on the front of the *Irish Times*, the day of his coronation ten years later.' Joanna glanced into the distance. 'It was the Duke of York. The man who would, when his brother abdicated, become the next king of England.'

He stared at her silently, then nodded. 'Yes. Well done.'

'So Michael thinks he might be able to get some serious mileage out of this. Maybe he visits the Duke at the coastguard's house, announces he knows who he is and of his affair with Niamh, and threatens to tell the Duchess.' Joanna rubbed her nose. 'I think that threat would be large enough to extract a serious amount of money, perhaps even enough for a London house, not to mention the promise of a new British identity and a fast track to acting success.'

'I think you might be right.'

'This, of course, precipitates a hasty departure by the Duke back to England, leaving his lady love high and dry and in the club with a royal baby. And that's really as far as I've managed to get. Could you . . . would you fill in the details? How you knew about the letter Niamh had written? I can only presume Michael O'Connell knew of its existence and had used it to safeguard himself and his family until he died.'

'The deal was the letter was to be returned to us on his death.' Simon nodded. 'We'd searched for it, obviously, high and low.'

'Why not in that house? Where Niamh had died? Surely it was an obvious place to look?' questioned Joanna.

'Maybe sometimes people don't see the things that are right under their noses. Everyone assumed that Michael would have kept it close, in his immediate possession.' Simon nodded in approval. 'Well done, Jo. Do you want my job?'

'Joanna stared off into the distance. 'And what about the child? Has anyone tried to trace Niamh's baby? The son or daughter of the king of England?'

'Yes, but to no avail,' Simon answered. 'The parents were paid a lot of money to have the baby disappear.'

'And to convince Ciara, their own daughter, that she was mad,' added Joanna. 'I must write to her, maybe go and see her, tell her the letter is gone, that it's all finally over.'

Simon covered Joanna's hand with his own and squeezed it. 'I'm afraid Ian wasn't the only casualty that night. Ciara died too. At Ian's hands.'

Joanna shook her head as she blinked away tears. 'This is all so . . . ghastly. Something that happened seventy years ago still destroying those that were unwittingly involved.'

'I know. I'm so sorry, Jo.'

She shrugged. 'And there are things that still don't seem right. For example, why on earth would the Palace send the Duke of York over to Ireland just after Partition? I mean, the English were hated, and the son of the sovereign must have been a prime target for the IRA. Why not Switzerland? Somewhere warm?'

'Possibly because it really was the last place anyone would think of looking for him. He was very sick, needed time to recover in complete peace. Whatever, it's time to close the book now.'

Joanna nodded as she ground a tuft of grass with her boot. 'You're right. You know, I can't help feeling bitter. All this, and where has it landed me? A wrecked flat, unemployed and lucky to be alive. Not to mention the nightmares I've had ever since that night.'

'Well, I do have one bit of good news for you.' Simon fished in his jacket pocket and handed her a letter. 'Go on, open it.'

She did so. The letter was from the editor of her newspaper offering her her job back on the newsdesk with Tom, as soon as she was fit enough to return. She looked at Simon. 'How did you get hold of this?'

'Oh, it was passed to me by one of them upstairs. Obviously the situation was explained and has been rectified. They do have some soul somewhere, you know.'

'I doubt it, but I am grateful for this.' She nodded.

'You deserve it. Speaking as Simon, I'm only sorry you can't go back in a blaze of glory with the scoop of the century. After all, it was you who beat us lot to the pot of gold. Come on now, let's go. I don't want you getting a chill.' He pulled her to standing and gave her a hug. 'I've missed you, you know. I hated it when we weren't friends.'

'So did I.'

They walked back down the hill arm in arm.

'Simon, there's one last thing I wanted to ask you about that night.'

'What?'

'Well, this sounds very silly, and you know I'm not a believer in any of this kind of thing, but . . . did you hear a woman's screaming coming from the house?'

'Yes. I thought it was you, to be honest. That's what alerted me to where you were.'

Joanna shook her head. 'Well, it wasn't me, but I think Ian heard it too. He had my head under water, then all of a sudden he let me go and put his hands over his ears, like he was hearing some dreadful noise. It was actually what saved me.'

'It had stopped by the time I arrived.'

'You . . . you didn't see a woman's face at an upstairs window, did you?'

Simon grinned at her. 'No, Jo, I didn't. I reckon you were hallucinating, sweetheart.'

'Maybe,' Joanna acknowledged as she stepped into the car. She sighed as she saw the woman's face as clear as day in her mind's eye. 'Maybe.'

*

Simon pulled his car away from the farmhouse, giving a last wave to Joanna and her parents. Before he headed to his own parents, he had to make a telephone call. A couple of miles along the moorland road, he pulled his car to a halt, pulled out his mobile and dialled the number.

'Sir? It's Warburton.'

'How did it go?'

'Well. She came close, but not close enough for any panic.'

'Thank God. You've encouraged her to drop the whole thing, have you?'

'I hope so. Sir, she did tell me something that I believe is very important. Something that William Fielding told Zoe Harrison before he died.'

'What?'

'The identity of our lady's emissary.'

'Not over the phone, Warburton. Use the usual route and I'll see you in the office at nine on Monday morning. Good evening.'

*

The day before Joanna was leaving to return to London to pick up the pieces of her life, she drove over to see Dora, her paternal grandmother in Keighley. In her mid-eighties, but still as sharp as ever, Dora lived in a comfortable flat in a sheltered-housing block.

As she was hugged and welcomed inside to great delight and a high tea of magnificent proportions, Joanna felt guilty that she did not visit more regularly. Dora had always been a constant in her life, up until five years ago living only four miles down the road from her son and his family. Joanna had treated her comfortable cottage as a second home, her granny as a second mother.

'So, young lady, tell me exactly how you landed yourself in intensive care, will you?' Dora smiled as she poured tea rather shakily into two fine bone-china cups. 'I know you fobbed off your parents with all that falling into the estuary and nearly drowning business, but you can't fool me. I remember all those badges and shields you won at school for swimming, even if they don't. Dora, I thought to myself when I heard, there's more to this than meets the eye. So,' Dora took a sip of her tea and eyed her granddaughter, 'who pushed you?'

Joanna could not help but smile. Dora was such a wily old bird. 'It's a long, long story, Granny,' she murmured as she polished off her second piece of parkin.

'I love a good story.' Dora nodded. 'And the longer the better,' she encouraged. 'Sadly, time is something I have in spades these days.'

Joanna weighed the situation up in her mind then, thinking that there was no one on the earth whom she trusted more and eager to put her still confused thoughts into words, she began to talk. Dora was the perfect listener. She rarely interrupted, stopping Joanna only if there was something her failing left ear had missed or misinterpreted.

'. . . so that's it, really,' Joanna concluded. 'Mum and Dad know nothing of course. I didn't want to worry them.'

Dora clasped her hands together in pleasure. 'My, what a tale. The best I've heard for years. Takes me back to the war and Bletchley. I spent two years there on the Morse code machines, until your grandad carted me off down the aisle and up to the wilds of Yorkshire to milk cows.'

This was a tale Joanna had heard many times before, but now she listened with renewed interest. 'It must have been an amazing time.'

'The stories I could tell you of things that go on behind closed doors, but I signed the Official Secrets Act and they'll stay with me till the grave. However, it made me believe that anything is possible, that Jo Public'll never know the half. More tea?'

'I'll make it,' Joanna offered.

'I'll help.'

The two of them wandered into the immaculate kitchen. Joanna put on the kettle as Dora doused the teapot under the tap.

'So, what'll you do?'

'About what?'

'Your story. You haven't signed any secrets act. You could go public and make a pretty penny.'

'I don't have enough proof, Granny. Besides, this is a secret that those in high places are prepared to kill to protect. So many people have died.'

'What do you have?'

'Rose's original letter to me, a photocopy of the love letter she wrote to Michael O'Connell, and a programme that seems to have little relevance to the story, apart from showing James Harrison using another name.'

'You got them with you?'

'Yes.' Joanna chuckled. 'They're in my rucksack and they go under my pillow at night. I'm still looking behind me to see if someone's lurking in the shadows. Tell you what, they're no use to me anymore. As they're connected, maybe you'd like them to put with the rest of your royal memorabilia.'

Dora's collection of old newspaper clippings and photos, betraying her status as an ardent monarchist, was a family joke.

'Let's have a look-see then.' Dora walked back into the sitting room with the teapot and settled herself in her favourite armchair.

'I'm surprised you'd allow yourself to think that one of your precious kings might have had a fling outside the marital bed, especially one that was married to your favourite royal,' Joanna commented as she dug inside her rucksack for the brown envelope.

'Men will be men,' countered Dora. 'Besides, up until recently, it was the done thing for kings and queens to have mistresses and lovers. It's a well-known fact there were a good few monarchs whose parentage was questionable. No birth control in those days, you know, dear. And I'd bet there are a whole heap of illegitimate children fathered by a royal. Most would never even know it. For example, I had a friend at Bletchley whose mother had been an undermaid at

Windsor. The things she told me about that Edward VII. It wasn't just Mrs Langtry he put in the family way, you know. Thanks, dear.' Dora reached out for the envelope and removed its contents. 'Now, what have we here?'

Joanna watched as Dora studied the two letters, then opened the programme.

'I saw him a good few times in the theatre. Looks different here though, doesn't he? I thought he was a dark-haired fellow. He's blonde in this picture.'

'He dyed it black when he became James Harrison and assumed his new identity.'

'What's this?' Dora waved around the photo Joanna had found in the attic in Kent and had not yet returned to Marcus.

'That's James Harrison, Noël Coward and Gertrude Lawrence, at some kind of first-night party, I'd imagine.'

Dora studied the photo intently, glanced at the other photo in the programme, then shook her head in wonderment. 'Oh no it's not.'

'Not what?'

'That man standing next to Noël Coward is most definitely not James Harrison. You wait here a minute and I'll prove it to you.'

Dora left the room. Joanna heard the sound of a drawer opening, a scuffling, papery noise before Dora arrived back, her eyes glinting in triumph. She sat down, laid the yellowing newspaper on the table and beckoned Joanna to her. She pointed at the faded, grey print, then at another one. Then she put Joanna's photograph next to it.

'See? It's one and the same person. No doubt about it at all. A case of mistaken identity there, dear.'

'But . . .' Joanna felt breathless and slightly sick as her brain tried to make sense of what she saw. She pointed to the face in the programme, the face of the young Michael O'Connell. 'Surely that can't be him too?'

Dora took her glasses off her nose and stared at Joanna intently. 'No, I'd rather doubt that the then second in line to the throne would be performing in a play at the Hackney Empire, don't you?'

'You're saying the man standing next to Noël Coward is the Duke of York?'

'Compare that photo of him with these: on his wedding day, in his Navy Officer's uniform, on his coronation . . .' Dora stabbed her finger at the face. 'I'm telling you, it's him.'

'But the picture in the programme . . . Michael O'Connell . . . they look so similar . . . I mean, they look like one and the same person.'

'Seems like we're seeing double, dear, doesn't it? Oh, and I brought you something else to look at too.' Dora brought out another cutting from under the other. 'I thought it sounded odd when you mentioned 1926. See, this shows the Duke of York and his wife as they left on a long tour of Australia and New Zealand. They were gone away a good few months. It's doubtful he could have been in Ireland at the same time as he was in the land of the Kiwis. Travel took far longer then, you know.'

Joanna sank to her knees, her hands going to her

head as her brain struggled to compute. 'So ... I ... then it couldn't have been the Duke of York in Ireland after all.'

Dora watched her granddaughter in silence.

'You know,' she said slowly, 'in those days, a lot of famous people used doubles. Monty was known for it, and Hitler of course. That's why they never could get him. They'd never know whether they'd killed the right man.'

Joanna looked up at her grandmother's wise old face. 'You're saying that Michael O'Connell might have been used as a double for the Duke of York? But why?'

'Search me.' Dora shrugged. 'But his health was never good. He was very sick as a young boy.'

'But surely someone would have noticed? All the photographs in the newspapers . . .'

'The quality was not like it is these days. No newfangled lenses pointing up your nose, and no television. You'd see the royals from a distance, if you were lucky. No, I'd reckon if there was some reason they wanted a stand-in, say if the Duke was sick or something, and they didn't want the country to know, they'd have got away with it easily.'

'Okay, okay.' Joanna tried to take in this new information. 'So, if that was the case, and Michael O'Connell was used as a double for the Duke of York, why all this fuss?'

'Don't know, dear.'

'Christ! I thought I'd made sense of it all and if what you've pointed out is right, then I'm back to square one. Why all the deaths? And what on earth was in that letter they were so desperate to get their hands on?'

'Joanna, you're the investigative journalist, that's your job.'

She stared into space, her heart beating hard against her chest. 'If . . . *if* you're right, Simon has sold me completely down the river.'

'Maybe he thought it was better than having you drown in it,' Dora replied sagely. 'Simon's a straight Yorkshireman who regards you as his sister. Whatever he's done, he's done to protect you.'

Joanna shook her head slowly. 'Oh no. Simon may care for me but his true allegiance lies elsewhere. Oh Christ, I don't know. I'm so confused. I thought it was all over, that maybe I could forget about it and get on with my life.'

'Well, you can, of course. All we've done is spot a similarity between one young man and another . . .'

'Similarity? In those photos you'd be pushed to spot the difference and it's too much of a coincidence. This means I'm going to have to go back and rethink everything.'

Joanna watched as Dora stifled a yawn. 'Excuse me, dear, I'm getting too old for all this excitement.'

'Of course. Can I borrow these cuttings?'

'With pleasure.'

'Thank you.' Joanna scooped everything up from the table and stuffed it into the envelope.

'Let me know how it goes, Joanna. My instincts tell me you're on the right track now.'

'God help me, so do mine.' She kissed Dora

warmly. 'This may sound rather overdramatic, but please don't say anything to anyone about what we've discussed, Granny. People involved in this seem to have a horrid habit of getting hurt.'

'I won't, even though half the old biddies in here are too senile to remember what day it is, let alone cope with a story like this.'

'I'll see myself out.'

'Yes. And you take care, Joanna. And I'll say it again: if you trust anyone, trust Simon.'

Joanna called goodbye from the hall, opened the front door and headed for her car. Dora may have unwittingly led her to the truth of the matter, but her final words of advice were fatally flawed.

chapter thirty-seven

The smell of perfume hung around Ian's desk, while his overflowing ashtrays and half-drunk coffee mugs had been replaced by a cactus in a neat yellow pot and a handbag slung by its strap on the back of the chair.

'Who's the new boy?' Simon asked Richard, the office's resident gossip and systems manager.

Richard raised his eyebrows. 'Monica Burrows. She's on secondment from the CIA.'

'I see.' Simon sat down at his own desk and switched on his computer. He'd been out of the office for most of the past month. He stared at Ian's desk, felt sick at the way his essence seemed to have been swept away with his few personal possessions. And it was on file that it was Simon who had ended Ian's life, shooting him in self-defence, even though it was Marcus Harrison who had actually fired the fatal shot. Jenkins had suggested it was cleaner that way, kept within the 'family'. He checked the time. He had fifteen minutes before reporting to Whitehall.

'Hi.'

A voice right behind his chair startled him. He turned round to see a tall, attractive brunette attired in an expensive suit. The brunette held out her hand. 'Monica Burrows, good to meet you.'

As Simon shook her hand, he noticed her smile was warm, but the perfectly made-up green eyes were cold.

'And you,' he replied.

'Seems we're desk neighbours,' Monica said as she sat down and crossed her long, slim legs. 'Maybe you'll help show me the ropes.'

*

He had the curtains drawn against the strong morning sunlight pouring in through the high windows. Simon thought for the first time how frail he looked, the desk lamp accentuating the deeply engraved lines on his face.

'Sit down, Warburton. Before we go any further, did you turn up anything through that private detective agency that James Harrison had engaged?'

'No, sir. The chap I interviewed told me James Harrison had asked him to investigate what had happened to Niamh Deasy, all those years ago in Ireland.'

'Guilt in the last stages of his life,' sighed the old man. 'I presume the chap came up with nothing?'

'No more than that she and the child died at the birth, sir.'

'Well at least I can take comfort that the British security service managed to cover their tracks sufficiently on that one. Now, this name that Miss Haslam gave you is interesting, very interesting indeed. I'd always wondered who it was she trusted enough to deliver the damned things. I've got a man on to it, but the chances are she's probably dead.'

'Possibly, sir, but at this point anything's worth a shot.'

'Yes. Anything else?'

'No, not really. I'm beginning to wonder whether he destroyed the letter, that maybe it just doesn't exist anymore,' commented Simon. 'We've turned both houses upside-down, looked in every conceivable place. It's obvious to me that the Harrison family know nothing of James's past. And—'

'Look how close the Haslam girl came to discovering the truth. We were only lucky that Harrison's Irish affair provided the perfect smokescreen.' The old man sighed. 'I cannot rest until that letter is found and destroyed. Mark my words, if we don't get hold of it then someone else will.'

'Yes, sir.'

'As there seem to be few other options, I'm putting you back on duty with Zoe Harrison. The Palace is still dithering as to how to play the situation. Prince George is resisting all attempts to bring him to his senses. The Palace are having to go along with him for the present, hope the relationship peters out.'

Simon studied his hands. 'Yes, sir.'

'We must hope that the infatuation ends. I would not relish having to personally put a stop to it, as I had to last time. Prince George is insisting that Miss Harrison be seen out officially in public with him. The Palace have agreed to her attending a film première with him in a couple of weeks' time. He's eager to move her into the palace, they are resisting. She's been away on a short holiday with her son for the past week.

You are to report to Welbeck Street next Monday morning.'

'Yes, sir. One last thing: Monica Burrows from the States, Jenkins told me she'll be working alongside us. I presume she knows nothing?'

'Absolutely not. Personally, I disapprove of all this getting into bed with other intelligence agencies, sharing methods and pooling ideas. Jenkins will put her on light surveillance work, spending time with members of the department, shadowing them.'

'Of course, sir.' Simon stood up, knowing the meeting was over.

'Thank you, Warburton. We'll speak at the usual time.'

Simon left the office thinking the old man seemed to have aged dramatically in the past few weeks. But then he'd carried the secret alone for many, many years. And the burden of that was enough to sap the strength of the strongest constitution.

*

'Joanna!' A pair of thick, hairy arms went around her shoulders and clasped her in a bear hug.

'Hi, Tom.' She was rather taken aback by this unusual display of affection.

He dropped his arms and stood back to look at her.

'How are you, love?'

'I'm fine.'

'You look peaky.'

'Thanks!'

'That's okay. You sure you're all right?'

'I think so. I've not been sleeping too well since I got back to London. Must be the noise. It's so quiet at home.'

'Hmm,' Tom said thoughtfully. 'Well now, as it's your first day you're to take it easy, and I'll see you for a sandwich next door at one o'clock. There's a few things I should fill you in on. Some . . . changes that have occurred since you went away. Go on, get off with you to your old desk.' He winked at her and returned to his computer.

Joanna wandered across the office, breathing in its fuggy smell. No matter how many 'NO SMOKING' notices the management posted, a cloud of cigarette smoke still hung above the desks in the newsroom. Glad Alice's chair was empty – she wanted some time to settle in without a barrage of questions – Joanna sat down.

Tom's comments were accurate. She was shattered. The past few days had been spent going through the motions of saying goodbye to her parents, travelling to London and back to her flat. These things she had done on autopilot as her mind ran over and over the new facts. She'd compared further photos of the young Duke with the one of the young Michael O'Connell in the programme. The two men were virtually indistinguishable. Taking Dora's idea of a double, Joanna had come up with a vague outline of what might have happened: a young actor, very similar in looks and age to the Duke of York, plucked to play the part of his life. Discounting the Duke being in Ireland due to the fact that he'd been in New Zealand at the time, it *had* to be Michael O'Connell who had travelled to Ireland to stay in the coastguard's house. And therefore Michael O'Connell who had the affair with Niamh Deasy. Poor Ciara had seen the picture of the Duke of York's coronation on the front of the *Irish Times* and understandably thought it was *he* who had been staying at the house across the bay, *he* who'd had an affair with her dead sister. And, Joanna thought sadly, the letter, hidden for so many years under the floorboards of the house, had probably been no more than the last few sad words of a dying woman to Michael, the man she loved.

If this was the case, why had Michael O'Connell changed his identity? What had he known that had provided him with a house the size of Welbeck Street, money, an aristocratic wife and almost overnight success as an actor? And what about the love letter to Siam from the mysterious lady that had begun her quest in the first place? Had it been written by Rose as she'd previously thought? And why, since James's death, had so many others died too?

The bottom line was that, even though the similarity between the two men was incredible, there was absolutely no proof.

Joanna glanced around trying to bring herself back to reality. The chances were that if she gave anyone so much as a sniff of the fact she was still 'interested', her number would be up. They'd given her back her life because they thought what she knew was safe. The big question was, did she have the strength and courage to pursue the truth? Even if she had no firm answers to a hundred questions, Joanna's instincts told her she was dangerously close to finding out.

*

'So, tell all.' Tom eyed her over his pint.

Joanna shrugged. 'Nothing to tell. I fell in the water during a storm, got carried away by the current and nearly drowned.'

'I know *that*, Jo. But what did you find out that had you fighting for your life?'

'Nothing, Tom, really. It's a complete coincidence. All my leads led to nothing. As far as I'm concerned the chapter's closed. I've got my job back and I intend to concentrate on digging the dirt on supermodels and soap stars, rather than getting carried away imagining fantastical plots fertilized by mad old ladies.'

Tom threw back his head and laughed. 'Joanna, you are a ghastly liar, but so be it. I accept that they've done a good job and you've been well and truly scared off. Which is a shame because I've done a little further digging myself.'

'Really? I wouldn't bother if I were you, Tom. The road leads to nowhere.'

'I don't like to pass rank on you, darling, but I've been in this business longer than you've been on the planet and I can smell a scandal from a mile. So, do you not want to hear?'

Joanna shrugged casually. 'Not really, no.'

'Ah, go on, I'll tell you anyway. I was reading through one of those autobiographies of our Sir James and something struck me as odd.'

Joanna continued to look disinterested so Tom continued. 'It recalls how close Sir James was to his wife, Kitty. How strong their marriage was and how devastated he was when she died.'

'Yes,' agreed Joanna. 'So?'

'Well, if your beloved died abroad, surely you'd want to collect the body and have it buried on home soil?'

'Probably.'

'Then tell me why Sir James didn't do that?'

'I don't know. Can I have my sandwich? I'm starving.'

'Sure. Cheese do?'

'Fine.'

Tom shouted the order over the noisy hubbub and ordered a couple more drinks. 'Anyway, she's over ninety by now, so the chances of her being compos mentis are slim.'

'Tom, surely you're not suggesting she's still alive?'

'Who knows? I just think it's mighty odd she wasn't buried here in England.'

'Tom, this is all very interesting, but as I said, I've come to the end of the line.'

'Your call, darling.' He shrugged.

'Besides, how would you go about trying to locate someone who's supposedly been dead for nearly sixty years?'

'Ah now, Jo, them's tricks of the trade. There's always a way to reel 'em in, if you word it right.'

'Word what right?'

'The ad, placed amongst the obituaries. Every old

crone reads those to see if anyone they know has copped the Big D. Come on, eat your sandwich, looks like you could do with putting on a few pounds.'

*

Joanna arrived home that night feeling exhausted. She picked her post off the mat and headed for the bathroom. Coming back from the clean, pure Yorkshire air made London feel even more dirty and grimy. As the taps ran water into the bath, Joanna munched an apple and opened her post. There was a sweet letter from Zoe Harrison, welcoming her back to London and asking Joanna to ring her so they could get together.

She thought about the suggestion as she soaked in the tub. Even though she liked Zoe enormously, she wondered whether she should give the entire Harrison family a wide berth. All her problems seemed to have stemmed from her association with them. Marcus had bombarded her with flowers in hospital and rung constantly asking to come up and visit her. She had instructed the nurses to say she was not well enough for visitors. She was aware Marcus had saved her life, which rather made up for his roguish behaviour of the past, but the thought of seeing him and subsequently having to relive the memory of that ghastly night was something she'd so far been unable to stomach.

Joanna stepped out and wrapped herself in a towel.

Of course, if she did ring Zoe it might be possible to slip in the odd question about Kitty and her unrecorded death . . .

Having eaten some toast and drunk a glass of wine, Joanna paced restlessly about her sitting room. She reopened the book on the house of Windsor she'd purchased from Waterstone's on her way home and stared at the photograph of the young Duke of York and his bride. Casting her eyes down, she noticed a ring on the fourth finger of his left hand.

She went to fetch a magnifying glass and placed it on the ring. Even though the photograph had it partly in shadow, the shape and the crest, that of a fleur-de-lys, looked awfully familiar. Joanna closed her eyes and scoured her brain. Where had she seen that ring before? Cursing out loud because the answer would not come to her, Joanna headed for bed.

At four o'clock, her eyes shot open.

'Of course!'

Too excited to sleep, she counted the minutes until morning came and it was an acceptable hour to put in a call to Zoe. She went into the hall and picked up the receiver.

*

'How are you?' Zoe stood up from her chair and embraced Joanna warmly.

'I'm well.'

'Sure?'

'Really.'

'Good. Sit down and help me with this bottle of champagne.'

Joanna took her seat at the table in the packed Kensington bistro. She noticed they were sat by the window, always considered the best tables in the place. She could feel eyes all around staring at Zoe, who was ignoring the attention stoically.

'This is such a treat! I've left Jamie at home with Marcus so we can take as long over lunch as we want. You know it was him that told the papers about me and Pip, don't you?'

'No, I didn't. Oh, Zoe, what a low-down thing to do.'

'Sure was. He confessed, very cleverly I might add, from his hospital bed. Said he'd been desperate for money. He looked so pathetic and penitent lying there.'

'Was he badly hurt?'

'The bullet lodged in the top of his arm and they had to use surgery to remove it. It damaged the nerves, so he's having to have major physio to get his arm back to working order. He's walking around like Nelson at the moment, enjoying the sympathy. I've told him he's an untrustworthy, mercenary pig, but I've forgiven him.'

'Under the circumstances, I think that's pretty decent of you,' replied Joanna as Zoe poured champagne into her glass.

'Well, he's offered to give the money that the paper paid him for the scoop on Pip and I to charity as penance. I can't ask for more than that can I?' Zoe grinned. 'And he's being so unbelievably nice and grovelly it's beginning to get on my nerves. The accident was a real shaker for him. I don't think Marcus has ever considered his own mortality before. And the fact you were involved, well, that really upset him. What did happen over there in Ireland to the two of you?'

'What did Marcus tell you?'

'Not much. That you were duck shooting in an

estuary and a gun went off by mistake. It hit him and caused you to tumble into the water.' Zoe raised her eyebrows. 'All sounded a bit far-fetched to me.'

'Zoe, it's a long story, and to be honest I'd prefer not to talk about it at the moment. It brings back some rather unpleasant memories. Let's toast to the future. Cheers.'

'Cheers.' They clinked glasses.

'Anyway, before I forget, I told Marcus I was seeing you today and he sent his love. He asked me if I'd ask you if you'd see him.'

Joanna sighed. 'Maybe.'

'Please, Jo. You should hear him bending my ear night after night, pining after the lost love of his life. Is Marcus over for you?'

'I don't know, to be honest.'

'Well, you should see him. It might help sort out how you feel. He's working really hard setting up the launch of the memorial fund next week. It's the first time I've seen Marcus put his mind to anything. He says it's keeping his mind off you.'

'I'm flattered. But I've only been back a few days and I'm still settling down. By the way, did you bring William Fielding's ring?'

'Yes.' Zoe reached into her handbag and pulled out a small leather box. She passed it to Joanna.

Trying to steady her trembling fingers, Joanna opened it.

'Well? Is it the one you saw in the catalogue? A lost heirloom from Tzarist Russia? A priceless ring stolen directly from the finger of some murdered archbishop during the Reformation?' teased Zoe.

'I'm not absolutely sure but, yes, it might be. Would you let me borrow it for a few days? I promise not to let it out of my sight.'

'Of course you can. It's not even mine to keep anyway. It seems poor old William had no living relatives. Maybe, if the ring is worth something, he'd like the money to go to the Actors' Benevolent Fund.'

'That's a nice idea.' Joanna closed the box and stowed it away in her rucksack. 'I'll let you know as soon as I find out for sure. Now,' she took a sip of champagne to calm the adrenalin that was racing round her body, 'tell me all about your prince.'

'He's fine.' Zoe nodded, reaching for the menu and studying it.

'Only "fine"? Not an apt word for the love of your life, the fairytale relationship of the decade, the—'

'I've not seen him in a while. I've been spending some time with Jamie over the Easter holidays. He's still shaken after what happened and he's nervous about going back to school and being ribbed.'

'Zoe, I've been away for weeks. I've rather lost touch. What did happen to Jamie?'

'Oh, he got teased at school about my relationship with Pip. I hadn't told him about it and while we were away in Spain together he ran away. It was Simon who found him, actually, lying asleep on his great-grandfather's grave.' Zoe's face softened. 'I'm still amazed Simon knew Jamie well enough to know where to look. He's such a kind man, Joanna. Jamie adores him.'

'But you and Pip, you're still okay, aren't you?'

Zoe sighed and took a sip of champagne. 'I'll explain after we've ordered.'

Over a lobster fettuccine for Zoe and lamb's liver for Joanna, Zoe tried to pinpoint how she felt.

'I was very angry with him when I left Spain. He just didn't seem to understand my fear, or to be honest care, that Jamie was missing. When he flew back to London he did the flower thing, apologized profusely for his insensitivity, promised to make sure Jamie was protected in the future.'

'So, everything's fine again, is it?'

'Supposedly, yes. Pip's moving heaven and earth to have his parents and the rest of the family accept me. He's issuing ultimatums, the lot. But' – Zoe twirled a piece of pasta round her fork – 'I'm seriously beginning to question my own feelings. I mean, I feel I'm under so much pressure to reciprocate. I'm desperate to believe that what I've felt for so long is real. Pip is all I've wanted for years, and now I've got him – well' – Zoe shook her head – 'I'm beginning to find fault with him.'

'That's very normal, Zoe. Especially when you've had this image in your head for all this time. No one could live up to the imaginary Pip of your dreams.'

'I know. I keep telling myself that. But, the truth is, Jo, I don't know how much we have in common. He never finds things that I find funny even vaguely amusing, in fact, to be honest he rarely laughs. And he's so –' Zoe searched for the word ' – rigid. There's no spontaneity at all.'

'Surely that's more to do with his position, rather than his personality.'

'Perhaps. But you know how with some men, you don't feel you're your true self? How you feel you're always acting? That you can never really relax?'

'Yes. I had one like that for five years, although I didn't realize it until he dumped me. I'm much happier now. Matthew just didn't bring out the best in me. We rarely had fun.'

'That's just it, Jo. Pip and I spend our lives having intense conversations about the future and never enjoying the moment. And I still haven't got up the courage to introduce him to Jamie. I just have this awful feeling that my darling son won't like him.'

'That's an awfully negative attitude, Zoe. And Jamie'll sense it.'

'Besides all that, it's the thought of the scrutiny I'll be placed under for the rest of my life. Having the media analysing my every move, having a camera lens pointed up my nostrils everywhere I turn.'

'I'm sure if you love Pip he can help nurse you through all that. It's your feelings for him that you must get straight in your mind.'

'Love conquers all, you mean?'

'Exactly.'

'Well, that's the bottom line, I suppose. I just don't know whether I love him or not. But I feel a bit like Pooh Bear stuck in the Rabbit hole. I've gone so far in that I'm wondering how on earth I can get out. God, it's times like this when I really wish my grandfather was still alive. He'd have some sane, wise words to throw on the subject.'

'You really were terribly close, weren't you?'

'Absolutely. I wish you could have met him, Jo. You'd have loved him and he'd have loved you. He adored feisty women.'

'Was your grandmother feisty?'

'I'm not really sure. I do know she came from a wealthy background. The White family were awfully grand, though. She was a Lady. Of course she lost her title when she married my grandfather. Quite a catch for an actor, especially one with supposed Irish origins.' Zoe raised her eyebrows.

'Kitty's maiden name was White?'

'Yes. She was awfully pretty, petite and dainty—'

'Like you,' countered Joanna.

'Maybe. Perhaps that's why James was so fond of me. Talking of dead wives, there's something else I wanted to tell you. I've been asked to play one.'

'*Talk to the White Knight's lady . . .*'

'Sorry?' Joanna forced herself to concentrate on what Zoe was saying.

'MCM are doing a major, multimillion pound remake of *Blithe Spirit*. They want me for Elvira.'

Joanna forced her mind back to the present. 'Blimey, Zoe, are we talking Hollywood here?'

'We sure are. The part's mine if I want it. They've seen a rough-cut of *Tess* and don't even want to audition me. They came through to my agent yesterday with an offer that borders on the obscene.'

'Zoe, that's fantastic! They must think you're something very special if they've offered the part on a plate without even meeting you.'

'I think they think their American audiences will think I'm something special, being the girlfriend of a prince. I don't wish to be cynical but I hardly think the offer would have come through if my face hadn't been plastered all over the papers with Pip next to me.'

'Zoe, don't belittle yourself. You are an extremely

good actress. Hollywood would have come calling eventually with or without Pip.'

'Yes. But I can't do it, can I?'

'Why not?'

'Jo, get real. If I marry Pip the most I'm going to be doing is chomping my way through numerous canapés and shaking endless hands in my position as ninth-best Royal figurehead, if they can't get one of my higher-profile prospective in-laws to do it.'

'Times are changing, Zoe, and you could be just what the royal family needs to bring them kicking and screaming into the twentieth century. Women have careers these days, end of story.'

'But maybe not careers whereby they maybe have to take their clothes off, or at best kiss their leading man.'

'I don't recall any nudity in *Blithe Spirit* myself,' chuckled Joanna.

'There isn't, but still you get my drift. No,' sighed Zoe, 'if I go ahead and marry him, I can kiss my career goodbye.'

'Have you told Pip?'

'Er, no, I haven't.'

'I suggest you do. Someone'll leak it to the press.'

'Exactly my point!' Zoe's blue eyes flashed. 'My life's not my own anymore. They've given me two weeks to decide. I'm taking Jamie back to school this Sunday, then I'm going to go down to Kent for the rest of the week to try to get my head straight.'

'Alone?'

'Of course not. Those days are long gone. Simon is joining me, not that I mind him being around. He's a great cook.'

Joanna looked at her watch. 'I know my boss told me to take it easy this week but even he might blanch when I arrive back at ten to five. I'd better go.' Joanna reached for her wallet, but Zoe stopped her.

'Don't be silly. This is on me. It's been so good to see you. I'm sorry I even thought for one minute it was you that gave me and Pip away to your paper.'

'Don't worry about it.' Joanna smiled. '*I* thought about doing it for at *least* one minute!' She leaned over and kissed Zoe on the cheek. 'You know where I am if you need to talk.'

'I do. Maybe you'd like to come to dinner next weekend at Welbeck Street. Pip's coming over and I think it's about time he met some of my family and friends. Then you can judge for yourself. I could do with a second opinion.'

'Okay. Give me a ring during the week. You take care.'

Joanna waved at Zoe as she left the restaurant, passing through the two paparazzi who were stationed outside, waiting for Zoe to make her exit. She saw a bus pulling into the stop opposite her. Taking her life in her hands as she dodged through the traffic, and with no idea where the bus was actually going, Joanna jumped aboard and climbed up to the top deck. Panting, she sat down and opened her rucksack. Reaching for the now decidedly crumpled brown envelope, she pulled out the photograph she had been studying so hard last night, then opened the box containing the ring. There was absolutely no doubt. The ring she held in her palm matched exactly the one that the Duke of York wore on the fourth finger of his right hand.

Joanna stared out of the window as the bus wended its way up Kensington High Street. Was this the proof she needed? Was this ring enough to guarantee that what her dear old granny had so innocently pointed out was the truth? That Michael O'Connell *had* been used as a double for the Duke of York?

And there was another thing . . . Tucking the ring safely back into her rucksack, Joanna removed Rose's letter. '. . . *if I am gone, talk to the White Knight's lady* . . .' James had been knighted. Kitty was not only a lady but a White.

Joanna felt her stomach churn. It seemed Tom had been spot-on.

*

Over a dozen national French newspapers had been listed in the directory, plus numerous local papers. She'd start with *Le Monde* and maybe a couple of others. If she received no joy from those, she'd move on to the next three, and so on. There was, after all, no guarantee that Kitty was still living in France. She might well have left soon after her death.

But how to word the advert so that Kitty would know it was safe to reveal herself? And, by the same token, not alert anyone who might be watching and waiting themselves? Joanna sat cross-legged on her bed far into the night, the duvet increasingly hidden by scraps of discarded paper, each one of which she must burn to a cinder before morning came.

As the dawn rose, Joanna moved to her computer and typed in the few words she would use, deleting them immediately after they had printed. On her way to the office the following morning, armed with a phone-card, she put in three calls to Paris. The ads would be placed in two days' time. All Joanna could do now was to wait.

chapter thirty-eight

'Hello, Simon.' Zoe reached up on tiptoe and planted a kiss on his cheek. 'It's lovely to see you. How have you been?'

'Well. You?'

'Yes, fine.' Zoe picked up his holdall from the floor of the hall and headed for the stairs, leaving Simon to follow in her wake. 'Jamie was so sorry to have missed you. I took him back to school yesterday. He was so nervous, poor thing, but I had a good chat with the headmaster and he promised to keep an eye on him. There.' Zoe placed Simon's holdall on the floor of his bedroom. On the table by the bed was a card with a felt-tip picture of two people playing on a computer. Zoe picked it up and handed it to Simon. 'It's from Jamie, to welcome you back.'

Simon took the card from her and read the childish inscription.

'That's sweet of him,' he answered.

'Now, you get settled, then come downstairs and have a drink. I've cooked us a meal, seeing as I owe you one.'

'Zoe, sorry to be a party-pooper, but I've already

eaten and I have a heap of work to do tonight. It's very kind of you, but maybe some other time, okay?'

Zoe's face fell. 'But Simon, I've spent all afternoon cooking. I . . .' She fell silent as she saw his closed face. She shrugged. 'Oh well. Never mind.'

Simon did not reply, but instead busied himself with unpacking his few possessions from his holdall.

'As Pip's away this week, I thought I'd go down to the house in Kent tomorrow, have a few quiet days there. Will that be okay?'

'Of course. Whatever you'd prefer,' he answered shortly.

Zoe felt uncomfortably as though her presence was undesired. 'Well, I'll leave you to it. Come down for a cup of coffee when you've finished your work.'

'Thanks.'

Zoe shut Simon's door behind her, feeling horribly deflated. She wandered down the stairs towards the yummy aroma wafting from the kitchen. She poured herself a glass of wine out of the bottle she'd chosen earlier from the vintage collection down in the cellar and sat at the table.

She'd been in such high spirits all day, running around the house tidying it up, shopping at Berwick Street market to get fresh ingredients for supper, coming home with armfuls of flowers to let spring indoors. Her excitement, all the things she had done today, were in anticipation of Simon's arrival at six that night. Zoe swallowed hard then drank some more wine. She groaned as realization hit her properly for the first time. Her actions today had been those of a woman elated by the thought of seeing a man she cared for, a man who was a prospective lover . . .

*

Simon did not appear downstairs that night. Zoe left most of the Stroganoff on the plate in front of her, preferring to drown her sorrows with the excellent bottle of wine.

Pip phoned at ten, telling her he loved her and missed her, reminding her that she was to face her first public outing with him in a week's time and should do something about a dress, which only served to aggravate her tension further. She tersely wished him goodnight and took herself off to bed.

Maybe, just like she had done with Pip for all those years, her imagination had run riot with Simon. She'd thought he cared for her, thought she'd felt his warmth towards her during the times they'd spent together previously. But tonight he'd been cold, distant, making it obvious to her he was there to do his job and nothing more. Tears of self-pity fell down her cheeks as she berated herself for the fact that it was not the love of her life she longed for beside her, but the man sleeping only a few feet from her in his upstairs bedroom.

*

The journey down to Kent the following day was conducted in virtual silence. Zoe, hungover and tense, sat in the back seat trying to concentrate on the film script of *Blithe Spirit*.

Having stopped off for supplies at the supermarket in Maidstone, they drove to the oast house. After

Simon had carried in Zoe's holdall and the shopping, he asked her curtly if there was anything else she required, then disappeared upstairs to his bedroom.

At seven that evening, as Zoe was sitting eating an uninspired pork chop with a covering of lumpy gravy, Simon wandered into the kitchen.

'Mind if I make myself a coffee?'

'Of course not,' she replied. 'There's a chop and potatoes keeping warm in the Aga if you want them.'

'Thanks, Zoe, but there's really no reason for you to cook for me. It's not your responsibility, so don't bother in future.'

'Come on, Simon, I was cooking for myself anyway.'

'Well, thanks. I'll take it upstairs, if that's okay.'

Zoe watched him reach inside the Aga and retrieve the plate.

'Simon, have I done something wrong?'

'No.'

'Are you sure, because it feels to me like you're trying to avoid me.'

He didn't meet her eyes. 'Not at all. I realize that it's difficult enough having a stranger staying in your house and invading your privacy without him foisting himself on you when you want some time alone.'

'You're hardly a stranger, Simon. I regard you as a friend as much as anything. After what you did for Jamie, well, how could I not?'

'All in the line of duty, Zoe.' Simon put his coffee and his plate on a tray and headed towards the door. 'You know where I am if you need me. Goodnight.' The kitchen door closed behind him.

Zoe moved her virtually untouched meal to one side and laid her head on her arms. 'All in the line of duty,' she muttered sadly.

*

'Good news. Our messenger is still alive.'

'Have you found her?' Simon asked, pacing across his bedroom floor.

'No, but we have located where she used to live. She moved several years ago when her husband died. There have been various owners since and the present ones don't have a forwarding address. However, I reckon we'll have tracked her down by tomorrow. Then we might be getting somewhere. I'll want you to fly across, Warburton. I'll be in touch as soon as we've pinpointed her whereabouts.'

'Okay, sir.'

'I'll call you in the morning. Goodnight.'

*

'Got a job for you this morning, my darling.' Tom's eyes twinkled as he hovered over Joanna's desk.

'What?'

'Get your backside over to the South Bank. It's the launch of the James Harrison memorial fund in the foyer of the National.'

Joanna looked up at Tom. 'Me?! Oh Christ, Tom, send Alice, will you?'

'We're running the interview you did with young Marcus Harrison tomorrow. As you wrote the piece, you'd better cover the launch too.'

'Tom, please . . . I . . .'

'I hope you're not refusing to do as your boss has requested, Miss Haslam. You can get fired for that kind of insubordination, you know.'

'I thought my interview with Marcus had been canned yonks ago. Why put it in now?'

'Because, my dear, the Harrisons have suddenly become strangely newsworthy. A shot of Zoe at the launch'll look good on the front pages. You never know, her boyfriend might put in an appearance too.'

'Zoe's in Kent.'

'Not a million miles away from London. Come on, Jo, get your arse into gear. It starts in an hour. Steve'll come with you for the piccies.' He threw an invitation on to Joanna's desk. 'See you later, alligator.'

'Sod,' muttered Joanna under her breath. She sighed, wishing that if she was going to have to meet Marcus face to face for the first time since the accident she'd worn something a little more glamorous than a pair of old jeans and a T-shirt.

*

The foyer was jam-packed with journalists and photographers, plus the odd television camera. It was a vast turnout for an event that would normally have warranted a handful of barely interested journalists.

Joanna took a glass of Buck's Fizz from a passing tray. She could see the top of Marcus's head peeping out from the middle of a huddle of journalists. Staying where she was, delaying the moment when she would have to glean a few words from his lips, she studied the large photos of Sir James Harrison that had been placed on boards around the foyer.

There he was as Lear, taken in dramatic pose, hands reaching to the heavens in askance, a heavy gold crown placed on his head.

'Art imitating life, or life imitating art,' she mused.

She turned and saw an extremely attractive woman standing no more than a few feet away from her. As their eyes met, the woman smiled at her, then moved away.

Joanna's attention was taken by Marcus, who had broken away from the crowd of journalists and was heading straight towards her. She hated herself for feeling her heart thud as he neared her. His brush with death had not impaired his looks, the arm in a sling half-hidden under his jacket giving him an air of vulnerability. She could see as he approached her that his eyes were full of anticipation, with more than a dash of apprehension.

'Joanna.' He kissed her warmly on the cheek. 'It's lovely to see you. I was hoping you might come.'

'The paper sent me,' she replied.

'Marcus!' A photographer was calling him.

'Look, it's chaos here, but please, Jo, would you hang around for a while afterwards? Let me take you to lunch. I really want to explain things to you. It's been driving me crazy for weeks.'

'I . . .'

'Surely at the very least you owe me an hour, in return for saving your life,' he urged, his eyes filling with mischief.

Her resolve disappeared. 'Okay.'

'Great!' He grabbed her hand, kissed it and began to move away.

'Is Zoe here?'

'No, but the thought she might have been has brought them flooding in in their droves. See you later.'

*

It was two o'clock before the last journalist had given up on Zoe arriving and left the theatre. Joanna was sitting quietly in a corner of the empty foyer scribbling notes on the launch taken from Marcus's short speech and the press statement she'd been issued with.

'God, I need a drink.' Marcus sank down beside her on one of the purple seats and proceeded to light up a cigarette with his good hand. 'How do you think it went?'

'About as well as any event of this sort possibly could. I reckon you'll get blanket coverage tomorrow. They'll just stick a past photo of Zoe next to your own.'

Marcus exhaled slowly. 'She offered to come, but we decided against it. She said it was my moment. She didn't want to upstage me or the memorial fund.' He stared at her. 'And how are you?'

'I'm well.' She nodded.

'Recovered?'

'Yes, virtually. No permanent scars, not like you.' She glanced at his arm.

'The doctors have told me they don't think I'll ever be scoring aces on the centre court at Wimbledon, but it will mend eventually. Shall we go?' He stood up and offered her his elbow.

As they left the theatre, Joanna noticed the woman

she had seen earlier reading a pamphlet on forthcoming productions.

'Who is she?' Joanna asked Marcus as they strolled into the warm sunlight of the spring afternoon.

Marcus turned to look, then shrugged. 'No idea. A journalist probably.'

'I don't recognize her,' remarked Joanna. 'And few journalists I know wear expensive designer suits.'

'Probably a bored housewife that just happened to be in the foyer at the time. Who cares?' He steered her along the Embankment, his arm going round her shoulders. 'I want to hear all about you.'

*

As the day was so warm, Marcus suggested they eat al fresco in the Embankment Gardens on the other side of the river. Choosing crisp baguettes and a bottle of Chardonnay from a delicatessen inside the nearby station, they lay on the grass enjoying the first taste of proper sun that year.

'It is so good to see you,' said Marcus as he poured the wine into two plastic cups. 'I nearly went demented when the nurses kept saying I couldn't visit you because you were so ill.' Marcus took a bite out of his baguette. 'Was that a rule for all visitors or just me?'

'Well I was very sick, but to be honest I just couldn't cope with seeing you right then.'

'Because of that ghastly night in Ireland? Or because of what Ian Simpson had told you?'

'Both, I suppose.'

'Joanna, for God's sake, if you never believe another word I say, I won't care, but believe this: I did meet

Ian Simpson, and yes, he did offer me money to do something for him, but it was only indirectly concerned with you. I agonized for ages about whether I should tell you, but because Simpson was so aggressive and insistent that I didn't, I thought it safer not to. I promise you, none of my feelings for you were a pretence.' Marcus sighed. 'To be honest, in the past few weeks I've bloody well wished they had been.'

Joanna stopped munching and stared at him. 'I want to believe you, of course I do, but both Simon and Ian Simpson confirmed it. I know how desperately you needed money, and what a rake you've been in the past. Romancing me for a few thousand must have been manna from heaven.'

'Jo, I'd fallen for you ages before any of this happened. The only mistake I made was not to tell you about my meeting with Ian Simpson. Then none of this would have happened. You wouldn't have gone racing off alone to Ireland, I wouldn't have been beaten up by a drunken, violent Simpson, or locked up in a police station in Rosscarbery. Never mind dragging you half-dead out of the drink and getting shot into the bargain.'

Joanna finished off her baguette and wiped her hands on a serviette. 'And have you any idea what it was all about?'

'Not really, no. Simon Warburton came to see me in hospital and explained that Ian Simpson was insane, drunk and vengeful, working outside his remit. But to be honest, I'm still as confused as before. And since I came back I've tried not to think about it, kept myself busy and pined for you.'

Joanna couldn't help but smile at Marcus's lack of guile. 'I think you're right. I'm not really any the wiser either. But just out of interest, what did Ian Simpson pay you to do?'

'They were looking for a letter, something to do with Sir Jim having an affair with a woman. From what Simpson said, she was well known and whatever was in the letter would compromise her family. He said it was meant to be passed to her family on his death and hasn't turned up. He wanted me to keep an eye out for it, see if I could figure out what Sir Jim might have done with it—'

'And keep an eye on me,' added Joanna.

'Yes.' Marcus shrugged. 'You'd got them really worried, Jo. Still, Simon told me the letter was found that night in the house, and that's the end of the matter I suppose. I'd love to know what was in it. Have you got any idea? Must have been something pretty hot for them to be chasing their tails the way they were.'

Joanna lay back on the grass and closed her eyes. 'No idea at all, Marcus.'

'You are so beautiful, Jo,' Marcus said softly.

'Flattery will get you nowhere.' She smiled, not moving. She felt him take her hand and stroke it.

'You know, that night when I pulled you out of the sea, I really didn't think you'd make it. I was so bloody frightened. I . . .' Marcus swallowed. 'I love you.'

She opened her eyes and saw he was leaning over her, his face close to hers.

'Thanks for saving me. I appreciate it, really.'

'Jo, please, is there any way we could forget the past

few weeks, start again? I've been so bloody miserable. I can understand how hard it is for you to believe me after what's happened, but I'd do anything to get a second chance, prove to you that what I'm saying is true. I need you, Jo, I really do. Zoe kept saying how good for me you were, and she's right.' Marcus paused. 'Would you give it another go? Please?'

Joanna studied his earnest face. No matter what he'd done before, he'd cared for her enough to put his own life in jeopardy. His body in such close proximity to hers had aroused her sufficiently to know the sexual spark was still very much there. And there was no doubt she'd missed him.

She put her arms around his neck and drew him towards her. 'Let's take it slowly, shall we? See how we go?'

His face lit up into a smile as he bent to kiss her. 'Just as slowly as you wish.'

*

He insisted on escorting Joanna back to the office in a taxi. She climbed out, Marcus hovering behind her.

'When can I see you again?'

'Zoe mentioned she was having a dinner party on Saturday night. I presume you're invited as well as me.'

'But, Jo, that's almost two whole days away.' Marcus groaned.

She kissed him lightly on the cheek. 'I must go. I have to write up your launch before Tom fires me after only a couple of week of being back. I'll give you a ring. Bye.' She skipped up the steps waving to him, then disappeared through the glass doors.

'And what time do you call this?' Tom growled at her as she passed his desk.

'I got an exclusive, Tom, okay?' she called.

'The way you're glowing, darling, it's obvious where you conducted the interview.' He followed her across to her desk.

'You couldn't be more wrong.' She sat down and turned on her screen. Tom sat next to her in Alice's chair.

'This arrived at reception for you today.' He handed her a small jiffy bag.

'Oh. Thanks.' She took it from him and placed it by her keyboard.

'You going to open it then?' he asked.

'Yes, in a second. I want to get this piece typed up.' Joanna turned her attention to the screen.

'Looks like a small incendiary device to me.'

'What?!' She saw he was smiling. She sighed resignedly and handed it to him. 'Cheers, Tom! You open it then.'

'Sure?'

'Yes.'

Tom tore the flap of the parcel open, and pulled out a small box and a letter.

'Who's it from?' Joanna continued typing. 'Does it tick?'

'Er, right. The letter says, "Dear Joanna, I have been trying to contact you, but I didn't have an address or telephone number. By chance I saw your name under a story in the daily paper yesterday. I enclose the locket that your Aunt Rose gave me last Christmas. I was having a spring-clean and found it in a drawer. As her niece, I think this belongs to you rather than me. Could you contact me to let me know you received it safely? Pop round for a cuppa sometime. It would be nice to see you. Hope you found your aunt. Best, Muriel."'

Tom handed Joanna the box. 'There you go. Want me to open it?'

'No, I can do it, thanks.'

Joanna took the lid off and removed the layer of protective cotton wool, revealing the gold locket with its delicate filigree pattern and thick, heavy gold chain. Joanna carefully pulled it by the chain out of its box and laid the locket on her palm.

'It's beautiful.'

'Sure is. Victorian, I'd guess. Worth a bomb, especially that chain. So, this belonged to the mysterious Rose,' Tom mused.

'Yes.' Joanna fiddled with the clasp that would open the locket.

'If it's anyone, my guess would be a picture of Sir James in there,' remarked Tom as Joanna's fingertips finally managed to win the war of attrition.

Tom watched as Joanna stared at whatever was inside. Her eyebrows puckered, then Tom watched as her cheeks drained of colour.

'Jo, you okay? What is it?'

She did not move, only stared at the contents of the locket as if in a trance. When she finally raised her head and stared at Tom, her hazel eyes shone huge in her pale face.

'I—' there was a catch in her throat as she tried to steady her voice. 'I know, Tom. God help me, I know.'

chapter thirty-nine

Marcus awoke feeling better than he had in years. He climbed straight out of bed, pulled on a tracksuit, a pair of trainers and headed out of his flat to the local newsagent. The day was beautiful and echoed his own high spirits. He collected a heap of papers, twenty Marlboro Lights, then left the shop to go to the café next door.

Over croissants and fresh coffee, Marcus read his way through the reports of his launch, ranging from a few column inches in the *Indy* to Joanna's centre-page spread in the *Morning Mail*. No matter that most of the headlines mentioned Zoe; if it took hanging on to his sister's coat-tails to propel the fund and subsequently himself to fame and fortune, then so be it. He was a mere twenty thousand away now from funding his film. Marcus decided he'd make an appointment with his bank. Armed with this kind of coverage, surely the manager would see he was someone who was going places, and change his mind about lending him the extra capital.

Ordering another coffee, Marcus sat and dreamed of the flat in Chelsea they'd buy for weekdays in town, the comfortable country house in which the influential film producer and his respected journalist wife would throw stylish weekend parties that the media world would vie to attend. Paying for his breakfast, Marcus stuffed his papers in a carrier bag and wended his way home. Having showered, he sat on the small balcony and contemplated whether he should ring Joanna.

He knew she wanted to take things slowly, ease back into their relationship gently, and he certainly didn't want to frighten her off. But on the other hand . . . it wasn't every day he got his face all over the newspapers and he wanted to celebrate with the woman he loved. He rang the newspaper and waited impatiently for the switchboard to put him through.

'Newsdesk.' A brusque voice answered.

'Yes, can I speak to Joanna Haslam.'

'Jo's not here today. She called in sick, said she'd probably not be back till after the weekend. Can I take a message?'

'No, I'll call her at home.'

Marcus tried Joanna's flat and got the answering machine. Deflated, he left a message asking if she needed him to smooth her fevered brow and to call him back immediately. An hour later, after ten further attempts and still no reply from Joanna, Marcus decided to hop in a taxi and call round to her flat. If she was too ill to answer the phone she might need a nurse and he quite fancied giving her a bed-bath.

*

Joanna's flat was deserted. Marcus stared through the un-curtained windows of her sitting room, then hopped over the hedge which he knew would lead him along a small path to the narrow lane which opened on to the street's back gardens. Opening the gate to Joanna's small and rather overgrown patch of grass, he checked for signs of life through the kitchen and bedroom windows. Unless she was hiding in the wardrobe, Joanna was definitely not at home.

Scribbling a note on the back of an old envelope, he posted it through the letterbox, then irritably made his way to the high street and the nearest pub.

*

'I've lost her, I'm afraid.'

Monica Burrows sat in the airy office overlooking the Thames.

'Where? At what time?'

'I followed her and her boyfriend back to the newspaper offices last night. She went inside and, hey, just didn't reappear.'

'She might have spent the night working on a story.'

'Sure, that's what I thought too. This morning, I went to reception and asked to see her. I was told she was not in the building, but off sick.'

'Then she must have slipped out of another entrance. There's bound to be numerous fire exits. Have you tried her flat?'

'Of course, but it's deserted. The boyfriend turned up as I was leaving, obviously looking for her too. I'm real sorry, Mr Jenkins, but I wasn't briefed she was the kind likely to slip the net.'

'No. Admittedly, we weren't expecting her to either. Okay, Burrows, write your report and I'll be down as soon as I've spoken to my colleague.'

'Yes, sir. Sorry, Mr Jenkins.'

Monica left the office and Lawrence Jenkins dialled the Whitehall office. 'It's Jenkins. The Haslam girl's gone AWOL again. I put Burrows on to her, seeing as you said it was a light surveillance job. Burrows lost her last night.'

*

Simon walked to the window of his bedroom and stared out at the garden below. Zoe was sitting in the rose arbour, a straw hat on her head, her lovely face upturned towards the sun. The past few days had been perfectly ghastly. Trapped in this house, the very nature of his job ironically precluding any kind of escape or respite from the nearness of the woman he loved, yet whom he knew was untouchable. He'd done what he thought best to retain his sanity and cut himself off, refusing all her kind offers of hospitality, loathing himself for the confusion and hurt he saw present in her eyes.

Simon's mobile rang.

'You heard from Haslam?'

'No. Why?'

'She's on the missing list once again. I thought you said she was off the case.'

'She was, sir, really. Are you sure she's missing on purpose? Her absence could be perfectly innocent.'

'Nothing about this situation is innocent, Warburton. When are you returning to London?'

'I'm driving Miss Harrison back this afternoon.'

'Contact me as soon as you arrive.'

'Yes, sir. Any news on the messenger?'

'The chap we sent found her house deserted. Gone away, on a long holiday, the neighbours said. Either it's coincidence or she's on the move. We're doing our best to locate her, but even these days the world is a big place.'

'I see,' Simon answered, unable to keep the disappointment out of his voice.

'Haslam's on to something, I know she is, Warburton, and we'd better bloody well find out what it is.'

'Yes sir.'

The phone went dead.

*

Joanna put the menu down and glanced at her watch. The string quartet began to play the first dance. From tables around her, elderly ladies and gentlemen, dressed in finery reminiscent of a more graceful age took to the floor.

'Would madam like to order?'

'Yes. Full afternoon tea for two, please.'

'Very good, madam.'

Joanna fiddled nervously with the locket round her neck, feeling uncomfortable in the pretty summer dress she had bought that morning. She had positioned herself so she had a perfect uninterrupted view of the entrance. It was twenty past three. With every minute that ticked past, her confidence was waning, her heartbeat growing ever faster.

*

The Earl Grey tea grew cool in the shiny silver teapot. The edges of the cucumber and potted-meat sandwiches, untouched on the fine bone-china plate, began to curl. It was ten past four.

*

At half past four, nerves and the fact that she'd polished off numerous cups of tea were making a trip to the lavatory an urgent necessity. The tea dance finished in half an hour. She had to hold out until then, just in case.

*

At five o'clock, after rousing applause for the musicians, the guests began to disperse. Joanna paid the bill, picked up her handbag and headed for the Ladies. After using the facilities, she straightened her hair, which she had rather inexpertly piled on top of her head with combs, and reapplied some lipstick.

Of course, it had been a ridiculous long shot. Kitty Harrison was probably long dead and buried, and even if she wasn't the chances of her seeing Joanna's advertisement, or replying to it, were minute . . .

She was suddenly aware of a face behind her staring into the mirror. A face that, through its obvious age, still showed traces of a noble lineage. Hair immaculately coifed, make-up carefully applied.

'I hear tell the King of Siam once stayed at the Waldorf.'

Joanna turned round slowly, gazed into the faded but intelligent green eyes and nodded.

'And his queen came with him.'

*

Joanna unlocked the door to the suite with the key the woman had offered her. She had obviously checked in, for inside the large, airy room was a small suitcase, open on the stand, and a bottle of pills by the bed.

'You first.' Joanna ushered the woman through the door then closed and locked it behind her. She went to the window, with its view of the busy London street below, and shut the curtains.

'Please, do sit down,' the woman said.

'Thank you . . . Er, may I call you Kitty?'

The woman eased herself into one of the comfortable easy chairs placed in one corner of the room and went off into peals of tinkling laughter. 'You may, my dear, of course, if it pleases you.'

Her heart sank. Even if Kitty looked in charge of her marbles, maybe appearances were deceptive.

Joanna sat down opposite her. 'You are Kitty Harrison, née White? Wife of Sir James, presumed dead over sixty years ago in France?'

'No.'

Joanna's stomach churned. 'Then who are you?'

The old lady smiled at her. 'I think, if we are to be friends, which I'm sure we are, you should just call me Rose.'

*

As soon as Simon entered his room in Welbeck Street, his mobile rang.

'I've just spoken to the editor of Haslam's paper. It seems it's not only her that's missing. It's the newsdesk editor as well, Tom O'Farrell. He told his boss he was on to something big and needed a couple of days to follow it up. They're on to us, Warburton.'

Simon could hear the barely disguised panic in his voice.

'I'm putting every available man on to this as of now. If we can find O'Farrell we'll make sure he tells us where Haslam has gone.'

'Surely they won't be able to break the story, sir? You can control that?'

'Warburton, there are two or three subversive editors who would clap their hands in joy to get hold of a story like this, not to mention foreign papers. For God's sake, it's the story of the bloody century!'

'What would you like me to do, sir?'

'Ask Miss Harrison if she's heard from Haslam. They had lunch last week. Then hold fast where you are. I'll be in touch later.'

*

Joanna stared at the woman.

'But you can't be Rose. I met Rose at a memorial service for James Harrison. And she wasn't you. Besides, she's dead.'

'Rose is a common enough name, especially for the era in which I was born. You are quite correct, my dear. You did meet a Rose. Except the one you met was Catherine Rose Harrison, more commonly known as Kitty.'

'That little old lady was Kitty Harrison?' Joanna asked in amazement.

'Yes.'

'Why did she use her second instead of her first name?'

'A flimsy attempt at protection. She would insist on going to England when he died. Then a few weeks later she wrote to say she was attending the memorial service. She was terribly sick, you see, had very little time left. She thought it the perfect opportunity to see her son for the last time, and view her grandchildren for the first. I knew it would stir up trouble, that it was dangerous, but she wouldn't listen. She didn't think anyone would be there to recognize her, that they'd all be dead and buried by now. Of course, she was wrong.'

'I was sitting next to her in the pew when she saw the man in the wheelchair. Kitty nearly had a seizure. I had to help her out of the church.'

'I know. She told me all about you in the last letter she wrote to me. I was expecting to hear from you, although I knew it might take you a time to work it all out. Kitty couldn't give you too much, you see, put you or myself in danger.'

'How did you know I was looking for you? I'd written my advertisement especially for Kitty.'

'Because I knew everything, my dear. Right from the beginning. When I saw your lines in the paper, asking for "The Queen of Siam to join her King at the Waldorf for tea," I knew it was meant for me.'

'But the clue in Kitty's letter – "Talk to the White Knight's Lady" – how did that refer to you?'

'Because, my dear, I married a French count. His name was Le Blanc and . . .'

'Blanc is French for White.' Joanna shook her head. 'I got it completely wrong.'

'No, you didn't. I'm here and all is well.'

Joanna shook her head. 'But why did she choose me?'

'She said you were a clever and kind girl, and that she didn't have much time. She knew it was over, you see, that he'd find her and kill her.' Rose sighed. 'Why she had to stir this up again, I really don't know. But she was so bitter, I suppose it was an act of revenge.'

Joanna stared at Rose. 'I think I know why she was bitter,' she said quietly.

Rose regarded her quizzically. 'Do you? You must have been doing some very careful investigation since poor Kitty died.'

'Yes. You could say it's rather taken over,' Joanna muttered.

Rose laid her small, neat hands in her lap. 'May I ask you exactly what you're going to do with the information you've gathered?'

This was no time for lies. 'I'm going to publish it.'

'I see.' Rose was silent as she digested this. 'Of course, it was the reason Kitty wrote to you in the first place. It was what she wanted. Retribution, for those that destroyed her life, to blow the establishment sky-high. Myself, well, let us say I still have some loyalty, though goodness knows why.'

'Are you saying you won't help me fit the pieces together? I think we're going to be offered an awful lot of money for this story. It would make you rich.'

'And what would an ancient old woman like me do with money? Buy a sports car?' Rose chuckled and shook her head. 'Besides, I'm rich already. My late husband left me excellently provided for. My dear, have you not wondered why so many around me have died? And yet here I am, still alive to tell the tale.' Rose leaned forward. 'And the thing that has kept me alive is discretion. I've always been able to keep a secret. Of course, I didn't expect I'd be harbouring the best-kept secret of the century in my bosom, but such is life. What I'm saying is that, for Kitty's sake, I can lead you there, but I can't tell you.'

'I see.'

'Kitty trusted you and so must I. But I absolutely insist on anonymity. If my name, or my visit here, or what we might subsequently discuss is ever mentioned I shall vehemently deny all knowledge. Remember, I still have friends in high places too.'

'Then why did you come?'

Rose sighed. 'Partly because of James, but mostly because of Kitty. I may have been part of the establishment, by accident of birth, but that does not mean to say I approve of the things they have done, the way other people's lives have been destroyed to keep the silence. I know I must meet my maker in the next few years. I'd like him to know I did the best I could for those I cared for on earth.'

Joanna nodded.

'Well now, why don't you put that sweet little kettle on to boil and make us both a cup of tea? Then you'd better tell me what you know and we'll take it from there.'

*

It took Joanna almost an hour to tell Rose everything, partly due to discovering she was partially deaf, as well as Rose wanting to clarify every fact Joanna had discovered twice.

'And when the locket arrived at the office yesterday morning and I saw the photograph of her inside, everything fell into place.'

Rose nodded sagely. 'Of course, it was the locket that convinced me downstairs that you were the young lady who had placed the advertisement. You could only have obtained the locket from Kitty herself.'

'As a matter of fact, she gave it to her next-door neighbour, Muriel.'

'Then she must have known they were on their way for her. The locket was mine, you see, a gift from her. Kitty always loved it. I gave it to her when she left for London, as a talisman. For some reason, I'd always felt it had protected me. Unfortunately, as we know, it did not work the same magic for her.'

*

Later that evening, Simon wandered down to the kitchen. Zoe was at the table, writing a list and drinking a glass of wine.

'Hello,' he said.

'Hi.' She didn't look up.

'Okay to make myself a coffee?'

'Of course it is, Simon. You know you don't have to ask,' she replied irritably.

'Sorry.' Simon went to the kettle.

Zoe put her pen down and stared at Simon's back. 'So am I. I'm tense, that's all.'

'Problems?'

Zoe sighed, then stretched. 'I dunno. I just feel . . . a bit unsure of things at the moment.'

He silently poured some coffee powder and sugar into the mug.

'Heard from Joanna recently?'

'No, not since our lunch. Should I have done?'

He shrugged. 'No.'

'Are you sure you're okay, Simon? I mean, I've not done anything to upset you, have I?'

'No, not at all. I've just been . . . dealing with some problems, that's all.'

'Women problems?'

'I suppose you could say that, yes.'

'Oh.' Zoe rather disconsolately refilled her wine glass. 'Love. It makes life so bloody difficult, doesn't it?'

'Yes,' Simon agreed.

'I mean . . .' She looked straight at him. 'What would you do if you were meant to be in love with one person, then found you were actually in love with someone else?'

The way she was gazing at him made Simon's heart begin to thump.

'May I ask who?'

'Yes.' She blushed and lowered her eyes. 'It's—'

Simon's mobile rang in his pocket. 'Shit! Sorry, Zoe, I'll have to take this upstairs.' He raced from the room and shut the door behind him.

Zoe could have wept.

He was back down ten minutes later, his jacket on. 'I have to go, I'm afraid. My replacement will be here any second. Monica's a nice girl, American. I'll be back later.' He smiled at her and left the house.

chapter forty

At Rose's request, Joanna had taken two small bottles of whisky from the mini-fridge, poured them into two glasses and added ice.

'Thank you, my dear.' Rose took a sip. 'I was feeling a little faint. Too much excitement for an old lady like me.' Rose settled back more comfortably in her chair, cradling her whisky glass in her hands. 'As you already know, I was working as a lady-in-waiting for the Duchess of York. Our families had known each other for years and so it was natural that I travelled down from Scotland with her when she married the Duke. Everything was fine, they were very happy, living between their houses in Sandringham and London. Then the Duke's health began to deteriorate. He had a bronchial condition, which, given the problems he'd had as a child, were cause for some concern. The doctors advised complete rest and fresh air for a number of months to help him recover. But there was the problem of what to tell the country. In those days, the royal family were in some ways regarded as immortal, you see.'

'So the idea of a double was put forward?'

'Yes. It is not unheard of amongst senior public

figures, as I'm sure you know. A senior adviser at the Palace happened to visit the theatre one night. And there he saw a young actor whom he thought could pass perfectly adequately for the Duke of York at state functions, factory openings and the like. The young man, Michael O'Connell, was brought in and given "Duke lessons", as myself and the Duchess used to giggle. The Duke was shipped off to Switzerland to recover. Pass me some more ice for my whisky, will you, my dear?'

Joanna did so. Rose put the glass between her shrivelled lips and took a small sip.

'Michael O'Connell was already an extremely talented actor, even in those days. He was installed into the Royal household and it all worked like a charm. Michael lost his Irish brogue completely, and literally, my dear, became the Duke.'

'Did many people know about this?'

'Oh no, only those that absolutely had to. I'm sure some of the servants guessed when they heard the "Duke" singing Irish ballads whilst shaving in the morning, but they were paid to be exceptionally discreet.'

'Was that when you and Michael became friends?'

'Yes.' Rose nodded thoughtfully. 'He was such a nice man, so eager to please. Took the whole situation in his stride. Yet I always felt slightly sorry for him. I knew he was being used and once he was no longer needed he'd be waved away without as much as a backward glance.'

'But it didn't quite happen like that, did it?'

'No. The thing was,' Rose smiled, 'he had such

charisma. He was the Duke with an added dimension. He had a great sense of humour, used to send the Duchess into fits just before they were about to meet and greet. I was always convinced that he laughed her into bed, if you'll excuse the rather tasteless expression.'

Joanna added more ice to her own whisky. 'When did you realize they were lovers?'

'Oh, not for ages afterwards. I thought, just as everyone else who knew had, that the Duchess was playing her part like the trouper she was. Then the Duke came home, fit and well, and Michael O'Connell was packed off back to his life as a roving thespian. And that would have been the end of it if it hadn't been for the fact that—' Rose caught her breath.

'What?'

'That the Duchess had fallen madly, head over heels in love with Michael. When he left the household, she did her best to settle back to the real Duke, but it was obvious she was terribly miserable. Then she came to me one day, asked whether I'd be prepared to help her, that if anyone found out she would make sure my name was never mentioned in connection with the matter. The darling burst into tears on my shoulder and confessed all.' Rose shrugged. 'What could I do but help her?'

'So you began to deliver the letters for her, and you met William Fielding?'

'Was that his name?' Rose queried. 'The young boy from the theatre, anyway. He'd give a letter to me, and I'd hand a parcel to him.'

'A parcel?'

'Yes, but I'll explain that later. Of course, at the

time I'd fallen in love with François, so the fact the Duchess was so in love too rather gave us a bond.'

'Did they see each other after he left the employ of the royal household?'

'Once, but that was later on. The Duchess was terribly concerned for him, for his safety, especially when her secret, one might say, exploded into public view.'

'Someone found out?'

Rose's eyes twinkled. 'Oh yes, my dear, more than one.'

'Was that when they sent Michael off to Ireland?'

'Yes. You see? You know most of the story already. The Duchess came crying to me one day, saying that he'd written to say he was being sent away, back to Ireland, that he didn't want to compromise her sensitive position. So he thought it best if he agreed and left the country as they wished him to do. Of course,' she raised her eyebrows, 'he wasn't meant to come back.'

'What do you mean?'

Rose gave a small sigh of irritation. 'Come, Joanna, don't you see? It was perfect for them. Him returning to Ireland, bearing this extraordinary resemblance to the Duke. Remember, Partition had just taken place. The Irish loathed the English. All they had to do was put it about locally that there was a member of the British royal family staying in those parts and goodbye Michael O'Connell.'

'You mean they wanted him dead?'

'Absolutely. Under the circumstances it was imperative they put him out of the way permanently. But it needed to be done discreetly, presented to the Duchess in a way she couldn't question. She was very volatile, you see. No one quite knew how she'd react.'

'So what happened then?'

'The person who saved Michael from certain death was his Irish lady love. She heard her own, and I might add, highly Republican father plotting and planning to kill Michael. So together they organized his escape back to England.'

'Niamh Deasy died. In childbirth, you know.'

'Oh dearie me.' A tear came to Rose's eye. She reached in her sleeve for a hanky and dabbed her eyes. 'Another tragic casualty in this twisted web of deceit. Michael always wondered what happened to her. He was expecting her to follow him to England, but she never came.'

'Please go on,' Joanna urged.

'Well, Michael came back to London and managed to contact the Duchess. He told her how they'd tried to end his life. The Duchess came back from the meeting, almost hysterical with anger and grief. Having spent a sleepless night trying to think how she could protect him, she came up with an idea. When she told me, I was completely against it. I tried to suggest that it would put her and her family in the most compromising position if it was ever discovered. But she'd have none of it. Michael O'Connell had to be kept from harm, regardless of her own or her husband's reputation and that was an end to it.'

'What was it the Duchess did?' asked Joanna.

She wrote him a letter, which I delivered personally to his lodgings, concealed in the usual way.'

'And Michael O'Connell used this letter to buy him

his safety, a new identity, a nice house and a brilliant future?'

'Spot on. I doubt if he'd have asked for anything, had they not tried so obviously to get rid of him. He was never a greedy man. But,' Rose sighed, 'he thought he'd be safer the more noticeable he was.'

'Yes. It's much easier to kill a nobody than it is a rich and successful actor.'

'After that, everything seemed to settle down.'

'You know, this is what has puzzled me in the past few days. The Duke and Duchess's marriage was always regarded as one of the success stories of the monarchy.'

'It's amazing, isn't it, what propaganda can do?' Rose smiled. 'A few years later as his career was blossoming, James Harrison, as he was now formally known, met Kitty. Out of complete coincidence I'd known her for years. We were presented at court together. And James fell head over heels in love for the first time.'

'You're saying he wasn't in love with the Duchess?'

'Oh, I'd like to believe he was, it would make the story more romantic. But when I attended his wedding to Kitty, I knew it wasn't the case. James glowed that day, in a way the Duchess had done a few years earlier.'

'It was a real love match then?'

'Absolutely. They worshipped each other. Kitty adored his outgoing, charismatic talent. He protected her against' – Rose thought for a few seconds – 'against a world that she'd never been very comfortable being a part of.'

Joanna frowned. 'What do you mean?'

'Kitty White was emotionally unstable, my dear.

Always had been. If she hadn't been part of the aristocracy, she'd have been tucked away in a funny farm years before. Her parents were just thankful to get her off their hands. However, with James she seemed to blossom. His enduring love steadied her somewhat erratic personality traits. They had their son, Charles, and all was going well for both of them . . . until the abdication.'

'I suppose then it was even more vital that the secret never came out.'

Rose studied Joanna thoughtfully. 'Oh yes, my dear, it certainly was. Confidence in the royal family was at an all-time low. The King had done the unthinkable, given up the throne of England to marry an American.'

'Which meant his brother was left to take over,' added Joanna.

Rose nodded. 'Even though I was in France, I felt the shock waves over there. Neither the Duke nor the Duchess had ever even considered that one day they would be crowned king and queen of England. Nor, and perhaps more importantly, had those that worked behind the scenes, those that knew exactly what had happened ten years earlier.'

'So what did they do?'

'Well, you remember the gentleman that so frightened Kitty at the memorial service?'

Joanna rolled her eyes. 'How could I forget?'

'He was a member of the British intelligence service, his remit the safeguarding of the royal family. He went round to the Harrison homestead and begged James to give up the letter the Duchess had written him, for the sake of the future of the monarchy. James, understandably, refused. He knew that without the letter he was unprotected.' Rose sighed. 'Unfortunately, Kitty came home before she was meant to and heard the gist of the conversation.'

'I see.'

'Perhaps it wouldn't have been so bad if she hadn't loved him so much. But she felt betrayed. Here was absolute evidence of her husband's previous, and obviously powerful, liaison with another woman. A woman whom Kitty thought she could never hope to compete with.'

'But James loved her?'

'Yes, madly. But she accused him of keeping secrets, of still being in love with the Duchess. You see, Joanna, you have to understand we are not talking about an ordinary, rational woman here.' Rose sighed. 'It sent her completely off the rails. She took to drink like a duck to water. Worse still, she started making drunken references in public to a secret that *had* to be kept at any cost. In short, she was becoming a liability.'

'Oh God. How awful. What did James do?'

'He wrote to me in France, confiding his fears, knowing I was a friend of Kitty's who also knew the truth of the matter. He was aware it wouldn't be long before our friend in the wheelchair and his cronies got wind of the fact Kitty knew, and of her indiscreet behaviour. James was desperately aware of what lengths they would go to to protect the secret, that even the letter he had could not save a woman who was in danger of spilling the beans anyway. So he decided to act before they did.'

'How did he get her out of danger?'

'Well with my help he took Kitty to France, bought her a new identity and tucked her away in a comfortable institution near Berne in Switzerland. We then made it known to those in England that Kitty had taken her own life whilst on holiday with me, her oldest friend. At the time most of London was aware of her instability. It made a believable story. We held a funeral in Paris with an empty box.' Rose shook her head. 'Let me tell you, my dear, she might as well have been in there for the difference it made to James. I've never seen a man so distraught. He could never see her again, he knew that.'

'Oh God.' Joanna shook her head sadly. 'How tragic. No wonder he never married again. His wife was still living.'

'Then, of course, we had the war. The Germans invaded France and my husband and I left for our house in Switzerland. I'd see Kitty as often as I could. She seemed to be deteriorating on every visit. She'd stopped ranting by then, just sat staring out of the window. I don't think she recognized me. My husband and I didn't reckon she'd see out the war. But she always was a tough old boot, physically anyway.'

'Did she stay in the Swiss institution for all those years?'

'Yes. I admit I stopped going to see her as often as I had before because it all seemed rather pointless. Then, one morning, seven years ago, I received a letter. It was from one of the doctors at the institution, asking me to go and see him. When I arrived, the doctor told me that Kitty, for some unknown reason, had suddenly improved. To the point where he suggested she was well enough to take a step into the outside world. I went to see her and there was absolutely no doubt that she was better. She knew who I was, and was able to talk rationally about the past and what had happened. She begged me to help her at least enjoy the final years of her life in some semblance of normality.' Rose sighed. 'What could I do? My beloved husband had recently died. I was rattling around in that huge chateau all by myself. So I decided I'd buy a much smaller house and have Kitty come and live with me. The doctor had agreed that any deterioration and Kitty would go straight back to the institution.'

'Did she deteriorate?'

'No, not mentally anyway. I'm not saying she was what you might call your average person. She was highly eccentric, as you probably realized when you met her.'

Joanna smiled. 'Yes.'

'We settled down to a life together; two old ladies grateful for each other's company, sharing a past that bound us tightly together. And then Kitty began to develop a cough that wouldn't go away. Tests revealed she had cancer of the lung. The doctor gave her a year to live.' Rose shook her head. 'I think that was the most tragic part of the whole tale. After all those years of incarceration, to finally find some peace, a little happiness and –' Rose fumbled for a hanky in her bag and wiped her eyes ' – Sorry, my dear. It's still very fresh in my mind.'

Joanna reached over and patted her hand, not

knowing what to say. She watched as Rose composed herself, before continuing.

'It was a few months later when Kitty took it into her head that she wanted to go back to England.'

'You should have seen the squalor she was living in. What on earth was in those tea chests?'

The comment brought a smile to Rose's face. 'Her life, my dear. She was the most dreadful magpie; she'd steal spoons from restaurants, toilet rolls and soap from powder rooms. Perhaps it was due to material deprivation in the institution, I don't know but she hoarded everything. When she left France, she insisted on having the tea chests shipped over with her.' Rose stared into space. 'I knew she'd never be back.'

Joanna watched Rose sink down, as if the telling of the story had taken from her slight frame. Rose yawned. From the way Rose's energy was visibly ebbing, Joanna knew it was now or never. 'Rose, do you know where this letter is?'

'Gosh, I'm hungry. I really can't talk anymore until I've had a good meal inside me. Shall we send for room service?' enquired Rose.

'Yes.'

There were so many more questions Joanna wanted to ask. She watched, trying to garner patience as Rose searched in her handbag for her glasses, removed the menu from the table between them and studied it intently. Then she stood up and crossed to the telephone by the bed. 'Hello there. This is suite four. Could you send up two sirloin steaks with Béarnaise sauce and plenty of French fries? Oh, and a bottle of good French white. Thank you.' She put the receiver down and clapped her hands together. 'Oh, I do so love hotel room food, don't you?'

*

If it was possible to mentally pace whilst sedentary in a wheelchair, then the old man was doing just that. He was not behind his desk, in fact he wheeled himself towards Simon to open the door, as if comforted by the sight of the only other human being who could share his anxiety.

'Tomorrow may be too late, dammit!'

'No sign of Haslam or Tom O'Farrell?'

'There's been a lead on O'Farrell's whereabouts which is being followed up at present. My bet is they're holed up in a London hotel somewhere, probably planning the sale of the century for their sordid little story.'

'What about our lady-in-waiting?'

'No flights into England from France have confirmed a passenger by that name, But of course it means nothing. She could have easily travelled in from another country. Christ, man! If Haslam gets to her first . . .'

'Sir, until they've found that letter, they don't have proof.'

He did not seem to be listening. 'I always knew we were headed for disaster, that the fool would never give it up. The bastard even got a knighthood on the strength of his promise.'

'Sir, I think you're going to have to widen the net, let others know what it is they're looking for.'

'No! They have to work blind. We just cannot risk a leak. I'm depending on you, Warburton. You must succeed where I failed.'

'I'll do my best. What do you want me to do?'

'I want you to stay exactly where you are. My gut has always told me, if that letter is anywhere, it's in one of Harrison's houses. If Haslam finds out where it is, she must come and get it. Both houses are under heavy surveillance. Go to the armoury on your way back to Welbeck Street and equip yourself. Do not under any circumstances let emotion cloud your judgement. Tell me now if you feel you are unable to finish the job.'

There was a pause before Simon said, 'No, sir, I can handle it.'

'If you don't, then someone else will. I hope you realize that.'

'Yes.'

'Carry on as normal. I don't want either Haslam or O'Farrell getting wind of the fact we're on to them. Let them lead us to it, understand?'

'I do, sir.'

He turned his wheelchair to face the Mall. 'You realize that if this gets out, it will be the end of the monarchy.'

'Yes.'

'Goodnight, Warburton.'

*

Joanna watched in an agony of suspension as Rose slowly munched her way through everything on her plate. She'd thrown hers down her throat, not even registering the taste. Finally, it seemed Rose was finished. She patted her lips with her napkin. 'Now I feel more like it. A cup of coffee while we chat, I think, my dear.'

Trying to control her frustration, Joanna put the kettle back on to boil.

Rose began again. 'It's well known that royals have had mistresses and lovers since the monarchy came into being. The fact the Duchess of York fell in love with her husband's double was not what the palace would have cared for, of course, but it could be dealt with. Even the fact she insisted on writing him dangerous letters of love, one of which you yourself saw, could be contained. At the time, it was unlikely she would be queen, or her husband king.' Rose chuckled. 'Ironically, history was changed overnight by the most simple yet potent force in the world.'

'Love.'

'Yes.'

'And she did become queen.'

Rose nodded and took a sip of coffee. 'So ask yourself, Joanna, what it could be, what could have happened between Michael O'Connell and the Duchess that could in turn become the most closely guarded secret of the twentieth century? And what would happen if proof of this secret was in letter form? Written, by design, from a woman who at the time loved him so much she was prepared to do anything to save him. Hidden somewhere, used as his only method of protection against the vast armoury of those who wanted and needed him dead?'

Joanna looked around the room for an answer. The

sound of the traffic on the street outside disappeared as the realization hit her.

*

It was Rose's turn to pour whisky down a shocked and shaking Joanna.

'Never let it be said I told you. You guessed.' Rose shook her head. 'I've only seen that kind of shock on one other face, and that was when I confirmed what Kitty had heard through the study door at Welbeck Street.'

'Surely you'd have been best to lie to Kitty? To make her believe she'd misheard? My God.' Joanna shook her head. 'I class myself as perfectly sane and I'm a gibbering wreck having finally discovered the truth.'

'I did consider it, of course, but I knew she'd not leave it there. There was a chance she'd go to the horse's mouth, to the man whom she'd heard James talking to that day in the study. A man who later became Sir Henry Scott-Thomas, head of MI5. A man capable of destroying both her and James if he found out she knew. A man who was later paralysed from the waist down in a riding accident.'

'I see.' Joanna felt as though her brain was frozen. She searched through the grey mists, knowing there were further questions she must ask.

'The letter . . . does it confirm . . . what we've just talked about?' Joanna could not bring herself to voice the words.

'I may have delivered it, but I didn't read it. However, if it kept James alive all those years, allowed him to amass fame and fortune right beneath the noses of those who wanted him six feet under, then yes, I rather believe it does.'

'And why did they never get to you? After all, you delivered the letters.'

Rose shrugged. 'I've always thought I was born under a lucky star. I was never even considered to be a party to any of it. That's why she used me to deliver them. The Duchess was awfully clever, until she couldn't hide her secret any longer. By then, I was engaged to my beloved François and on my way to the Loire.'

'You mentioned earlier you always delivered a package, rather than a letter?'

'Correct.'

'What was in that package?'

Rose yawned. 'Oh my goodness, I'm getting sleepy. It's way past my bedtime. Well, the thing was that obviously these letters were highly sensitive. If they had fallen into the wrong hands, it could have been disastrous. So the Duchess and I thought up a very clever way to disguise them.'

'How?'

Rose wagged her finger at Joanna. 'Come now, you're slowing down. You saw the letter that Kitty sent you, a letter she herself had found quite by accident in James Harrison's house. Even though it was old, there must have been something odd that you noticed about it?'

She racked her brains. 'I . . . yes, if I remember, there were tiny holes around the edges.'

'As you've tried so terribly hard and been so

resourceful, maybe I should help you with the final piece of the jigsaw. Remember, I am only doing it for poor Kitty's sake.'

Joanna nodded her head wearily.

'Well now, the Duchess had two passions in life, not counting poor dear James of course. One of them was the cultivation of the most marvellous roses in her garden at Sandringham, the other, exquisite embroidery.' She eyed Joanna, who looked back at her blankly. 'Now, I think it's high time I was on my way. I am not quite so silly to think that my presence in London will not soon be noted.'

'Rose, please! Don't do this to me! Tell me where the letter is.'

'My dear, I *have* just told you. All you must do now is use that quick little brain and those pretty eyes of yours.'

Joanna knew there was no point in begging. 'Will I see you again?'

'I doubt it, don't you?' Rose's eyes twinkled. 'I thought it best if I made myself scarce for the next few months, until the dust settles. So, I have booked myself on the Orient Express and will take what I am aware will be my last opportunity to see a little more of the world before I die.'

'Did they know it was Kitty who died, not you?'

'Of course.'

'Then yes, you must take every precaution.' Joanna's eyes widened with fear. 'I told Simon you were the messenger. I thought you were dead.'

'Quite. Oh, don't worry, my dear. I'm old enough not to care particularly for my own safety.' Rose laid a hand on Joanna's shoulder. 'But I should think you are in the most ghastly danger. Still you have eyes like a cat and they have nine lives.' Rose kissed her gently on the cheek. 'Goodbye, Joanna. If you survive to tell the tale, you'll leave your mark on the world, of that there's no doubt. See yourself out, will you?' Rose walked towards the bedroom and closed the door behind her.

chapter forty-one

'Hi, Simon, what time did you get back last night?'

'Just after midnight.'

'Oh. Has Miss Burrows gone?'

'Yes, she left as I arrived. I somehow didn't fancy sharing quarters with her.'

Zoe dipped her finger into the sauce she was stirring on the hob. 'She's an attractive girl.'

'Not my type, I'm afraid,' Simon answered shortly, as he filled a cup with coffee granules and hot water. 'What are you cooking?'

'What do you cook for a prince?' She smiled. 'I'm struggling to provide something more sophisticated than my dinner party staple of pasta and salad.'

'Oh God, of course! Your dinner party's tonight! I'd forgotten all about it.'

'Pip called last night. He said he'll expect you at Sandringham at six. The others are arriving around eight so that should time nicely.'

'Others?'

'Yes. Marcus and Joanna. They're back together, you know. She's decided to give him another chance. He's over the moon.'

'Have you spoken to him this morning?'

'No, but he did call last night, said he'd managed to lose Joanna for a day, but hoped to have found her by tonight. I hope they do come. I'm cooking enough food to sink a battleship.'

'Then do you not think you should call and find out?'

Zoe stopped stirring. 'Yes, I suppose I should.' She wiped her hands on her apron. 'Keep stirring, will you?'

She was back a few minutes later. 'No, he's heard nothing.' She shrugged, watching Simon searching her cupboards for something. He turned around with a bottle in his hand. 'Add some Tabasco, it gives the sauce that extra zing.'

*

Later that morning, Simon's mobile rang. 'We think we've located O'Farrell. Knew he couldn't stay without whisky too long. He signed a credit card to buy supplies at an off-licence in the Docklands.'

'I see.'

'We ran a check of his numerous friends and acquaintances and it seems he has a journalist pal in the States who has a flat near the off-licence. My men have checked, and there are signs of life in the supposedly empty apartment. They have it under heavy surveillance at the moment. We've got hold of the telephone number. If he's going to use a modem to send the story, we can stop it instantly.'

'And Haslam?'

'Not a sniff.'

'Do I continue as usual for the present?'

'Yes. If nothing's come to light, collect HRH this evening as planned.'

'Miss Haslam's been invited tonight, although I doubt she'll turn up. It would be rather like walking into the lion's den.'

'Just make sure you're armed, Warburton. I'll be in touch.'

*

Simon arrived outside the secluded house on the Sandringham estate and pulled the car to a halt. He opened the door, climbed out and saw the butler was already opening the front door.

'The Prince will be delayed, I'm afraid. He's on the telephone. Would you step inside? As he might be some time, the Prince suggested you might wish to wait inside and take some tea.'

'Oh, right.' Simon followed the butler into the house, along the hall and into a small but beautifully furnished ante-room.

'Earl Grey or Darjeeling?'

'I really don't mind.'

'Very good.'

The butler left the room. Simon stood up and paced, wondering why on earth, on today of all days, the Prince had to be delayed. Monica Burrows was covering for him at Zoe's, but every second away was making Simon more and more edgy.

The butler brought his tea and left again. Simon drank it, pacing distractedly up and down the room. Something on the wall, sitting innocently amidst the myriad of other, probably priceless, small paintings, caught his eye. He moved closer to study it and the hand holding his teacup began to shake.

He was sure it was identical, down to the last detail.

Simon pulled out his mobile phone to dial, but at that minute the butler arrived in the room.

'Prince George is ready to leave now.'

The teacup was removed from his hand and he was ushered out of the room.

*

From her vantage point inside the telephone box, Joanna dialled a mobile number. 'Steve? It's Jo. Don't ask where I am, but if you want a pretty piccie, get your backside to Zoe Harrison's house in Welbeck Street. The Prince is about to arrive. Yes, really. Oh, and there's a back entrance if you want an interior. It's usually unlocked. One last thing, Steve, wait outside Zoe's house until you hear from me. Bye.'

She then dialled another number, and another, until she had informed every picture desk of every daily London newspaper of the whereabouts of Prince George's supper engagement that evening. Now all she had to do was wait for them to arrive.

*

One of the photographers spotted the Prince as soon as Simon turned the car into Welbeck Street.

'Oh Christ!' the Prince swore as he saw the barrage of cameras placed outside Zoe's house.

'Would you like to move on, sir?'

'Bit late for that now, isn't it? Come on, let's get on with it.'

Joanna watched as the door to the Jaguar opened and the photographers clustered round the Prince. She made a dash for it, across the road and into the scrum, emerging on the steps just in front of Prince George and Simon. As she knew it would, the door opened like magic and she stumbled inside before the door shut closed behind her.

'Jo! You did manage to make it after all. What a pretty dress, and I love your hair like that.' Zoe kissed her on the cheek, then turned her attention to Pip. 'Hello, darling. How are you?' she said as they all jumped at the hammering on the front door.

Simon went to open it. Marcus, looking dazed and clutching a bottle of wine under his good arm, joined the party in the hall.

'Blimey! They must have known I was coming,' he joked.

'Please everyone, come through to the sitting room where I can introduce you all. Simon, would you shut the curtains for me, please?'

Simon moved reluctantly into the sitting room. Joanna turned to Zoe. 'Excuse me, I just must go to the loo.' And she dashed upstairs before Zoe could answer.

'Simon, would you mind bringing the champagne through? It's on ice in the kitchen.'

'No, of course.'

Simon ran along the corridor, zoomed into the kitchen and collected the champagne. He deposited it on the table. 'I'll leave you to it, now.' He nodded, left the sitting room and mounted the stairs.

Monica Burrows was waiting at the top. 'She's here. I've just seen her, in Zoe's bedroom. She went into the bathroom when she saw me.'

'Okay. Leave this to me. Go downstairs and station yourself by the front door.'

'Sure. Shout if you need me.'

Simon watched Monica run down the stairs. Then he settled himself outside the bathroom to wait for Joanna.

A scream from Zoe echoed up from the kitchen. 'Simon!' she yelled.

'Warburton!' The Prince's voice joined hers.

Simon careered down the stairs, along the hall and into the kitchen.

Joanna breathed a sigh of relief and unlocked the bathroom door as soon as she heard Simon leave the landing.

'Get him out of here!' Zoe yelled, staring at the man stoically taking photos, even as Simon man-handled him to the ground and removed the camera from his grasp.

'Only doing my job, guv.' He grimaced as they shoved the camera back into his grasp and marched him to the front door. Simon pulled the man's wallet from his jeans pocket and took a note of the name on his credit card.

'You'll be charged with breaking and entering, Mr Vincent. Now get the hell out.' Simon opened the front door, virtually threw the photographer down the steps and slammed the door behind him. Zoe was in the kitchen being comforted by a shaken Prince George.

'You okay?'

'Yes.' She nodded. 'It's my own fault. I hadn't locked the back door.'

'Hardly. It's Warburton's job to attend to security matters. Bloody shoddy of you, if I might say so.'

'My apologies, sir.' Simon nodded.

'Don't blame Simon, Pip. I said it was my fault. Simon's been absolutely wonderful and I don't know what I'd do without him,' Zoe said defensively.

'Hear, hear. He's a great guy, aren't you, Simon?' Joanna entered the kitchen behind him.

Simon turned and knew then, in that instant, that she'd found it.

'Well, great guy or not, I'd rather like to settle down and get on with the evening,' Prince George remarked irritably. 'We'll call you if we need you, Warburton, okay?'

'Yes, sir.' Simon made his way upstairs. It was as he'd expected. The empty frame lay on Jamie's bed, the delicately embroidered nursery rhyme, chanted by thousands of children, belying its hidden depths, had vanished.

'We all fall down,' muttered Simon under his breath as he left the room to climb to his own.

*

'She has it, sir.'

'Where is she?'

'Downstairs, enjoying a pleasant dinner party with

the third in line to the throne. We can't touch her and she knows it.'

'We've made sure O'Farrell won't help her. He was all set to sell it to the *Sunday Times*. We found the story on his computer. All he was waiting for was the letter.'

'At present, with HRH in the house, there's very little we can do here.'

'Then we must remove him immediately.'

'Yes, sir. And, if you'll excuse the impertinence, I have come up with an idea.'

'Fire away.'

Simon told him.

*

'This evening has only proved to me what I already know. Zoe, you can't continue to stay here. I'm moving you into the Palace where at least you'll be safe. Anyway, apart from the little interruption at the beginning, it's been most awfully pleasant. I think a toast to the hostess is in order, don't you? Zoe, for a fine dinner.'

'To Zoe.' The rest of the table joined Pip and raised their glasses.

Zoe stood up to remove the dessert plates. Joanna joined her in the kitchen.

'Well done, Zoe. That was a wonderful dinner.'

'Thanks.' Zoe put the kettle on to boil for coffee. 'What do you think?'

'Of what?'

'Pip, of course.'

'He's nice.'

'You mean it?'

'Yes. I mean, he's a bit . . . royal and everything.'

Zoe filled the percolator with fresh coffee. 'He is, isn't he?' She shook her head. 'I . . . I'm really just not sure anymore,' she whispered.

'Is there someone else?'

'Yes, I really think there is.'

'Oh dear. I don't know who'll be more disappointed if you end it, Pip or your gallant protector.'

'What do you mean?'

Joanna looked at her watch nervously. 'I . . . er, nothing. Look, Zoe, I . . .'

'You okay, Jo? You've been awfully jumpy this evening.' Marcus had slipped into the kitchen behind them. He put his arms round Joanna's waist.

'Have I?'

'Yes.' Marcus turned her around and kissed her gently on the lips.

'Excuse me, you two lovebirds, but I need to take the coffee through.'

Joanna and Marcus moved out of the doorway to let Zoe pass.

'What is it, Jo? I know something is wrong,' he said gently.

'No, I'm fine, really.' She nodded and smiled up at him, then caressed his cheek. 'I need to pop to the bathroom. I'll be down in a second.'

'I'll be waiting.' He smiled, kissing the tips of her fingers.

Her eyes filled with sudden and unexpected tears

and she drew away from him, disappeared into the hall and up the stairs. Marcus went back to join the others in the dining room.

*

Monica signalled to Simon as Joanna passed her in the hall and climbed the stairs. He nodded and picked up his mobile.

'Now, sir.'

*

In the bathroom, Joanna feverishly dialled Steve's number.

'It's me. I'll be out in two minutes. Get the bike ready, okay? Just don't hang around to ask questions.'

Then she heard the sirens wailing.

'This is the police. We have a bomb alert in Welbeck Street. Would all residents and those on the street kindly leave their homes immediately. I repeat, would all resi—'

Joanna banged her knuckles on the floor in despair. 'Shit! Shit! Shit!'

*

Simon appeared in the dining room. 'Ladies and gentlemen, would you kindly come this way?'

'What is it? What's happened?' Zoe let Simon steer her towards the door, Pip and Marcus following behind.

'What's going on now?' said Pip irritably.

'Bomb scare, sir. I'm afraid we'll have to evacuate

seeing double

the building. If you'd like to follow me, sir, there's a car outside already waiting.'

'Where's Joanna?' asked Zoe, as she was hustled to the front door by Simon.

'She's up here, in the bathroom. I'll see her out,' called Monica Burrows from the top of the stairs.

'Then I'll wait here for her,' said Marcus.

Joanna felt the cool steel press hard into her back.

'Tell him to leave,' the woman whispered.

'I'll see you outside, Marcus, okay?' she called shakily. 'I . . . I love you.'

The front door slammed and the house fell silent.

'Don't move, okay? I'm under orders to shoot to kill, ma'am.'

Joanna bit her lip. She heard the front door open and slam shut again. Monica steered her into Jamie's bedroom. Simon followed them a few seconds later.

'Let her go, Monica, I've got her covered.' Simon raised his arm and Joanna saw his gun. The nozzle poking into her back was removed and she sank down on to the bed.

'Joanna.'

She stared at him. 'What?'

'Why couldn't you leave it alone when you had the chance?'

'Why did you lie to me?'

'Because I was trying to save your life.'

'You're too late, anyway,' Joanna said, with a bravado she didn't feel. 'Tom knows it all. By now he's probably sent the story down the line. And if anything happens to me, he'll know why.'

'Tom's dead, Joanna. They found him and stopped him in time. The game's up, I'm afraid.'

Joanna's bottom lip quivered. 'Apart from the fact that I have the letter and you don't.'

'Search her, Monica.'

'Get off me!' Joanna struggled free from Monica's grasp. The sound of a bullet rang out from Simon's gun. Joanna and Monica turned and saw the bullet had shot into the wall and embedded itself in the plaster. Raw fear appeared on Joanna's face as she looked at Simon's cold, hard eyes.

'Rather than putting you through the indignity of a bodysearch, why don't you just give me what I want? Then no one will get hurt.'

Joanna nodded brokenly, not trusting herself to speak. She rolled up her skirt and delved into a pocket she had sewn into the lining, withdrawing a small, rolled-up square of material. She handed it to Simon. 'There. You bastards have finally got what you wanted. How many have you had to kill to retrieve it, Simon?'

Simon ignored her, concentrating instead on unrolling the material. '*Ring A Ring O' Roses . . .*' The words were exquisitely embroidered on to the material. Simon turned the material over. A piece of cream backing was neatly stitched on, covering the embroidery ends beneath. Simon took a pen-knife from his trouser pocket and cut away at the stitching. Despite her gnawing fear, Joanna was mesmerized that, after all these years, the truth would finally be revealed. The lining came away in Simon's hand. And there, tacked on to the back of the embroidery itself was a piece of thick cream vellum paper, identical to that which the original letter had been written on.

Simon snipped again at the neat tacking stitches and the paper came loose. He read it and nodded to Monica. 'It's the one.'

Carefully folding it into his inner-jacket pocket, he turned his gaze to Joanna.

'So, Joanna, what are we to do with you? Strikes me you know a bit too much.'

She couldn't look up into those eyes that had become cold, grey flints of steel.

'Surely you can't kill me in cold blood, Simon? Jesus, we've known each other for years, been best friends for most of our lives? I . . . Give me a chance to run away. I'll . . . I'll disappear. You'll never see me again.'

Monica Burrows watched Simon waver. 'I'll do it,' she said.

'No! This is my job.' Simon raised his gun and took a step forward, as Joanna crept backwards on the bed.

'Simon, for God's sake!' She screamed, then rolled off the other side of the bed and cowered against the wall. He leaned across the bed until his face was close to hers, the gun pointed at her chest.

'Simon, please!' she cried.

He shook his head. 'Remember, Joanna. This is *my* game. We play by *my* rules.'

She stared at him, her voice husky with dread. 'I surrender.'

'Bang. Bang. You're dead!'

She screamed as he fired two shots, the bullets

entering her at point-blank range. Then she slumped to the floor, gave a high-pitched moan and said no more.

Simon moved round the bed and took her pulse, then listened to her heartbeat. 'She's dead. Call in, please, tell them mission accomplished in all respects. I'll clean up. We've not got long to get her out to the car.'

Monica studied Joanna's prone body from where she stood. 'You knew her from way back?'

'Yes.'

'Jeez,' she breathed, 'that sure took some guts.'

He stared at her. 'You know the rules of service, Monica. No sentiment allowed.'

*

Fifteen minutes later, the street was still deserted as the door opened. The surveillance team in the office across the road monitored Warburton and Burrows as they supported the body between them, heading to a car which was parked a few feet along the road.

'They're en route now,' one of them mouthed into his walkie-talkie.

Ten minutes later, with a back-up car tailing them some distance behind, they parked in a street on the edge of a gated industrial estate. Transferring the body from their car to the one parked a few feet away, they climbed back into their own car and drove off at top speed. Twenty minutes later, the sound of an explosion shattered the peace of the surrounding streets.

*

Simon reached into his pocket and pulled out the letter. He handed it across the desk.

'There you are, sir. Safe and sound at last.'

Sir Henry Scott-Thomas read through it without a hint of emotion. 'Thank you, Warburton. And the body? It was placed successfully?'

'Yes.'

Sir Henry studied Warburton. 'You look exhausted, man.'

'I'll admit it was a pretty unpleasant thing I had to do.'

'It won't be forgotten. That kind of loyalty is rare, let me tell you. I'll be recommending you for immediate promotion. There'll also be an excellent bonus placed in your bank account for all your hard work.'

Simon's stomach churned.

'I think I need to go home and get some sleep, sir. Tomorrow will be another difficult day when they work out exactly who was killed in the bomb blast.'

Sir Henry nodded. 'After the, er, funeral, I suggest you take a couple of weeks off, fly away somewhere hot and sunny.'

'I was thinking of doing just that, sir.'

'Just two other things before you go: how did Burrows cope?'

'She was pretty shaken up afterwards. I got the feeling she'd never seen anyone killed in cold blood before. When I dropped her home, she was reconsidering her position.'

'This kind of thing does tend to sort out the

men from the boys. Did she see the contents of the letter?'

'No, sir, she didn't.' Simon paused, then added, 'I can assure you she had no idea what the hell was going on.'

'Good chap. You've done a fine job, Warburton, a fine job. Now, goodnight.'

'Goodnight, sir.'

Simon just managed to hold it together until he reached the men's toilets further along the corridor. There, he vomited continuously, then sank to the floor, wiping his mouth on his sleeve. Only now could he empathize with the gut-wrenching despair that had driven Ian Simpson over the edge.

He was not a man, but a machine, trained and programmed to kill. He'd never forget the fear in her eyes, the look of betrayal as he pulled the trigger. Simon put his head in his hands and cried his heart out.

*

Sir Henry Scott-Thomas sat at the breakfast table the following morning and studied the headline on the front of his newspaper.

JOURNALIST KILLED IN BOMB BLAST
A car bomb exploded near an industrial estate in Bermondsey last night, killing the driver, a 27-year-old journalist. The explosion came after an evening of hoax calls, which resulted in part of the West End being closed to traffic for two hours. The victim is believed to have been Joanna Haslam, who worked for the *Morning Mail* and had recently been on a visit

to Ireland. Police suspect that she and her boss, Tom O'Farrell, may have been en route to uncovering a terrorist plot. Tom O'Farrell was found shot dead in a friend's Docklands apartment late yesterday afternoon. The victim's parents were being comforted last night by relatives. Miss Haslam's boyfriend, the film producer Marcus Harrison, brother of the Duke of York's actress girlfriend, Zoe, was too distressed to speak to reporters. Police are continuing with their investigation.

He sifted through the other articles in the newspaper, until his eyes fell on a short piece at the bottom of page fourteen.

RAVENS RETURN

It was announced this morning by the Tower of London that the ravens have returned home. The ravens, who have by tradition guarded the Tower for 900 years, mysteriously vanished 6 months ago. A nationwide hunt ensued, but to no avail. Although during the Second World War the disturbances of the bombing reduced their number to one bird only, at no time has the Tower been without a raven to guard it. Protected by the Royal Decree of King Charles II, legend has it that should these birds ever leave the Tower, the monarchy would fall.

So it was with considerable relief that the raven keeper found Cedric, Gwylum, Hardey and the rest of the ravens back at their lodgings near Tower Green late last night. After a good meal of dead flesh, the keeper pronounced them in excellent physical condition, but was at a loss to explain their sudden disappearance.

The Queen, we are told, has been informed. After a difficult few months, she is bound to take comfort from the news of their safe return.

Sir Henry saw his gnarled hands were shaking. He folded the newspaper neatly in two and reached for his cup of Moroccan coffee.

chapter forty-two

Marcus watched the coffin as it made its way into the ground. Huge gut-wrenching sobs emanated from him. Zoe put her arm around his shoulder and tried her best to comfort him. She looked at the drawn, pale faces of Joanna's parents, standing opposite her by the head of the grave, and at Simon, whose face was a mask of misery.

When it was over, the crowd began to disperse, some heading for the tea provided at the Haslams' farmhouse, others straight back to London and their newspapers.

'Come on, Marcus, we'd better go now,' Zoe said softly.

'She k . . . knew she was go . . . oing to d . . . die.'

'Marcus, I'm sure she didn't.'

'She told me she loved me as I left the ho . . . house. Go . . . God I was so happy!' He spat the last sentence out. 'They wouldn't even let me see her at the mortuary. Said . . . said there was nothing left of her. That, she was . . . blown to p . . . pieces.'

Zoe tried to steer him away but he shrugged her off. 'No, I want to stay just a bit longer, okay?' He wiped his nose on his sleeve. 'See you by the gate,' he mumbled.

She walked back slowly towards the church gate, thinking what a peaceful, beautiful spot this was, tucked away on the edge of a small moorland village.

'Hello, Zoe. How are you?' Simon had caught up with her.

'Middling to absolutely ghastly.' She sighed. 'But nowhere near as bad as Marcus. It's destroyed him. He just won't accept it.'

Simon sighed heavily. 'He's not the only one. I keep going over and over it in my mind, wishing I'd not let her drive off alone that night.'

'You can berate yourself for ever and a day. Nothing's going to bring Joanna back.'

'No, you're right.' Simon stopped by the gate and looked back at the huddled, lonely figure of Marcus, still static by the grave. 'I've asked for a sabbatical, I want to take a little time to think things through.'

'Where will you go?'

'Oh, the States, probably, do a bit of travelling.' He smiled at her wanly. 'I don't really feel there's anything to keep me here.'

'When are you going?'

'In the next couple of days.'

'I'll miss you.'

He nodded. 'Me too. How's Pip and the Palace?'

'Okay.' She nodded. 'I suppose it was sensible to move me in there after what happened.' She scratched her nose. 'To be honest I haven't really settled, but it's early days yet. I have my first official public engagement with him tomorrow. A film première, of all things.'

Simon sighed. ''Ain't life ironic.'

'It sure is,' she agreed.

'Are you coming back for some tea? I can introduce you to my mum and dad. They're very impressed that I know you.'

'No, I promised Pip I'd get back. My driver awaits.' She smiled, indicating the long, black stretch limousine in the car park. 'Well then. I suppose this is goodbye.'

'Yes.'

She reached up and kissed him on the cheek. He squeezed her hand as she walked swiftly away from him, not wanting him to see her tears.

He mumbled something under his breath. She stopped and turned back, her expression hopeful. 'Did you say something?'

Simon shrugged his shoulders. 'No, not really. Good luck.' He watched as she climbed into the limousine. 'My darling,' he whispered as the car drove away and out of sight.

*

'Good afternoon. I have an appointment with Sir Henry at three.' Simon smiled at the woman, but she did not return the courtesy. Instead her eyes filled with tears.

'Oh, Mr Warburton.'

'What?'

'It's Sir Henry. He died last night. At home. It was a massive heart attack. Nothing anybody could do.' The woman's face disappeared into her sodden lace handkerchief.

'I see. Well, I am so sorry to bother you. It's unfortunate I wasn't told.'

'I think news is only just beginning to leak down the ranks. They're announcing it on the six o'clock news tonight. But,' she sniffed, 'the show must go on. Mr Jenkins is waiting for you in Sir Henry's office. Do go through.'

'Thank you.'

'Simon.'

'Hello, sir,' He smiled at the sight of Jenkins grinning at him from behind the table. 'Fancy meeting you here.'

'Want a drink, Simon? Been a bit of a roller-coaster day, as you can imagine. Sorry to see the old boy gone, but I have to admit we're all a little relieved. Sir Henry would hang in here. We all indulged him, of course, but we've been doing his job for years. Not that I'd want that to go out of this office, of course. There we go.' Lawrence handed him a tumbler of brandy. 'Your health.'

'Your new position?' Simon raised an eyebrow questioningly.

'I'd like to believe so, but – ' Lawrence Jenkins tapped his nose ' – you'll have to wait like the rest for the official announcement.'

Simon looked at his watch. 'Sorry to hurry you, sir, but I'm getting on the nine o' clock flight from Heathrow and I still haven't been home to pack.'

'Of course.' Lawrence offered him one of the comfy leather chairs in a corner of the room and the two men sat down. 'The thing is, Simon, I know you've asked for three months' sabbatical, and there's no doubt you fully deserve it, after that, er, little upset. But it just so happens we might have a little job for you while you're in the States.'

'Sir, I . . .'

'Call me Lawrence, man. One thing I intend to do is dispense with the ridiculous formality that harks back to another era entirely. The point is, if you would do this job for us, we could justify paying all your expenses. Rather than bumming around, you could treat yourself to the best, for only a tiny spot of light investigative work you could do standing on your head.'

Simon sighed. 'What is it?'

'Well, the problem is that our little American lady, Monica Burrows, has gone AWOL. We know she took flight and ran back to the States the day after the Welbeck Street affair, because passport control in Washington have a record of her entry. But so far she has not turned up at her White House office.'

'Surely, sir, if she's returned to the States, then she is no longer our responsibility? We can't be accountable for the fact she's decided to move on.'

'No. But would it not be true to say that poor Monica found herself witnessing some fairly unpleasant scenes for an agent fresh into the service?'

'Yes, I admit that was bad luck, sir.'

'Besides which, are you absolutely sure she had no idea what it was all about?'

'Pretty sure, sir.'

'Obviously, under the circumstances, I'm uncomfortable about information of such a sensitive nature escaping across the Atlantic.'

'Yes,' Simon agreed.

'The CIA are wanting to know what happened to Monica over here. She'd apparently been their star graduate. As a gesture of détente, I promised to send someone over to see them, plus I'd like a little investigating of our own done. I can think of no one more qualified than yourself, especially as you're going there anyway.'

Simon nodded. 'Okay, but I want four months.'

'Don't push it.'

'I'm not.' Simon shrugged. 'To be honest, I'm not keen on doing it anyway.'

Lawrence sighed. 'All right. It's my first day and I'm feeling generous. Take your four months and sign for a company credit card on your way out. Don't go too mad.'

'I'll do my best not to, sir.' Simon put his glass on the table and stood up.

'When you get back, there'll be a nice promotion waiting for you.' Lawrence shook his hand. 'Goodbye, Simon. Keep in touch.'

Lawrence watched Simon leave the room. He was a talented boy, that one, worth giving some leeway to. Sir Henry had him earmarked for great things. Given the Haslam saga, the chap had certainly shown his metal. Lawrence had a top-up and surveyed his new domain with a slightly guilty pleasure.

*

Zoe looked at her reflection in the mirror. She tugged at her hair, piled tightly into a French pleat by the hairdresser who had come to her rooms at the Palace.

'*Too* tight,' commented Zoe irritably as she

attempted to loosen and soften the style. Her make-up was still not right either, although Zoe had to admit her dress, a Givenchy sea of midnight-blue chiffon, was stunning.

The reason she felt so disgruntled was that Pip had called her an hour ago to say he was running late at another function. This meant they'd have to rendezvous at the cinema. Which in turn meant she'd have to initially face the press all alone. And even worse, Jamie had called her earlier, sounding downright miserable. He just wasn't settling back down at school, finding the jibes of the boys too hard to take. Besides all that, she had twenty-four hours before she had to say no to Hollywood and a possible glittering film career.

'And Joanna is dead and Marcus is useless and Simon's gone!' she shouted, then sank to the floor where she was and burst into tears, guilty for her self-pity, but managing to justify it anyway. Zoe thought back again to yesterday, after Joanna's funeral, when she thought she'd heard Simon mutter 'I love you'. No. She shook her head, he'd been distraught, she'd probably misheard . . .

'Oh God! I bloody love him! I miss him,' she moaned, wiping her tears away with her hand. She looked up and stared at her pitiful reflection in the mirror. As she did so, she suddenly remembered something she'd forgotten after the terrible trauma of the night Joanna had died. They'd been in the kitchen. She'd talked of leaving Pip, and Joanna had remarked she didn't know who'd be more disappointed . . . *Pip or your 'gallant protector . . .'* Joanna must have been talking about Simon.

Zoe looked at herself carefully in the mirror. She hated it here at the Palace, Jamie was miserable and the truth was – Zoe swallowed hard – she didn't love Pip. What was she waiting for? The worst he could do was to turn her down. What would she have lost? Nothing, except perhaps a slice of pride.

Standing up, she raced to the telephone. Her fingers hardly able to dial, Zoe called the number Simon had given her while he stayed up in Yorkshire in the aftermath of Joanna's death.

'Hello, is that Mrs Warburton? Yes, is Simon there? No? He's gone?' Tears came to Zoe's eyes. 'Oh, you mean he's gone to London . . . What time?' Zoe looked at her watch. 'Oh God! Give me that number again. Okay. Thanks, Mrs Warburton. You too. Must fly.'

*

Simon barely made it to the check-in on time. His meeting with Lawrence Jenkins had delayed him considerably, but had at least provided him with a seat in Club Class.

'Would you mind going straight to the gate, Mr Warburton? Your flight is already boarding.'

'Of course.' Simon wandered through the crowds towards passport control. He'd just handed his ticket and passport over when he heard his name being called.

'Simon, wait for me!' The crowds parted like the Red Sea to let the vision of beauty, clothed in a cloud of blue chiffon, her blonde hair flying, reach her love.

Simon stood there, rooted to the spot as she ran towards him, her face radiant with happiness. He held out his arms as she neared him, but she slowed down and came to a halt a few feet away from him.

'Tell me what you said yesterday, just before I got into the car.'

'I said, "I love you."'

'I thought you did. Well guess what?'

'What?'

Those watching held their breath with Simon.

'I love you too.'

A round of spontaneous applause broke out as Simon walked towards her, kissed her, then swept his very own fairytale princess into his arms.

epilogue

Two months later, Los Angeles, California

Zoe was still sleeping as Simon came back into the bedroom. He dressed as quietly as he could so as not to disturb her. She hadn't arrived back from the studio until two last night. After a week of similar late nights, she was exhausted.

'Simon?'

He was just tiptoeing out when she called him.

'Morning, darling.' He walked back to the bed and kissed her.

She stretched. 'What time is it?'

'After ten.'

She pulled him towards her. 'Come back to bed. It's Saturday, remember?'

'There's nothing I'd like more, but I have to go out, I'm afraid.'

'Where?'

'I told you I had an old pal from school contact me last week. He's on his way through the States and he called last night to say he was in LA. I'm meeting him downtown. We'll have some brunch and I'll be back straight after. Jamie's awake and is, guess where?'

'In the pool.' Zoe smiled.

'He's been told not to bother you. Consuela's keeping an eye on him.'

'Okay. Don't be long.'

'I won't.' Simon rose and walked towards the door.

'I love you.'

'I love you too.'

*

Simon walked into the Cabana café, its exotic name belying its scruffiness. The area he had driven through in the taxi was undeniably seedy, graffiti sprayed on the wall opposite, a group of young men of mixed race lolling against it looking for action. He ordered a double espresso from the Mexican sweating behind the bar, then took himself off to a table by the window.

He was waiting a good half an hour before a tall, attractive female walked through the door. She had the typical lithe-limbed, golden-brown body and blonde hair of the Californian woman. He watched as she walked up to the bar, ordered a milkshake, then turned and surveyed the tables.

'Anyone sitting with you?' she asked as she strolled across.

'No, but I'm waiting for someone.'

She sat down, and in a broad Yorkshire accent said, 'Yes, Simon, you dozy git. You're waiting for me.'

*

Simon was still stunned by her transformation. He, who had known her since she was a toddler, would not have recognized her in a million years. The only things left of her past self were her hazel eyes.

They left the café soon after, took a taxi, then a bus, then walked down to the beach and sat by the waves. She wanted to know everything, as she always had done, in minute detail.

'Was my funeral good?'

'Extremely moving, yes. Everyone in floods of tears.'

'I'm glad to know they cared.'

'They did.'

'How were my mum and dad?'

'Distraught.'

She kicked off her sandals and dug her toes into the sand. 'I wish . . .' She shook her head. 'I wish I could tell them.'

'Joanna, it was the only way.'

'I know.'

The two of them sat in silence and stared out at the sea.

'And Marcus?'

'A shadow of his former self. Devastated. I obviously underestimated his feelings for you. Belated apologies for that.'

She sighed. 'So much happened during the time we were together. It didn't strike me until it was too late how much I cared for him.'

'There'll be another man, some day.'

She shrugged. 'Maybe. You don't think I could write to Marcus and . . .'

'No! Jo, please, don't even think about it.'

'No, of course not.'

'How are you . . . surviving?'

'Oh, I'm managing, just. It's pretty hard being a nameless person. I did as you asked and ditched Monica's passport and credit cards the minute I arrived in Washington.'

'Well, at least it got you out of the UK alive and into the States.'

'Yes. The problem is, you can't get work here without a social-security number, so I'm having to take anything they offer me cash in hand. I've been washing dishes at a local diner for the past three weeks, but I'm fast running out of money.'

'I have something for you.' Simon dug in his pocket and produced an envelope. 'As promised.'

Joanna took it and pulled out an American birth certificate, a United States passport and a card with a number on it. 'Margaret Jane Cunningham,' Joanna read. 'Born, Michigan 1968 ... Hey, Simon! You've made me a year older! Charmed, I'm sure.'

'Sorry. It was the closest I could come on an "off the shelf" identity-kit basis. You have a social-security number there, too. That should sort out your work problems.'

'Are you positive it's all kosher?'

'Joanna, trust me, it's kosher, but you'll have to add a photo. I left the plastic open so you could. I'm glad I did, as you now resemble something out of *Baywatch*. I rather fancy you like that.'

'Well, it remains to be seen if blondes have more fun. Talking of blondes, how's Zoe?'

'Happily ensconced with Jamie in a sumptuous villa in the Hollywood Hills. Courtesy of MCM.'

'She left the Prince?'

'Yes. Didn't you read about it?'

'No. I've been too terrified to even pick up a

newspaper in the past few weeks. I kept thinking I'd see my picture on the front and a headline saying "Wanted!" above it.' Joanna nodded. 'I knew Zoe was wavering about Pip though. Was it the offer of the film that finally made her decide?'

'That, and the fact she realized she was in love with her very own "Buttons", I suppose.'

Joanna stared at him. 'You mean . . .?'

He smiled. 'Yes. And we're outrageously happy together.'

'I'm thrilled for you both. Can your old pal Margaret Cunningham come to the wedding?'

'Too late. We married a month ago. I'm in the process of legally adopting Jamie at the moment.'

Joanna lay back and looked at the blue sky. 'Thank God this whole saga has had one happy ending. I'm still having the most ghastly dreams about that night I "died". I was absolutely convinced, right up until the very last moment, that you were going to kill me.'

'I absolutely had to make it look real, Jo, to convince Monica. I needed a witness to call in and say I'd done the dirty deed.'

'All those silly Cowboy and Indian games we used to play on the moors when we were kids,' she mused. 'You were so bossy, making me be the one who had to die all the time. "This is my game, we play by my rules," and then I had to say "I surrender," and you'd say . . .'

'". . . Bang, bang, you're dead,"' Simon joined in, chuckling. 'You were a girl, Jo. I couldn't let you win all the time. Anyway, thank God for those games. It provided me with the perfect way of telling you to "die".'

'When you fired that bullet into Jamie's bedroom wall, it was real, wasn't it?'

'Absolutely.' Simon nodded. 'I can tell you, even though the next two were dummies, some sweat poured off me. I'd not had time to go through the usual rigorous procedures. I had to load the gun on the way up the stairs to Jamie's bedroom. If I hadn't have moved quickly, Monica would have killed you and I couldn't risk that.'

Joanna sat up on her elbows and studied Simon. 'And to think I ever doubted you. What you did for me that night . . .' She shook her head. 'I can never repay you.'

'Well, I just hope that, when my day of judgement comes, he'll forgive me. Monica was the first . . . I ever . . .' He swallowed hard and shrugged. 'The bottom line was, it was her or you. Fancy a beer?'

They strolled up to the bar at the edge of the beach, ordered two Buds and sat down.

'Was your boss thankful to get hold of his pot of gold after all this time?' Joanna asked.

'Yes, extremely. It may sound stupid, but I actually felt sympathy for him towards the end. He was only doing his job. Trying to protect what he believed in.'

'No, Simon, never, ever could I shed one tear. Think of those he's murdered: Kitty, William, Ciara, Niamh, poor Tom . . .'

'But it wasn't him that caused all this in the first place, was it?'

'No, I suppose not.'

'Well,' Simon shrugged, 'the old boy died the day after I handed him back the letter.'

'Don't expect me to mourn.'

'I won't. But the odd thing was, only a couple of hours before you turned up at Welbeck Street, I'd suddenly realized where the letter had been hidden.'

'How come?'

'I was waiting in York House for the Prince, to bring him back to London, and I saw a framed sampler on the wall. It was absolutely identical to the one I'd seen hanging above Jamie's bed a few weeks earlier.' He sighed. 'If I'd have got there sooner, then all this could have been avoided.' He took a slug of his beer. 'I know how you found out where it was.'

'Do you?'

'Yes. A wily old bird, by all accounts.' Simon's eyes twinkled.

'Is she okay?'

'I believe so. Sir Henry went to his grave taking her identity with him.'

'I'm glad. She's one hell of a lady.'

'And so are you, if I might say so. Maybe Margaret Jane Cunningham should think about joining the intelligence services over here. It seems she may have a nose for it.'

Joanna shook her head. 'No, but maybe now I'm a bona fide American citizen I could look for a career in journalism. Something gentle, maybe, like a problem page. I intend to keep my slate clean in my new future, stay out of trouble.'

He laughed. 'That really will be a first, but I certainly suggest you try it.'

'I hate the name Margaret.' Joanna sniffed. 'I shall become a Maggie.'

'So, Maggie, will you stay here in LA?'

'Maybe, maybe not. The temptation to visit you and Zoe, the connection with Marcus, might be too strong. I quite fancy New York.'

'It might be for the best. Zoe and I have decided to stay here for the foreseeable future. We thought it was wise to make a new start, and it looks like Zoe will be inundated with work offers when *Blithe Spirit* is released. We went to see a school for Jamie a couple of days ago. He was so unhappy at his last place. Here, everybody's mum and dad are celebrities.'

'What about your job?'

Simon shrugged. 'I haven't decided yet. The service has offered me a transfer over here, but Zoe has this mad idea of me opening a restaurant. She wants to back me.'

Joanna giggled. 'Well, we always did talk about it. But could you leave your old way of life behind, do you think?'

'The truth is, I'm not a killer. The fact I took another person's life will haunt me for ever.' He shook his head. 'God help me if Zoe ever found out what I did that night, or Jamie.'

Joanna laid her hand on his. 'You saved my life, Simon, that's what you did.'

'Yes.' He took her hand in his and squeezed it. 'You know that for your own sake, I can't see you again.'

'I know.'

'I'd better go. You just never know who might be watching. Oh yes, I have something else for you.' From his shorts pocket, he drew out an envelope and handed it to her.

'What's in it?'

'Twenty thousand pounds in dollars, the bonus I was paid for finding the letter. It's yours by rights and it might help get you started.'

Tears filled Joanna's eyes. 'Simon, I can't take this.'

'Of course you can. Zoe's earning a fortune and my boss insisted on paying for all my expenses while I was here investigating Monica's disappearance on her arrival back in the States.' He shrugged sadly. 'Seems my investigating is done.'

'Thank you, Simon. I promise I'll make good use of it.'

'I'm sure you will.' He watched Joanna fold the envelope up and put it in her rucksack.

'There's something else in there too, something I thought you should at least have the satisfaction of reading.' He pulled her up to standing and hugged her tight to him.

She wept on to his shoulder. 'I can't bear the thought of never seeing you again.'

He pulled her from him. She saw he was crying too.

'So long, Butch.' He chucked her cheek.

'Take it easy, Sundance,' she replied.

Choked with tears, Joanna watched as he left the beach. Only when he was a tiny spot in the distance did she pick up her rucksack and walk back down to the water's edge.

Kneeling on the sand, she found a hanky to blow her nose. Then she reached inside the envelope he'd given her, took out the sheet of paper and unfolded it.

York House
Sandringham

10th May 1926

My darling Siam,

Understand that it is only my love for you that compels me to write this, the fear that others might wish to hurt you overriding care for myself or common sense. With God's grace, let it be delivered to you without incident in the secure hands that bear it.

I must tell you the joyful news of the arrival of our baby girl. She has your eyes already, and perhaps your nose. Even if the blood that runs through her veins is not royal, your child is a true princess. How I wish her real father could see her, hold his child in his arms, but of course that is an impossibility, a dreadful sadness I must live with for the rest of my days.

My darling, I implore you to keep this letter safe. The threat of its existence to the few that know the truth should be enough to see you safely through life. I trust you will dispose of it when the time comes for you to leave this earth, for the sake of our daughter, and so that history may never record it.

I cannot write again, my love,

I am, yours for ever,

The letter was signed with the famous flourish, the photocopy not diminishing the magnitude of what Joanna had just read.

A baby princess, born into royalty, sired in the most extraordinary circumstances by a commoner. A baby that at the time was fifth in line to the throne, the chances of her succession tiny. But then, through a twist of fate, which ironically saw others putting love before duty too, the baby princess had become a queen.

Joanna stood up, the letter in her hands, temptation to exact revenge for her own and other lives destroyed holding her tightly in its grasp. The anger left her, as fast as it had come.

'It's finally over,' she whispered to the ghosts who might be listening.

Joanna went to the water's edge, tore the paper and watched the pieces as they fluttered in the wind. Then she turned, picked up her rucksack, and headed into her new life.